Soap Opera DIGEST

THE STORY OF A WOMAN.
A DREAM.
AND AN ENDLESS LOVE.

STACY THOWE

Copyright © 2025 Stacy Thowe.

All rights reserved. No part of this book may be reproduced, stored, or transmitted by any means—whether auditory, graphic, mechanical, or electronic—without written permission of both publisher and author, except in the case of brief excerpts used in critical articles and reviews. Unauthorized reproduction of any part of this work is illegal and is punishable by law.

ISBN: 979-8-89419-914-6 (sc)
ISBN: 979-8-89419-915-3 (hc)
ISBN: 979-8-89419-916-0 (e)

Because of the dynamic nature of the Internet, any web addresses or links contained in this book may have changed since publication and may no longer be valid. The views expressed in this work are solely those of the author and do not necessarily reflect the views of the publisher, and the publisher hereby disclaims any responsibility for them.

One Galleria Blvd., Suite 1900, Metairie, LA 70001
(504) 702-6708

This book is dedicated to my mother and her Ritchie.
I know you will see each other again, one very special day.

CHAPTER ONE

THE YEAR: 1981

*Screech...*the muffled sound of a radio tuning in. *"This is KCBQ coming to you from the lovely city of San Diego, California. How are all you listeners doing out there? We are coming at ya from the happening location of 7th and Ash, so come on down and visit me here in the DJ booth. If you are lucky, I will give you a wave, and if you are one of the beauties I see walking around here in a bikini, maybe even a wink. Here is a tune from Kool & the Gang coming off of last year's hit 'Ladies' Night.' Here it is; let's celebrate! And I intend to do just that. Anyone want to join me?"*

Ritchie drummed on the steering wheel as the music played, tapping his fingers to the tune. His tan, muscular arms were still strange to him as he fumbled with the knob on the radio. The cool breeze from the ocean's edge floated its way into his light green Chevy Camaro as he danced to the beat drifting from his radio. His window rolled down, Ritchie glanced out toward the shimmering waves of the Pacific, listening to them crash in the distance as he made his way through the winding turns, the wind rushing through his hair.

He peeked over at the small black box in the seat next to him and thought of Julia. It had been two long years since they first met at the Tropicana Dance Club. He was serving his first year in the Marine Corps and was stationed at MCRD, and Julia had just graduated from high school earlier that year.

Ritchie thought about the first time he ever saw her. She was dressed in a white one-piece jumpsuit and danced as if she owned the dance floor. The disco globe flashed sprinkling lights onto the floor that reflected off of her skin like sunlight on the ocean. It all seemed like yesterday. From the very beginning, he couldn't take his eyes off her.

Ritchie loved to dance, coming from a Puerto Rican mother who would salsa around the kitchen as she prepared supper every night, blaring the radio as she cooked to the tune of a cumbia beat. She would often snatch Ritchie or one of his brothers and begin to salsa with them as they attempted to stumble along, dancing to the bubbling sound of boiling water.

She danced as if she didn't have a care in the world, and at that time in their life, they didn't. His father owned a butcher shop that was located below their three-bedroom apartment. The business provided the family with a good living. Ritchie and his brothers never wanted for anything.

Ritchie concentrated on the busy traffic before him. The sun was fading, and he hadn't gotten out of the barracks early enough to call Julia and let her know that he was able to meet her that night. His evening duty had been canceled, and he was able to acquire a pass, so he thought he would surprise her.

He wasn't sure if it was the full moon that floated over the ocean or the thick salty air, but the possibility of Julia saying yes got the best of him, and he decided that tonight would be the night he would ask her to marry him.

He envisioned her sauntering across the floor with her girlfriends. They would be giggling and whispering to one another as they herded their way through the crowd like a school of swans on a smoke-filled morning.

Julia stood out among the others. Her brown wavy hair flowed down around her shoulders in soft ringlets that bounced every time she turned her head. She had recently trimmed her bangs, which made her look older. But not in a negative way; she looked sophisticated, like one of those models in Vogue. She didn't have any height to speak of, only standing about five-foot-three, but when she moved across the dance floor in those platform heels, she stood as tall as any runway model.

Ritchie admired Julia for the mere fact that she had no clue how truly beautiful she was. She was silly and kind and at the fine old age of twenty, was having the time of her life.

Ritchie did not care for the fact that she would be sitting at the club with her friends, alone, giving the impression that she had no one special in her life. The men in the room would often flock to her, asking her for a dance, and for her phone number, but she would always tell them that she had a boyfriend and just came along with her friends to dance.

To this day, Ritchie was not sure why she had selected him. Why with all the choices before her, she said yes, to only him.

He was not bad looking with his thick Italian hair and glistening brown eyes that came from his mother. His height came from his father, who stood about six-foot-one. His athletic father played high school basketball and football and continually pushed Ritchie to participate in sports. His father believed that to win in life, you had to push your limits. You had to go for the win. You had to grab fate by the reins and not let it decide the road for you. His father often said that you should always choose your road in life. On purpose.

He advised Ritchie to live his life as if there would be no tomorrow, and that was what Ritchie tried to do. He joined the Marines to see the world. Little did he know, his world would begin and end with Julia.

They talked for hours about all they desired in life. All they hoped to accomplish. Julia wanted to write magnificent stories. She was currently attending the local community college to complete her general requirements. Her dream was to someday be a published author.

She had written and submitted many stories and had been turned down again and again for various reasons. Facing this rejection, Julia decided that she needed some type of direction if she was going to succeed in this competitive profession, and Ritchie encouraged her to pursue her dream and finish college.

He had read almost everything she had ever written and believed she was so gifted. He was not sure why her work was turned down. If he had been a publisher, she would already be published. She was so intelligent, so free, so young, and so beautiful. These are all reasons why he couldn't imagine what she was doing with the likes of him.

Ritchie figured that he would finish out his four years in the military, and then they would decide what they would do from there. He had always dreamed of retiring from the Marines, but maybe that was not Julia's dream. His dream had begun to change the moment he met Julia.

Like destiny, they just clicked. It was as if she were the part of him that he had been searching for all of his life. The half of him that had been missing all of those years.

He looked over at his future, sitting next to him in that empty passenger seat.

But how would she feel about getting married so young? Would she think she was throwing her life away? Would she throw the ring in his face, or worse, would she cry and say she wasn't ready for this? He could wait. He could wait forever. But would she let him?

Ritchie caught sight of the beams of light flashing out across the sky from the dance club at the top of the hill. He thought if she would only say yes. If she would only be his, he would not ask God for anything else in this world. She made him a better man. He couldn't imagine his life without her. But with one word from her, it could all end…or it could all begin. His heart throbbed through his chest with the anticipation of the night.

He recollected the day he introduced Julia to his mother, who was visiting from New York. Julia wore a green dress that day because he had told her that green was his mother's favorite color. The green dress could not save them when things quickly started to go awry. Ritchie decided to take his mother and Julia out for dinner. Julia—wanting to make a good impression—helped Ritchie's mother into the car and held the door for her. Julia, feeling very nervous, shut the door behind his mother a little too soon and failed to see his mother's fingers gripping the door jam, and well, as fate would have it, as you can probably guess, there was a trip to the emergency room involved. His mother's fingers were swollen but not broken. Thank goodness for small miracles because his mother may not have warmed up to Julia had she been proven to be bad luck. His mother was a little superstitious that way.

Julia apologized profusely, and his mother got to see a side of Julia that Julia does not show to everyone. The side that is vulnerable and sweet. You see, Julia grew up quite fast. She started working to help support herself in high school. Her mother—being a single mother—was always away working. Julia and her sister often had to manage things at home on their own. They made their daily meals and drove themselves to school events. Julia was captain of the dance team in high school and was also in the top ten percent of her class, all the while holding down a part-time job.

She often told Ritchie how she wished her mother would have made it to more of her dance performances in high school. She was voted most likely to end up on Broadway due to her dancing ability. She said that in all the years she danced, her mother only made it to one performance. It was the final performance of her senior year, and Julia had to beg for her to attend. Julia's mother just didn't see attending the dance performances as a priority. She said she was just too tired. She believed putting food on the table for Julia and her sister was just a little more important.

Ritchie thought that Julia's history with dance was why she loved it so much. She had a passion for it. It was part of her soul. When she danced, it was as if she were the only one in the room. She would take over the dance floor. Julia, and whatever poor soul she chose to be her partner, was always the center of attention. She rarely found a partner that could keep up with her. Ritchie tried, but he never quite made it to her level of skill.

Julia would usually slow down whenever she danced with him. Every time that they danced, it was as if everyone else in the room disappeared, and they would melt into each other. They became one soul swaying to the tune. His other half. The one that completed him.

He was two blocks from the dance hall when he began to rehearse how he would propose to her. He considered dropping to one knee in the middle of the dance floor. He began to run scenarios through his mind, picturing what would happen. Somehow the scenario always faded into a humiliating disaster. He thought, what if someone bumped into him and the ring he had saved for six months to purchase went flying into oblivion, never to be found again? What if he tripped the couple next to him, and the man standing twice his size beat him senseless, and he ended up spending the night in the emergency room? Or what if she said no, and the crowd around them gasped and whispered about what a fool he had made of himself?

In the end, he was determined to take a chance. He decided that he would pull her out to the balcony, where it was only the two of them. They were at their very best when they were alone. When the rest of the world disappeared. Whenever they were alone, they would plan their future. Alone was where they would dream about what each other would achieve.

They had spoken about marriage, but never in a serious nature. Ritchie believed this was because she had such big dreams. A novelist. A journalist. Ritchie only hoped that she would allow him to tag along for the ride.

The light turned green, and Ritchie looked over at the ring one last time, thinking, *yes, the balcony, that is where it will happen. That is where she will say yes.*

He stepped on the gas pedal, and the world began to spin from all the promise that lay before them, and in that one moment in time, he saw two bright lights blaring toward the left side of his vehicle, and he turned to see Julia's face for the very last time…

CHAPTER TWO

PRESENT DAY

"What's wrong with this stupid thing?" Julia grumbled. She melted into the old leather recliner, engulfed in her fuzzy blue robe. She kicked her heels down, bringing her feet back onto the carpet just as the sun flared its way through the beige blinds of the dimly lit room. Particles of dust danced in the sunbeams as Julia fiddled with the remote control. "Why isn't this stupid thing working?" she asked the empty room.

A white light projected from the television, which sat on a black entertainment center lining the east wall of the living room. The screen, white and snowy, sent out a deafening hum of defiance. Julia stood behind the pine coffee table that displayed a white-laced table runner. She marched back and forth in front of the sofa, rotating the remote control like a magic wand, hoping to magically summon a clear picture on the screen.

"What are you doing?" her mother's voice interrupted the silence. The disruption was so abrupt that Julia almost dropped the remote control.

Carmen's red-dyed hair was wrapped up in large curlers, forming a pink roadmap of her scalp. Carmen poked her head around the wall as her blue poke-a-dot house dress swayed to the side.

"The wedding is today," Julia whined.

"What wedding? Are you going to a wedding?" Carmen asked.

"No, Mom. Michelle and Darren's from *One Moment in Time*. What did you do to the TV?"

"I didn't do anything. I can never get it to work. There are too many buttons."

"Awww…figures," Julia cried, throwing her head back. Her brown curly hair bounced onto her shoulders. She moved around the room with the remote control in her hand, desperately pushing the buttons, trying to summon some type of force that would somehow bring the picture back to the screen. "I'm going to miss it!" she cried.

"You watch that thing too much. Your brain cells are dying as we speak. What's wrong with you? Get out. Enjoy life. I wish I was your age again."

Rolling her eyes, Julia flopped down in her recliner just as the picture cleared on the screen. "Yes!" she shouted.

"Yes…yes," her mother repeated. "Now, I'll never get you away from that thing."

"Oh, Mom. Sit down and watch this with me. It's just starting. We haven't missed it."

"I have better things to do with my time. I'm going to take out the trash."

"Shhh…you are going to make me miss it."

"Ahhh, I give up," her mother said, plopping her hands into the pockets of her house dress. She glared at her daughter, shaking her head back and forth in disbelief as she headed to the laundry room where the trash can was kept.

Julia kicked her feet up and gazed at the screen. A bronze woman with blonde hair made her way across the screen in a white strapless wedding gown that hugged her hips and flared out toward the floor.

Julia scooped up a couple of miniature-sized candy bars that were sitting beside her and got lost in the episode. In her mind, she abandoned the small confines of the dusty, dreary living room and was transported into the church. Julia imagined she was sitting next to her favorite character, Solomon. She blushed as she felt his eyes scanning her from the side. "If only…," Solomon said. Julia was then jolted back to Earth by the sound of her mother yelling at her from the other room.

"Don't you have to work today?" Her mother shouted.

"Yes, but I don't go in until 1:00."

"I don't know why you still work for that store."

"Mom, please, I'm trying to watch this," Julia said as she scooted to the end of the recliner and leaned into the television, straining to hear over her mother's voice.

Julia nestled back into the old leather recliner that her mother had bought when Julia was still in high school. Her mind wandered back to when she was young, and her mother would come home from work and sit in the recliner with her feet up. They would eat chocolate cupcakes with the white swirl on top and watch late-night television shows like *Love Boat* and *Fantasy Island*. Julia would curl up on the floor right in front of the television and watch all those beautiful people as they set off to exotic places and fell in love over and over again.

In their world, everything was perfect. It was a place where broken hearts were always mended, and prince charming rescued you, riding a white horse. In this fantasy world, there was always a happy ending, a new road, and fantastic adventures, and no one was alone in a living room, living with their mother.

When the episode ended, Julia slowly dragged herself from the recliner and made her way to the bathroom to get ready for work. She looked at her face in the mirror, stretching her skin in various directions, scanning her face for new wrinkles. She felt the lines separating her nose and cheeks deepening. She placed her hands on each side of her mouth, lifting her skin. Julia remembered that face. What was staring back at her in the mirror today was some stranger. Some loner. Someone she didn't recognize.

She squeezed into her favorite black skirt and white lace button-down top and placed her name tag across the pocket, staring at the image looking back at her.

Julia had been married once to a liar. She knew he was a liar shortly after she met him. That was part of his charm. He told her whatever she needed to hear. He knew exactly what to say to her to get what he wanted. He knew she needed to hear that he would love her forever, that he would give her the world, and that he would never leave her.

Maybe the sagging skin and the pounds she gained from having their two children drove him away. But down deep, Julia knew that she would never discover the truth because, with him, the truth did not exist.

Scott, her ex-husband, was a good father when their children were babies. But as they grew, he seemed to lose interest. He took a job in sales and soared to the top of the ladder. Being very charismatic, his charm instantly won people over. Just as it had done with Julia. People usually bought two or three of whatever he was selling and gave one to their neighbor, who in turn also bought from Scott. He was that good.

Being in the spotlight inflated Scott's ego to the point where he couldn't see Julia anymore. He started to spend less and less time with her and their children. He began drinking more. He would often arrive home in the early wee hours of the morning and would be so drunk he couldn't even make it up the stairs.

Julia would often have to make up stories about where Daddy was. He was working. He was entertaining clients. He was out late because he was providing for them. He was the reason they had all these beautiful things. And then, one day, he just stopped coming home. And on that day, the children discovered the truth. And Julia finally had to face the truth. That was the day she came to terms with the fact that he just didn't love her anymore.

They had two children, a boy and a girl. Her son, Bobby, unfortunately, acquired her husband's gift for gab. He also stretched the truth. He stretched it so far that it quite often came back and slapped him right in the face.

But it was too late. Scott's genetics were already formed, and her son became his father's boy. It was inevitable. Julia tried to reason with her son, but it was to no avail. He always felt God had a deaf ear when he spread his versions of the truth. Just like his father, the fantasy was always better than reality. And when you think about it, it probably was. Why face this reality when you could remain in the fairy tale? Live in the lie. The lie was just so much more attractive than reality.

Lauren, on the other hand, was placed in Julia's family by her own misfortune. She was everything Julia once was. She was always joyous, loved to dance, and got good grades. Julia often felt bad that Lauren was stuck with the likes of them, but Lauren didn't seem to mind. She loved her family, the good and the bad. But the day her father left blackened her sun. The day her father left, a piece of her died. Just like it did for Julia. And Lauren found herself looking for someone to fill the void her father left. The men she brought home were almost a mirror image of Scott.

Gazing into the mirror, Julia sighed and turned her face to the left and to the right. She colored her eyes and placed foundation over the lines she assumed everyone could see. In reality, Julia looked young for her age. When her husband left her for Sky, and that was actually her name, Julia suddenly dropped twenty-five pounds. That was the one thing she could thank Scott for. Well, besides their children, Bobby and Lauren. She never dreamed she would be a size six again. But there she was, drowning in her old clothes.

After the divorce was final, and her ex and his next victim rode off into the sunset, Julia went out and bought herself a whole new wardrobe. After all, you have to look good to sell perfume.

Perfume. Julia never imagined her part-time job at the perfume counter would lead to a full-time job at the perfume counter. She looked at her face again and applied some mauve lipstick. *What are you doing with your life?* She would shout at the image looking back at her. But at forty-seven, Julia thought life had abandoned her, just like Scott and just like Ritchie.

She never told many people about Ritchie.

Not even Scott.

When Lauren was about six years old, she was shuffling through one of Julia's dresser drawers and accidentally ran across some pictures of a man with her mommy. The pictures were made especially for Julia. Ritchie had given the photos to her just before the accident as if it were a premonition of what was about to happen.

The pictures were hidden in a black folder set inside a plastic bag in one of Julia's drawers. Lauren thought he looked like a prince. Julia told her that he was a friend of Mommy's that she knew before she met Daddy. But from then on, Lauren always referred to him as "the prince."

Julia often found herself drawn to the pictures. She would examine them, sometimes for hours, without even realizing she was doing it. It was just that he never seemed to age. In the photos, he was forever twenty-two. Forever young, forever the way she would always remember him. The love of her life. The one she was meant to be with. The one that fate had stolen from her before she had a chance to know. And now she would never know.

Ritchie had given the pictures to her as a two-year anniversary gift. In the pictures, he was sitting there in his marine uniform, looking straight at the camera, straight at her with that beautiful smile and that short, thick, black hair, frozen in time as if time no longer existed. And in the corner of the photo, there were tiny bubbles leading up to a cloud-like image. And in the cloud was a picture of Julia. It was almost as if the accident was predestined. As if he wanted her to know that she would forever be in his heart and his thoughts. Always a part of him.

He gave the photos to her two weeks before he was killed.

She never showed them to anyone. Selfishly, she was afraid his mother would want them. It was the last photo ever taken of him. But Julia could not bear to part with them. It was the very last part of him that she would ever own. The only thing that confirmed she just didn't dream him up. That he was real. He existed. And at that moment in time, he loved only her.

As for Julia, she didn't have faith in love anymore.

For her, love existed in its most perfect form on the screen. Where hearts mended. Where soul mates strolled together into the sunset. And where love developed like flowers in the spring.

Julia exited the house that day with thoughts of Ritchie surrounding her. Sometimes she swore she could see him driving up in his lime-green Camaro. One hand on the wheel as he leaned over into the passenger seat to open the door for her. What she would have done to see him driving toward her one more time, and how she wished she would have been able to say goodbye.

She climbed into her gray Toyota Camry and started the engine. She gazed into her rearview mirror and could almost see his smile. She pulled out and headed to the department store at the mall. To the perfume counter where she was now the manager. With nothing to face but the young college girls that worked for her. Each with their lives before them, as Julia viewed her life from a rearview mirror.

CHAPTER THREE

"Whoa! You got a date later?" Julia heard her best friend Lisa shout out from behind her. Julia was busy opening a glass case to add new merchandise to the emerald, pink, and purple designer perfume sets that were already displayed on the shelf.

"Lisa, I'm trying to work here. Stop kiddin' around," Julia said as she placed the boxes on the clear shelves, careful not to leave fingerprints on the shimmering glass.

"All I'm saying is you're probably going to be selling a lot of perfume tonight, girl."

"What are you talking about? Don't you have something you are supposed to be folding in the women's department?"

"That skirt, man, I remember when my rear end looked that good." Lisa, who was Julia's age, stood about two inches taller than Julia. She was a full-figured-women who liked to dress in the latest fashion. Lisa also looked young for her age. She had a flawless bronze complexion and short black hair that she tended to place behind her ears.

"What are you talking about?" Julia said as she backed up to view the results of her labor.

"Maybe I need to get married and divorced if that's what it will take to look like you do at our age."

"You really need to stop. You are making a fool of yourself," Julia said as she looked around for customers who might be eavesdropping.

"Girl, you need to get you a full-length mirror because you are looking fine in that. The men are going to be lining up. Take my word for it, watch!"

"Okay, you are getting a little crazy here; you need to get to work before Dan sees you goofing off. Where's my six o'clock?" Julia announced, looking at her phone. "That's why I hate working this late shift. Those girls never get here on time. Who's working today? Dang it, it's Brooke. She's never on time."

"Go on with your bad self. I will be right over here holding back all the guys waiting to see you."

"Guys?"

"Yeah, guys. They will be lining up to buy perfume from you."

"No, that would be when Brooke gets here."

"Brooke, smook! They will be lining up to see you."

Julia tossed the empty cardboard box behind the counter as she turned with her eyebrows raised, now facing Lisa.

"Okay, I will leave you alone now. Off I go before I get fired from this wonderful job that I love. Where I'm living the dream at minimum wage. But whatever," Lisa said as she danced her way to the women's department.

Julia walked around the counter and watched as Brooke made her way down the escalator, looking at her nails as if she hadn't a clue what time it was. Brooke was a sophomore in college and had the world at her feet. She had long blonde hair that framed her face and these incredible big blue eyes set within her crystal-clear skin.

Brooke was born into a wealthy family. She explained that her family decided she needed a taste of reality and told her she needed to get a part-time job if she wanted any extra cash because they were cutting her off. Well, the funny thing was, Brooke does really well with sales at the store. She barely had to look in a man's direction, and he was put under her spell. He couldn't get to the perfume counter fast enough. She had the highest sales in the department and worked the fewest hours.

Yet, Brooke truly had no interest in dating anyone, which Julia thought was incredibly adult of her. She was just happy hanging out with her friends and going to class every now and then. She was not looking for a relationship. And why should she? She was only twenty years old. She had her whole life ahead of her.

When Julia was twenty years old, she was in love. She was ready to give up everything to spend the rest of her life with Ritchie. At that age, Julia already had both of their lives planned out. He would stay in the service, and they would travel the world, and she would take classes in every country they were stationed in. Germany, Italy, China, England, anywhere the service took them, and she would write her stories based on their experiences. But her story ended that day. As if destiny had come up and slapped her right in the face and said, "Take that, dreamer." And she did.

Oh, it wasn't that she didn't love her family. Even her crazy mother and irresponsible son. She wouldn't have traded them for anything in the world. But she would have given anything just to have been Ritchie's wife for just one day. One beautiful day.

Yet, life had a different ending for Julia. She had finally come to the conclusion that love just wasn't in the cards for her. She eventually had to face her reality. There were enough people around her living in fantasy land. Julia just didn't have that luxury.

"Julia, pssst...Julia," her friend Lisa whispered from the women's department. "How about we go out for drinks after work? I know a good place."

"No, you don't," Julia answered her as she unpacked some boxes and placed the perfume in the cabinets across from Lisa's department.

"No, really, there's this dance club. It's phenomenal, and there are people our age there. It plays '80s music all the time."

"I don't dance anymore," Julia responded.

"You don't dance? I have seen you swaying behind the counter to the store's music. Don't tell me you don't dance."

Julia glanced at Lisa as if she just realized that someone had been watching her. "I'm just messing around with that. I don't like to go out. It's complicated. I just don't want to go."

"Complicated? It's just a night out. We're not taking off for a weekend in Paris. Although, I would be up for that. Come on, girl. What else do you have to do this evening?"

"I don't know. My show is on tonight. And…well, you know I don't like to miss it."

"Oh, okay, let me get this straight. The show you watch every single day that plays reruns every single night is the one you can't miss?"

"Yeah, I like it, okay. It's just something I like doing."

"No offense, girl. But you got some messed-up notions of what fun is. Come on, girl. I don't want to go alone."

"I'm sorry, I just don't feel comfortable going."

"Ohhh…come on. What do you have to lose but a night alone with your mother?"

Just as Lisa said that, Brooke strolled over to where Julia was standing. "Ahhh…Julia, can I get off early? I told some friends I would meet them later and they don't want to wait on me. I was hoping since we are kind of slow here, I could get away early since it's kinda your night to help close anyway."

Julia glanced over at Lisa, who was smiling back at her. "Okay, I'll go," she said to Lisa. She then turned toward Brooke. "No, you can't get off early. You got here late. You're required to work your whole shift."

"Okay…okay. I just thought I would ask," Brooke said as she moved back behind the counter and took out her nail file, waiting for her next victim, just as a young man walked up to her, asking her about some cologne.

Julia looked over at Lisa, who was now dancing behind her counter, and shook her head as she said, "What did I get myself into?"

The store was like a ghost town that night, so Julia had time to venture outside her department. She strolled over to the jewelry section to see if her friend Annie was working. Since all the customers were drawn to Brooke anyway, she figured she would just let Brooke have whatever few sales there were.

Julia loved the jewelry department. Not that she bought jewelry, ever. It was just the way the whole area glimmered and shined. The jewelry department was honestly like walking into Tiffany's. They had clear glass shelving lined with black felt. Earrings were placed on silver racks that sparkled under the lights. There were huge silver-plated mirrors on every counter, and all the women were dressed in black and white.

Her friend, Annie, had worked at the department store most of her life. She was quite a bit older than Julia. Julia had never had enough guts to ask Annie her exact age. She figured Annie worked there because she desired to keep busy. Her husband had died about ten years ago, and her kids lived in different parts of the country. Julia got the impression that Annie didn't see them very often because she never mentioned her kids. She honestly believed that Annie worked there so she wouldn't be alone, and Julia, more than anyone else, knew that was a pretty good reason.

Annie dressed in the latest styles. She always looked very professional, almost as if she owned the place. And Annie would never have been caught without her deep matte lipstick and mauve blush. Julia thought Annie had aged beautifully. She often thought about how nice it would be if Annie actually met someone. But who was she to talk? She had been alone for almost as long as Annie.

"Hey lady, how are you?" Annie said upon catching sight of Julia.

"I'm good."

"What? That's not a very enthusiastic 'I'm good,'" Annie said as she walked toward Julia, stopping to straighten some earrings now and then.

"Ohhh…it's just Lisa talked me into going out dancing with her. And, well…I'm starting to rethink the whole thing. Sometimes I wonder why Lisa and I are friends. She's always trying to push me to do things I just don't want to do. Oh…why the heck did I say I would go?"

"Why? Did you have other plans?" Annie asked, placing some earrings on a shelf.

"Well, no. But the show I like to watch is on tonight. And…well, I had the whole night already planned."

"Your show? Really, Julia. When I was your age, my husband and I went out dancing all the time. Oh, how I miss that. You should go."

"I'm forty-seven years old, Annie. I have no business out there. It's for the young."

"And the young at heart. Julia, you should live a little. Lisa's just pushing you so you can see a different part of life. What's the harm in that? You might enjoy it."

Julia frowned. "I doubt it, but I already told her I'd go."

"I bet you'll have a better time than you think. I thought you told me you used to love to dance."

"That was ages ago. That was a whole other life. A whole other world."

"Well, your old world will be waiting for you at the end of the night. I guarantee it. What do you have to lose?"

"My sanity," Julia smirked as she helped straighten some of the necklaces hanging on a display.

"Ohhh…it's not that bad," Annie said as she strolled over to a display of earrings and picked one off the rack. "Here…I want you to wear these tonight. They are on me. I think they will go with your outfit perfectly."

"I don't need earrings. I'm just going to be sitting there anyway."

"Well, humor an old friend and wear them. Please?" Annie then walked Julia over to one of the large silver mirrors and held the earrings up under Julia's brown hair. "See, they are perfect for you."

"All right. I will wear them. They're beautiful," Julia said, looking down at them. The earrings brought her back to a time, years ago, when she danced under a large disco ball. The shimmer and shine that reflected off anything that the light touched.

"Okay, Annie. Thanks for the earrings. I will let you know how it goes."

Julia made her way back to the perfume department. She debated on whether she should wear the earrings or not. After all, how would Annie know if she decided not to wear them? She put them on to see how they looked and decided to wear them for a little while to see if she liked them.

She bent down and started to wipe down the bottom cabinets when she felt someone standing over her, staring at her. She squinted her eyes, looking up toward the fluorescent lights as a shadowed image of a man formed above her, the beams of light coming through his arms and around his head. He was standing on the other side of the counter, waiting patiently for her to notice him.

"Hello," he said.

"Hello. Oh, I'm sorry. How may I help you?" Julia stuttered as she stood up.

She instantly felt a familiarity with this stranger. Like when you run into someone you have seen somewhere, but you can't remember where. You even believe you may have spoken to them, and still, you are unable to place them.

"I'm looking for a particular perfume for my girlfriend."

"Well, you have come to the right place," Julia said. She couldn't seem to hear herself speaking. She was so taken by the man's smile. After every sentence, he would light up with this huge grin. He seemed to be older, possibly her age. He had dark hair that had begun to gray on the sides, which Julia found quite attractive.

He had a distinguished air about him. He was sophisticated but sweet.

"I'm afraid I procrastinated and have been everywhere looking for this certain brand of perfume and can't seem to locate it. I hate ordering online because it takes forever to arrive, and I kind of need it tonight."

"Well, what's it called?"

"Joy. It is by Jean Patou. I am not sure if I'm pronouncing that correctly."

Julia had only heard that name twice since she had begun working at the store ten years ago. Once was when her former manager told her never to go into the case behind her unless she had a legitimate customer. And the other time was when she sold a bottle to a young woman who came in dressed in a business suit. The young woman looked like some type of swimsuit model with her tan complexion, slim build, and long legs. The woman wore a skirt that ended just before her knees. She strolled around in matching heels and had a man in a black suit behind her, carrying all of her bags. All Julia could think about at that time was how her feet would have been killing her if she walked around the mall in those types of heels. But this young woman walked around in them as if she were barefoot, putting one foot in front of the other, gliding across the floor.

Julia took a gulp and looked down at the locked metal box that contained the key that would open the case to what they all called "the good stuff." Someone had even humorously placed a note on the outside of the metal box that stated, "Enter at your own risk!"

"Yes, we have it. Let me get the bottle for you." Julia then looked back up at him. He was wearing a dark gray jacket and matching slacks. His white button-down cotton shirt was open at the collar just above his chest hair. He stood looking over the other perfumes and colognes with one hand in his pocket, strolling back and forth in front of the display like a runway model. He would stop now and then and smile that gorgeous smile at her. "So, is this for a special occasion?" she asked, trying to make conversation.

"Yes," he said abruptly and looked down at the gold badge over her pocket. "Julia?"

"Yes, it's Julia." She smiled and waited for him to finish his explanation of the night that awaited him, which of course, he didn't, so she opened the metal cabinet and grabbed the key for the display cabinet behind her. She placed the key in the slot as smoothly as she could, nervous about taking out the expensive bottle of perfume. She grabbed the box and quickly closed and locked the cabinet door behind her.

"Here you go," she said, laying the box down on the counter as if she sold one every day of the week.

"Wonderful, you are a lifesaver, Julia. What a pretty name," he said.

"Well, thank you," Julia responded, trying not to blush.

He proceeded to take out his wallet and removed a credit card. "Here, you can use this," he said.

Julia carried the card to the register and proceeded to scan the perfume. She noticed how this man continued to move back and forth in front of her, eyeing their different products. She caught him glancing up at her a couple of times when he thought she wasn't looking.

Julia thought it was because she was taking so long to ring up the sale. She hadn't rung up this large of a sale in a while. This one purchase would cover her quota for the next two weeks.

When the sale was completed, she went to tear the receipt off, and it somehow got stuck in between the metal teeth. She tried to tug at the receipt, and it still would not budge. She quickly pulled out the scissors they kept in the bottom drawer of the register and cut the receipt from the roll, stuffing it in the bag where the perfume was held, and quickly turned back toward the counter.

"Thank you so much for your purchase. I hope she is surprised."

"Me too," the man said, and he stood there for a second, looking into Julia's eyes.

Julia, uncomfortable, placed a piece of hair behind her ear and smiled back at him. "Please come back," she said awkwardly, hoping she didn't seem too obvious.

"Thank you, Julia. I will." He then turned and took a few steps toward the escalator and turned back around. "Oh, and nice earrings," he said, flashing that gorgeous smile.

"Thank you," Julia said awkwardly, grabbing onto the earrings she had forgotten she was wearing.

He then floated up the escalator and was gone and out of her sight within seconds.

After coming out of her love-sick gaze, Julia scanned the area and realized that Brooke was standing behind the counter the whole time. This guy didn't even notice her. He seemed to deliberately search out Julia. She looked over at the escalator one last time, stroking her new earrings, and watched as people continually disappeared in and out of her sight.

CHAPTER FOUR

Julia and Lisa pulled up to the '80s Explosion—a local '80s-themed dance club. The buildings—set in the Old Downtown section of San Diego—were slowly being modernized and refurbished into restaurants and nightclubs. The '80s Explosion was located in an old red brick paper warehouse. The exterior windows were recently covered with a black tint to prevent outsiders from peering in.

As soon as the two women parked their vehicle, they could smell the salty air making its way in from the Pacific. Locals flocked toward the mile-long line that awaited them on the newly laid stone walkway in hopes of making it into the dance club before dark.

Cooled by the breeze that made its way around the swaying palm trees, guests usually found themselves in deep conversation or resting on the many bronze benches that lined the path just outside the front doors. Every so often, a miniature dance floor exploded within the line, drawing in most of the people waiting into an impromptu dance party right outside the ticket booth. Couples swayed to tunes coming from the exterior speakers as the relaxed mood of the San Diego nightlife made waiting in line part of the ambiance.

"I can't go in," Julia said, feeling her temperature rise and her cheeks flush to a rosy red as she tried to cool them frantically with the back of her hand.

Lisa, sitting in the driver's seat, looked over at Julia, rolling her eyes in disgust. "What do you mean you can't go in? You promised me. Now get out of the freakin' car."

"Okay…okay, but let's not stay long."

"Whatever, Julia. Just give it a chance, girl. I bet we're going to have the time of our lives. When was the last time you had the time of your life? Huh?"

"I don't remember," Julia said, in a state of panic. "Seriously, I don't remember."

"Girl, get out of the car. You need this. And I definitely need this."

"Okay…okay," Julia said as she slowly reached for the door handle.

They steered their way through the parking lot like they were on an African safari and headed toward the end of the line. Julia peered at all the—what seemed like—teenagers surrounding her and tried to melt into the crowd, eventually taking a seat on one of the bronze benches.

Lisa scanned the crowd, bouncing up and down while in line. Trying to see over the crowd, she constantly checked the front of the line to see if they were getting any closer. After slowly making progress in line, the two friends finally reached the woman with blue hair that sat behind the ticket booth.

After buying tickets, they walked into a large, dimly lit hall that flashed multi-colored strobe lights. There was a massive dance floor in the center of the room and tall round tables placed strategically throughout the nightclub, making it look like a pinball machine.

Lisa grinned as if she had just found Neverland, her eyes skimming the crowd. "Girl, look at all these fine young men."

"That's just it, Lisa," Julia whispered while trying to duck back into the shadows. "They're all young."

"Not all of them. I think there are some men our age over there." Lisa pointed to the corner of the room, drawing Julia's attention to where the pool tables were located. The overhead lamps, made up of different brands of beer bottles, lit up the area like a bus stop on a dimly lit street. Each pool table was surrounded by ten to twelve people, men and women. One of the men in the group that was nearest to the dance floor turned around and stared at the two women as they passed by.

"Oooh…girl, I think you have an admirer," Lisa teased.

"What are you talking about?" Julia asked as she crept out of the shadows, squinting her eyes to see across the faintly lit room. Julia turned her head toward the light just in time to spot her fan. There stood before her a tall, blonde Greek Adonis looking right at her. She immediately avoided his stare, looking in the opposite direction as if she were looking for someone in the deep sea of bodies. "That kid is young enough to be my son. In fact, I think he may be a friend of my son's."

"What are you talking about, girl? He is at least thirty-nine…forty. Take my word for it," Lisa screamed out at Julia as the lights flashed around them and the crowd grew thicker. The two women struggled to stay together as they searched for an empty table.

"Let's go," Julia begged.

"Oh, come on, we just got here. Give it a chance."

Julia reluctantly followed Lisa across the floor, turning every few seconds to see the same man staring at her. They made a path toward a small empty table near the bar. A waitress, who had on torn jean shorts and a small white tank that barely covered the red-laced bra, came over to take their order.

"What can I get you, ladies?"

"Ohhh…I will have a Pink Lady, please," Lisa said, turning to whisper to Julia. "I always wanted to try one of those. What are you going to get?"

"Ahhh…I'll take a margarita, please."

"Great, I'll get those right away," the young woman said as she balanced an empty tray with one hand.

Julia scanned the club, still uncomfortable with her surroundings, feeling like a wallflower in a sea of roses. Believing everyone she laid eyes on was thinking the same thing, *What in the heck is she doing here?*

Her heart was pounding to the beat of the music as she watched the young crowd before her make their way off and onto the dance floor. The music was so loud that the two women found themselves shouting at one another across the small table, trying to hold some kind of a conversation.

After a few songs, their drinks finally arrived. Lisa danced on her stool as the songs played one right after the other, snapping her fingers to the beat. Julia—who continually refused Lisa's invitation to head out to the dance floor—got lost dissecting the people surrounding her. The young crowd continually made their way on and off the dance floor, laughing and giggling and loving life. Julia did notice that there was a wider age span of attendees than she thought there would be. The '80s music seemed to draw an audience from all decades.

Strobe lights flickered as the DJ announced the next melody. "I know all you lovelies out there can't wait to hit the dance floor, so here is a song just for you, 'Wake Me Up Before You Go-Go,' by my man, George Michael, better known as Wham."

Upon the announcement of this particular tune, there was an eerie silence. The dance floor suddenly went black. The two women looked around as a stillness ensued, and the crowd turned mute. The dance floor brightened slowly, and lights started to flare in every direction, consisting of rainbows of reds, blues, yellows, and greens, glittering the dance floor like raining confetti. Julia watched as the crowd parted, and several young women scurried out onto the center of the dance floor. The girls were outfitted in leg warmers that lay at their ankles, resting upon pink and turquoise tights. The young girls all wore black and white T-shirts displaying the phrase "Choose Life," just like the one George Michael was wearing in his video that was playing on a screen above the dance floor.

At that moment, the entire crowd burst into song. Everyone in the place rushed onto the dance floor, mimicking George Michael's signature moves. Julia—not realizing she was doing it—found herself moving her feet to the beat of this iconic song.

Lisa swayed to the music while standing on her barstool, trying to see the dancers over the crowd.

The music, the lights, and that song suddenly brought Julia back to a time in her life she thought she had buried deep down inside her. A time she had chosen to forget, as memories came pouring back, and a life she intentionally chose not to remember flared up before her once again.

Sent back in time, she imagined herself under the disco globe. She was twenty years old again, moving across the dance floor as the music took control and everyone else in the dance club disappeared. Everyone but Ritchie. He was there in the corner of the dance floor, making his way over to her as the lights flashed across his beautiful skin. The replaying of this memory seemed so real that Julia reached out to touch what she thought was Ritchie heading toward her and accidentally hit Lisa in the back of the head.

"Ouch, what are you doin'?" Lisa screamed over the crowd.

Before Julia knew it, she found herself up on her feet, clawing her way through the celebrating crowd, trying to find the exit. The air seemed to escape the room as Julia found it hard to breathe. The music blared as everything in the room started to blur. She felt Lisa behind her, trying to grab at her, yelling her name as she surged forward. Both women were being knocked around and pushed back as they moved against the massive wave of people trying to reach the dance floor.

Julia suddenly grabbed at her throat, her breath becoming labored as she struggled to breathe, and everything became hazy. The room began to spin, slowly at first and then as if she were on a rogue merry-go-round. Julia looked to the left and the right and found herself unable to focus as she turned toward the lights over the dance floor and saw that beautiful smile once again. She reached out toward it, but the image disappeared, leaving her reaching toward the young man from the pool table that she had noticed earlier.

"Are you okay?" he asked in what seemed like slow motion. Julia felt herself falling as the young man reached out and grabbed her under her arms. Lisa came up behind them and helped to hold Julia up. The two struggled to get her to a stand. They each placed one of Julia's arms around their shoulders, dragging her toward the exit. They maneuvered her through the crowd the best that they could. Once outside, Julia began to come to, feeling the cool, fresh ocean air hitting her face.

"Julia," Lisa said as she leaned over her, pulling Julia to an upright position. "Are you okay? You seemed to lose your balance in there."

Julia heard Lisa's echoed words come to her as if from a distance. "Yeah…yeah, I'm fine. Sorry, I just got a little dizzy, that's all. I don't know what's wrong with me. I think I need to sit down."

"Well, I think you almost passed out," the young man said while helping to move Julia to a nearby bench.

Julia then realized that the handsome young man, whom she had caught a glimpse of earlier near the pool table, was now attempting to hold her up. She took her hand down from his shoulder, pulling herself onto the bench. "I'm so sorry. Thank you for helping me out."

"Are you sure you're okay? Do you need to go to the hospital?" the young man asked. He was broader and taller than most of the other young men there. Julia thought he looked possibly thirty-six to thirty-eight years old. His torso and arms were bursting out of the blue T-shirt he was wearing, and he had on a baseball cap that had what looked like deer horns on it. Underneath the cap, his bleach-blonde hair was cut within inches of his scalp.

Julia noticed how the young man answered every question with a "Yes, ma'am" or "No, ma'am." She thought that he was either in the military or from the South. He didn't have an accent, so Julia figured that he was possibly a Marine.

"No, no, I'm fine. Just a little embarrassed," Julia said, hugging her stomach with her arms as if she were chilled. "Maybe I shouldn't have had that margarita."

Lisa smiled at the handsome young man, squinting her nose, and said, "We don't get out very much."

"Well, I'd be glad to escort you home," he said, looking down at Julia.

Julia blushed as Lisa nudged Julia with her hip as if telling her to say something.

Julia, taking the hint, answered, "I'll be fine. I appreciate the offer, though."

"It's not a problem. I have my GPS, and I can get you wherever you need to go. I can take both of you home if you need a ride."

"No, no, really. We'll be fine," Julia said, now a little more flattered to have the attention of this young, handsome soldier.

"Okay, well, can I at least get your phone number so I can check on you tomorrow?" the handsome young man said. "Oh, and by the way, my name is Brad, Brad Anderson. Just in case you were wondering."

Julia then shook her head, embarrassed that she hadn't asked his name before now. "Oh, I'm so sorry. I'm Julia Melrose, and this is my good friend, Lisa Arnold."

And before Julia had a chance to say anything else, she heard Lisa rambling off a phone number to him. She thought for a moment that Lisa was giving him her own phone number. It took Julia a second to realize that the number Lisa was reading off was actually Julia's phone number.

"Hold on, Lisa," Julia protested, just as she saw Lisa leaning over Brad's shoulder to make sure he got the number correct. "I didn't say I wanted my number given out."

Lisa looked over at Julia and then back at Brad, realizing that she might have just crossed the line. "He just wants to check on you, Julia. He is not asking for your hand in marriage."

Julia, now angry, stood up and pulled Lisa to the side. "Have you lost your mind? What are you doing?"

Lisa whispered back, "I am trying to help you, my friend. Now, just shut up and let me do it."

Julia turned around to find Brad walking up behind them. "Julia, right?" he said.

"Yes, it's Julia."

"I promise. I'm not any kind of psycho. I really just want to make sure that you're okay. Can we start over?" Brad said, with such sincerity, that Julia found herself putting her borders down. "I'm Brad Anderson." Brad stuck out his hand for her to shake it.

"Nice to meet you, Brad," Julia said as he shook her hand.

"Oh, and I'm the good friend, Lisa, if anyone is interested," Lisa said.

"Nice to meet you both," Brad said, turning to each one of them. "I would honestly like to check on you tomorrow, Julia, if you're sure you will make it home okay," Brad said so sweetly; Julia smiled and gave him a reassuring nod.

"I'm fine, just a little embarrassed," she said, now looking over at Lisa, who was smiling and in some sort of a trance, staring at this poor young man so hard that Julia had to nudge her to bring her back to reality.

While the group was engrossed in small talk, Julia spotted someone she thought that she knew out of the corner of her eye. Curious, Julia squinted her eyes so that she could focus on what looked like a familiar face. There was a man, who looked about her age, who was waiting to get into the club. She thought she recognized the gentleman from somewhere and continued to try and place him. Then as if a light bulb had gone off, she realized it was the man she had waited on earlier that day. The man who bought the expensive perfume. He was wearing the same jacket and button-down shirt, so she was sure it was him. He was with a young brunette woman wearing a mini dress. The woman looked to be half his age. It didn't seem to be his daughter as he held her by the small of her back, which was completely bare. He leaned down to whisper in her ear as they waited to enter the club.

Julia was so surprised by the sight of the man that she found herself intensely staring at him. So much so that Brad and Lisa turned to see who she was glaring at.

"What?" Lisa suddenly asked.

Julia narrowed her eyes as the stranger felt someone staring at him from his side and turned to look back toward her.

Julia, realizing he had seen her staring at him, ducked down behind Lisa.

"What…do you know him, Julia?" Lisa asked.

The man she had sold the perfume to started to wave toward the group as Julia turned her head to look in the other direction.

Brad then nodded toward the man in line, acknowledging his wave, and turned to let Julia know the man was waving. "I think he's waving at you, Julia."

Julia glanced at Brad and looked reluctantly back at the stranger she had helped earlier that day, giving him a slight grin and a wave while trying to casually continue a conversation with Lisa and Brad.

The man in line, getting the impression she was trying to stay out of his view, smiled and entered the dance hall with the young woman, looking back once before he was out of sight.

Julia—trying to play off her strange reaction to seeing this man again—suddenly asked, "So, where are you from, Brad?"

"Oh…I'm from a small town in Kansas," Brad said, staring straight at Julia as if trying to get her attention back on him.

"A Midwesterner, huh?" Julia said, trying to seem interested.

"Yeah…don't miss it, though," Brad continued.

"You don't?" Julia asked. "Why not?"

"Well, there's no ocean back there. Miles of flat land, beautiful pasture land, but no ocean. I love it out here. Not sure how long I will be stationed here, but I am hoping to stay for a while."

"Stationed? So, you're a Marine?" Julia asked as if it somehow bothered her.

"Are you not a fan?" Brad said awkwardly.

"No, I'm sorry. I admire the military. I…I'm just surprised, that's all."

"Surprised?" Lisa huffed. "Julia, the man is built like Dwayne Johnson. I knew he was a Marine the moment I laid eyes on him."

Julia, becoming more and more annoyed with Lisa, grabbed her arm and yanked it as if they had to suddenly leave. "Well, Brad, I really have to thank you for all you've done, and it has been awfully nice to have met you, but we have to go now. I have to…yeah, work tomorrow, and we were going to make this an early night, especially with me almost passing out and all," Julia said, trying to convince Brad of their sudden need to leave.

"Well, I will check on you tomorrow, so answer my call. It is Brad Anderson. Just so you know the name when you hear my voice."

"Yeah, well, Brad, you have been a real lifesaver. We have to go now. It was a real pleasure meeting you," Julia said as she tried to move away, dragging Lisa along behind her.

"I wanted to stay awhile," Lisa tried to whisper to Julia.

"No…no. Have to work tomorrow, must get home early, Lisa,"

"Yeah, whatever. We have to go now," Lisa said reluctantly. "You know, my friend here almost passing out and all."

"Oh, yeah, I totally understand," Brad yelled back at them as they moved away. "So, I'll talk to you tomorrow, Julia."

Julia smiled reluctantly as she grabbed Lisa's arm, pulling her toward their car. "Yes, tomorrow. I will answer your call tomorrow. Thanks again, Brad."

"What are you doing? Let go of my arm," Lisa said as she was shuffled toward the parking lot. When they were out of range, Lisa turned toward Julia. "Did you really almost pass out in there? Are you okay? You had this weird look in your eye."

Julia did not answer. She just kept moving toward the car. "Everything went dark. I don't know what happened. I saw…"

Lisa stopped for a minute, waiting for a response. "You saw what?"

"Nothing…I just got dizzy, that's all. It was nothing."

"Really, 'cause you turned white as a ghost. If Brad hadn't been there, you would've face-planted right into the floor. Are you sure you're okay?"

"Yeah…I'm okay. I just got woozy, the lights and everything. You know we're getting too old for this."

"Hey, speak for yourself. Old? What are you talking about? You just had a thirty-something male bodybuilder get your phone number and was begging to drive you home. And who was the other guy in line? He wasn't bad-looking, either. You have some luck. I didn't even have time to meet one guy. That's okay. That's okay. I get it. You don't feel well, so we should go home, but you owe me another night out."

"What? No, I'm not coming back."

"Why not? Here you have two mystery guys, and I didn't even meet one. You owe me another night out."

Julia didn't answer as her thoughts turned to the mystery man from the store. The woman he was with looked so young. *Figures,* she thought to herself. *Men our age are always looking for someone my daughter's age. But why did he wave? Was he waving at someone else? No, even Lisa and Brad saw him waving. Was he waving at me?* Julia questioned. *Was the young girl the person he had bought the perfume for? She had to be. He said it was for a special occasion and he needed it that night. Was she his girlfriend?*

Julia was suddenly brought back to reality as she heard Lisa's voice, "Are you listening to me?"

"Yeah, yeah," Julia heard herself saying.

"Who was the guy in line? You never go anywhere, huh? Then where did you meet him?" Lisa asked.

"He was a customer I waited on earlier today."

"A customer? Why was he waving at you? Why was he so buddy-buddy? And who was the young girl he was with?"

Julia felt her world starting to spin again as she grabbed onto Lisa's car. "I don't know. You were the one that wanted to come out here, so we came. Now I have this young guy calling me, and the man in line thinks Brad is my boyfriend or something."

"What do you care what he thinks? Who is that guy?"

Julia thought about her question for a minute. *Yeah, why did she care what he thought? He was with some teenybopper. Why should she care what he thinks of her?*

"You're right. I don't know him. He just seemed interesting, that's all."

"Interesting, huh," Lisa said, realizing she had struck a chord with Julia. "Well, you still owe me another night out."

"Okay…okay, can we go home now?"

"Yeah, I guess. Man, is Brad fine. If you don't want him, can I take him?"

"He's just a kid."

"That's no kid, Julia. He is old enough."

"I'm old enough to be his mother, Lisa."

"He doesn't have to know that."

Lisa rambled on as Julia rewound the last few moments of her life. She wondered why she had met both of these men on the same day. She thought about her favorite show, *A Moment in Time*, and her mind flashed to what Michelle would have done in her shoes. She knew what Michelle would have done. She would have taken Brad's hand and gone back into the dance hall and danced the night away right in front of her mystery man and his "so-called" teenage girlfriend.

Maybe Lisa was right, Julia thought. *Maybe this was what living was all about.* Julia felt a tingle move up her spine as she felt a giddiness she hadn't experienced in quite some time overtake her. She stretched her arm out of the open window and laid her head back on the headrest, hearing the ocean crash against the shore in the distance, and felt something coming alive in her for the first time in a very long time as Lisa drove the long-distance home, rambling on about their night, and how life was so unfair.

CHAPTER FIVE

"Hello, anyone home?" Julia recognized Bobby's voice vibrating down the hallway. Checking her alarm clock, she slowly rose from her bed, rubbing her eyes as the first morning light made its way through the beige window shade. Julia covered her eyes, regretting her late-night clubbing. Grabbing her blue furry robe, she scrambled to cover up her nightgown. In the rush of trying to maneuver the robe around her body, she tangled her feet in the dangling belt and almost fell to the floor. Moments before falling, she reached up and grabbed the bed rail, which left her dangling like a zoo monkey.

"Mom?" she heard Bobby call out again from down the hall. "Are you up?"

"Yeah, on my way!" she yelled back, jerking at her robe while trying to untangle the belt wrapped around her leg. Julia glanced over at the luminescent numbers on her digital clock that read 7 a.m.

Julia stood up in front of her mirror and tried to smooth down her untamed hair with a brush. She then wiped away the mascara embedded under her eyes, recalling the humiliating events of her girl's night out with Lisa.

She stumbled out into the hallway, hearing voices floating out of the living room, which should have been a warning to her that Bobby was not alone, but she thought he might be talking with his grandmother, so she didn't give it a second thought.

"Hey, Mom!" her son said as a wide-eyed Julia walked into the room. "I want you to meet Ashley."

Ashley was a cute blue-eyed redhead with freckles across her nose. Julia noticed immediately that she was different from most of the other girls her son had dated. For one thing, Ashley still had her natural hair color, and Julia couldn't pick out any nose rings or eyebrow piercings. She found herself smoothing down her hair and wiping the remnants of the mascara from under her eyes as she came into close proximity of the young couple.

"Hey, son. You didn't tell me you were bringing someone over this morning," Julia said, smiling at the young woman. "So, who do we have here? I'm sorry I'm in my robe," she quickly apologized to the young woman.

"Oh, no, you're fine. I'm sorry we woke you. I told Bobby you all might not be up yet. We're just coming from the gym."

Julia furrowed her eyebrows, staring at her son as he smiled back at her. She knew he had never been to a gym before, especially at this hour. Julia thought immediately that he must really like this one. "Well, it's so nice to meet you, Ashley. You're more than welcome here any time. Have you all eaten?"

The young woman spoke up for them as her son, who was usually the person gabbing away, stepped back to let Ashley do the talking. "We just hit the coffee shop and had an egg and biscuit with some fruit. We were in the area, so Bobby wanted to stop by. I've heard so much about you."

Julia found this to be a rare moment. She assumed Bobby said nothing about her to his friends. Her son told her nothing about his life, so she just assumed he didn't care to speak about her to his friends. His father was even less informed, but Julia considered her children's lack of contact with their father their father's fault.

Bobby and Lauren had almost no relationship with their father. If their father said he was coming to meet them, there was always a question as to whether he would show up or not. Julia wasn't sure if this was due to Scott's drinking or his women. Sadly, the kids learned early in life that they just couldn't depend on him.

Even though Bobby swore he was nothing like his dad, Julia knew better. He had unfortunately inherited some of Scott's questionable characteristics. Bobby, like his dad, didn't know how to distinguish between what a person wanted to hear and the truth.

"Well, I'm so glad you both stopped by. I think Grandma may still be asleep."

"What's going on out here?" Julia heard her mother yell from the back of the house. "Who in the heck's here at this hour?"

"That would be Bobby's grandmother," Julia said, trying to smooth the comments she heard sailing their way from the back of the house. "She's not a morning person," Julia whispered.

"What are you talking about? I've been up since 6 a.m.," Carmen announced. "Is that Bobby? Who's with him?" she announced to the room.

"Mom, this is Ashley, a friend of Bobby's," Julia said before her mother could say something embarrassing.

"Friend, huh? Well, nice to meet you, young lady. We don't get to speak with too many of Bobby's girls."

"Grandma! I don't have girls," Bobby interjected.

"Well, yeah, that's not what I would call them either. You seem pretty normal. What's your name again, sweetie?"

Ashley laughed and answered, "Oh, I'm Ashley. Very nice to meet you, Grandma Carmen."

"Oh, just call me Grandma. Everyone does."

"Okay, Grandma," Ashley said reluctantly.

Bobby, feeling embarrassed, slowly tried to move Ashley toward the front door. "Well, we just wanted to stop by. I'm going to work later, so we have to get going," Bobby said, afraid of what his grandmother would say next.

"Oh, did you find a job?" Grandma Carmen asked. "He's been looking for quite a while. We didn't think he'd ever find one."

"Mom, you know Bobby's working. He's selling cell phones now," Julia said, trying to redeem her son's honor.

"He's selling what?"

"Cell phones. You know, like the one I got for you that you refuse to use."

"Oh, yeah. I can't figure that thing out. All those buttons and rings and crazy pictures. If someone wants to get a hold of me, they will call my house phone."

Ashley stepped back toward Carmen for a minute and said, "Well, maybe we need to sit down with you and show you how it works."

"That would be nice, young lady. No one ever takes the time to do that around here."

"Well, that's what we will have to do then," Ashley said as she found herself being pulled toward the front door by Bobby.

"Okay, Grams. We are heading out now. I love you both." And Bobby did something he hadn't ever done with anyone. He opened the door for Ashley and let her walk through first. He also reached down and grabbed her hand before she had a chance to get past him. Before he walked out the door, he turned back around and winked at Julia, and somehow, she knew. She knew he had found his someone.

Now, if he just doesn't screw it up, she thought to herself.

Being that it was Sunday and the department store was not opening until noon, Julia dressed for work and sat down for breakfast. She had to go in a little early on Sundays to turn on all the computers and make sure that everything was balanced from the night before. Since Brooke had closed, she never knew in what condition the department was left.

She thought about the mysterious man who had bought the perfume from her yesterday. She wondered how his night went and if he was still seeing the young woman that she saw him with. He seemed very taken with her, but the young woman seemed a little like Brooke; like she could take him or leave him.

What would she be doing with him anyway? Julia thought.

Just as Julia was about to take a bite of her toast, her phone rang. She looked at the screen and dropped her toast onto her plate just as her mother walked into the dining room.

"Isn't that your phone ringing?" Carmen asked.

"What?" Julia said.

"Your phone's ringing. Are you going deaf? Answer it," Carmen said, turning to go into the laundry room.

The screen lit up with a phone number Julia didn't recognize. With all the commotion, Julia had forgotten that Brad said he would call today. She was still racking her brain, trying to figure out why a nice young man like that would be interested in calling her. There were so many beautiful young women at the '80s Explosion last night. Why would he want to talk to her?

"Hello," Julia said, checking to see if her mother was listening as she heard the washer begin to fill with water. Julia then made her way into the hallway bathroom and locked the door behind her.

"Hi, Julia. It's Brad from last night. You remember me, don't you?"

"Yes, Brad. Thank you again for helping me," Julia said, trying to whisper.

"Oh, don't give it a second thought. Are you feeling okay?"

"Yes, thank you for asking, but I feel like there's something I should tell you," Julia said, whispering so her mother couldn't hear.

"Sorry, I'm having a hard time hearing you," Brad said, finding himself whispering too.

"Oh, sorry, can you hear me now?" Julia reiterated, trying to speak a little louder.

"I have to ask, so please don't take offense, but you aren't married or something, are you?" Brad asked in such a way Julia couldn't help but take it as a compliment.

"No, nothing like that." She giggled.

"Well, neither am I, just in case you were wondering. Well, I'm not very good at this, but would you like to have dinner sometime?" Just then, Julia heard a pounding on the bathroom door.

"Julia, are you in there?"

"Is someone calling you?" Brad asked.

Julia looked toward the door with a panicked look on her face. "Yes…yes, it's just my mother."

"Oh, you live with your mother?"

"Yeah, she's not…well," Julia stumbled.

"Oh, I'm sorry to hear that."

The pounding started to get more intense as Julia found herself needing to get off the phone.

"Julia, Lauren is on the house phone. What do you want me to tell her?"

"I have to go, Brad. She needs me."

"Well, how about Friday night?"

"I have to work."

"Okay, how about Saturday?"

The banging on the door became increasingly louder. Julia struggled to hear Brad over the noise. "Okay, I guess," Julia said, trying to get to her mother before she broke down the door.

"Great. If you'll text me your address, I will pick you up at six. Is that okay?"

"Yeah…yeah," Julia said, trying to end the conversation.

"I know you have to go, so I will see you then."

"Ahhh…that's fine, see you then, Brad, goodbye."

Julia hung up the phone and opened the door.

Her mother almost fell onto the floor from having her ear pressed against the door so closely.

"Mom, what are you doing?"

"I told you, Lauren's on the phone."

"Okay, I heard you. You don't need to be listening in on my conversations."

"But that's the only way I find stuff out around here."

Julia made her way to the phone but had to be brief because she was now running late for work.

"Mom, can we meet after you get off work?" Lauren quavered, almost panting as if she were losing her breath. "Maybe for dinner?"

"Yeah, sweetie, that's fine. Is six-thirty okay? Are you okay?"

"I'll explain later. How about Manfield's Café?"

"Yeah, that's fine. I'll see you then, sweetie," Julia said, looking at her watch as the minutes ticked away.

Her brilliant, fun, beautiful daughter found herself in a relationship with what Julia would call a real loser. Lauren was a fixer, just like her mother. Lauren was sure she could fix her boyfriend, Jake, and make him into her ideal boyfriend and possibly, regrettably, her husband. Julia knew differently, but she also realized that voicing her opinion would only throw Lauren into his arms faster. So, she held her tongue.

She only hoped Lauren was not bringing her news that she didn't want to hear. Like she was planning on marrying that loser or something.

Yet, what could Julia say? She just made a date with someone not much older than her daughter. Julia thought, *What a fine group of lunatics her family had turned out to be, and she was the queen lunatic.*

As she walked out the front door that day, she stood and looked at the neighborhood that she had settled for. It was the same one her mother had settled for. She wondered if her children would end up here, too. Julia looked around at the '50s-style homes that made up the quaint neighborhood she had grown up in. The concrete porches and brick homes that were inhabited by couples her mother's age.

She giggled as she thought about the one good thing about living here. Somehow being surrounded by people her mother's age made Julia feel young. Because she was the youngest person on the block. She sighed, took a deep breath, and headed toward her vehicle parked just outside the chain-link fence.

As she started the engine, Julia's thoughts drifted to her past. She thought about the fact that her life, with all that she had lost, was quickly withering away, along with her many dreams, which were left unanswered and unsung. She took out a notebook that she kept in her purse and looked around at the clear blue sky. She began to write down the beginnings of a poem as she often did when things just didn't make sense. When life was going a little sideways. The notebook was filled with many verses of dreams, doubts, and questions. She sent them out into the universe, like a silent whisper or scream, unseen and unheard, dying, oh so slowly inside the lines of this small book.

CHAPTER SIX

"I'm pregnant," Lauren sniffled, sitting across from her mother in a brown leather booth, a tear rolling down her cheek. She immediately turned her head toward the parking lot to avoid her mother's reaction. The waiters ran around them carrying food and taking orders, unnoticed at this moment by Julia or her daughter. The hazy lights from the restaurant and choosing to not wear her eyeglasses forced Julia to strain to see her daughter across the table.

Julia searched through her purse as if she were trying to find a solution to her daughter's dilemma, as if the answer would somehow magically be found at the bottom of her bag.

The crowded restaurant slowly began to disappear as Lauren and Julia felt alone in this large room. The heavy weight of the words still circling above them. She placed her glasses on her nose and looked at her daughter, lowering her eyebrows as if trying to sort out what she thought she had heard.

"Pregnant? Are you sure?"

A series of sobs followed as Julia stretched out her arms, taking Lauren's hands in hers. "It's...going to be okay, sweetie."

"I don't know what to do. How can I raise this child when I am still raising myself?" Lauren said as her eyes searched the room for the answer.

With those words, Julia was sent back to a memory. It was when Lauren was three years old. She had placed a pillow under her sundress and walked around pretending to be pregnant, shouting, "*Look at me, Mama! Look at me!*"

She squeezed her daughter's hands tight, trying to remove the pain she saw swelling in Lauren's eyes. "Have you told Jake?"

"He's gone."

"What do you mean he's gone? Gone where?" Julia huffed.

"He left about two weeks ago. He doesn't know. He said he was moving to Hollywood with his uncle to make a go of his acting career. Whatever that means. We had a fight again. At the time I thought it was for the best, but now…"

"Does he still have his cell phone?"

"No, it got shut off."

"Can you tell his mother?" Julia asked, scrambling to find a ray of hope in her daughter's current situation.

"I don't want anything to do with him," Lauren said and then looked down at her belly, slowly caressing it. "Well, except the baby. I can do this, Mom."

"Oh, Lauren. I know you can. I just hate that you are going to do this alone."

"I have you guys."

"Yes, yes, you do."

"This baby will never feel unwanted; I swear that. This baby will never know it wasn't planned. Swear to me, Mom. Swear you will never tell my child the truth."

"I promise."

"Jake was a mistake, but this baby isn't. I will just have to figure it all out, that's all."

Julia got up and made her way to Lauren's side of the booth taking her daughter into her arms. She sat there hugging her brave daughter, rocking her back and forth, unable to take the hurt away. Unable to change the past. They sat there in that booth as the rest of the world disappeared. Julia held her daughter until she felt her wanting to let go. In the dim of the light, she sent out a prayer to the unknown and waited, again, for an answer.

How could her baby be having a baby?

Julia did not want this for her daughter. She did not want this to be her reality. Lauren had so many dreams.

Yet, in a way, she was proud of her daughter and the way she was handling the pregnancy. She was handling it like an adult. Julia, on the other hand, wanted to get up and run around the restaurant, shouting, "This can't be happening."

She could immediately tell that Lauren already loved this child. The child would never know its beginning because it would never be unwanted. *Grandma*, she thought to herself. *Am I going to be a grandma?*

A grandma looked like her mother, not her. *I can't be a grandma*, she thought to herself. *I'm too young.*

She tried to convince her daughter to come home with her, but Lauren said she had to work the next day and then had to go to school, so it would just be easier for her to go home.

Lauren seemed so brave. Julia thought if she had been in Lauren's shoes, she would have been at home in bed with the blankets pulled up over her head, but her daughter seemed to have no doubts. She was going to have this child, and the child would never know it was unplanned. Julia knew that Lauren would see to that. She already knew Lauren would die for that child. Yet, Julia also understood that Lauren didn't know all that she would be facing, raising a child alone. How could she?

After they said their goodbyes, Julia found herself crying uncontrollably on the long road home. She sniffled as she hit the steering wheel of her car, shaking it uncontrollably as her car swerved into the other lane. What was it that life wanted from her? Would it ever end? Her daughter's pain was just a reminder of the lack of control they all had in life. Or in love.

She was angry.

She felt helpless.

Her daughter was going to be a mother, and as fate would have it, she would be forced to raise this child on her own. "It's so unfair!" Julia felt herself screaming out to the universe. Into the silence of an empty car.

She wiped her eyes, trying to see the road before her. As luck would have it, it started to rain. Julia watched the streams slowly make their way down her windshield. She drove, finding it hard to distinguish between the tears in her eyes and the raindrops on the glass. She watched as the rain slithered down, forming paths, blurring her view of the world.

Exhausted by her daughter's new reality, Julia knew it would all work out if she could just make it home. As soon as she walked through the door, the rest of the world would disappear. She didn't have to be the manager. She wasn't the mother or the ex-wife or the grandmother. When she was home alone, she could just be Julia, and the world outside couldn't touch her. Within the safety of her home, the rest of the world did not exist.

That was until the moment that the world would come bursting through again, as the world always tended to do.

When she arrived, her mother had already gone to bed. Julia plopped down on her favorite leather recliner and thought about her own life. She felt guilt overtake her for the way her children's lives had turned out. Just like in her own life, her children were letting the road choose them.

She clicked on the television to a recently recorded episode of her favorite soap opera and sat back in her chair, ready to leave the truth that surrounded her behind and disappear into the world of make-believe.

She grabbed the remote control and turned up the volume as she entered the lives of the characters she loved so dearly. She watched as Michelle, her favorite character, made her way across the screen. She envied how confident Michelle seemed, how she never let the past define her. She had not been perfect. She had made mistakes, and had losses in her life, but she always bounced back. She always found love again. She was not afraid of anything, and she never thought of the consequences.

Julia was nothing like Michelle. She was afraid of everything because everything did have consequences. Every choice, every turn, every road had her world turning upside down. *When would it all end?* she thought, as tears again filled her eyes. She realized at that moment that she had not done one thing in her life that she had set out to do. The minutes and the hours were constantly ticking away, and to top it all, she was now going to be a grandmother.

She stood up and walked over to the large oval mirror that hung in the living room, critiquing the image before her. She wondered what Ritchie would have thought of her choices. Would he have been disappointed in her?

She became increasingly distraught. She turned back around and threw the remote control with all of her might toward the sofa, watching it bounce off the cushion and hit the floor.

At that moment, she realized it really didn't matter what Ritchie would have thought because he was dead. Dead and gone. She couldn't go back and change the past. It was there, just like everything else in her life that couldn't be altered. The past just kept bleeding into her future, like an unhealed wound that stabbed at her, over and over again, straight at the heart.

Julia climbed into bed that night and brought the covers up to her chin. She felt her special drawer calling to her. She got up and walked over to her dresser, opening the drawer to her past. She took out the plastic bag that held the secret black folder. She removed the folder from the plastic and delicately opened the cover.

Julia gasped at the sight of Ritchie. She gazed at his smile and big brown eyes that never seemed to age. She would never know a Ritchie of advanced years. She thought he might be graying by now. He wouldn't have many wrinkles, his face being so long, maybe a few toward the ends of his eyes. She ran her hand over the image and up to her own picture that he had placed in a cloud beside him. She was so young. So beautiful. So strong. So full of life.

She brought the folder back to her empty bed, placing her head on the snowy, white pillow. She then moved the open folder next to her, staring at it until she could no longer keep her eyes open.

Her mind then developed shapes and colors that formed themselves into images and, eventually, memories, pulling her back in time to a dance club. Ritchie was holding her hand and leading her in. They giggled as their feet moved forward in rhythm. The globe shimmering over the dance floor spun around and around, causing lights to flicker in and out of their eyes. The movement of the globe was so rapid it caused the specks of colors to race across their complexion.

"Wait," she shouted as he let go of her hand.

He turned and smiled, "Come on, babe."

She laughed as she began to run toward him, but the closer she got to him, the further he seemed from her. She ran faster and faster as the globe began to spin out of control, circling so fast the lights became a blur. A magnificent light then formed on the ceiling, and a spotlight hit Ritchie as if he were standing center stage. He smiled and looked up toward the light.

"I love you," he said. "It's so beautiful here. *I would like to dance with you.* That's what he will say, babe."

"What did you say?" she asked.

He mouthed other words to her, but Julia couldn't hear him. The crowd, ignited by the bright light, quickly drew in around them.

Julia turned to search the crowd and then turned back toward the spotlight, and Ritchie was gone.

She screamed Ritchie's name as she clawed her way through the crowd toward the spotlight. Finally standing in the center of the floor, she reached toward the light, watching the glistening sparks dance along her arm.

Julia sprung up from her pillow, his name swelling in her chest, making its way out of her throat as it burst into the silence of the dark room, "Ritchie!"

CHAPTER SEVEN

Julia muddled through another exhausting week with the realization that Lauren was going to be a single mom and she was going to be a grandmother. Lisa was the only person she confided in with the news of Lauren's pregnancy.

Julia was always extremely guarded around people, especially when it came to her family. She felt she had to be. Outsiders always had to prove themselves to her before she would let them in. Maybe it was because she had so many people in her life taken away or so many that didn't hold up their end of the bargain. Whatever the reason, Julia took it upon herself to guard what was left of her mended heart.

Saturday rolled around, and Lauren called to see if she could visit. She didn't sound well on the phone. Julia's mom intuition kicked in, and she realized that this was probably the first day that Lauren had a chance to slow down and think about her situation. It was the first time that she did not have demands being made of her by work and school, giving her time to think. Lauren was carrying the weight of the world on her shoulders, and Julia knew she had been placed here to ease a little of her daughter's pain, if only for a moment.

"Hi, Mom," Lauren said as she walked into her grandmother's living room for the thousandth time. The room was still lined with the original green and pink wallpaper that formed alternating diamond shapes that Lauren had been fascinated with as a child. The diamond shapes were outlined by a silver border that she grew up running her fingers along. She would start in the living room and would follow the border along the wall as if it were a highway guiding her to a mystical world. Eventually, she would reach the point of infinity, the hallway, where she would then take off, running into the abyss, following that silver lining until it ended just outside the entryway to the dining room.

Julia gave Lauren a huge bear hug as her daughter went limp in her arms. "It's going to be okay, sweetie. I promise. I know it doesn't look like it right now."

"Thanks, Mom. Awww…how did I get here?" Lauren said, throwing her head back and placing her hands over her eyes. "How did I become this person?"

Julia ran her fingers through her daughter's hair as she thought of the long road that awaited her daughter. She tried to pass along words of wisdom. Something that would reassure her daughter that she still had a future ahead of her. "Sweetie, it's all going to be okay. I know it doesn't seem like it now, but I promise you, it will get better."

"Oh no, is Grams here?" Lauren asked as Julia's words went floating by.

"Yes, she's here. You know your grandmother doesn't go out much anymore."

Lauren raised her head to look directly at her mother. "Do you think I should tell her?"

Julia plopped down on her recliner, pulling the lever that swung her feet up. "Well, this is probably something she will eventually notice."

Lauren sat down on the couch, her eyes debating the question before her. "I…I just don't know how she will take it. I don't want to disappoint her."

"Well, sweetie, she's going to find out eventually."

Lauren could hear the door to her grandmother's room open as the bird clock in the living room chimed nine o'clock. The clock had twelve images of different species of birds, replacing the numbers on the face of the clock. Every bird had a distinct chirp upon the arrival of the hour. The nine o'clock hour happened to be the blue jay, Lauren's favorite. Lauren grinned as she heard the nine chirps singing from the clock. She secretly counted each chirp in her head as she had always done.

Her grandmother loved birds. Always had. She owned a huge birdcage that was set in her room and was home to two parakeets. No one else but grandma could feed them. They would bite the hand of anyone else who tried. How they knew the hand didn't belong to her grandmother, Lauren wasn't sure.

When her grandmother was in the hospital for her knee replacement, her mother had to feed the birds. Her mother would use cooking tongs to refill the water dish and the bird feeder; otherwise, the birds would attack her hand like it was a worm peeking its head out of the soil. Julia and Lauren were not fans of the birds, but they made Carmen happy, so they did everything they could to help keep them alive.

Carmen came into the living room and lit up as soon as she saw Lauren. It was no secret that Lauren was her favorite. Lauren was always very sweet. She had not given Julia any trouble growing up. Lauren always did the right thing, worked hard, and got straight As. That was until she met Jake. No one in the family cared for Jake. Not even her brother, Bobby. And Bobby got along with everyone.

"Well…Lauren, sweetheart," Carmen said, "we weren't expecting to see you today. So, where's what's his face?"

"You mean Jake, Grandma?"

"Yeah, that's him."

"We aren't together anymore."

"Hallelujah!" Carmen clapped her hands. "You've come to your senses. I always knew you would. Thank God you did it before it was too late. I knew you would wise up."

"Yeah. But there's a small issue," Lauren said, looking at her grandmother and then at her mother.

Julia just nodded in affirmation and looked over at her mother.

"Something tells me I better sit down," Carmen said. She walked over to the sofa and grabbed the arm, slowly lowering herself to the puffy gray cushion. "Okay, I'm ready."

"I'm pregnant."

"Lord, child," Carmen said, bringing her hand up to her mouth as if to prevent herself from saying something she would regret. Looking into Lauren's confused eyes, her heart softened. "Well…what's done is done. And what's his face?"

"Jake, Grandma."

"Yeah, that's him. What'd he have to say about all of this?"

"He's gone. I'm actually not sure where he is right now. I think he might be living in Hollywood, but I'm not positive."

"Well, that's the best news yet," Carmen said, smacking her knee.

"Mom…" Julia blurted out.

"Well, it is. Ain't no great-grandchild of mine needin' to be around that…well, you know what he is."

"I've decided to raise the child on my own."

"Well, it won't be easy. You're going to stay in school, right?"

"Yep, that's the plan, Grams."

"Well, that's somethin' anyway. Can't turn back time," Carmen said, seeing Lauren's face turn toward the ground.

Carmen stood up and walked over to Lauren taking her face in her hand. "You don't have anything to be ashamed of. It's very brave what you are doin'. I went through the same thing with your mother here. I hadn't told you, but I married your mother's father after we conceived her," Carmen said. "He did walk out on us shortly after your aunt Charlotte was born, but that's beside the point. I still lived my life, and you will, too. You'll see. Everything will be just fine. God always has a plan."

"Oh, Grandma," Lauren said. "I love you."

"I love you too, sweet pea. Now, don't you go a worryin'. We will help you through this."

At that moment, Julia's phone screen lit up with a text. Julia glanced down at her screen and read it to herself. *Hi Julia, it's Brad. Just checking to see if you could text me your address. I am so excited about tonight. See you at six.*

"Oh, my, I forgot," Julia absentmindedly said out loud as her daughter and mother looked over at her, wondering what in the world she was talking about.

"Sorry," Julia said. "It's a text from work," Julia lied, trying to calculate how in the world she would explain Brad to Lauren, and there was no way she was letting her mother find out about Brad.

At this point, Julia realized that going out with Brad would probably be a huge mistake. She started to text Brad back when she suddenly gazed inconspicuously at Lauren.

"Huh," Julia said to herself. *Lauren was twenty-five years old. And Brad was possibly thirty-three or thirty-four; that's not so bad.* And the wheels in Julia's head started turning.

She immediately started going over scenarios in her mind of how she could arrange to have Brad and Lauren meet and possibly even…date. After all, he was such a nice guy, and Lauren looked a lot like Julia. It could work, she thought.

Julia shook her head back and forth, realizing that a plan like that would be ludicrous. She couldn't set her pregnant daughter up with someone she had just met and made a date with. Could she?

The more she thought about it, the more the plan seemed plausible.

She figured she would have Brad come over when Lauren was still there, and then she would bow out by saying that she was not feeling well. That would leave the two of them alone.

No, she thought to herself. This was insane. Too strange. Lauren would kill her.

She looked over at her beautiful daughter again and thought, *Why not?* Michelle would have done it in a second. Lauren obviously can't be trusted to find a man on her own. Jake proved that, and Julia had her grandchild to think about. But how to get them together?

Julia had no idea. She only knew that this road, her daughter's road, was not going to determine Lauren's future anymore. Not if Julia had anything to say about it.

Julia—now more determined than ever—quickly texted Brad her address.

Just as she was about to put her plan into action, Bobby came through the screen door with a colorful brunette under his arm. The two of them stumbled in the door and stood swaying together as if they were standing on some type of merry-go-round, trying to hold each other up. The girl was wearing dark eyeshadow with a rainbow of colors lining her upper brow area, and some type of metal was sticking out of her upper lip.

The group turned to acknowledge them just as Bobby slurred out an introduction.

"Hey, fam…family," Bobby said as Julia turned toward the clock that read 9:45 a.m.

Carmen and Julia turned toward Bobby and said in unison as if they had planned it. "Where's Ashley?"

"Oh…her," Bobby slurred as he turned and smiled at the young girl under his arm. "She's kinda not in…in the picture any…more…more, but this is my new love."

"What'd you do?" His grandmother asked. "And what's Ashley's phone number?"

"Oh, Grams—I love you so much," Bobby said, stumbling forward.

Julia had never seen her son so out of it. She figured he had really blown it with Ashley.

"What happened?" Julia asked.

"I don't know. She said she couldn't trusss…me or something crazy like that. I don't need her. I don't need anybody," he stumbled through his words, smiling at the girl under his arm. "Except you, of course," he continued, trying to backtrack from his last statement.

Lauren walked over to her brother and his new friend and fanned her hand in front of her face as she hit Bobby's breath. "Drinking a little early, are we?"

"Yeah, we hosted a party last night," the young brunette said, more articulate than her counterpart. "Oh, and by the way, my name's… Star."

"Is that your real name?" Lauren asked.

"Yeah. My mom said I reminded her of the stars."

"Oh, how sweet," Carmen said sarcastically.

"How'd you get here?" Julia asked.

"Oh, I drove," the young brunette said, raising her right hand as if she had a question.

"I'm calling you both a cab," Julia announced to the room.

"Mom, we're fine," Bobby said as he swayed to the silence in the room.

"No…no, you're not, Bobby," Julia argued, picking up her phone. "This is not fine. I thought…"

"You thought what, Mom?"

"Never mind," Julia said, disappointed in her son. "Didn't you have to work today?"

"Nope. I told them I was ill." Bobby laughed. "Which I am. I don't feel so good."

Julia dropped her phone. She walked over to Bobby, obviously disappointed and annoyed by her son's condition. "Well, then maybe you both should sleep it off here. You can take the spare bedroom."

"Ahhh…thanks, Mom," Bobby said and slowly made his way down the hall, balancing himself against the walls, leaving his newfound love standing in the entryway.

"Could I get that cab?" the girl in the goth clothing said. "I have to get home to my son."

"I'll call," Lauren said as she went and picked up her cell phone.

"Thank you so much," the girl said as she swayed beside the sofa. "Do you mind if I sit down?"

"By all means," Grams said. "Sit down before you fall down."

"Here's my address," the girl continued. "You know. Just in case I fall asleep." And she took out an envelope from her purse and handed it to them. The official-looking letter had her address written across the front of the envelope as if someone had written it there for a moment just like this.

"The cab will be here in fifteen minutes," Lauren said. She turned and looked down at the girl, who was fast asleep on the pillow.

Julia shook her head. "Why is he so much like…." And she stopped and looked over at Lauren. "I'm going to make this girl some coffee to go."

She left the living room and moved down the hallway, stopping in front of Bobby's sixth-grade baseball picture. Her mother had it hanging on the wall just outside the spare bedroom. The picture was taken when he was about twelve-years-old. He stopped playing ball soon after his dad left. Baseball was their love. Scott had coached Bobby since he could pick up a bat. When Scott left, Bobby refused to play anymore. It was like her son was looking for ways to hurt his dad, and he had found a direct vein to his dad's heart. He knew his dad loved to watch him play. Scott was always bragging to his friends about how good Bobby was. Bobby knew his dad would be devastated that he had stopped playing. Bobby wanted his dad to hurt as much as he was hurting, and he succeeded. Both of their lives and their relationship were changed forever.

Julia never saw Bobby pick up a bat or glove again.

She took a few steps and looked in on her son, who was passed out face-first on the bed. Julia wondered if things would have been different had she and Scott stayed together. If he hadn't stopped loving her. If he hadn't left his family. Scenes ran through her mind of a forgotten family that hadn't been ripped apart.

She stared at her son and wondered how in the world she was going to fix this, how she was going to repair this emptiness in Bobby's heart. Guilt took over, as it always did, and Julia debated about how she was going to erase the damage that they and this world had already done.

…And a silent prayer left her lips.

CHAPTER EIGHT

With Bobby sleeping it off and his Cinderella on her way home, Julia's mind wandered as she went through scenario after scenario on how to place Brad and Lauren in the same place at the same time. She intentionally chose to ignore the fact that Lauren was pregnant. By another man. Who had abandoned her.

Julia figured, what did she have to lose? It could all work out. After all, Lauren wasn't even showing yet. How would Brad know?

Julia knew that she would have to create one believable story. One that Lauren would not question. She truly believed that once Lauren got to know Brad and discovered what a great guy he was, her plan would all fall into place. And Lauren was so adorable. Julia knew Brad would fall madly in love with Lauren once he got to know her. It just had to be planned in a way that left no room for doubt.

And the answer appeared to her.

Michelle from *One Moment in Time* was faced with a similar situation. Her daughter was pregnant, and the father was this gangster, mobster dirtbag who would have destroyed Michelle's daughter's life, but her daughter couldn't see the truth. She couldn't see this loser for who he really was. Just like Lauren. So, Michelle set her daughter up to meet one of the executives in Michelle's law firm, and after a miscarriage, one affair, and a bout with cancer, the two were finally married. Julia thought to herself, *This could actually work.*

Later that afternoon, Julia entered the living room, determined to get Brad and Lauren in the same room. Lauren was watching television, resting her head on a decorative pillow, drowning herself under the knitted blanket her grandmother had made for her when Lauren was just five-years-old when Julia set her plan into motion.

"Sweetie?"

"Yeah, Mom."

"I have a dilemma," Julia announced as Lauren turned her head, waiting for her mother to finish her statement. "Well, you won't believe this, but your aunt Lisa and I were out the other night, and we met this wonderful young man who is in the Marines, and well, he is new to the area," Julia fabricated, somewhat.

"Okay? So what does this have to do with me?"

"Well, you know your aunt Lisa," Julia said as she maneuvered herself around the sofa so she would be in Lauren's direct line of sight.

"Yeah, I do," Lauren said, hugging the pillow in front of her.

"Well, she got it in her head that we should go dancing."

"You two went dancing?" Lauren asked, now sitting up on the sofa.

"Sadly, yes."

At that moment, Carmen's eyes moved from viewing the television to viewing her daughter without turning her head as she blurted out, "You went dancing?"

"Yes, Mom."

"Well, miracles do still happen." Carmen laughed, now on the edge of her seat in anticipation of the rest of the story.

"As I said, it was Aunt Lisa's idea, and we met this very nice young man while we were there, and well, we got to talking to him, and he said he really didn't know anyone in town and wondered if we would like to show him around. And, well, you know your aunt Lisa, she, of course, said yes, and now she has to work tonight and can't go, so I was hoping you could come with me to, you know, show him around."

"He tried to pick you up? Gross," Lauren said, throwing the knitted blanket to the side.

"Yeah, was he young and blind?" Carmen said sarcastically.

"No, Mom, he was just being nice, and he seemed…you know, kind of lonely. And he wasn't trying to pick us up. He is from the Midwest and doesn't know anyone here. Come on. It might do you good to get out."

"I just don't think I am up for it, Mom. You go."

"I'll go," Carmen interjected.

"Mom…" Julia answered, through her teeth, turning back to Lauren. "Oh, come on. It might be fun. You need to get your mind on other things. Besides, I don't want to go alone. Please," Julia begged.

"Well, where does Mr. Wonderful want to go? And what's his name?"

"Yeah, I want to know that too," Carmen blurted out, trying to join in the conversation.

"Brad, ahhh…wait…he told me, Brad Anderson. He said something about a rooftop theater. I think."

"Oh…" Lauren said, looking off into the distance as the realization of her situation suddenly hit her, and she rubbed her belly, "I have always wanted to go there."

"Well then, here's your chance," Julia said, seeing a twinkle in Lauren's eyes. Julia held her breath as she waited for the verdict, hoping Lauren wouldn't see right through her scheme.

Lauren, looking as if she had an epiphany, exclaimed, "You're not trying to set me up, are you?"

"No, I told you, he invited me, and Aunt Lisa can't go. I really don't want to go alone."

Lauren scooted to the end of the sofa as if she were about to stand up. "Well, when?" Lauren asked.

"Tonight."

"I can't go like this," Lauren protested, looking down at her sweats and T-shirt.

"I can run you home to pick up something," Julia blurted.

"Well, I guess it wouldn't hurt, but if he turns out to be some type of weirdo, I'm out of there."

"Okay, I'll tell him that we will meet him there. Does that sound fair?"

"Yeah, well, that's better. I can't believe you are picking up young Marine guys, Mom," Lauren said, throwing the pillow to the side of the sofa.

"It's not like that. He was just so nice."

"All right. What time do we meet Mr. Wonderful?"

"Ahhh…in about two hours. So, we better get moving."

"You two are never going to make it on time," Carmen added as the two women frantically tried to gather their belongings.

Julia stumbled through a text to Brad—leaving out the fact that her pregnant, twenty-five-year-old daughter was tagging along—and she and Lauren traveled through the San Diego traffic to Lauren's apartment.

After convincing Lauren to wear the blue velvet dress that gave her brown eyes specks of gold, Julia and Lauren arrived at an old historic building in the scenic district of downtown San Diego called the Gaslamp Quarter. Julia pulled next to an antique street lamp and shut off her vehicle. Nervous about the evening ahead of her, she sat in her vehicle, scanning the people passing outside, and debated on whether to move forward with the plan or not.

As Lauren checked her lipstick in the visor mirror, Julia contemplated making up some type of story about not feeling well and hitting the gas pedal as fast as her foot could get there and speeding back home.

She then turned and looked at her daughter. Lauren—who, even though she wouldn't have admitted to it—seemed excited about a night out. She was finally happy.

Julia's mind then drifted to what her idol Michelle would do about now. Michelle would not hesitate to get her daughter out of the car and sweep her up to the ball or dance or whatever she believed would bring the two lovebirds together. Michelle was always ready to do whatever it took to create a happily ever after for her daughter. In fact, Michelle would probably have already begun making plans for their wedding. Julia smiled into her visor mirror as she visualized Lauren's happy ending while checking her lipstick, and she clicked the car doors to open.

"Let's go," Julia proclaimed.

Julia wore the most conservative gray dress she owned. The dress buttoned up so high it pressed against her neck. She also wore her black tights and her wide black leather flats that made her look like a librarian. She put one foot in front of the other as she led her beautiful daughter, Lauren, to her future. No one would be slapping them in the face today. Not even that dang no-it-all, destiny.

They entered the wood-framed, stained-glass doors. The stained glass consisted of red-petaled roses held up with deep green stems that swirled in every direction. Julia strained to see through the glass onto the white marble floor. The floor was surrounded by authentic maple wood walls that had been refinished so beautifully they glowed below the hanging black brass chandeliers.

As they walked through the entryway, scenes flashed in front of Julia's eyes of the multitude of things that could ultimately go wrong with her plan. Julia looked over at her daughter, and her daughter smiled back at her, almost floating across the floor in her deep blue velvet dress, so Julia kept moving forward.

They entered the metal elevator doors. It took only moments after pressing the rooftop button to reach their destination. They found themselves stepping out onto the blue cloud-filled sky—as if they had reached heaven itself. A slight breeze had begun to blow as the women felt their hair lifting into the cool evening wind.

The rooftop displayed a bar and restaurant on one end of the roof and a large blue movie screen that bled into the sky on the other. There were several small wood chairs, dressed with red cushions, sitting on the other half of the roof, facing the screen. A glass rail consisting of glittering silver poles aligned the roof top's edges, giving the area a look of limitless sky. Faces turned and floated by as laughter and conversation filled the end of the day.

The sight was so spectacular Julia and Lauren froze in place as their breath seemed to evaporate as if the wind had rushed their gaping lips, whisking the air away. The wind attempted to lift Julia's dress away from her body, separating the deep pleats in her skirt. Julia reached down to keep it in place. She quickly turned back to see a large body headed her way. The gleam of his smile was caught by the sun, and she actually thought she heard her daughter gasp.

"Julia," the voice said as Brad moved toward them, looking even more handsome in the daylight. His blonde hair blew in the wind, and his blue eyes blended in with the sky. "How are you?"

Julia suddenly found herself in a massive embrace as she struggled to get Brad to release her. Upon letting go, Brad looked over toward the young woman standing beside them. Lauren stepped back with a sudden realization of what this reunion actually was, embarrassed that she had agreed to come along.

"Um…Brad. This is my daughter…Lauren."

Brad, surprised, turned toward Julia and, without thinking, blurted out, "This is your daughter?" He tried to amend his thoughtless statement by quickly introducing himself to Lauren, shooting his hand out toward her as they both awkwardly grasped hands. "Nice to meet you," he said, staring at Lauren and then looking back toward Julia, noticing the obvious similarities.

"Likewise," Lauren said. "So, my mother tells me you are a Marine."

"Yes…yes, I am," Brad said, confused about what was happening. He quickly took a drink from his glass, not sure what to say next. "Well, would you both like a drink?" he said politely.

Julia, taking this chance to keep the conversation going, shouted out an enthusiastic, "Yes, please. Margaritas." She smiled.

Brad, who was debating on whether to hop on the elevator or get the drinks, excused himself and walked over to the bar to place the order.

Lauren, taking full advantage of Brad's absence, moved closer to her mother. "You said this wasn't a date, Mom."

"It isn't. He's just being nice," Julia lied under her breath.

A little hesitant, Brad walked back up with the drinks and handed them to the ladies. "So, Julia. I didn't know you had a daughter."

Lauren then chimed in. "Yeah, she has a son too. There are two of us."

"Oh, really," Brad said, taking a big gulp of his drink.

"So, Brad, how are things on the base? Are you adjusting to the area?" Julia continued, shooting a glance toward Lauren, hoping that her daughter was not about to make a run for it.

"Well, as I said, I love it here. I'm not sure I would return to the Midwest, well, except to visit family, and well, we have a farm and all."

"A farm. Well, that's interesting, wouldn't you say so, Lauren."

"Yeah, that's amazing," Lauren said as she handed her mother her drink. "Give me the car keys, Mother."

"Honey, you aren't staying for the movie?"

"No," Lauren said, pressing her lips together and grinding her teeth. She then grinned at Brad. "I was just walking my mother up here to, you know, check out the place. It's very nice. I'm going to be going now. It was nice meeting you, Brad."

"Nice to meet you," Brad said as the wind picked up Lauren's hair, sweeping it across her face. Lauren brought her arm up quickly, removing the hair from her eyes as if the hair was adding to her irritation.

Brad then looked toward Julia and stepped back, not sure what to do or say. "I'll let you all say goodbye."

Julia took a couple of steps toward Lauren. "Why don't you stay?"

Lauren looked at her mother. "He's here to see you, Mom. I'm sorry about that crack about me and Bobby. I'll see you at home. He seems really nice."

Lauren then turned toward the elevator and pressed the down arrow button as Brad returned to the two women. And to Julia's surprise, Brad spoke out into the night air, almost in a whisper, as if he were afraid to let Julia hear. "You don't want to stay?" he said to Lauren.

Lauren turned back toward both of them; her hair picked up in the breeze as she attempted to put it behind her ear. Her blue dress now dancing in the wind. "No, I don't. Nice to have met you, Brad. You two have a good time."

Lauren stepped into the elevator and disappeared behind the elevator doors, leaving her scent in the air as Brad turned back toward Julia.

"Can I ask you something?" Brad said.

"Yes," Julia said, trying to hide her embarrassment.

"What are you up to?" he asked. "And don't lie to me. I always know when someone is lying to me."

"I just thought. Well, it doesn't matter what I thought. I'm so sorry, Brad. You must think I'm a horrible person."

"No…I wasn't thinking that. I was thinking you were a very loving mother. A little crazy, maybe, to try and pull this off. But a good mother."

Julia, embarrassed at Brad's realization of her scheme, could do nothing but smile. Trying to avoid Brad's stare, Julia looked away, trying to figure out her next move. Just as she glanced out toward the sky, Julia felt someone tap her shoulder. As she turned around, a bright smile greeted her, and she heard the most-lovely words, "It's Julia, right?"

And there he stood once again. The man from the perfume counter. The one who had bought the expensive perfume. The one that made her heart skip a beat every time she saw him. Julia almost forgot her name as she felt the words come up slowly, finally remembering who she was. "Yes, it is."

"I was there the other night. The bottle of perfume. Do you remember?" he said with one hand hidden in his pant pocket, his jacket gathered up at his waist. A drink of caramel-colored liquid in his other hand.

Julia stumbled with her words as she forgot that Brad was even standing there. "Yes, I remember. You bought it for your girlfriend, if I remember right."

"Yes, that was me. I thought I recognized you. Well, I just wanted to say hello."

"Hello," Julia stammered as if in a trance.

"Well, my girlfriend is waiting for me. I just thought…"

"What?" Julia asked.

"I just thought I had seen you the other night. At the dance club. That was you, wasn't it?"

Julia hesitated for a moment while trying to wrap her head around what was going on around her, struggling with the reason that she kept running into this man. This man, who left her more breathless every time she saw him. It was like he had some type of magnetic pull on her. Julia couldn't remember the last time she had ever felt this way as she struggled to remember what he had just asked her.

"Was it you?" he asked again. "You were with another woman, and I believe this gentleman."

Julia was then able to think clearly enough to decipher what he was asking her. "Yes, yes, that was me. I saw you." She then turned toward Brad. "I'm sorry. I am being terribly rude. Brad, this is…"

"Andrew. Andrew Harrington, but everyone calls me Andy." Andy then took out his hand from his pocket and shook Brad's hand. The two men gripped each other's hands as if they were about to arm wrestle, and Julia was the prize.

"I'm Brad Anderson. Nice to meet you, Andy." Brad said, returning the strong grip and looking Andy straight in the eye without any fear.

Brad, noticing Julia's obvious attraction to Andy, played along with the charade. "I'm Julia's date."

"Ohhh…" Andy said. "Well, I'm sorry for intruding. I just wanted to say hello," Andy said, staring at Julia as if he were trying to remember something.

"No, you're not intruding," Julia said. "So, where's your girlfriend? I mean…did she like the perfume?"

"Yes, she did. Thanks for asking. She's sitting over there, speaking with some friends of ours. Are you staying for the movie?"

"No, we just—" Julia started to say.

"Yes, we are," Brad chimed in, putting his arm around Julia's waist and pulling her closer. "We wouldn't miss it…Andy."

"Well, good. Maybe I can introduce you to Zoey. Sorry, that's her name, my girlfriend, I mean. We are staying for the movie. Should be a good one. I believe they are showing *Sleepless in Seattle* tonight."

"Oh, I love that movie," Julia said, glancing up at Brad, who still had his arm around her.

"Me too," Andy said. "One of my favorites."

"Well, we hope to see you both a little later, Andy," Brad continued, grinning and pulling Julia a little closer to his side.

Andy smiled and raised his glass to the couple as if he were confirming Brad's statement.

As Andy left, Julia turned toward Brad. "You don't have to do this. I'm so sorry, Brad. I didn't mean for any of this to happen. I just thought that you and Lauren…."

"I know what you thought. That's sweet in a weird way. I don't know why I said those things. You just seem to kinda like this guy. Am I wrong?"

Julia looked over at Andy. "It's something. I don't know what it is. Oh, I'm acting like a love-sick teenager. I'm so sorry; we don't have to stay."

"Hey, I came to see a movie. Might as well see it. Anyway, I may need a phone number from you later on."

"A phone number?" Julia asked, lowering her eyebrows.

"Yeah, your daughter's."

CHAPTER NINE

"Shall we?" Brad said, holding out his arm for Julia as they made their way past the red cushioned chairs finding two seats next to the center aisle, about six rows back from the enormous blue screen mounted in a black frame.

"I think you have an admirer," Brad said, smiling and glancing back toward Andy.

"Stop it," Julia said, hitting his arm. "He's going to think you're watching him." Julia caught sight of Andy through the corner of her eye. She noticed how he turned around every few seconds and glanced back toward where she was sitting.

"That's what I want him to think. Wow, his girlfriend," Brad said.

"I know. I don't have a chance," Julia admitted, watching as Andy's young girlfriend shifted her stance, causing her gold, form-fitting mini dress to shimmer in the setting sun.

"I wouldn't say that. He sure can't seem to keep his eyes off you. If I didn't know better, I would say he is a man in love."

"Love? No…he's with her. Why would he? There's just no way," Julia said as if she were trying to convince Brad of how ludicrous this notion was.

"Julia?"

"Yeah."

"Have you looked in the mirror lately? Because you should, you're kind of nice to look at. Take it from someone who knows." Brad winked at Julia.

Julia smiled. She could feel her face turning red. She hated it when she blushed. For her, it was an automatic response when she was embarrassed, and there was nothing she could do to halt the rosy flare-up. All of a sudden, her face would light up like a red-light bulb on Christmas morning, and no matter how she tried to prevent it, it only got worse.

"I'll go get us some popcorn. This will give Mr. Smooth a chance to make his way over here."

"Oh, you, he's not going to come over here."

Brad winked at Julia and made his way back to the counter to order two more drinks and a large container of popcorn.

Julia glared at the cloud-filled sky as people began to gather around her. The natural theater was so beautiful. She watched as the clouds floated by, disappearing behind the large screen. Birds flew overhead, squawking at the people below them as if they were objecting to the intrusion of their space on this planet.

The clear railings brought a sense of empyrean grandeur. There was a feeling of weightlessness, as if you could float off the side, cradled by one of the surrounding clouds. The scene resembled what Julia had always imagined heaven would look like. She wondered if Ritchie could see her here, between the clouds, and if he had somehow lured her to this rooftop for that very reason.

A man caught Julia's attention as he sat down behind the projector to start the movie. She turned back around toward the screen to find Andy and his girlfriend, Zoey, taking a seat right in front of her.

"Julia, hey," Andy said, making an effort to take her hand in his, slowly releasing it. To Julia's amazement. Her heart began to quickly pulsate from his touch, so much so that Julia grabbed at her chest to try and slow her heart rate. "I would like to introduce my girlfriend, Zoey

Monaco. Zoey, this is the woman I told you about from the department store." Julia watched as Andy held Zoey by the small of her back.

Zoey peered at Julia as if she expected Julia to look different. "This is the woman?" Zoey said bluntly with a Spanish accent. "Oh, I am so sorry. But from what my Andy told me, I expected an older woman. Thank you so much for helping my Andy. He is just lost when it comes to buying gifts for me. The perfume is truly spectacular," she said as if she were searching for someone, anyone, but this boring little woman in front of her.

"I'm so glad," Julia said, a little thrown off by her accent and puzzled as to why they would have discussed her at all. "It was my pleasure."

Just as Julia finished her sentence, Zoey caught sight of some friends exiting the elevator. She waved to them excitedly as if to let them know where she was sitting. "If you will please excuse me, several of my friends have just arrived. They have never seen this type of movie theater before. Andy has been telling me about it, and we are all so excited to be experiencing it for the first time. Excuse me, please, will you?" And Zoey sauntered off before Julia had a chance to answer. Zoey, and a group of people around her age, hugged and laughed, pointing toward the phenomenal view surrounding them. The group, who seemed thrilled to be together, acted as if they had never seen clouds before.

"She's very excited to see the film," Andy said, somewhat embarrassed by his youthful girlfriend's reaction to it all.

"I can tell. So great your friends could join you," Julia said, still watching the group giggle and hug.

"Yeah, it's great. Zoey knows so many people in the area. I was a transplant here."

"Oh, really. So, what do you do?" Julia finally got the nerve to ask. "I mean, you already know what I do."

"Well, I started out as a professional baseball player a few years back. I grew up in Nebraska but got offered a position to play in the league out here."

"Oh my gosh, I didn't know that. That must have been so exciting. What position did you play?"

"I played right field. And yes, it was certainly a dream come true. But I got hurt early on in my professional career and never played again."

"Oh, I'm so sorry, but you pursued your dream and saw it to the finish. That's something not many people can say," Julia said, forming a mental picture of all the dreams that she at one time wanted to accomplish.

Andy smiled. "Yes, I'm very proud of that. I just wish I had been able to play longer. But, I now run a fast-food chain."

"Really, which one."

"A & B Burgers."

"Oh my, that's you?"

"Yep, been in business twenty years now with twelve locations up and down the coast."

"Well, Andy, that's wonderful," Julia exclaimed, followed by an awkward silence. "So, you said you were from Nebraska. Did you stay out here because of your business?"

"I love the life out here. You wouldn't know it, but I was quite the party guy when I was younger. I mean, I saved and started my own business, building it from the ground up. I wasn't dumb; I knew my career could end at any moment, and well, then destiny stepped in, and everything just kind of fell into place for me to stay and live here. Oh, I go home every now and then, but I have fallen in love with the San Diego area and the people." And he looked Julia straight in the eye. "This area is just unique. The people are so vibrant. I've never thought about living anywhere else."

"So, ever married?" Julia asked before she had a chance to talk herself out of the question, surprised at her forwardness.

"Yes, but unfortunately, it didn't work out. You?"

"Yes, I was married for sixteen years to the wrong guy, but we had two great kids."

"Wow, sixteen years. What happened, if you don't mind me asking?" Andy asked casually, hiding one of his hands in his pants pocket.

Julia had to intentionally concentrate on what he was saying because she kept getting lost in those deep brown eyes of his. They just seemed so welcoming, so gentle. His thick brown hair kept feathering up on top of his head, trying to distract her from their conversation. "He fell in love with someone else, and I realized I don't think I ever really knew him. Maybe that was the problem," Julia said, surprised that she had announced this to a perfect stranger. At that moment, she thought the only other person who knew this about her was Lisa.

Andy's attention suddenly turned to Zoey, and her crew headed right toward him. "Oh, I'm supposed to be saving seats. Well, Julia, it has truly been a pleasure." He then reached into his pocket and pulled out a card. "Here is my card, just in case you ever need a tour of A & B Burgers. I hope that we run into each other again," he said and winked at her.

Brad then came up on the other side of her, announcing loudly, "Here is your popcorn, sweetheart."

Julia looked at Brad, trying not to laugh at his serious tone, and decided to play along, announcing, "Oh, thank you, dear."

"Anything for you, my love," Brad said while glancing over at Andy.

Andy smirked at Brad and narrowed his eyebrows in question as Zoey and her entourage plowed their way over to him like a herd of lost chickens, taking their seats in front of Brad and Julia.

Brad handed Julia her drink and sat down with the popcorn in between them.

"Told you so," Brad whispered.

"Okay, I'll give you that one," Julia affirmed, looking over at Brad. "And great improv, by the way."

"Thank you." Brad smiled.

"I have been sitting here wondering what is wrong with you. There has to be something. You seem too perfect. How is it that no one has snatched you up yet?" Julia asked Brad.

"Still looking for the right girl, it seems. We Kansans are a little picky," Brad said, putting a fist full of popcorn into his mouth and placing an arm around Julia, "You know, I haven't ever seen this movie before," he announced.

Julia looked over at Andy, who was busy explaining the movie to Zoey's friends. "It's a love story," she said.

"A love story, huh," Brad said. "And who's Meg Ryan? She's the star, right?"

Julia looked over at Brad as if he had just arrived from Mars. "You are kidding me, right? She's a pretty big star. I'm surprised you don't know her."

"I think my mom has mentioned her." Brad smiled and winked at Julia.

"Oh, you," Julia responded, shoving Brad with her shoulder.

When the movie started, Julia caught Andy turning around and stealing glances at her and Brad as he finagled his arm around his girlfriend. Zoey, oblivious to Andy's curiosity, continued to giggle and laugh with her friends.

Julia found Zoey's reactions very annoying and wondered how it was that Andy didn't feel the exact same way. *She was obviously too young for him*, Julia thought to herself. Julia had to admit Zoey was very beautiful. Very young. Very exotic, in a way. She spoke Spanish to her friends, and they all giggled throughout the movie.

Julia found herself watching more of what was going on in front of her than the movie.

After the film ended, Brad and Julia made their way out of the crowded seating area, losing sight of Andy and Zoey as everyone blended together. The lights from the outdoor theater dimmed, giving patrons the opportunity to take in the night sky. Julia took one long last look at the sky, which had now darkened to a twinkling black palette that even an artist would gasp over. The moon hung over the rooftop like a bright white and gray marble. The stars glistened through the darkness, and silence filled the crowd as everyone stood looking up in awe at the night sky.

Brad left Julia's side to throw the leftovers away as she made her way to the glass rail inhaling the cool night air and slowly letting out a prolonged sigh.

"Shall we go?" Brad said, extending his arm to Julia.

Julia took one last look at the stars and grabbed onto Brad's arm. "Yes, of course." She smiled.

They strolled toward the elevators, and Julia glanced back just before stepping through the doors. She caught sight of what appeared to be Andy. He was waving at her, his arm extended high in the air, over the crowd, as if he didn't want her to leave without saying goodbye. Julia faintly waved back, surprised by his gesture, just before the elevator doors shut in front of her.

Brad dropped Julia off at her home and said he would consider giving Lauren a call. He explained that he wasn't sure how Lauren would feel about him due to the interesting way that they met, being he was her mother's date and all.

Julia understood and left it at that, feeling bad for lying to Brad. Then there was the fact that Lauren was expecting another man's child. She knew she should have told Brad, but she just couldn't bring herself to do it. Besides, Julia thought to herself, Michelle would have never divulged that information, especially if her daughter's happiness hung in the balance.

The next morning, Julia received an expected early morning call from Lauren. Given how she deceived Lauren into thinking that Brad had no feelings toward her, she was expecting a call from her daughter, but not at this hour of the morning.

"Hi, sweetie," Julia said, trying to remind Lauren that she was indeed still her mother.

"Mom, what were you thinking? You have really lost it this time. Honestly, Mom, you watch too many soap operas. Life's just not like that. You cannot fix your daughter up with the guy who asked her mother out. Life just doesn't work that way."

"I know, sweetie. I'm…"

"Anyway, that's not the only reason I called, even though we need to have this conversation."

"Well, what is it?" Julia's demeanor suddenly changed as she knew whatever was more important than Lauren yelling at her about last night must be something life-altering.

"Bobby showed up here last night," Lauren said in a whisper.

"Yeah, so…" Julia inquired.

"He was out of it. I don't think he was just drunk. He's doing something or using something I don't know anything about. He didn't even know where he was."

"What are you talking about? What's he doing or using?"

"I don't know, Mom. That's what I'm trying to tell you. I think he was high on something."

"What?" Julia said, sitting straight up on the edge of her bed. "Well, is he all right?"

"I guess. I just don't want to confront him about this by myself. Can you come over?"

"Yeah, I can come right now, but where would he get the money for that anyway?" Julia asked as she looked around her room for the closest pair of sweats to throw on.

"I don't know, but you need to come over. I don't know what to say to him. He didn't look good last night. He kept rambling on about Ashley."

"Okay, I'll be right over."

"Oh, and Mom…"

"Yeah?"

"I called Dad too."

CHAPTER TEN

Lauren's apartment was dark, except for the light streaming in from the outside as Julia stepped into the entryway. She looked around at the pristine apartment, everything in its rightful place. Not a speck of dust. Where Lauren got this gene, Julia was not sure.

Lauren had always been an overachiever. She was going to do it all. Get her graduate degree, work in counseling, and marry the love of her life. She had it all figured out. But now…now with the baby on the way, no one had anything figured out. Julia the least of all.

As she moved forward, Julia spotted Lauren sitting on her loveseat, wrapped in a blanket with her legs crossed.

"Where is he?" Julia asked.

"He's in my guest bedroom."

"Well, what makes you think he wasn't drunk?" Julia said, sitting down on the sofa behind her.

"I've never seen him like this. He wasn't himself. He pretty much demanded that I let him stay," Lauren said, kicking her feet out from under her.

"Well, I'm glad you did."

"To be truthful, Mom, I was a little scared of what he would do if I didn't. He had that look in his eye."

"What look?"

"You know, with the wide, red eyes. Like he was getting ready to go berserk at any moment. The look Dad used to have. That look."

Julia was a little stunned by her daughter's comment. She hadn't realized how much Scott's addiction to alcohol had made its way into her children's world. She had tried so hard to protect them from it. It seemed the alcohol was able to seep its way into the lives of her entire family, no matter how hard she had tried to cover it up.

Julia placed her purse down on the coffee table. Just as she began to rise, the two women heard a faint tapping noise in the distance. Afraid that Bobby had already awakened, the two women stood like statues with their eyes widened, trying to pinpoint where the sound was coming from. They then realized the noise was coming from the front door.

Julia knew who it was before his shadow appeared in the doorway. Normally she hated being in the same room with Scott, but today was different. She was actually a little relieved that her ex was there. She had no idea how to deal with whatever it was Bobby was doing to himself.

She was out of her element, and she knew it. She couldn't ground him. She couldn't take away his phone. Julia somehow hoped Scott would have some magical solution to whatever was developing in their son's life.

Julia held her breath as her daughter walked over to open the front door.

There he stood, Julia's past. With the passage of time, her former life with Scott seemed almost like a dream. If it hadn't been for the reality of the kids, she might have thought it was all just a figment of her imagination.

She barely remembers what she was like with him. She had memories with the children, but Scott was almost never a part of those memories anymore. It was as if she had entirely erased him from her memory. He was just something she had to put up with at birthday parties and during the holidays, and he rarely showed up for many of those. So, in the past, his presence or absence at family events had never really been a problem. She went on with her definition of living, and he lived out his life with other women. Ones he thought that he loved.

"Hello, Julia," Scott said, always with an apologetic tone as if he somehow needed to apologize to her every time he saw her. As if he somehow now understood the damage that he had done.

"Hello, Scott," Julia said. Scott, who stood only a couple of inches taller than Julia and his daughter, had developed a mid-sized belly that was slowly making its way over his belted jeans. He wore his polo shirt out over his belt to try and camouflage the obvious lack of healthy eating and exercise his current lifestyle has led him to.

Scott glared over at Julia and wondered how she stayed so trim. She seemed to look younger every time he saw her. He secretly wondered how it was that she had not found anyone else.

"So, where is he?" Scott asked, turning his attention to Lauren.

"He's in my spare bedroom," Lauren answered.

"How's he doing? Do we really know if he's using? I mean, do we have any proof?" Scott asked as if he had all the answers rolled up in his sleeve.

Julia sighed, knowing all too well that Scott would react like this. He came in like the white knight and then would leave as soon as things got tough. She hoped with all her strength that she was wrong about him this time. She wasn't sure she could handle this one alone. She wasn't sure she could survive losing her son.

"We don't know what he's using or if he's using. We were hoping you could help with that," Julia retorted.

Scott stood there, trying to seem stronger than he was. Trying to be strong for the family he walked out on. Hoping no one could see through his facade. "I would have to see him or talk with him. Even then, it would be hard to tell unless he came right out and told us."

"Well, that's not going to happen," Lauren announced to her parents as they both turned their heads toward her in unison.

"We don't know for sure that there's a problem, do we? It could have been anything. He could have just had a bad day. He's still so upset about losing Ashley," Julia said.

The group suddenly heard the sound of the floor creaking in the back of the apartment. The noise sent their heads flashing toward the guest bedroom. Terror filled their eyes as they realized that they were only moments away from a confrontation with Bobby.

"Well, what did he say last night?" Scott whispered to Lauren.

"He was angry when he walked in and said I had to let him stay here. He said he had no other place to go," Lauren blurted out, feeling that it was okay to physically back away from her parents. Sensing that her parents were—at this particular moment—more concerned with Bobby than their own petty differences.

"I say we ask him," Scott declared.

"He's just going to deny it," Lauren smirked, pulling one leg behind her as she sat down on the sofa, bringing her other leg across her knee, drowning herself in her blanket again.

Julia stood silent, hoping that this was all some type of misunderstanding. Wanting her choice in their father not to be the reason her son has chosen to destroy his life. Guilt, shame, a resounding voice in her head, started to sing. And she listened.

The group felt an awkward silence come on as they suddenly heard some rattling coming from the back of the apartment.

"Looks like he's awake," Lauren said, adding a "dunt…dunt…dun…."

Julia looked over at her.

"Sorry." Lauren grinned.

They heard the door to the backroom open as footsteps made their way from the bedroom to the bathroom. The door then shut. After a prolonged silence, they heard the toilet flush and a door open. They all braced themselves as the rapid footsteps traveled toward them.

An image formed in front of them as Bobby stopped abruptly in the entryway to the living room, shocked to see his entire family standing in front of him. "Mom? Dad? Who died?" Bobby asked, sensing the gloom in the room.

Scott, noticing Julia's reluctance, spoke up first, trying to ease the stress he sensed emanating from her. "Your sister called us."

"What for?" Bobby asked, now turning his attention toward Lauren, whose eyes widened.

"Well, she was worried about you," Julia explained.

"Why?" Bobby said, turning his head back toward Lauren.

"I thought," Lauren said, feeling she had betrayed her brother, "well, you didn't look like yourself last night. The way you came in and…well…your eyes."

"My eyes?" Bobby asked, still standing under the arched doorway to the living room. "What are you talking about?"

Lauren stood up, looking straight at Bobby. "I'm talking about crazy eyes. You can't stand there and tell me you are not doing drugs."

Bobby looked around at everyone. Everyone but Julia. "You're crazy. So, I had a few too many to drink. I made it over here, didn't I?"

Julia then spoke up, "She was just worried about you. You need to tell us the truth, Bobby. How much did you have to drink, or what are you on? We can't help you if you don't tell us the truth."

"I'm telling you the truth. Why would I lie? Where would I get that kind of money?"

"Well, that was my question," Julia said.

Scott took a step toward Bobby. "I don't believe you."

Bobby, stunned, slowly turned his head to face his father as if he couldn't believe what he was hearing. "You don't get to say that to me. Not after all the crap that you put us through. You do not have the right!"

"Oh, I have the right. You're my son. No matter how much you would like to change that, I will always be your father."

"No. I was your son. You left me behind just like you did everyone else. You were my father. You aren't anymore. So, you don't get to say that to me."

Scott stood in place, not knowing what to say as Julia spoke up, "He's your father, Bobby. He's here because we are worried about you. All of us came together because we believe you may have a problem."

"Oh, that's a big surprise. I'm always the one with the problem, right? I'm the screw-up. I've always been. I'm the son of a screw-up. I don't need you all to tell me what I already know. So, if you will excuse me, I'm going to get my things and get the heck out of here!"

"Bobby, wait," Scott said, moving toward him, grabbing his arm to try and prevent him from leaving. "You have to be honest with us, son."

Bobby, feeling his father's grip, sprang around, grabbing his father's arm and pushing him away. Scott stumbled back, and Julia instinctively grabbed Scott under his arms to prevent him from falling to the ground.

"Bobby!" Julia shouted out.

Bobby looked at Scott with a glare his family was very familiar with. One with red, widened eyes of rage. His arm trembled as if he were fighting the urge to move across the room and strike his father once more. "I'm sorry, Mom. But honest? Really, Dad? Ha. That just came out of your mouth. You don't know the definition of the word. I can show you your type of honesty. I can do that all day long."

At that, Bobby turned around and left the room. The group, still stunned, heard some rustling coming from the back room. Not sure what to do next, they stood there, stealing glances at one another, lowering their eyebrows in question as the sound of rapid footsteps headed back toward them, as they prepared for another outburst, secretly thinking about the fact that Bobby was the only person in the room who had most of what went on with their family right.

Bobby returned with his tennis shoes on and a jacket in his hands. He didn't say a word to them. He passed right by them, like a gust of wind, without even a glance and flew out the front door, letting it slam behind him.

In the silence, they heard the revving of his car and then the screeching of his tires as he hit the gas. No one said a word until they could no longer hear the roar of the engine in the distance.

"Ahhh...well, that went well," Lauren said. "What the heck? Drama. That's one thing this family is full of. I'm going to get some breakfast," Lauren said as she headed toward her miniature kitchen.

Julia then turned toward Scott. "What are we going to do now?"

Scott took a few steps away from her and turned around, announcing to the room, "It's all my fault. I'm so sorry. I'll find a way to fix this."

Julia looked back at him. "He's our son. We'll have to find a way to fix this."

"I don't deserve to be part of his world—or your world. I really screwed things up this time, and Bobby's paying for it," Scott confessed.

Julia wanted to scream at him that that's exactly what happened. His selfishness. His lust. All of these things were stepping stones to this moment, but she just couldn't bring herself to do it as she looked into his teared-up eyes. At this moment in time, she knew she needed him. She knew Bobby needed him, and she just didn't want to face this craziness alone.

"We'll find a way. I can't do this on my own, Scott," she said.

Scott, fighting tears, immediately realized the lifeline she had thrown him. It was rare, but there were moments when Julia would let him in. Let him be a part of the family again, and this was one of those moments.

He grabbed it with all of his might and tried to think of something wise to say to help Julia understand that he was not going to leave her to deal with this on her own. This time, he would be there for his family. For his son. For Julia.

"You don't have to. I promise you. I won't let you all down this time. I will be here for you and the kids." Scott moved toward her as if he were going to take her hand, like he had, in a world far away from where they currently are. Julia automatically stepped back, leaving Scott standing in his tracks.

She had heard all those words before. The day he told the kids he was leaving, "I will always be here," he said as the kids teared up. "Nothing is going to change. Daddy will just be living somewhere else."

The strange thing was she felt Scott truly believed the lies pouring out of his mouth. It was as if he entered this world where he couldn't distinguish between what he wanted to be true and the truth. She only hoped that this time, this one time, Scott was actually being truthful for all their sakes. But especially for the sake of their son.

Julia and Scott stood there staring at one another. Knowing their history. Knowing that they both would do anything to save their son. They stood in silence, wondering to what extent Bobby had truly fallen, and questioned what exactly it would take to somehow get him back, if that was even possible.

CHAPTER ELEVEN

Julia called into work on Monday, too miserable to face a day of needy shoppers or staff drama. She wore her pajamas all morning and ate chocolate out of a multi-colored plastic bag that she left on the end table for times just like this. It was either chocolate or a margarita, and she thought it was a little early to break out the Jose Cuervo.

She watched the screen with a blank stare as contestants won prizes on game shows, and reruns flashed before her eyes, projecting episodes she had seen a thousand times before. Her mother entered and exited the room, picking up various items while pretending to be dusting. At one point, she even started vacuuming. Carmen finally stopped cleaning long enough to inquire what Julia was still doing at home.

"Well, did you get fired?" her mother asked, unable to hold back her curiosity any longer.

Julia lazily rolled her eyes toward her mother, almost too exhausted to answer. "No, Mom. I just don't feel well."

"You looked okay yesterday."

"Yesterday is yesterday; it's not today. Do you want me to go to work, Mom? Is that what you are telling me?" Julia said while continuing to deplete the small plastic bag of chocolate.

"Go to work. Stay home. Makes no difference to me," Carmen said, throwing her hands up in the air. "No one tells me anything around here. If you are sick, go to the doctor. I'm going to the store."

Julia heard her mother's voice fade as it traveled down the hallway, turning into drowning syllables of nonsense. The sparrow from the bird clock chirped eleven times, signaling her to change the channel on the television. The chirp was a set reminder that her favorite show, *One Moment in Time*, was about to begin. She sat back in her recliner with her legs twisted up beside her, wearing her fuzzy blue robe and fluffy white slippers, drowning into the back of the chair. She grabbed her robe and tightened it in front of her chest as if she had a chill, melting into the softness of the cushion.

A sliver of light made its way in through the vinyl blinds as she saw her favorite character appear before her. It was Michelle. She had her thick blonde hair tied up in a French twist. Her diamond earrings sparkled against the highlighted streaks of her hair. The gray business suit that adorned her body announced to everyone that she was the boss. As the CEO of her company, she always looked very professional. Michelle made her way past her male assistant, who was secretly in love with her, turning to look back at him before she entered her office. This young man was ten years her junior, but his obvious infatuation with her was clear to everyone. Their eyes met as Michelle came out of her office and asked him to bring in a client's file.

At that moment, Julia was reminded of her lowly job. Her mind wandered to her co-workers, and she felt a sense of guilt for not going to work. Yet, another part of her wondered if anyone would even notice that she wasn't there. Besides Lisa, that is.

Julia thought about her daughter, Lauren, and sighed, picturing Lauren making her way to her classes that morning. She thought about what her unborn grandchild would look like. Julia tried to think of names the baby would call her besides Grandma. Nana…Ona…Mimi…. She then thought, *What difference did it make?* They all added up to Grandma. She was going to be a grandma.

Julia rose and slowly made her way over to the mirror that hung in the entryway and began to stare at the image looking back at her, tugging and pulling at her skin, finally giving up, feeling the fight was useless.

She intentionally avoided thinking about the situation with Bobby. She just didn't have the strength to deal with it at the moment. She knew that her son was good at blaming others for his bad decisions. Blaming his dad for not being around was one of the ways Bobby justified what he was allowing to happen to him. His behavior—Julia worried—was a means to a devastating end.

His behavior was a process of hurting his dad by hurting himself. He knew by destroying himself, others, like Ashley, his dad, and possibly Julia, would suffer. It was the only way. The only way to make others feel the hurt that he was feeling. The hurt that he blamed them for.

Julia sat back down and let the world drift from her shoulders. She snuggled back into her cushioned recliner, with her chocolate in hand, and began to enter into the lives of the characters she adored. The elegant gowns, the business suits, and the exotic vacations were all a part of this world.

Oh, the character's children on *One Moment in Time* would get into trouble, like everyone else, but they always seemed to manage to land on their feet. Of course, thanks to the millions of dollars their parents had at their disposal. And everyone on the show took part in guiltless extravagant spending on the most frivolous of things.

Julia imagined herself as a part of their world, as part of that community, if for only a moment, living life to the fullest. In their world, she wasn't home alone, divorced, living with her mother, facing being a grandmother, her daughter pregnant, and her son addicted to some unknown substance. In this fantasy world, she wasn't who she found looking back at her in the mirror. She was successful, attractive, and not afraid of anything. In this dream world, she looked life in the eye and said, "Bring it on." She wasn't sulking, in her furry rob, watching the world slowly dwindle, moment by moment, right in front of her.

Julia peered around the living room at the many pictures of her and the kids. Her mom even had a picture of Scott, Julia, and the kids when they were all still a family. They were at an amusement park. The kids had cotton candy splashed all over their faces, and Scott held her close with one arm. All four of them were smiling into the camera. This moment seemed ages ago, long dead and forgotten. She wasn't that wife anymore. She wasn't that mother anymore. She wasn't sure who she was now, but she was painfully aware of who she wasn't.

The last scene of *One Moment in Time* ended with Michelle, in an evening gown, alone with her assistant at her Malibu mansion. Disgusted, Julia clicked the television off, got up, and walked into her bedroom. She knew exactly where she was going. She headed straight toward her closet and took out a large box she had intentionally stuffed away in the back. The box, covered by her clothes, her shoes, and random scarves, was brilliantly hidden from curious eyes. Magically camouflaged from the present. A place where her past was buried from everyone, especially herself.

She lugged the large box out and opened the flaps of the cardboard box, taking out a leather binder and several large notebooks. She sat on the floor outside of her closet, with the closet light making its way into a small section of her room.

She unsnapped the binder and took out several pieces of paper, and began to read them. She smiled and giggled and cried as she read, bringing the papers up to her chest and hugging them as if they were a long-lost child. She looked through another section and another until she got lost in the moments she had created. These were her stories. Stories she had intentionally left untold and unsung.

As a writer, she felt a deep yearning for her stories to be told, to be cherished, to be known. Like a newborn child that everyone cannot wait to celebrate the birth of, she waited for them to be discovered. In the closet, under her clothes, in the brown cardboard box, hidden away in the dark crevasses of her room.

After hours of reading, she reluctantly gathered them all up and carefully placed them, one by one, back into the box as she had done hundreds of times before. But this time, she left one of the newer notebooks out and walked over to her bed, scooting onto the bedspread and grabbing her pen.

She began to write about her daughter, about her son, about her mother, pages about Lisa and even Scott, and she poured it all out on her canvas, and she gasped at the wonder, the magic, of what the words told the world.

She continued to write as fast as her hand would allow. All the pain, all the happiness came thrusting onto the small, thin, white sheets as they struggled to hold it all in, and before she knew it, she had written twenty pages, thirty…until her hand finally collapsed from exhaustion.

She looked down at her bed and the pages and pages of words, each page leading to the next, and she laid back onto her pillow, surrounded by the words of her life, the words of her past, and the many roads destiny had placed before her, and the world began to spin as she closed her eyes.

"Julia," a voice said. "Hey, babe."

Julia rose up on her bed to a darkened room, hearing the sheets of paper crinkle underneath her, and looked over toward a bright light beaming in from the window. She put one hand over her eyes, trying to see past the gleaming light, and a dark silhouette formed out of the scintillating light.

"It's me. Wow…you're still so beautiful."

"What? Who are you?" she asked, thinking she was dreaming.

"You don't recognize me? I look exactly the same, don't you think?" the image said as he moved out of the light.

Julia quickly backed away, scurrying toward the headboard on all fours until she could not back up any further. She reached down and grabbed a bat she kept by her bed, bringing it up and balancing it on her right side as if she were about to blast a ball out of the park. "Who are you? Don't come any closer!"

"Babe," the image continued, "you don't recognize me? Come on."

"Get out!" Julia cried out.

The image began to move toward her as Julia tightened her grip on the bat, bringing her knees underneath her and kneeling on the top of her bed.

Then she saw his face.

She saw that smile.

He flipped his hair back with one hand, standing there in a pair of worn-out jeans.

"It's me," the image said with his hands spread wide as if preparing to hug her.

Julia squinted her eyes, rubbing them frantically as if to clear her view. "What? It can't be. I must be dreaming."

The image moved closer to her, the glittering dust that surrounded him now sprinkling to the floor behind him as if to leave a trail for others to find. "I only have a few minutes."

"What do you mean a few minutes?"

The image moved closer to her.

"Don't come any closer. I'm not afraid to…to use this," Julia shouted out into the night.

Then he said something only he would say. Something he used to say. "I love us."

Julia stared at the image, lowered the bat to the bed, and felt the room starting to spin, her knees collapsing onto the mattress. "How…?"

"Hey, beautiful. How about a dance?"

At that, Julia moved her feet off the side of the bed and sat at its edge, staring at the fluorescent image before her that somewhat resembled what looked to be…Ritchie.

"It's me. Wow, you look great," the image said, lowering his hand to take hers.

When Julia reached out to the translucent hand, it slowly melted into hers as glimmering light shot out in every direction of the room, lighting up the translucent face.

The image moved closer to the light, and Julia gasped in wonder. "My only wish would be that I could hold you again, if only for a moment," the image said.

Julia squinted her eyes, trying to see through the image before her. "Your wish?"

"Of course. What are you sitting on, my love?"

Julia looked down and around her, "My...my stories."

"Why are they here?" the image said, pointing down to the bed.

"They...they were in the box," she said, still dazed.

"Well, take them out," said the glowing image.

"Why?" she asked.

And the image looked up at her, staring into her eyes. "Because the world needs to hear them."

"What are you talking about? How?"

The image then smirked and placed his glowing hand on the side of Julia's face as if trying to clear a strand of hair from her eyes. "You'll go back to school."

And with that, the image vanished, leaving glowing dust particles floating to the floor. Julia immediately darted backward on all fours toward her headboard and dove under her covers, rubbing her eyes as if she had just awakened.

With a new awareness of what had possibly just transpired, Julia suddenly threw off her covers and frantically looked around the room. She stood up and hurried over to her bedroom window and whipped open the curtains, sending them flying in both directions. She looked out of the window that faced toward the neighbor's fence. She looked past the wood fence, around the neighbor's house, and into the front yard, banging on the window several times, screaming, "Ritchie! Ritchie...don't go! Please don't leave me here again!"

CHAPTER TWELVE

After a sleepless night, Julia tiptoed around her room like a burglar afraid of waking a homeowner. She looked in closets and underneath her bed, not really sure what she was looking for. She sensed a presence around her, almost as if something or someone were watching her. She gazed into her mirror at the image staring back at her, replaying her spiritual encounter over and over again in her head. *Was it a dream?* she asked herself. *Or am I truly finally going mad?*

Should she tell someone? Her mother possibly? She thought that was probably not a good idea. She wasn't sure if she should tell anyone. If someone were to find out, she thought they might lock her up and throw away the key. Julia tried to recall all that the spirit had said. But like most dreams, the words dissipated in the night—as specific details of dreams do—but she did recall the last words the image or spirit or whatever it was said to her, and she replayed the words again and again in her mind. "You'll go back to school."

Back to school at my age? Julia thought to herself. *At my age? Could I?*

The next thing Julia knew, she was racing toward her laptop to look up local universities. She had completed two years at the city's community college before she met Scott…before Ritchie died. Julia had always planned to go back to school, but all of that was diverted when she met Scott and started a family. It wasn't that Scott made her quit. It wasn't that she didn't have enough time or money. She had used the marriage as an excuse. An excuse to give up.

At the time, what she loved, what she dreamt of becoming, didn't make sense anymore. Not even to her. She felt she wasn't good enough to fulfill her dream. *So why even try*, the young version of herself would say, *if failure was almost guaranteed?*

Julia typed the name of the local university into the keyboard and stared at the screen. She looked around the room, wondering if the spirit was still there, watching her. She called out to the silence, wondering if he was still there, "Hello." But the room never answered.

With the excitement of a high school senior going to a college site for the very first time, she clicked away at the keys. She felt a pain in her stomach and a lump in her throat, and she couldn't seem to move her fingers fast enough as the images on the screen began to appear before her like dreams being unlocked.

Julia stopped for a moment, wondering what her family and her friends would think about her returning to school. She thought they would probably think that she had lost her mind. Who does this? Who goes back to school at her age? But her fingers just kept on tapping on the keys.

English Department, the college site read. That led her to a screen that listed the various degrees. First, there was literature and then teaching, of course, and she scrolled down to the bottom, "Emphasis in writing." *That's it*, she thought to herself. *I'm going back to school to be a writer.*

Julia looked through the various required courses for the degree. Her eyes brightened as she skimmed the name of each course. She noticed how lovely all the titles sounded. There was: beginning poetry, beginning fiction writing, English literature, American literature, world literature, and on and on. Julia felt an excitement blooming inside her that she thought had died long ago. She couldn't seem to hide her giddiness as she dove deeper into the specifics of each course.

She maneuvered her mouse over to the application page and began to fill out the lengthy form, hesitating every now and then, debating all the reasons why she shouldn't go back. All the reasons she may fail. Still, something inside of Julia pushed her to trudge forward. And she did.

She wondered, for the first time in a long time, what exactly her future would hold. Julia knew that in order to be looked at seriously as a writer, she would need a degree.

Completing all the necessary forms, she hesitated for a moment, staring at the screen, holding her finger over the keyboard, and closed her eyes, finally letting her finger fall, sending the application into the unknown.

When she opened her eyes, she sat back and was brought back to the words from the spirit. How did he know? How did he know what was hidden in the deepest part of her heart?

It had to be him.

Julia hugged her chest as a chill came over her. Looking at her hand, she remembered how her fingers passed through his, almost as if they were one.

Lost in her daydream, Julia was awakened when she heard her mother shout from the kitchen, asking if she was going to eat breakfast or not. Julia rose from her bed and quickly got dressed. She flew by her mother, kissing Carmen on the cheek as she passed by her.

Carmen was so stunned by Julia's joyous spirit that she didn't say anything for a minute and then asked the question, "What's gotten into you?"

Julia answered with a reassuring, "I'm going back to school, Mom."

Carmen's demeanor slowly changed as she froze in place as if she were debating if she had heard her daughter correctly or not and responded, "Well…good. It's about time."

Julia smiled and grabbed her purse, heading toward the front door. "I'll pass on breakfast, Mom. I have to run some errands before work," Julia said, and she headed out the front door. After all, if she was going to go back to school, she was going to do it in style.

Still, as thrilled as Julia was, she couldn't help but hear that familiar voice inside her head. The voice of failure. This voice she knew all too well. Familiar to most. It is the voice that tells you not to even try.

For some reason, Julia thought of a phrase that she had heard Michelle on *One Moment in Time* repeat to herself when she was trying to make a life-altering decision. *If not now, then when?* And Julia ran that phrase, like a videotape stuck on rewind, repeatedly in her mind until it became a natural reaction to any of her doubts.

If not now, then when? If not now, then when?

After running her errands, Julia rushed into the department store so she could share her good news with Lisa. The store was exceptionally busy that day, and Julia found herself running back and forth to restock the shelves as soon as she clocked in. The store was having a huge sale, and it seemed that the community had turned out in droves. Julia didn't have time to make it over to Lisa's department because there was already a line to buy perfume and cologne when she arrived.

The crowd started to diminish around dinner time, and Julia took this opportunity to restock shelves as her evening staff arrived. She was so busy she didn't notice a shadow that was approaching her from behind. When she stood up from the glass cabinet, she almost ran into a man standing right beside the counter.

"Hello, again," the voice rang out.

Julia grabbed at her chest, startled by the image in front of her. It was Andy.

Her heart skipped a beat. She battled to steady her breathing as the man that left her breathless stood before her once again.

"Oh, It's you, Andy. How are you? So sorry, I didn't see you standing there," Julia said, embarrassed that she had almost run into him.

"Oh, no, you're fine. It was my fault. I shouldn't have been standing so close to you. I hope I didn't scare you," Andy said, standing within inches of Julia. She had to squirm through the small area between them to get to open space.

"No, no, of course not. It has been a madhouse around here today," Julia said, placing a box on the counter and nervously placing a piece of her hair behind her ear. "I wouldn't have noticed my own mother standing behind me." Julia laughed.

"I know. I came in for a few things, and the lines were crazy," Andy said, moving closer to where Julia stood as he leaned against the counter.

"So, are you shopping for something special?" Julia asked, curious as to what brought him to her department.

"No, I just have some business trips coming up, and I felt like I needed something less dated to wear. You know us bachelors, shopping is not high on our priority list."

"Oh…well, we're having some amazing sales."

"Yes, I saw that. So, how've you been?"

"Really good, busy, but it keeps me out of trouble," Julia said, still trying to figure out why Andy kept showing up wherever she was.

"So, do you maybe get a lunch or coffee break or something? I was just thinking of getting something to eat and wondered…well, I wondered if you might want to join me?"

Julia, stunned for a moment, lowered her eyebrows, trying to make sure she heard him correctly. "Oh, you mean right now? With me?"

"Well, yeah, if you are available, that is. I totally understand if you're too busy."

"No…no," Julia said, looking around at the counters where the girls were just standing around at the moment. She looked back toward Andy, wondering if this was something she should do, and she heard that voice go off in her head again. *If not now, then when?*

Julia then replied, "Sure, I have a lunch break. And well, I am the manager, and it looks like things are under control at the moment, so I would love to."

"Great, I'm not familiar with what's around here, so I'll have to depend on your expertise."

"Oh, I have been to every eating establishment within a ten-mile radius of here, so I'm sure we can find something that we both would enjoy," Julia said, trying not to sound too anxious.

Andy stood there beaming as if he didn't know what to say next and suddenly blurted out, "Wonderful. My dinner prospects are in your hands."

"Well, you are in good hands. Let me just get my things," Julia said, and she left to retrieve her purse behind the counter.

They decided to eat at a Chinese restaurant called The Great Wall. The restaurant, being very authentic, had you check your shoes at the entryway. The Great Wall displayed large oriental pieces of art, highlighted by red and black accents. As you walked in, you were immediately surrounded by orange and gray lighting that beamed through the black cast iron decor and carved oriental wood architecture.

They followed their hostess, who, like the other wait staff, was wearing a beautiful silk kimono outlined with blue chrysanthemum accents.

Julia thought the female staff looked so beautiful, each wearing a different vibrant color made up of blues, yellows, pinks, and greens. Each waitress had their hair slicked back into a French twist which was held in place by several floral hairpins.

Julia and Andy chose to sit back in the grill area, where the master cook created their meal right in front of them. The large metal grills were set in between tables that lined the grill in a sort of "U" shape. The captive audience sat and watched their chef perform and prepare their meal right in front of them.

The gleam of the blades shimmered in the reflection of the overhead lights as the chef, who was wearing an oversized white hat, alternated throwing the glowing blades upward in front of him, teasing his audience with near-death antics. Suddenly, the grill lit up in a blaze of whites, golds, oranges, and reds as the flames danced back and forth over the grill.

Julia, taken off guard, turned her head to avoid the flames from getting too close to her face. Andy, trying to make sure she didn't fall from her stool, instinctively grabbed her shoulder, bringing her close to him as if it were a natural thing to do. The two simultaneously burst out in laughter, realizing that the flames diminished almost as quickly as they had ignited.

Julia peered over at Andy as he smiled and put his face so close to hers that she thought that he might kiss her. She reactively turned her face, looking back toward the chef.

Embarrassed that she had turned her head away, Julia sat and wondered what would have happened if she hadn't.

"I'm sorry," Andy said. "I didn't mean to make you uncomfortable."

"No…you didn't. I was just surprised by the fire being so close," Julia lied, watching as a loose strand of Andy's thick hair fell onto his forehead.

They watched the chef perform until their meals were sitting right in front of them. Then they both ordered a glass of wine.

"So, how long have you worked at the mall?" Andy asked.

"Since my divorce, which was about…ahhh…around ten…or so years ago," Julia answered, quickly taking a drink from her glass, embarrassed that she had been working at the mall so long.

"So, do you enjoy it?" Andy asked.

"It's fine. It's not my dream job, but becoming a manager has helped. I have a little more freedom, and of course, the extra money comes in handy. It filled the need at the time and allowed me to have flexible hours when my children were young," Julia said and then tried to change the subject. "And you, so how long did you play baseball?"

"I played for three seasons before getting injured. I was injured actually at the beginning of my fourth season."

"Really? That's still a long time. I'm sure not long enough for you," Julia said, noticing the five o'clock shadow that she found so attractive on Andy, making its way onto the lower portion of his jaw.

"No. When I stopped playing, my life just seemed so empty. I mean, I was one of the smart ones. I realized my career could end at any time, and I planned for it. I began A & B Burgers after my second season and planned to go into it full time once I retired from baseball, but I had no idea that would be nearly a year later."

"It must have been exciting, though, seeing your dreams come to pass, knowing that you succeeded."

"Yes, that part was. I never dreamed that I would be propelled to the major leagues."

"So, you had mentioned you were married at one time," Julia said, wondering if Andy would think she was prying too much.

Andy answered honestly without even blinking, "Yes, actually twice."

"Really? What happened? If you don't mind me asking."

"Well, one was my fault, and the other, well, let's just say she didn't marry for true love."

Julia wondered about Andy's current dating status, something she had failed to ask before agreeing to have dinner with him. "So, are you still seeing, was it, Zoey? I mean, she seems really nice."

Andy looked over at Julia, almost as if he knew what she was trying to get at. "No, that didn't exactly work out. We didn't really have much in common. She didn't want anything serious, and I am a little tired of dating."

"So, you broke it off?" Julia asked, surprised by her boldness.

Andy hesitated for a moment, looking straight into Julia's eyes. "I'm tired of searching. Tired of being alone. I know that sounds cliché, but I just didn't see myself ending up where I am. Divorced twice. Never finding the right one. I mean, at first, dating was fun, and well, when you are in the major leagues, I have to say, it isn't all that hard to meet… well…women."

"I'm sure it wasn't," Julia said while playing with her food, not sure at this point if she wanted to eat because she was so enthralled with Andy's story.

"I had a good time, and then it wasn't so good. Time flew by, as it tends to do, and you find yourself suddenly out of time."

"So true. It goes so fast. It's almost like you're afraid to blink."

"Yeah, blink, and you're catapulted into the next chapter."

"Yes," Julia said, feeling an unusual connection to Andy at that moment. They had been through similar situations. He had lost his ability to play ball. Julia gave up on her dream to write. They both had relationships that didn't work out for reasons they should have seen before they got into them. There were similarities in all that life had thrown at them. But they both had survived. Maybe came out a little battered and bruised. But they were surviving.

"Well, anyway, I found myself to be what you're now looking at. I'm not that young, hot baseball player anymore, and Ms. Wonderful never showed up. I mean, there was one girl years ago, but nothing ever became of it."

"It didn't. Why not? If you don't mind me asking."

"She was already taken."

"Oh…well, you shouldn't give up. Maybe you aren't looking in the right direction," Julia said, trying to lighten the mood.

Andy smiled, "Are you referring to Zoey's age?"

Julia smiled back. "Andy, I'm certainly no one to judge anyone else, but I have boots older than her."

"Ahhh…huh. I saw you."

Julia turned back toward him after taking a bite, "What?"

"That night, I saw you. Then you showed up with him at the movie the other day. That younger-looking mountain-like man," Andy said, rubbing his hands on his napkin and taking a drink from his glass.

"Mountain man?" Julia thought for a minute. "Oh, you mean Brad."

"Yeah, Brad…you know exactly who I'm talking about," Andy snickered while placing his glass back down.

"That was nothing, really," Julia said, trying to convince Andy that she was telling the truth but failing miserably.

"It didn't look like nothing. He looked like a man in love," Andy said, taking a quick bite from his plate.

Julia hesitated for a moment before answering, wondering if she should set Andy straight or not. She decided there were enough lies surrounding her life, so telling the truth seemed almost refreshing. "No, not a man in love. He's just a friend. Brad's very sweet."

"Yeah, sweet. I thought he was very sweet, too," Andy said. He said it in a way that made Julia believe that he may be jealous of Brad.

She took another bite of her meal and decided to satisfy her curiosity regarding Andy's past. "And you. Why do you suppose it never works out?" Julia asked.

"What? You mean my marriages?"

"Yeah, your marriages."

"I don't know. All the good ones are already taken?" Andy joked.

"And how old were your wives at the time? If you don't mind me asking," Julia said, taking a drink from her glass.

"Well, they were old enough," Andy explained.

Julia then flashed back to the night Lisa dragged her out to the dance club. The night she met Brad and saw Andy in line with Zoey, and she couldn't help but laugh out loud.

Andy snickered, thinking she was laughing at him. "What?" Andy said, now smiling.

Julia laughed so hard she grabbed her napkin holding it over her mouth, trying not to spit out her food, "It's just what you said. My friend Lisa said the same thing to me the other night."

"See...," Andy said, pointing right at Julia. "See, you can't tell me you weren't attracted to Brad," Andy joked, nudging Julia with his shoulder. "I think you're doing exactly what I was, well, I mean, I am doing."

"Oh yeah," Julia said. "And what is that?"

"We are both looking for love in all the wrong places."

They both began to laugh as if they were old friends. As if their dinner was an everyday occurrence, and they had known each other their entire lives as the people around them smiled at the fun-loving couple who looked as if they were the best of friends.

After dinner, Andy drove Julia back to the department store. Julia noticed that Andy would glance over at her every now and then when he thought she wasn't looking. For some reason, she felt so drawn to him, as if it were a natural thing for her to be sitting right beside him.

When they arrived at the mall, Andy got out and opened Julia's door for her, walking her back to the public entrance of the store. Julia turned around to face him just as the wind picked up, lifting her skirt in the breeze as she tried to hold it down, brushing her hair from her face.

Julia smiled as Andy looked around at the sky, seemingly searching for the right words.

They stood awkwardly for a moment smiling at one another, not knowing what to say next, and then Andy said something unexpected.

"I saw you," Andy said.

"What?" Julia said. "You mean the other night?"

"No. This was in another life. We were both in our early twenties. I was playing ball, and a couple of us would visit the Tropicana Dance Club pretty regularly."

"What?" Julia said, her mind flashing past scenes from the Tropicana when she was with Ritchie. "You did?"

Andy looked around, placing his hands inside his pants pockets as if he wasn't sure he should continue. But he did. "You really don't remember me, do you?"

"No…I'm sorry, I don't think I do," Julia said as she turned her head, looking deeply into Andy's eyes as if she were trying to remember him.

Andy stared at Julia as if he were trying to figure out if she was telling the truth or not. "You were always there with a bunch of girls, or you would show up with this tall guy. I think he was in the service because he would wear his tags occasionally. I think he might have been a Marine."

Julia lowered her eyebrows as if trying to figure out how Andy knew all this. "Yeah, that was me…, and yes, his name was Ritchie."

"Yeah, I think I heard you say that once."

"How do you remember that?" Julia asked, moving closer to Andy so that she could look deeply into his eyes. Trying to determine if he was telling the truth or not.

"Because I asked you to dance a couple of times when Ritchie wasn't around, and you always turned me down cold."

"I did?" Julia said, lowering her eyebrows, straining to remember a past she had worked so hard to forget.

"Yeah…you were, and I mean you are now, really something. I used to watch you dance across the floor. I would try to get close to you, but you never gave me the time of day. No matter what girl I was with, trying to make you jealous. You never even looked my way."

"You were there?"

"I was there. I would always say I would like to dance with you, and you would never even respond."

"Wait…," Julia said as she flashed back to a recent dream she had when Ritchie came to her. She remembered that Ritchie had also said those exact words to her, *I would like to dance with you.*

"Could you say that one more time?" Julia asked.

"What? You mean, I would like to dance with you? But you never…."

Suddenly, Julia felt as if she couldn't breathe, like the other night when she almost passed out at the dance club. Everything started to blur around her. "I'm sorry, Andy, I need…to…get back to work."

"Wait…did I say something wrong? I didn't mean…," Andy said, reaching for Julia's hand as she quickly moved away from him, backing herself into the glass doors.

"No, you didn't do anything. I just need to get inside. I'm sorry. Thank you for this evening," Julia apologized, but before Andy had time to respond, she turned toward the mall entrance and opened the outside doors to go in.

Once inside, she turned back around, staring at Andy before entering the second set of doors. She caught sight of him as the parking lot lights suddenly turned on behind him, and Julia thought she spotted another image standing right beside Andy. Julia stared harder, squinting her eyes, as she saw that smile, that hair, through the glass, standing right there, almost as clear as day, with his arm around Andy's shoulder. It was Ritchie.

Julia's eyes widened. She immediately panicked and tried to open the second set of doors as fast as she could. Short of breath, Julia struggled to get the large glass door open.

Andy, wondering what he had said wrong, looked around the parking lot, trying to figure out what Julia was looking at. Wondering why Julia looked at him as if she had just seen a ghost.

CHAPTER THIRTEEN

As Julia walked toward the center of the store, she was so flustered by the image of Ritchie she saw standing next to Andy she didn't hear the loud commotion happening right in front of her.

"Let go of me!" she heard a familiar voice shout out. "Get your hands off me. My mother works here!"

Julia stopped for a moment as the world went into fast forward. She saw what looked like her son being slammed to the floor, face first, by one of the security guards. The officer was now sitting on top of Bobby, trying to place handcuffs on him. A young woman—who appeared to be with Bobby—stepped back, falling to the floor on her back, roaring with laughter. The chain hanging from her nose caught the reflection from the overhead lights as she hit the floor. One of the officers behind the young woman instinctively slid onto his knees, skidding across the floor, trying to keep the young woman from crashing her head onto the marble.

Julia looked on as her staff was gathered around the young couple like a mob cheering on a bar fight. Julia felt a lump in her throat as she went mute, unable to speak or command her body to move forward, and then he recognized her.

"There she is!" the boy, the man, announced to her colleagues, her friends, and her staff as they all turned to look back at her. "Mom! Tell them. Tell them who I am!"

Julia couldn't breathe; she felt herself moving forward but couldn't feel her legs alternating beneath her. She thought about diving behind the closest counter but knew she had already been spotted. She looked at what resembled her son as he squirmed to get himself loose from the officer's grasp. She heard herself whisper to him under her breath, "What are you doing?"

"I came to see you. I needed to borrow some money, that's all. They're lying! All of them. I wasn't taking anything. Mom! Mom, tell them!" he said as he struggled to get loose.

Julia began to come out of her dreamlike state as the lights from an overhead display hit her, and she felt someone grab her from behind. She turned and realized it was Annie.

"Julia, Bobby tried to break the glass cabinet. I'm sorry, sweetie, but they are taking him in. Do you want me to drive you to the police department?"

Julia looked around as all eyes were focused on her. She could hear Bobby and his girlfriend being dragged off in the distance as the officer's rubber shoes squealed across the gold and black marble floor, trying to keep a hold of her son, who was still trying to fight off the officers. Sirens could be heard in the distance as the lights started to flash outside of the building, creating circulating lights that beamed through the glass doors into the interior of the store, signaling for people to gather around, and all Julia could manage to say was, "Yes, Annie. Could you, please?"

Julia turned toward her staff, not sure what to say, and saw Brooke—of all people—making her way toward her. Brooke looked at Julia and said something that Julia couldn't make out. It was as if she were suddenly in the middle of a silent movie, and everyone was moving around her and speaking to her, but she couldn't hear what they were saying.

"Julia...Julia, do you need me to close tonight?" Brooke asked very softly, with a sense of compassion Julia didn't know Brooke possessed.

"Yes, Brooke," Julia said very professionally, "that would be great. Thank you."

Annie put her arm around Julia's shoulder and helped her to the door. Julia looked out the glass doors as her son continued to wrestle with the police. The police, now having to become more physical with him, slammed him against the police car with his face pressed against the window. The girl he was with was now trying to run away. It took two officers to hold her in place, and all Julia could hear through the glass was her son as he yelled out, over and over again, "Mom, help me! Why aren't you helping me? Do something! Why are you letting them do this to me?"

Annie kept her arm around Julia's shoulder as she guided her toward her vehicle. Julia, unable to focus, watched as the world around her started to spin again, and Annie had to physically hold Julia up, guiding her steps across the parking lot.

When they arrived at the police department, the officer at the front desk looked up at Julia, annoyed to have another walk-in. He barely acknowledged them as he shuffled papers from one shelf to another. The officer then glanced at Julia and asked, "Who are you here to see?"

Annie ushered her toward the officer's window as Julia answered, trying to keep her head held high. "My son…um…he was brought in here a few minutes ago. I need to know what's going to happen to him."

"And his name?" the officer asked as if it were routine.

"Bobby Melrose."

The clerk looked up at her as if he knew exactly who she was talking about. "Yeah…yeah, he's here," he said as if he was having a visual flashback of Bobby being brought in. "We're holding him for testing. You can wait over there." And he pointed to a waiting area made up of black plastic chairs and a magazine rack filled with an array of pamphlets.

Julia looked at Annie and then back at the officer. "Do you know how long it will take?"

"No, ma'am," the officer said sternly. "I do not."

Annie scooted Julia into the waiting area, guiding her as if Julia might somehow fall at any moment.

Julia looked around at other people in the room, who she assumed were there to pick up a loved one, a relative, or a spouse, and felt the confusion in most of their eyes. Looking at them was almost like looking in a mirror. Then there were others who walked around as if they were all too familiar with places like this, situations like these, and the waiting was just part of the process. They walked around with the plastic cups from the water dispenser, laughing and making jokes as if they were at some type of family reunion.

After about two hours of waiting, a female officer, whom Julia remembers from the department store, came out and told them that Bobby was being charged with possession of methamphetamine and would not be able to bond out until the morning. The female officer, obviously seeing how upset Julia was, brought a chair over and sat down in front of her, looking Julia directly in the eye.

"Bobby has tested positive for meth, and we found a small baggie in his coat pocket. He is claiming that this was his first time using, but he is being charged with possession of narcotics, destruction of private property, and resisting arrest. Do you understand what I'm explaining to you, Ms. Melrose?"

Julia, now even more numb, shook her head up and down as Annie leaned forward.

"Will we be able to bond him out tomorrow?" Annie asked.

Julia looked over at her, grateful for the question.

The female officer wearing a badge that read, Officer Howard, turned her head toward Annie and answered, "Yes, he can bail out tomorrow if his record checks out, and this is indeed his first offense, and there's nothing else on his record," she said. "We should know more by morning."

Julia, trying to think clearly, asked, "If he bails out tomorrow will he need to go to court?"

"Yes," Officer Howard said. "He will be assigned a court date in four to six days, and the judge will decide how to proceed."

"What will he be looking at?" Julia said, trying to sit up straighter to look the officer in the eye.

"Well, if this is his first offense, and he doesn't have any priors, it is a misdemeanor in the State of California, and he will be looking at entering mandatory drug treatment, which would probably override the fine and any jail time. It all depends on his criminal history."

"So, I can pick him up in the morning?" Julia asked.

"Yes, ma'am. If everything checks out, you can bond him out in the morning," the female officer said, trying to console what the officer could tell was an overwhelmed mother.

Julia, grateful for the news and the obvious compassionate way the officer treated her, thanked the officer for all of her help.

"It's my pleasure," Officer Howard said, handing Julia a card. "You let me know if you have any questions at all."

Julia took the card and placed it in her purse, where she would be sure not to lose it. Julia and Annie then headed out of the police station in silence, walking toward Annie's car.

"Well, at least he will not serve any real jail time," Annie said, trying to console her friend.

"Thank you so much, Annie, for being here with me through all of this. You were a godsent."

"Oh, sweetie. You're very welcome. Would you like for me to bring you in the morning?"

"No, you have done more than enough. I have another person in mind for that job." Julia then took out her cell phone and dialed a number, letting it ring. Suddenly a sleepy male voice answered.

"Scott?"

"Yeah. Julia?" Scott asked, hearing a sense of desperation in her voice. "What's wrong?" Scott's voice rose as he cleared his throat, knowing that Julia would never call him, especially at this hour, if something wasn't desperately wrong.

"It's Bobby."

"What happened?" Scott asked.

"He's...he's been arrested."

"Arrested?" Scott blurted out as Julia heard some shuffling of what sounded like covers in the background. "For what?"

Julia reflected back to the incident and the officers literally dragging Bobby out of the store. "He tried to steal something from the store."

"From your work?" Scott gasped.

Julia felt his blood pressure soar through the phone.

"Yes...I believe...sorry, I just can't relive it right now," Julia sighed, hearing herself breathing into the phone, trying to slow her heart rate down. "And well...."

"What?"

"He's using. He's using meth."

"How do you know? Is that what the police said?" Scott said as if he was having a hard time breathing.

Julia walked around the parking lot, placing one hand on her forehead. "Yeah...that's what they said. They are testing him. He's in deep."

"Okay...what do we do now? Are they releasing him?" Scott questioned.

"Yes, he can be picked up in the morning. I'm sorry, I just can't go over the details right now. Can you be at my place first thing in the morning?" Julia asked. "They said we could bond him out then."

"I'll be there. I'll make a few calls before I get there to try and figure out what we need to do."

"Okay. Well, I'll fill you in then. Oh, and Scott..."

"Yeah?"

"Bring some cash. We're going to need it."

She lowered her phone, staring at the device, as the images of the day flashed before her, and her familiar, old friend, failure, whispered to her loud and clear.

CHAPTER FOURTEEN

The past filled Julia's thoughts as her regrets played over and over again in her mind. All the what-ifs that build in the dark places of our souls, the should-have-beens that later seem so clear to most when we are looking back in retrospect. She blamed Scott. She blamed herself. She blamed God. She blamed the world. Yet, the sun rose in the early morning hours of a new day, and she was left with the fact that she felt she had failed her family. Failed her son.

Kicking the blankets off, Julia looked at her television and thought about the wasted hours she had spent in front of it, wishing and hoping to be like the pretty, strong people she watched every day in that world that called out to her relentlessly. *Such wasted moments*, she thought to herself. Such wasted time. So much missed opportunity.

Julia wanted to scream out loud. So loud that everyone around her would hear her, so they would know that she still existed, in this little room, in her mother's home, as her family, her world slowly fell apart.

Julia's daughter, now pregnant, would soon be a single mother, raising a child on her own. Julia's own marriage failed. The love of her life, dead and buried. Now…now her son, who was hanging on by a very thin thread, addicted to a white powder that held him in the palm of its hand. How disappointed she was in her life…her family. And how she blamed herself for it all.

Julia thought, how could she possibly go back to school with all this chaos around her? She had to fix it. She had to control it. After all, it was all entirely her fault. If only she had been a better wife, a better mother, a better daughter, a better woman. If only Ritchie hadn't died and left her with this life. This was not supposed to be her life. She was supposed to be doing so much more. Where did it all go so wrong?

Her hands formed fists as she paced back and forth in her small bedroom, wanting, begging to hit something…someone. She felt the walls crumbling down around her, and she looked over at the baseball bat she kept in the corner by her bed. She grabbed it, taking it into her fists, passing it back and forth between her hands. She felt so helpless. So angry. Suddenly she stopped and raised the steel bat over her head and brought it down—quick and hard—letting the bat's exterior form into her mattress, feeling the energy from the contact vibrate through her body as she slammed the bat down over and over again onto the innocent sheets, screaming out into the silence until she could no longer feel her fingers.

Bringing the bat back up to her chest, she hugged it like it was one of her own. Moving the bat over her shoulder like a major league slugger, she visualized swinging it into the television screen and watching it explode into a million tiny pieces. She vividly saw the whole scene happening in her mind. She imagined the bat crossing her chest as she felt her heart leap into her throat and then, as if in slow motion, slowly releasing it from her fingers.

She visualized how the bat would crash through the face of the television, and the source of her failure would be dead. Dead and gone. It would torture her no more. She would be left with only the echo vibrating through her small room as the glass embedded itself into the carpet like water falling from a waterfall. At that moment, she decided that she would wait no longer. Julia was just about to release the bat from her shoulder when she heard her bedroom door creak open.

"Julia, what in the heck are you doing?" her mother screamed out.

Julia stopped in mid-swing and looked over at her mother, then instantly collapsed onto her bedroom floor with the bat still in her hand, silently weeping, tears forming pools in the lower parts of her eyes.

Carmen walked over to her and kneeled beside her daughter, as she had done when Julia was a little girl. She sat beside her, trying to rock her adult-sized daughter in her arms.

"Julia, what is it? What has gotten into you?"

"I'm so sorry, Mom. I'm sorry you have to take care of me. I'm sorry I'm such a failure. I'm sorry for not being what everyone needs me to be. I can't do it. I can't. I just can't. It's all falling apart."

"What's falling apart?"

Julia looked up at her mother as if her mother were joking. How could she not see? Julia thought, doesn't she see all that is happening? Doesn't everyone see? "My world. The kids. All of it."

"Sweetie, nobody expects you to be perfect. And those children of yours are adults, making adult decisions. Honey, look at me." Carmen brought her daughter's eyes up to hers. "Julia, you are my daughter, but you're certainly not responsible for everyone. Heck, you are not responsible for me, although I know you think you are, for Lauren or for Bobby, and you're certainly not responsible for Scott. You're only responsible for yourself. Dang-nabbit, you've got to start worrying about yourself. Now...," Carmen hesitated, "what kind of life do you want for you?"

"I don't know. I just know I can't do this anymore. This was not supposed to be my life. I was supposed to do so much more."

"Julia, what have I told you since you were a little girl? This is not your practice life. It's all or nothing. How do you want to finish it? There are no do-overs here. The Lord did not promise you that it was going to be easy."

Julia sat for a moment, drying her tears. "I know. I don't want to be this person. This isn't who I am. What does God expect of me?"

"He expects you to love Him and be the best you, you can be. So… what are you going to do about it?"

"I…I don't know. It's just all so crazy right now. There's Lauren and Bobby and me…."

"Julia, I had to learn this the hard way, so I guess you might have to, too, but is it your life that is really crazy? Or is it the world around you? The world you are holding on to. The world that you have no control over."

Julia looked up at her mother, wiping her nose with the back of her hand as she slowly released the bat and let it roll onto the carpet. "Mom?" Julia grinned. "How did you get to be so smart?" Julia smirked, wiping her nose.

"I've always been smart. I'm just the only one who knows it." Carmen smiled.

Julia laughed, and Carmen held her and rocked her back and forth. "What do you say? How about you get started on you for a change, huh? I can't do everything around here. You're going to have to step it up, sweetie. It's your life, not mine."

Julia shook her head in confirmation and then looked up at her mother while wiping away her tears. "Well, Mom. Looks like Bobby has got himself into a mess?"

Carmen looked down at her. "Oh no, what now?"

"He's in jail. They're charging him with possession of narcotics."

"Oh, Lord. No wonder you're on the ground. Well, I guess I'll have to get him straightened out too. Lord, I don't know what any of you would do without me," Carmen said, releasing her grip on Julia and making her way to a stand. "Well, get up and get dressed. We need to go pick his behind up. And I have a few choice words for that boy."

Julia looked up at her mother and sighed. "Yep, we got to go get him."

Carmen turned around, "Well, get up. We don't have all day."

"Oh and…,"

"What now?" Carmen asked, obviously more irritated, having to turn back around.

"Well, Scott's coming. He should be here any minute."

"Lord, that's all we need. Well, no, I take that back. He should be a part of this. He's the real reason these children's all screwed up. Yes, let's wait for Scott," Carmen said as she opened the door and headed out toward the hallway, screaming back, "And get ready!"

Julia was dressed in minutes. She was heading out of her room when she heard the doorbell ring. Scott stood there, looking as if he hadn't had a wink of sleep all night either.

"So, what happened?" Scott asked, making his way into the living room.

"He's apparently using drugs. He came into the store and was on something. Our security officers had to restrain him. I think he tried to steal some merchandise. I'm not even sure if I still have a job."

Scott's face whitened as he seemed overwhelmed by all of the information. He took a deep gulp and quickly looked away from Julia and then turned back, looking directly into her eyes. "I'm so sorry, Julia. What did they arrest him for?"

"I don't understand it all; possession of narcotics, resisting arrest? Apparently, they found meth on him. I am not sure what to do," Julia whined, looking to Scott for some type of guidance. Then as if the past came creeping up on her, Julia realized who she was entrusting this information to and walked away from Scott as she tried to compose herself.

Scott, having seen this blank stare from Julia before, realized that she had immediately regretted asking him to come. "I'm here, Julia. Please let me help with this. Were there any signs?" Scott asked.

"Signs? What are you asking me, Scott? Why wouldn't you know any of this? You're his father."

"I'm sorry. You're right. I should've been there. I don't mean to blame you for any of this. I realize I'm screwing up," Scott said, trying to redeem himself. He waited a few minutes to let Julia cool down before asking her any more questions. "So, they found meth on him?"

"Yes, that's what the officer said," Julia fumed, now more irritated than grateful that he was there.

"Man, this is bad. He could do time. This could go on his record. How will he find a job?"

"I don't know, but he's not going to be able to con himself out of this one," Julia said, making her way to the coffee table to retrieve her purse.

"So, we just bail him out? Will he stay with you?" Scott asked.

"I hadn't thought that far ahead," Julia admitted. "He can't go home if he's going to be using again. He has a court date coming up in a few days, but yes, we bail him out, I guess. What else can we do?"

"Let him sit in jail. Let him think about it," Scott said more forcefully than he intended. "Stop bailing him out of everything."

"I don't know," Julia said. "He's expecting us to get him out."

Scott hesitated as though he were thinking about his next words carefully. "I think we should let him wait there until his court date. He got himself into this mess, and he can get himself out. You can blame me for it. I will take the heat."

"No, Scott, I don't want him there for four or five days. I just can't leave him there."

"Julia, he won't learn if we keep bailing him out. I know this from experience."

"I don't want him there. The officer said he would be going to court in a few days and probably be sentenced to drug treatment. I think that all this legal stuff lingering over his head will make him realize just how much he screwed up."

"You don't know what drug addiction is like. I do. I had to hit rock bottom. I had to lose all of you before I realized how much I was destroying myself. And…well…everyone around me. This is not something you are automatically cured of. Once an addict, always an addict. You can fall off the wagon at any time. I'm telling you he needs to be in jail."

Julia peered at him, considering his last words. She didn't know what the right thing to do was. She didn't know what their next move should be. She just knew her son was in trouble, and she just couldn't sit around doing nothing. "I just can't, Scott."

"I will do whatever you want to do," Scott said, finally giving in, reactively placing his hands on both of Julia's shoulders as she looked up at him, and for one rare moment, she didn't fight him. "But I'm telling you, hon; it's a mistake to keep coming to his rescue. Rock bottom is sometimes the only thing that saves you."

Julia stood for a moment, letting Scott's words sink in.

Carmen then came racing around the corner of the hallway and announced to the room, "Are you two done? Let's go get my grandson."

Julia and Scott looked at one another as Scott slowly lowered his hands to his sides, acknowledging defeat, as they both slowly made their way out behind Carmen.

When the three of them arrived at the police department, the waiting room, which was full just ten hours ago, stood empty. There was a single female officer behind the window who approached the counter as soon as she saw them.

"Are you here to post bond?" she announced to the room as the sound of her voice vibrated down the long hallway for all to hear.

"Yes, we are," Scott answered her.

Scott approached the window. "We are here to pick up Bobby Melrose. We were told he would be released today."

The officer began to shuffle through some papers and look through a filing cabinet. "Here it is. Looks like the bail is set at $300. His court date is scheduled for Friday with Judge Conner." And the officer handed Scott a pile of papers. "Please look these over. This information will give you the courtroom, the time, and what to bring with you. Do you have any questions?" Scott looked down at the paperwork as a thousand—a million—questions went through his head, but only a few that the police officer could answer.

"Will he be released to us immediately?" Scott asked.

"Yes, I will just get this entered into the system and give them a call. They should bring him up shortly after that. He has been informed of the charges and what the consequences will be should he not show up for court," the officer announced to the room.

"I'll take care of the bail," Scott said and handed the officer the cash.

The officer took the cash, counted it, and handed Scott a receipt. "Here you go. They should be bringing him up anytime now."

The three took a seat on the black plastic chairs that lined the concrete wall. A few minutes later, the glass doors behind the female officer opened, and two officers escorted Bobby into the police report area.

Bobby scanned his surroundings and discovered his family sitting right outside the glass. He turned his head toward each of the officers on either side of him as if he were wondering what was going to happen next. He looked as if he had got about as much sleep as they had. His five o'clock shadow across his jaw was now the beginnings of a full-grown beard. His shirt was ruffled as if he had tossed and turned in it all night, and it was ripped at the bottom as a reminder of the struggle that he had with the officers the night before.

As he came closer to the outer glass doors, his family could see that he was still handcuffed.

He turned to have the officers release him. One of the officers said something to him as he was being released, and he nodded, rubbing his wrists. The door then automatically opened to allow Bobby to walk out into the waiting room.

His family stood there, still stunned by what had transpired in the last twenty-four hours, not sure how to react as an awkward silence followed. Bobby looked up at them and said repentantly, "Thank you for coming to get me."

Scott, obviously still angry, mumbled, "They said they gave you some paperwork. Do you have it?"

"Yes, Dad. I know what I need to do."

"Apparently, you don't, or you wouldn't be here," Scott retorted.

Julia trying to prevent an argument, spoke up, "Are you okay?"

"Yes, Mom. I'm fine. I'm sorry. I didn't mean for all this to happen. I hope I didn't get you in trouble at work."

"It'll be fine. It'll work itself out one way or the other."

"What the heck were you thinking?" Carmen exploded into the conversation, grabbing at her grandson's torn shirt.

"Mom!" Julia protested, grabbing Carmen's arm and lowering it back down.

"No, she's right," Scott said. "Do you know what you put us all through? How could you allow yourself to get involved with this stuff?"

Bobby looked at Scott, "I guess I am just the spitting image of my dad."

Scott took a couple of steps toward Bobby as the female officer looked up from behind the glass, and Scott pulled back. "You can't continue to blame me for all your bad decisions. You're an adult now, Bobby, so start acting like one."

"Oh…I have seen how adults act. No thanks," Bobby proclaimed. "I'm getting outta here."

"Outta here?" Julia said. "You aren't going anywhere. You're coming home with me. If you think I'm going to let you roam around town after getting you out of jail, you're sadly mistaken."

"Okay…okay, let's go or whatever. I want to get outta here," Bobby said, and he started to walk toward the front doors.

The three followed close behind him, not sure what to expect next. This just didn't seem like the Bobby they all knew and loved. He had no remorse for his actions. He didn't seem to care how he had hurt them or if he had hurt them. It was like watching a walking mummy.

He seemed to have no feelings one way or the other about all that had happened. He seemed...hollow.

Bobby rode home with Julia without a word being spoken. Every time Julia asked him a question, Bobby would not answer. He would just sit there and stare out the window.

"Your mother is speaking to you, Bobby," Carmen told him after hitting the back of his seat, irritated at his disrespect.

"Sorry," he said. "Mom, what do you need?" These words were followed by an even deeper silence.

Scott followed the group in his car.

Upon pulling up in front of the house, Bobby suddenly seemed to magically come out of his morbid state. He got out of the car and stopped his family before they all had a chance to enter the gate outside of his grandmother's home and confronted them.

"I just wanted you all to know that I'm so sorry for everything I put you all through and that I ever tried this stuff. I promise you it was the first time and the last time," Bobby said sincerely, taking time to look them in the eye. "I understand the implications of my actions now. Being in jail was such a wake-up call for me. I never want to go back there ever again." He then turned toward his father. "I'm so sorry for saying those things to you, Dad. Thank you for getting me out."

Scott looked at him, wanting to believe him but having doubts. Scott, a victim of alcohol addiction, felt that he would have said those exact same words had he been caught at his lowest point. "Okay, son. But you have to realize what that drug can do to you. To your life. We don't want that life for you," Scott pleaded.

"I know. I wasn't thinking. It was a one-time stupid mistake. I still can't believe I did it," Bobby said, with tears forming in his eyes.

With her son's seemingly heartfelt words, Julia was somehow a little more comforted. She felt her son had possibly finally hit rock bottom and was ready to turn his life around, his destiny. She believed that Bobby's experience in jail had taught him just how short life was. "Let's get you inside, Bobby. I'm sure you are exhausted," Julia said, leading the way through the gate.

Carmen stood there looking at her grandson, "Bobby, do you really know what you have put your mom, your dad, and me through the last couple of hours?"

"Yes, Grandma. I know I really screwed up. I know I disappointed you. I don't ever want to go back to that jail cell again. I get it."

"Well, I really hope you do. Because let me tell you, your mom and dad will not be here forever. And Lord knows, I will not be. Do you know how much we love you?"

"Yes, Grandma. I do," Bobby said. "I'm so lucky to have you all." The group stood there for a moment, looking awkwardly at one another, when Bobby looked toward his grandmother. "Grandma, do you have any leftovers? I'm starving," he joked, just like he had all of his life. Ever since he was a little boy, Carmen had always called him her little food disposal.

The four of them sat down that afternoon to spaghetti and tuna salad. They laughed and talked as they always had since Bobby was a little boy. The morning faded from their thoughts as the afternoon was filled with food and conversation. The upcoming court date seemed months away as they all tried to put the last twenty-four hours behind them.

Scott stayed a while to watch television with Bobby and Julia.

Julia got a call from her boss, who said to take off as much time as she needed to deal with her family issues. She told Julia her job would be waiting for her when she was ready to return. This was the boost Julia needed. She could now commit her time to Bobby without worrying about work.

Scott stayed late into the evening. He felt good about Bobby's decision to stay with his mother. He felt that Julia would probably be able to keep an eye on him.

When it was time for him to leave, Scott asked Julia to follow him to the front door. "You call me if anything happens. I'm still not sure about all of this," Scott said. "Do you want me to stay the night?"

Julia looked at him with her eyebrows narrowed.

"I meant I would sleep on the couch."

Julia looked back toward Bobby, who was talking with his grandmother as they watched television. "I think he's okay."

"Okay, if you're sure...," Scott said as he continued toward the door. He then abruptly stopped and turned around. "Maybe I should stay just in case."

"We'll be fine. I'll call you in the morning."

"No, I'll be here first thing. I'm going to take a few days off of work," Scott said as he awkwardly patted Julia's shoulder.

"That would actually be great," Julia said.

After dinner, Bobby convinced Julia and Carmen to join him in a game of Monopoly, one of Bobby's favorites. They spent the evening laughing as Carmen cleaned out both Julia and Bobby within the first two hours.

When the game was over, Julia and Bobby discussed his legal options right before going to bed. She wanted to make sure he understood just how much trouble he may be in.

"You know, son, you gave us quite a scare."

"I know, Mom. I know better than to get involved with drugs. I still can't believe I did it. It was just all the stuff with Ashley. I just didn't know how to handle it. I felt like...like a failure."

"Everyone goes through that, and you're not a failure. You're my son. I believe in you. What is it you want for your life? Your dad and I can help you. You have the rest of your life in front of you."

"I know that now. I just felt worthless. I just couldn't seem to get anything right. I'm so sorry," Bobby said, looking away from his mother for a moment. "I'm so sorry I put you through all of this. If I could change the past few days, I would."

"Well, it is what it is. We just need to concentrate on moving forward. Both you and I. Let's make that our goal, huh," Julia said, now feeling more relaxed after hearing Bobby's words of repentance.

"Yep…that's my new goal, Mom. I'm really tired. Do you mind if I crash now?"

"Yep, but just remember that you have court in four days. You need to be at your best. You're not out of the woods yet," Julia said, trying to gently remind him of all that lay before him.

"I know," Bobby said, seemingly tired from the day.

"You know I love you, don't you?"

"Yes, I know, Mom. I love you too. Don't worry. It'll be okay," Bobby said, and she watched him head to the spare bedroom, turning to smile at her as he closed the door.

As Julia headed off to bed, she had a sense of peace that everything was going to work out for the best. Bobby would get the counseling he needed, and Julia could start preparing to go back to school.

Her mind wandered to Scott and how supportive he was being. She wondered if it was all for Bobby or if he somehow still had feelings for her. She thought to herself, no…there's been too much between them. He has to know that there's no way she would even consider anything regarding the two of them again.

And for some reason, at that moment, Julia thought of Andy. She secretly hoped she would hear from him. Julia thought about possibly calling him. She had left so abruptly last night. Had she really seen Ritchie again? And she said out loud without realizing it, "Oh my gosh, I think I saw Ritchie next to Andy. What does that mean? Am I losing my mind?"

By this point in the evening, Julia was so exhausted she didn't have the energy to think about all the craziness going on around her, so she headed off to her room. She climbed into bed, reaching for a book she had been wanting to finish, and soon found herself in a deep sleep. But as midnight approached, she heard a voice calling out to her from the darkness.

"Julia, wake up, babe," a voice whispered in the night.

"What?" Julia said, half asleep.

"Julia, babe," the voice said again.

Julia opened one eye as she saw something glowing in the corner of the room.

"It's me," the voice said.

Julia tried to close her eyes, thinking that she was dreaming, but the voice cried out again in a thunderous tone, "Julia, wake up!"

Julia sat up in her bed, and the light in the corner was gone. She heard things being knocked over or tripped over in the dark. She got up and reached for her robe, wrapping it around her. She then reached for her baseball bat as she made her way out into the darkened hallway.

She quietly rapped on the door of Bobby's room, hoping to wake him so he would join her in searching out who or what was making such a racket. She tiptoed toward the door to the guest room, pressing her body to the door so as to not be seen or heard, still hearing sounds coming from the living room.

She gently turned the doorknob and opened the door calling out to Bobby in a whisper when the noises coming from the living room suddenly stopped. She then flicked the light switch on to find Bobby's disheveled bed empty. She flashed on the hallway light and made her way to the living room with the baseball bat just above her shoulder, hoping that Bobby was out of harm's way.

She then heard the front door open as she inched her way into the living room.

She flicked the light switch on just in time to see someone in a hooded sweatshirt leaving with a trash bag full of items. The person looked back at her once and quickly escaped through the gap in the door. The intruder was moving so quickly that he tripped on the door frame, losing his balance, plummeting to the floor of the porch, and dropping the bag, which was followed by a series of loud clanging noises as the metal items banged against each other, making their way across the front porch, rolling off the edges into the yard.

Julia ran to the door and opened it, seeing the items rolling across the wood planks of the porch.

Confused, she looked up and saw someone making their way through the gate with what was left in the trash bag. In a single moment, she caught sight of his face under the street light as her heart sank to her stomach.

It was Bobby.

He must have seen her because he quickly turned back around, running out of the yard.

Julia's mind went blank as she tried to talk but couldn't seem to form the words. Finding her voice, she felt herself screaming out into the dead silence, "Bobby!"

He turned once and looked back at her and took off in a strong stride across the lighted street, not looking back, not even once, until he was out of sight.

Julia just stood there, looking into the darkness. Unable to move.

Carmen came out of her room just as Julia let the screen door close in front of her, staring out into the street as if in a trance.

"What in the heck is going on out here, Julia? Is that you? What are you doing at the front door?" Carmen came up beside her and opened the door, seeing their things spread across the porch. "What happened? Those are my things. Julia, what happened?" Carmen asked as she looked to the left and right of the porch, searching for the culprit, still dazed from being awakened from her slumber.

Julia didn't say a word; she turned around and re-entered the living room, almost having to drag herself toward her room in a zombie-like slow stride, heading toward her cell phone. She could hear her mother shouting out at her in the background, asking her what was going on.

Julia picked her phone up, dialed a number, and waited for someone to answer.

"Hello," a sleepy voice said.

"It's me, Scott. I'm sorry, he just left. I don't know where he's going. Can you come over?"

"I'll be right there," she heard him say as she heard the call end.

And Julia's phone dropped from her hand, bouncing once onto the brown carpet that lined the small confines of her room.

CHAPTER FIFTEEN

That night Julia sat in her recliner as if the world was resting on her chest. She couldn't find the strength to move, so she sat staring off into space, trying to make sense of all the lies. She wondered how she could have been so gullible. So, trusting. Scott convinced her that it would be best if she remained at the house just in case Bobby came back. She dialed her son's cell phone number so many times her finger became numb. At one point, someone—whose voice Julia didn't recognize—answered the phone, and when she asked them to identify themselves, they quickly hung up.

She paced the living room floor most of the night, debating if she should call the police. Scott was against it. He said that, at this point, it would only get Bobby into deeper trouble with the law. She stared at the clock as the minutes melted into the early morning hours, and she feared what the morning sun would bring.

She pictured Bobby walking through their door, defeated and broken and begging for their forgiveness. Part of her would want to hug him and tell him that everything would be okay. The other part of her wanted to slap him across the face and scream at him for taking advantage of their love. How could he have done this to his family, she questioned over and over in her mind until the echo of her thoughts verged on madness. How was it that she had failed with him so badly that he had stolen from them? Her family had officially graduated to one of those families that everyone talked about. That poor family with the pregnant, unmarried daughter and the son hooked on drugs.

After a night of drifting in and out of slumber, Julia abruptly awoke, catching a thin stream of light making its way in between the blinds. Still hazy, she rotated her eyes around the room, hoping that the previous night had all been a nightmare. She suddenly felt her stomach turn and immediately knew that she was going to be sick. Julia raced out of the living room, heading toward the kitchen, passing her mother without a word, trying to make it to the bathroom in time. Her mother stood in the sunlight, staring out the sliding glass door with a cup of coffee in her hand.

There was a flush and a rush of water from the sink as Julia exited the bathroom with a towel resting in her hand, patting her face with the cool water. Her mother didn't even flinch. She stood and continued her gaze out into the backyard, choosing not to face Julia.

"Did you know he took Grandpa's wedding ring?" Carmen murmured.

"Oh, Mom, I'm so sorry," Julia apologized.

Julia walked around the table, noticing her mother's blank stare. Carmen looked as lost as Julia felt. She looked as if a piece of her had been stolen, along with the ring. This only added to the anxiety and sadness that consumed Julia. The guilt so overwhelming.

"Mom…he doesn't know what he is doing. I'm afraid his addiction is worse than any of us imagined. Scott's out trying to find him now."

"Ohhh…it's not the dang ring," Carmen flustered. "It's just…."

"I know. I can't believe he did any of this either," Julia said, placing her hand on her mother's shoulder.

"I would have given the ring to him had he asked me for it. I didn't need it," Carmen said as she continued to look out the door.

"I know you would've," Julia acknowledged, trying to console her mother but unsure of just how to do that since she herself was still in denial over the whole ordeal. "Mom, I think I'm going to join Scott and try and locate Bobby. If we don't find him before the court date, he could do some real jail time," Julia said, stretching her head around to see the front of her mother's face, not sure if her mother was listening. "But maybe that's what needs to happen. Maybe that's the only thing that will wake him up. I just don't know what's the right thing anymore. Mom, do you think you could call us if he comes back here?"

Carmen didn't answer. She stood, gazing at the trees swaying in the yard, only moving to lift her coffee cup up to her lips.

"Mom," Julia reiterated. "Are you okay?"

"Yes, I'm fine. Go, go find him. It's just a different world out there. What a mess…what a mess it all is…," Carmen said, shaking her head back and forth in disgust.

At that moment, Julia's phone lit up, and she looked down at it thinking it might be Scott with news of Bobby's whereabouts. Julia didn't recognize the number but decided to answer it anyway, thinking it might be Bobby.

"Hello," she said frantically.

"Is this Julia?" a familiar voice said.

"Yes, this is Julia."

"It's Andy. Sorry to call you so unexpectedly; I got your number from your friend, Lisa. I happened to run into her at the department store, and, well, she told me you were taking some time off."

Julia, still frazzled by everything going on around her, had to take a moment to compute what the voice on the other side of the phone was telling her. "Yes…yes, I'm taking some time," Julia said, not sure how much she wanted to reveal to Andy. She quickly turned and walked into the hallway so that her mother couldn't hear the conversation.

"I don't mean to pry, but…are you okay?"

"Yes…it's not me," and Julia hesitated, forming her next words carefully, afraid to send them out into the world. Afraid of how Andy would respond. "It's…well, it's my son."

"Oh…I'm sorry, Julia. Is there something I can do? Can I help in any way?"

For some reason, Julia felt a sense of comfort in Andy's voice. He seemed genuinely concerned. She somehow felt she could trust him with the truth. Something she hadn't felt towards someone since Ritchie. With all the craziness around her, she had forgotten the way she had left things with Andy. His last words. The image of Ritchie beside him flashed back into her mind, but she quickly pushed these thoughts aside, knowing that she did not have the time to deal with any of that right now.

"Well, he's missing. I'm sorry, I have to go help find him. It's a long story," Julia revealed before she had a chance to think about it.

"Well, I'd like to understand. I'd love to help you if you will allow me to," Andy offered.

Julia sat on the phone. Afraid to release the words that sat on the tip of her tongue. In the deafening silence of her increased heart rate, she wondered if she could trust Andy with the truth. She hesitated and took a deep breath. "He's not doing well. He's making some really poor choices, and he's well…we believe he's hooked on meth."

Julia hesitated, waiting for the phone to click, closing her eyes after she released what she thought would be the last words she would say to Andy. She sat waiting in silence, hearing Andy breathe into the phone, thinking why in the world did she just blurt that out.

"What's your address? I can come over and drive you around. You're probably in no shape to be driving. I have experience with this. A buddy of mine was an addict for several years. I would really like to help, Julia, if you will allow me to."

For some reason, Andy's words brought a sense of peace to Julia. She suddenly felt as if a weight had been lifted. She wanted so much to say yes but hesitated and tried to give him an out. "You really don't have to. It's not your problem and…."

"Julia, give me your address. I can help with this. Really, I can. And I want to. I will be right there," insisted Andy.

Julia rambled off her address and heard Andy say it would only take him a few minutes to reach her house before they hung up. Julia glanced over at her mother, who was still standing and staring out the sliding glass door. She walked over to her mother and put her hands on her shoulders, rubbing them.

Her mother reached over and grabbed her daughter's hand, and sighed. "Go, go get ready. You need to find him before it's too late. I'll be all right. I'm a tough old bird." She grinned.

"I know, Mom. But even tough old birds need a hug every now and then. I'm so sorry he hurt you."

"As you said. He doesn't know what he is doing. Go, go bring him home. I'll be praying that he will come back to us. I'll be okay."

"Are you sure? Cause I can have Lauren come over and stay with you."

"I'm sure. Now go," Carmen said, waving her daughter away.

Julia went into her room to change her clothes. She was barely putting her shoes on when she heard the front doorbell ring.

"Julia, I'm so sorry," Andy said upon the door opening.

"Thanks for coming, Andy. I really don't know what to do. Where would we look?"

"I know of a couple of spots to start looking. There's one close to here; I think he might have headed there," Andy said with confidence. They hurried out of the house and climbed into Andy's SUV. Julia was not used to sitting up so high and had to reach for the leather strap above her head to pull herself in.

"Do you think he will come with you voluntarily?" Andy asked.

"Oh, he's coming with me. If I have to drag him kicking and screaming," Julia said, her anger at her son finally coming to the surface.

Andy hesitated for a moment and started the engine. "I know this is hard for you. I've been there; you have to prepare yourself. He may not come. He may be too far gone. There's something more powerful than you, his family, or even his own welfare now. He's addicted. I hate to tell you this, but the drug probably means more to him than even you do."

Julia looked at Andy as if she was sorry that she had accepted his offer to help. How dare he make these assumptions? She then vocalized the first response that came to her mind, "I know my son. He will come with me."

"Okay, I'm sorry. I just want you to be prepared," Andy apologized.

"I know you do. I'm sorry. It's just…," Julia said, realizing Andy was just trying to be helpful.

"Don't apologize. I get it. This is all so overwhelming. I just want to help."

"I know you do."

"This place I'm thinking of is close by. My buddy I used to play ball with got hooked. He used to hang out there. He'd call me and ask me for a ride or cash every now and then. I would pick him up there."

"What happened to him?"

Andy looked toward Julia. "He didn't make it out. I'm really not sure where he is now."

Julia looked toward the dash as her world began to spin out of control. She pictured her son lying in an alley somewhere, possibly dead from an overdose. Feeling as if she might break down, Julia looked out the window.

She then felt a hand reach over and place itself over hers. She was so shocked by his touch that Julia jumped, and Andy clenched her hand as she looked over at him and gave him a reassuring smile.

They drove across town and pulled up to a street that Julia had never paid much attention to before, even though she had probably driven by this area a thousand times. She, like others, had never given much thought to the people she saw wandering the sidewalks of these lonely streets. It was a forgotten part of the town with empty buildings that displayed boarded-up windows. The exterior decorated with broken glass and trash. Graffiti speckled the exterior walls of several of the buildings.

They pulled into an abandoned hotel's parking lot and saw a group of young men turn their heads toward them in unison as if they were expecting someone else, disappointed by the two outsiders they saw intruding on their turf. Julia looked over at Andy and then back at the young men who were making their way to the back of the building.

"Well, shall we go in?" Andy asked. "Or would you like to wait here? I'm just not sure how safe it's going to be. There is a campsite just past those trees." Andy pointed to a park path leading into overgrown shrubs and trees. "I know the police are here a lot and patrol the area, but that doesn't mean that our safety won't be at risk."

Julia sat frozen in the front seat as the options just presented to her ricocheted through her mind. To see him or not, to do nothing, to let him die. *No*, she said to herself.

"I just don't know what he looks like. Do you have a picture of him?" Andy asked.

"I'm coming with you. He's my son. I need to be there if you find him," Julia replied.

"I just want to warn you that it will not be pretty. Don't bring a purse or anything that they would consider valuable," Andy advised while checking his pants pocket for his pocket knife.

"Okay," Julia tried to state bravely as she tucked her purse under the seat, still not sure how she would get through all of this.

They got out of the car and started to walk toward the dirt path. Julia and Andy were just about to enter the park when a patrol car pulled up to the curb beside them and sent its blue and red lights flashing across the bushes and trees. The police car let out a foghorn sound, which startled the two outsiders.

The officer driving the police vehicle rolled down his window and yelled out at them. "Can I help you?"

Andy looked over at Julia, and she turned toward the officers. "I'm looking for my son," she said.

The officers looked at each other and seemed to know exactly why she was there. They reacted as if she were the tenth parent that day that had been out looking for their child.

"We're patrolling the area. Would you like some help?" the officer said, sensing the fear and hesitation coming from the couple.

Andy whispered under his breath, "They'll need to know his name."

Just as Andy said that, Julia realized this would mean that they would run him through their systems. She turned and smiled at the officers.

"Thank you so much, officers, but we've been here before. I think I know where he is."

The officer—uncertain whether to believe them or not—got the sense that the couple did not want police involvement. "Okay, if you're sure," he said, throwing the vehicle into park. "We'll just be parked here if you need us," the officer added, and his partner, who was seated on the passenger side, leaned forward for extra reassurance. They both gave a sigh of relief as they waved to them, and Julia mouthed a thank you to the officer at the window.

The two then heard a rustling behind some bushes as the boys that they had seen earlier scattered, now aware that the police were parked just outside of the tree line.

The path curved under overhanging trees and was shadowed by several overgrown bushes and tree limbs. Bursts of sunlight hit the couple—shimmering onto their skin—where the trees opened and allowed the sunlight to peek through. Low tree branches and bushes fought back at them as they worked their way through the secluded area.

Originally meant for a jogger's path, the hidden area was now filled with an array of trash. Julia looked down at her feet as she viewed mangled tin cans scattered around the area. There were several empty ballpoint pens and cut-up straws in certain areas. Julia's eyes searched the ground as she moved forward. She saw something glimmering in the sunlight and discovered what appeared to be small square pieces of tin foil scattered about the ground. They both walked carefully, listening for any unwanted advances, as they made their way through the brush.

They entered a dense area of trees where they witnessed shadows bopping up and down through the brush in front of them. They stopped listening to the rambling of voices before them, trying to make out what was being said. The two then slowly crept forward, hearing the sound of laughter and cursing as the group spoke to one another like campfire buddies. The two intruders stopped kneeling just outside the campsite area, debating on their next move.

Julia's heart was beating so loud she could hear it above the campsite clatter. Andy squeezed Julia's hand and looked down at her for her confirmation to proceed. Andy—now leerier of moving forward—took out his pocket knife and held it in his hand. Andy started to clear a path when there was a sudden tug on Julia's jacket. Julia froze in place, afraid to look behind her. Andy immediately noticed her being pulled backward and slowly turned back around, wondering if she had somehow gotten caught on a nearby branch. A shadow then made its way over the couple, inching its way forward as they both held their breath in fear of what was coming toward them.

"What are you doing here? I told you to wait at your mother's," Scott scolded Julia.

The couple gave out a sigh of relief as Julia caught her breath, grabbing at her chest. "What are you doing? You scared me. We're here looking for Bobby," Julia whispered.

Scott then looked down at Julia's hand, which was resting in Andy's palm. "Who's this?" Scott asked as if he were still her husband.

Julia whispered, "He's a friend. We don't have time for this. Did you find Bobby?"

"I followed him here. I was just about to go in when I saw the two of you."

Andy, aware of what the group on the other side of the brush was capable of, spoke up, "Look, we don't have time for introductions. Do you want to find your son or not?" He whispered, glaring at both of them.

Silenced, Julia and Scott both nodded their heads yes, as Julia's hand dropped to her side. Andy put his finger up to his lips, signaling for them to be quiet. He opened a branch, and they found a group of people—consisting of various ages—sitting around a small fire. There was a large man in the center of the group who stood up immediately upon seeing the three intruders enter their campsite.

"What do you want?" the large man yelled in a voice that sent a chill down the intruders' spines.

The trio, not sure of what to say next, were overwhelmed by the smell of what appeared to be marijuana floating toward them. The fog slowly made its way into their system. Julia, already feeling woozy, felt a sudden high from the haze as the world started to blur.

A young man wearing a hooded jacket suddenly turned around to face them. It was Bobby.

Scott took a few steps forward as Andy grabbed ahold of Scott's arm holding him back. "Let go of me," Scott said as he shook his arm loose.

Julia watched in horror as Bobby quickly turned back around, sniffed something through a straw, and suddenly threw his head back. He stood for a minute and turned back around, staring at his parents as if he didn't recognize them in this new realm. As if they didn't fit into this world. Julia's heart dropped as she saw him dusting the white powder from his face.

Bobby then shouted at them, waving his arm in defiance, while stumbling forward, "Go away. I don't want you here!"

Julia moved toward her son as Bobby reactively backed up, moving away from them. "Bobby, it's me. You have to come with us. It's the only way. Please, son," she begged.

He dropped the straw he had been holding and began to sway as if he were losing his balance and cried out, "This is all your fault. I don't want to have anything to do with you. Do you understand me? Get away from me! I'm not your son anymore! I hate you. I hate all of you!" And then, without warning, he took off in a run, like a lineman trying to reach the quarterback, heading back toward the tree line that was hidden behind the large man who was blocking it.

Julia started to run after him, but Andy grabbed her from behind, circulating his large arms around her as Scott looked on.

Scott then moved forward, ready to follow Bobby, when the large brown man with tattoos under his eyes pulled out a knife and started to approach Scott yelling out. "Hey man, are you here to party? I have a present for you, Daddy! Come and get it!"

Andy dragged Julia from the rear back toward the trees. "No!" Julia pleaded, trying to get away. "Bobby!" she shouted. "I'm sorry!" And she burst into tears, clawing at Andy as he attempted to keep a hold of her.

The large man signaled for the other men standing around him to circle back around the three outsiders. "Hey, pretty lady. I would like to party with you. Come on over, I got something for you," the large man smirked and started to walk toward Julia. He suddenly stopped when he saw the tree line open up behind the intruders, and the two officers from earlier stepped into the campsite.

"Anything wrong here, Harry?" Officer Wilson, the officer who was driving the police car, asked.

"No, man, these crazy people just walked into our place. I have no idea what they're doing here. We ain't doing nothin' to nobody," the large man said, already stepping back to where he was earlier. He then sat back down, discreetly placing the knife into his pants pocket.

"Are you all right?" Officer Wilson asked Julia as Andy released her.

"Yes, I'm fine," Julia whimpered, straightening her blouse that had lifted in the struggle.

"Can we help you find someone?" the other officer, whose badge read Officer Garcia, said. "Is your son still in the area?"

Julia thought for a moment. "No, he's not here. We thought he was, but it wasn't him."

The officers swung around, hearing the other young men behind them, making their way through the brush, now headed in the opposite direction.

"Harry, you all need to get out of here. You know you are not supposed to be here. I do not want to get a call about this area again. Understand me? And put out that fire," Officer Wilson ordered them.

The men nodded and began to pick up their belongings that lay on the ground as they threw dirt on the fire, staring at the intruders with rage, knowing that they had caused the disruption. The campers then moved into the tree line in the same direction that Bobby had traveled.

Julia dropped to her knees, sobbing as the officers looked over at her.

"Ma'am, we can't help you if you don't help us," Officer Garcia said.

Julia nodded her head, unable to respond, staring at the clearing that the men had just disappeared into. "I know. I'm sorry."

"We'll walk you all out of here. You shouldn't be here alone," Officer Garcia advised.

"Thank you so much, officers. We'll leave now," Andy said, and the officers turned to lead the way out.

Andy dropped down beside Julia as Scott looked on, sad that he had not thought to help her up himself. Scott's head was now going back and forth, seemingly still debating on whether or not he should follow Bobby or leave with the officers.

"Sir," Officer Wilson stated, looking at Scott as if he were reading Scott's mind. Scott turned back around and looked at Officer Wilson. "It's time to go, sir."

Scott turned with tears in his eyes. "My son…" he said.

"We know, sir. But there's nothing you can do. He's gone," Officer Wilson stated.

"We have to leave, Julia," Andy whispered to her.

Julia took one more look at the hole that the men had disappeared into, considering the same thing that Scott was…if she should follow them. Wondering if she should take off in a strong stride and disappear through the brush.

"You won't find him today," Andy said. "We can come back."

He slowly lifted her and helped her back through the tree line. Scott followed reluctantly, turning every now and then to see if he spotted anyone. When they reached the parking lot, the three of them stood silent, exhausted from their altercation.

"These people do not play," Officer Garcia said. "They take an intrusion very seriously. I don't recommend you all come back."

The three nodded in confirmation.

"Thank you, officers," Andy said.

"I'm sorry, but we need you all to leave at this time. We don't trust this group. They'll be back," Officer Wilson ordered.

"We understand officers. We're leaving," Andy confirmed.

The officers then walked back to their vehicle, discussing something by the curb, looking back at the three, who were making their way toward Andy's vehicle.

Once they reached the vehicle, Scott turned toward Andy and asked him, "Who are you, and why did you bring her here?"

"I wanted to come, Scott," Julia said in Andy's defense.

Scott looked over at her. "I'm sorry. It's just I almost had him. I was going to go in. I had spotted him entering the campsite. Now, I don't know where he's gone," Scott said as he turned toward Andy, and Andy met his gaze.

"He's my friend," Julia said to Scott. "Andy, this is my ex-husband, Scott."

Andy glanced over at him with this new realization. "I'm sorry, but we were just trying to do the same thing you were. I just wanted to help."

"Well, you didn't," Scott fumed.

"Scott, that's not fair," Julia objected.

"Oh, I don't know what's fair anymore. I just know we just lost him again. I'm going back to my vehicle. I'll call you if I find out anything. I just can't stand the thought…," Scott said, and he took a few steps forward and turned back around, directing his comments toward Andy. "I'm sorry. Thank you for being with her."

Andy bowed his head in response as he and Julia watched Scott move toward the street where his vehicle was parked.

"We should go," Andy said.

Julia looked back toward the path, toward the brush, as Andy took her hand, gently pulling her toward his vehicle.

"We'll keep looking," Andy said, "but he's lost for now."

Julia responded, looking back toward the path, "I know."

CHAPTER SIXTEEN

The house seemed exceptionally quiet as Julia placed her key in the front door of her home. Exhausted, Julia dropped her purse and keys on the table that lined the entryway, turning back to make sure that Andy was still behind her. She found it hard to concentrate. Her mind wandered to the events of the day. Nothing made sense. It hurt to think. It hurt to relive the past and what could have been done differently. She debated if she had made a mistake by not having Bobby remain in jail. He would probably still be there had she listened to Scott. Another mistake. Another bad decision that may cost her her son.

Andy walked in behind Julia and sat with her on the sofa. They both sighed at the same time, exhausted from recent events. Andy was not sure whether to take her hand or not. He wanted to put his arm around her and comfort her but was not sure if she would allow him to.

"Would you like me to go? Do you need to be alone?" Andy asked.

"No. I'm sorry. I'm just trying to stop my world from spinning. Not sure if there's any way I can do that." Julia grinned.

"Would you like me to get you something to drink? Possibly water or maybe something stronger?" Andy grinned.

Julia sat and stared off into space as if the words floating toward her didn't exist. She thought about her mother and how Bobby's actions seemed to have affected her. She now understood how numb her mother felt. How rejected. Because she now felt all these things and more.

"Water would be great," she finally said, squeezing his hand. "Thank you so much for all that you've done. I'm so sorry about Scott. He's just worried about Bobby."

"Hey, I understand, and you're most welcome. I've been there." Andy hesitated for a moment as if wondering in which direction he should go to get a glass of water. "The kitchen is in the back, right?"

"Yeah," Julia said absentmindedly, "I'm sorry, it's to the right and down the hall."

She watched as Andy turned the corner. Once he was out of sight, Julia placed her head in her hands, rubbing the sides of her temples, trying to stop the throbbing migraine she felt coming on. She listened to Andy's steady resounding footsteps make their way down the hallway, maneuvering his way to the kitchen. At that moment, she wondered what made him stay and why he cared so much.

Suddenly she heard his footsteps come to an abrupt stop. She listened as she thought she heard Andy scream her name. And then she heard it again, but in a louder, more desperate tone, "Julia!"

His voice was so jarring Julia snapped her head toward the doorway like a Beagle who had spotted its prey. She felt her heart leap from her chest as she yelled back, "What happened?"

"Julia, come here now!" she heard his panicked voice scream out once more.

She dragged herself off the couch and made her way down the hallway, bouncing between both walls, terrified of what awaited her at the end of her destination. She turned the corner and was witness to her mother's still body lying on the linoleum floor, her cup broken, the pieces scattered around her mother's head. The mocha-colored coffee flowed in a river across the linoleum.

"Oh, God, no!" Julia shouted out, collapsing at her mother's side.

"Julia, I'm calling 911," she heard Andy murmur as he disappeared behind her.

Julia picked up her mother's arm and leaned in toward her open mouth. "She's still breathing," she said to herself.

Andy returned with his phone in his hand. "They're on their way."

"Mom…Mom! Can you hear me?" Julia said over and over again. The seconds flew by as if time stopped in this single moment. She wanted to scream but couldn't find the strength. She listened for a pulse, a heartbeat, and somewhere in the midst of all that was happening around her, she heard the deafening sirens approaching.

Julia didn't remember Andy leaving to open the front door or the sound of equipment being rattled down the long hallway. But when she looked up, the EMTs were surrounding her. They gently moved Julia out of their way so they could reach Carmen.

Julia stood up and felt two hands on either side of her shoulders, and then a voice quietly whispered behind her, "I'll drive you to the hospital."

Julia didn't answer as Andy guided her back outside to his waiting vehicle.

After helping her into his car, he walked around and got into the driver's seat. Julia watched as the EMTs loaded her mother into the back of the ambulance.

It was as if everything were happening at a distance, as if she were in a movie, not real life, seeing the story unfold right before her eyes.

The neighbor's homes were lit up with the red and yellow lights of the ambulance. The lights flashed in every direction. The sirens brought the occupants of the neighboring homes out to their front porches as they whispered about the woman on the corner who lived with her middle-aged daughter.

Andy started the engine as the road before them became a blurred vision of lights and distorted images flashing across the window's gleam.

When they arrived at the hospital, the smell of antiseptic surrounded them, hitting them like a cold winter breeze. Julia felt as if she were floating from one area to the next. From the waiting room to the sterile hallway, past the many nurses and doctors, all huddled over computers, and finally to a small room with a sliding glass door. As everything came to a halt, they became witnesses to various colors of beeping lights from a machine that was now attached to her mother's arm and chest. All of this set over a laminate tiled grey floor made to resemble some type of white marble.

Once the world settled on its axis, Julia was able to concentrate on the reality before her. Her mother, lying in a bed of snowy white linens, looked as if she were in a deep sleep. Julia looked toward the man she barely knew who was sitting beside her and realized that he was the only thing keeping her from falling off the edge. How grateful her heart felt toward Andy at this moment.

With everything appearing to be crashing down around her, Julia—in an effort to retain her sanity—reverted back to what was familiar. She turned to the one thing that had stayed constant in her life as she drifted off to her favorite television show, her favorite character, and how exactly Michelle from *One Moment in Time* would be handling all of this. Julia knew exactly how Michelle would be handling this chaos. She would be falling into her hero's arms. She would be telling the doctors exactly what she needed them to do, and Michelle would go out and single-handedly drag her son off of the streets and toss him into treatment, and she would do it all with no regrets.

Regret was Julia's middle name. So, unfortunately, Julia sitting there beside this stranger, looking at her mother's still body, felt she just didn't have the strength. Once again, she fell short of what she felt life expected of her and what she expected of herself.

"Thank you," she said, turning toward Andy.

"It's nothing. You've got a lot going on right now. I'm just glad I could be here," Andy said sincerely.

"I don't know how I would have done any of this without you… so thank you," she said again, feeling a sense of guilt for keeping him there with her, as Andy smiled at her, gripping her hand tightly in his.

Julia had texted Lauren about what had happened when they arrived at the hospital. She hoped that Lauren's arrival would give Andy a break from all the craziness surrounding her. She thought he was probably ready to run out the door as fast as he could and escape this looney bin she called life at any minute. He just needed an excuse.

Once all the tests were run, it was a waiting game. Her mother's vitals had leveled off, but she still lay there, unconscious. Andy sat holding Julia's hand. Julia felt that same sense of peace she always had come rushing in from his touch.

Suddenly, without warning, the sliding glass door opened. Andy and Julia's heads lifted toward the opening, wondering if it could be the doctor with news of Carmen's condition.

Julia's face lit up as she saw Lauren's face peek around the corner. Julia jumped up, rushing over to give her daughter a hug as she felt suppressed tears come flooding down her cheeks. Lauren grabbed onto her mother as they both fell into each other's arms, wrapping each other in a blanket of uncertainty.

Andy rose, unsure of what to do next, when a shadow came creeping in behind Lauren through the sliding glass door. Julia didn't see the image until she heard a voice speak out into the aseptic air.

"Hello, Julia," the voice said. "I'm so sorry."

Julia looked behind her daughter at the stranger who seemed to recognize her. Julia's eyes widened as the voice suddenly clicked, and a familiar face walked into the light.

"Brad?" Julia questioned.

"Yes, it's Brad, Mom," Lauren answered for him. "So sorry, but I wasn't sure if I could drive myself, and Brad was there, and well…."

Julia, now mute, waited as the words floating toward her got lost in translation. *Brad was there*—slowly registered as his image came into view. "No, it's fine," Julia said, still unsure of what to say next. "Hi, Brad, come in…. I was just surprised, that's all."

Julia looked back at Andy, who stood shrugging his shoulders as he lowered his eyebrows. Andy stepped forward and shot his hand out toward Brad's.

"Good to see you again, Brad."

Brad, with his usual innate good manners, looked at Andy, "Good to see you again, Andy."

"Well, aren't we one big happy family," Lauren said, turning toward her mother. "How's Grandma?"

"She's hanging in there. She hasn't woken up, but her vitals are good right now. We're just waiting to hear from the doctor."

"What happened with Bobby?" Lauren asked as Julia noticed Brad standing awkwardly behind Lauren.

"I'll tell you about it later. Brad, please come in and sit down," Julia said as she tried to make room for everyone in this small area.

"Thank you, but I can stand, Julia. You all take the chairs."

"Don't be silly; there are enough chairs. Everyone, sit down…please," Julia said, trying to make everyone feel as comfortable as possible in this unusually strange situation where Julia's former boyfriend was obviously now dating her daughter. And her current love interest, Andy, was now wondering why the young man he had seen with Julia just a couple of weeks ago was apparently now with Julia's daughter. And Julia's world just kept spinning, a balancing game, tilting every now and then, continually asking her if she would like to…get off.

Just as the group took a seat around Carmen's hospital bed, the emergency room doctor caring for Julia's mother entered the small room through the sliding glass doors. "Well, we have quite a group here," the doctor said, with an Indian accent, as he greeted who he presumed was Carmen's family. "I'm Dr. Patney. I have been in charge of your mother's care since she arrived. We have the results back, and I'm sorry to say that she has suffered what we believe to be a stroke on the right side."

Julia heard the word "stroke" pulsate through the room like a bouncy ball, slamming against each of the adjacent walls as her mind went blank. The word seemed to hang in the air as all other communication was lost, and Julia wondered what exactly this meant for her mother's future. Lauren, sensing her mother's confusion, grabbed Julia's hand. Julia, still in disbelief, looked back at her daughter and saw Brad start to rub Lauren's arm to comfort her.

Julia, forcing herself to concentrate, listened to the doctor's prognosis.

"We won't know the extent of the stroke until your mother wakes up. We are admitting her now and will be moving her shortly. We are probably looking at rehabilitation somewhere down the road," Dr. Patney communicated. "At this point, we may expect to see a lack of use of the right side, and she may be non-verbal at first, but this is nothing certain; I just want to prepare you."

After digesting the grim prognosis, the group was then shuffled up to the fifth floor of the hospital, where Carmen still lay in a comatose state. The doctor's words continued to float through Julia's mind. Stroke…anxiety…lack of use of the right side…she may be non-verbal as she questioned if this was all really happening and if she would be able to get her mother through it all.

Julia finally convinced Andy that he should go home. She explained to him that she would be staying the night so she could be there should her mother awaken. Andy offered to remain with her, feeling that she should have someone there, but Julia knew that he probably had to work the next day and believed that he was only trying to be nice. Besides, she didn't know how her mother would react to her prognosis, and Julia knew in her heart that it would probably not be pretty. She told Andy that she would contact him later when she knew more about her mother's condition. Andy reluctantly left, stating that if he didn't hear from Julia, he would call her.

Julia was not used to a man being so honest. Andy, at least from what she had seen, always held to his word. But even with all of Andy's good intentions, part of her was still somewhat reluctant to trust him.

Lauren and Brad waited around with her at the hospital for a couple of hours. Brad finally excused himself from the hospital room to get them all something to eat. This allowed Julia time to find out what exactly was going on between the two of them. Could it be that Julia was right about them? Could it be that Brad was truly falling for her Lauren? Julia had to find out.

"How long do you think she will sleep?" Lauren asked in a whisper.

"I'm not sure. The doctor didn't know, but I would like to be here when she wakes up. I'm sure she will not take all of this well. I know I wouldn't."

"So, were you shocked?" Lauren grinned, nudging her mother.

"Yeah, lucky we were already in the hospital because I thought I was going to pass out." Julia smiled at her daughter, taking her hand. "But really, I'm so very happy for you both. He's so great. At least what I know of him."

"No, I have to give you credit on this one, Mom. You were right. I mean, at least he has good taste in mothers and daughters, right?" Lauren teased, speaking as quietly as she could.

"Oh, you. I don't know how we're going to explain this to people. But whatever. Ahhh...so, how did it happen?" Julia whispered, nudging Lauren's shoulder back.

"Well, I was at work when, who do you think walks in? My mother's ex-boyfriend, Brad."

"Oh...you. He was not my boyfriend by any means."

"I know, Mom. I'm just teasing you. Well, anyway, he's enrolling in some classes to finish up his criminal justice degree and was having trouble getting into a couple of classes, and well, long story short, I helped him out," Lauren said.

"And..."

"Well, he asked if I could show him where the bookstore was, and it happened to be time for my break, and the next thing I knew, I was agreeing to have dinner with him."

"That's wonderful, honey," Julia said, now glancing over at her mother.

"It'll be okay, Mom. You know Grams. She's a fighter. She will be up and bossing us around in no time."

"I hope so, sweetie. I really do."

"Sooo…speaking of mysterious men, who's the guy?"

"Oh, Andy?"

"Yes…."

"He's a friend. I mean, I knew him when I was younger. I don't know. He just sort of fell back into my life."

"Wow, so how did you know each other?"

"It was a long time ago. Honestly, I didn't remember him. But I guess he remembered me."

"And?"

"And he's sweet. He's good-looking. Seems financially stable, I don't know; there's just something."

"What? What's the something? He sounds fabulous. Why can't you let yourself be happy?"

"I can't talk about this right now."

And there was a silence between them as the beeping of the machines filled the air. "Well, I'm almost afraid to ask, but did you find Bobby?"

Julia continued to look toward her mother.

"Mom?" Lauren said again as if her mother hadn't heard her the first time.

"Yes, we did, sweetie."

"And?"

"He didn't come back with us."

"Is Dad still looking for him?"

"Yeah, he is. I'm afraid we may have lost him," Julia said, tears welling up in her eyes. "Did you know he took Grandad's wedding ring?"

"He what?"

"When he left last night, apparently, it was among the things that he took. Mom just couldn't understand. She didn't understand that he was doing it for the drugs. They've taken him over."

"That's his choice, Mom. It has nothing to do with us. You have to stop making excuses for him. He's a man. He's not your little boy anymore."

"I know. My head tells me that. My heart's another story."

"Oh, if I get my hands on him."

"You need to settle down. You don't need to be getting upset in your condition. And by the way, did you tell Brad?"

"Yes, he knows about the baby. We've agreed to see how things work out. We are taking it slow. So, don't be getting any ideas about us just yet, but he is wonderful."

"Yeah, he is."

"Mom, what do you think he will do?"

"Who, Brad?"

"Yeah."

"I think only you can answer that one, sweetie. But I'm hoping that you will find someone that will love you and the baby as if the baby was his own. It's what I'm praying for anyway."

"I'm kind of scared to hope for that. It just seems so…impossible."

"I know," Julia said, trying to concentrate on the conversation before her. "And well…," And at that moment, the two women heard groaning coming from the bed in front of them as Carmen began to move around, straining to open her eyes.

"Mom?" Julia called out.

And they saw Carmen's eyes open wide as fear flashed across her face, and she immediately tried to speak, her vocal cords failing her. Carmen squirmed frantically, grabbing at her throat, commanding the sounds to be released as they refused her. She gurgled and hissed at them, not understanding why there was silence. At that moment, Julia and Lauren rushed to either side of the bed, trying to comfort her.

Julia grabbed her left hand as Carmen shook her hand free, flailing her good arm and pointing toward her throat while trying to lift her right arm that lay dead beside her.

She started trying to twist from the left to the right and raised her left arm but couldn't lift her right arm. Carmen's eyes widened as she grabbed onto Julia's blouse with her left hand, her eyes demanding Julia to explain what was happening.

Julia could see the terror in her mother's eyes and tried to comfort her by holding onto her mother's left hand and stroking Carmen's hair back out of her eyes.

"Mom…Mom, look at me. You're in the hospital. You're okay. Can you talk?"

Carmen began to point at her mouth with her left hand.

Julia turned toward Lauren, "Lauren, get the nurse."

Lauren left the room, frantically trying to locate someone.

"Mom, you're in the hospital."

Carmen looked at her, shaking her head rapidly back and forth, stopping only to point at her mouth. Julia, at a loss of what to do, tried to remain calm while explaining to her mother what had happened. "Mom, you're going to be okay. Listen to me. You've had a stroke, but it's going to be okay. The doctors are going to work with you so you can regain the use of your right side and your speech."

Carmen continued to frantically flail around, her eyes wide open as if she had seen a ghost.

"Mom, Mom, did you hear me? You're going to be okay."

At that moment, the nurse rushed in, heading straight toward Carmen's right side. "Carmen…," the nurse said as Carmen still fought to get up. "Carmen, I need you to listen to me, sweetie. Your daughter and granddaughter are here. We can't understand you, hon, so you will need to try and help us figure out what you need. You've had a stroke on your right side, and it may affect your speech for a while. Can you point to what you want?"

Carmen then stopped struggling as she looked around the room, and on the bed tray, there was a cup. Carmen quickly pointed at the cup.

"I'm so sorry, hon, but the doctor has taken you off of solids and liquids. I can get you some ice chips to suck on. Would you like that?"

Carmen, frustrated with the response, closed her eyes tight, rapidly shaking her head no. The nurse rubbed Carmen's hair and spoke very softly to her, "Carmen, sweetie, you need to calm down."

And Carmen shook her head, no, as tears were released, streaming down her cheeks.

The nurse then asked her, "Does it hurt somewhere?"

And Carmen shook her head, yes.

The nurse continued, "Where does it hurt?"

The nurse looked up at Julia and Lauren as Carmen pointed at her heart.

Julia pulled Carmen's hand up to her face and looked directly at her mother, "I'm here, Mom. I'm here. We're going to take care of you," she said, fighting back tears.

And Carmen closed her eyes tight and shook her head no, grunting and squirming as if she never wanted to open her eyes again.

CHAPTER SEVENTEEN

Julia sat on the vinyl recliner in her mother's hospital room, staring out into space as images of the last few hours revolved around her like ghosts on a merry-go-round. The unknown that she faced with each new tilt of the universe left her asking, *why?* She wanted to pray but couldn't seem to find the words or the strength. Her first impulse was to scream at the top of her lungs, but in her current surroundings, that just wasn't an option.

She jumped as the phone in her hand started to vibrate. Juggling her phone in her hands, she quickly answered it.

"How's your mother?" Scott's exasperated voice asked through the cell phone, presumably exhausted from the ongoing search for his son.

"She's not doing well," Julia grumbled, speaking softly into her phone. "The doctor said it's all to be expected, though. She seems to have dropped into some type of depression, but who wouldn't? You wake up, and your whole world is turned upside down. I mean, she can't speak, she can't eat…"

"I'm so sorry, Julia. Let me know if I can help in any way."

Julia got up and walked out into the hallway so as not to wake her mother. "Do you have any leads on where he might be?"

"There's a house near the park where we found him the first time. For lack of better words, new users hang out there. I've been showing his picture around, and one guy said he saw him there."

"What makes you think he will come with you this time?" Julia said, discouraged by her current world.

"I don't know if he will come with me. I'm just, you know, hopeful…"

"Yeah. I get it. Sorry, but my hopefulness is a little weary right now. God, what happened to him, to us, all of us? I don't even know what to expect next. In fact, the thought of what could happen frightens me to death."

"I'm sorry you have to do this on your own. Is Lauren there?"

"No…sorry, she will be here later. I'm just having a little pity party right now. Just find him, Scott. Can you do that? Can you please find him?"

"I'm looking, hon."

And he said that word that always sent a chill down her spine. It would slip out every now and then, and Julia would pretend the word was never spoken. Scott acted as if it were something natural, something that he said habitually. When they first divorced, Julia would correct him, stating that he had others to whisper endearments to, and she was not one of them anymore. It would infuriate her that he had the nerve to try and keep his foot in the door at her home while he was off with whatever girl would have him at the moment. Right now, that day, she didn't have the strength to correct him. Today she would let it go stating, "Just please find our son."

"I'm not giving up. I won't let them take him. I promise you that."

Julia thought back to the past and the years and years of promises Scott declared as the truth. She felt she wasn't any closer to believing him now than she did back then. But she had no choice. She couldn't leave the hospital and would have to depend on him, at least for now. Her mother needed her. And truth be told, Julia didn't think she could add one more thing to her plate without crumbling and climbing into bed right next to her mother.

Julia was able to get a couple of hours of sleep after they finally sedated Carmen.

She watched as the woman, who was stronger than anyone she had ever known, became this person she didn't recognize anymore. She had stopped acknowledging any of them. She seemed angry. Her mother seemed to have decided that she didn't want to live anymore. No matter how much Julia and Lauren tried to convince her that she was still needed. Their efforts went in vain. She had made up her mind to stop living, and it was going to take a true miracle to convince her that her current life was one worth saving.

The doctors were concerned as Carmen, time and time again, refused to acknowledge them or work with the nurses to communicate using the laminated pictures she had been given. The pictures displayed parts of the body that she could use to communicate with the medical staff and with her family to show them if something was hurting or if she was uncomfortable. Carmen was also given pictures of everyday objects, like a hairbrush and a toothbrush, so she could let them know what she wanted. Carmen would violently shove the sheets on the floor with her left hand and would stare off into space as if she had checked out of this world. Her hollow stare told the world that she had had enough and was choosing to depart with no intentions of returning.

Julia's mother didn't respond to anyone, not even Lauren. She stared out the window as if she were searching for something she had lost. Something she felt she couldn't get back. Not being able to swallow, Carmen continued to be unable to have solid foods and liquids, and the strange thing was she didn't show any interest in wanting to eat or drink on her own anyway. She was being fed intravenously. Her lack of interest in wanting to regain her ability to eat on her own concerned the hospital staff. Carmen was able to use her left arm and leg but rarely did so. They had even noticed some movement in her right arm and leg, but she didn't encourage her body to move the limbs that had abandoned her.

The first couple of days came and went in the blink of an eye with no improvement. Julia stayed in constant contact with Scott, hoping for some good news regarding Bobby, but every lead seemed to turn up empty, and without police support, there were areas that Scott just couldn't get into, although he said he had tried.

Julia's mother showed no signs of improvement. She had stopped acknowledging that Julia and Lauren were even in the room. Julia figured her mother saw no use in half a body. She saw no use in half a life.

Looking at the dawn of a new day through the large window in her mother's hospital room, Julia felt the weight of the world overtaking her. She had sent Lauren home to rest, worried that the recent events—in her ever-changing world—would cause irreversible damage to her unborn grandchild's tiny growing body. And again, Julia turned toward the road in front of her and succumbed to her inability to freely choose what road she should travel. The road—regardless of her efforts—was forever being placed before her without any regard for what road Julia desired to take. She found herself with her head in her hands, sobbing silently, her unresponsive mother in a deep sleep after taking her antidepressant medication.

Julia cried out to the heavens, who looked down on her, asking the question, *why?* Why was this all happening? Julia felt she was a good person. Her children were good people. Her mother certainly was, so why? The question of why rang out over and over again in her head as she looked outward to that sun of yesterday, the same sun that had pushed her to the edge of sanity over and over again. She thought about her son throwing his life away in a world of drugs and about her mother, who had given up her will to live, both so consumed with what they had lost, they couldn't see Julia there, fighting, struggling to save them.

Frustrated, Julia picked up the box of tissues and threw it against the wall. Standing there with her fists clenched, she heard a knock at the door.

"Can I come in?" she heard a gentle voice make its way into the room.

Julia turned to see Andy juggling two bouquets of flowers in one hand and a small brown paper bag in the other hand.

Julia quickly wiped her eyes, irritated that Andy had found her in her current condition.

"Andy?" she said, and she quickly took one of the vases from him, wondering if he had been a witness to her outburst.

"Ahhh…these are for you. I was never able to bring you any since our second date was more of a rescue mission," he said jokingly, waiting for her reaction as Julia grinned while adjusting some of the flowers. "No, but seriously, I wasn't sure what you needed, so…"

"This…this is perfect," Julia struggled to say, holding back the tears as she grabbed a Kleenex to wipe her eyes.

"Ohhh…but I have more. Coffee and an egg and cheese biscuit sandwich. I wasn't sure what to get because I didn't know what you liked to eat for breakfast. Do you drink coffee?"

"On occasion…and yes, this is an occasion," Julia said, trying to pull herself together. "Thank you so much. You have been exceptionally kind to me and to my family."

"Well, you know a guy will go through a lot to get that first dance."

Julia looked up at him remembering their conversation the other night. "Yes…the first dance. I remember now. You were there at the club. When Ritchie and I were there."

"I'm sorry. I was just joking. I didn't want you to worry about that right now. How's she doing?"

"Not so good. She seems to have, well…given up."

"I'm sorry. I wish there was more I could do. And you? How are you doing?"

"I'm…I'm not sure. I just can't seem to think straight right now. You know, it's strange, but I can't seem to dig myself out of this one."

"Anyone would feel the same, Julia. Can I help in any way?"

"You already have. I really don't deserve…"

And Andy reached over, placing his fingers on her lips. "No, you do."

Julia, growing more irritated by the minute, reactively swiped Andy's hand from the front of her face. "No, I don't, and if you knew what was good for you, you would start running in the other direction. I'm quicksand, and I take anyone and everyone around me down with me. You don't know. You don't know what being with me is like. Look around. Everyone that I love is slowly dying. And it's all—"

Andy then interrupted Julia, "It's not your fault."

"You don't know what you're talking about. You don't know me. The real me."

"Julia, I'm a big boy. If you haven't noticed, I want to be here for you."

"Yes, like Zoey."

"What does she have to do with this?"

"Nothing. It's just. I'm not young like that. I don't giggle at movies. I'm a mother and soon to be a grandmother."

"What?"

"Yes, a grandmother. I'm going to be a grandmother," Julia said, heading over to the large picture window that looked out over the city. "So, what do you think of that? Your disco queen is going to be a grandmother."

"A grandmother, huh," Andy said, not realizing how angry Julia was. "Well, you will make a beautiful one. Julia, I want to be with you. Whatever that looks like."

"No, you don't get it. I just can't do this. You…you deserve better. You deserve a Zoey. That's what you want. What you are looking for. What happens when I'm not good enough for you? When I'm not what you want anymore?"

"What do you mean?"

"I mean. I don't know what I mean. I don't have it in me to do us right now. Can you understand? I just don't want you dragged into all of this."

"Julia, I know what I'm doing. I know what I want, and I would like to see this through."

"I'm so sorry, Andy, but you should leave."

Andy stood for a moment and tried to walk toward Julia, grabbing the ends of her fingers. "Julia?"

Julia shook off his hand, turning toward him, now angry. "No, please, Andy. This is the right thing for all of us. I have to take care of my mother, my son, my family. I don't have the strength to do this right now. I'm so sorry, but I just can't."

"Julia, don't do this."

"Ahhh…do what? There's nothing here. There can't be. I won't allow it. I'm not this fantasy girl you have in your head. I'm not the twenty-something disco queen anymore that you saw at the dance club. I'm sorry to destroy this fantasy you have about me, but that's just not who I am anymore."

"I think that you're wrong about that. I think that…that maybe life has thrown you some curveballs, excuse the pun, but it has thrown us all some. You don't see yourself as others do, and I don't get that. You see, you are that girl that I saw at the club. You have all the fire and passion that I remember, and it's not just me. I see you with your mother, with your kids, and even with your ex-husband, and…well, you're a good person. You're a strong woman. I don't know how you don't see that."

"Because it's not there anymore. You're seeing what you want to see. That girl you fell in love with twenty-five years ago died a long time ago."

"I don't think it's me that has it wrong, Julia. I think it's maybe you. And I'm not sure why you can't see yourself the way that I do. Anyway, you deserve to be happy, Julia. That's all I ever wanted for you."

"It's not in the cards. Can't you see that? Not with me."

"No, I don't see that, and I'm sorry that apparently, you do. I'll go," he said, and took a few steps forward and leaned over and kissed Julia on the top of her head. "Goodbye, Julia." And Andy walked slowly toward the door looking back once before he exited the hospital room.

"Goodbye," Julia whispered as she looked out the large picture window, watching that old friend of hers bring in another day, another morning, and Julia felt her heartbreaking all over again, and Ritchie had died all over again, and there was no future to look forward to, and Julia closed her eyes trying to drown out the rays that were making their way into the room.

CHAPTER EIGHTEEN

Julia and Lauren spent hours staring at one another as Carmen refused to acknowledge either of them. The doctors visited frequently, attempting to communicate with Carmen, trying to get her to react to their various forms of stimuli. Julia would converse with her but found herself being passively blocked out. Lauren would read to her and brush her hair, and still, there was nothing. Yet, her body was doing remarkably well considering the lack of enthusiasm of its host. Carmen's body would naturally respond to certain stimuli. However, she made it clear that she was an involuntary participant in her body's obvious will to live.

The doctor would tickle her left foot, which would automatically react to the touch. The right foot even reacted slightly to the stimuli by the nurses and doctors. It was small, but there was some feeling on the right side. Yet, Carmen still refused to acknowledge that her body wanted to live.

Carmen sat there—amongst the white sheets—with a blank stare, angry at the constant care and fuss over the body she felt had abandoned her. At one point, Carmen tried to pull out all the tubes and needles that were helping to keep her alive. Her depression concerned the doctors. With therapy, they felt Carmen could start to eat on her own, but would she allow her body to take in the nourishment? Would she feed this body that she had disowned?

Her silence was a painful rebellion to those who loved her. It was as if she were saying she no longer wanted to be a part of their lives.

The doctors and nurses looked on gravely as the woman who had so much promise of recovery withered ever so slowly away. Julia—who was alone with her mother that day—sat near Carmen, rubbing her hands, her feet, her legs, and still received the same blank stare. Her mother's eyes would barely open anymore as she tried to drown out all the noise and the life around her.

In the silence, something snapped inside Julia as if she had finally had enough. Overwhelmed with the world around her, she decided to take a stand while she still could. "Mom," Julia blurted out. "Mom. It's me, Julia. Remember me, your daughter?"

And her mother didn't even flinch.

"Mom! I know you can hear me!" Julia raised her voice. "How can you give up like this? Is that what you taught me? I know that's what I've been doing. I'm sorry. But you're the strong one. Not me. You have to fight, Mom. You have to fight for me. Did you hear me?"

Carmen glanced over but didn't move. She didn't try to speak.

"Mom, I can't do this without you. I need you. Please don't do this!"

Carmen blinked and buried her head deeper into her pillow, unable, unwilling to respond. A tear made its way down her cheek. At that moment, amongst the beating of her mother's machines, Julia felt the need to escape. She had to get away. She couldn't breathe; it was as if she were drowning, and the only lifeline was a trillion-pound anchor.

And the situation with Bobby was no better. She would talk with Scott frequently but didn't look forward to his calls because they always brought such bad news. He's not there. He just left. He ran out of the room when he saw me.

What did this life expect of her? She felt the walls closing in as she rushed frantically out of her mother's room and out of the hospital into a courtyard where she thought there was no one around, and in the silence of that moment, she grabbed the opportunity to let out a fierce scream at the top of her voice that echoed up and over the building, reaching up high, as a head turned back toward her in the shadows.

"Why? What did I ever do to deserve this?" she shouted as she fell to her knees and sobbed over and over again, hugging her body with her arms, rocking herself ever so gently, as the breeze rushed around her, surrounding her in its arms, trying to dry her tears.

An elderly man, who sat in the shadow of a large tree a few feet away from her, lifted his head after hearing her cry out. The man, moved by this woman's great sadness, came over to her and knelt down beside her. "Miss, can I help you in any way?"

Julia, startled by the presence beside her, looked up at the stranger who had a book in his hand. "No. You can't help me," Julia fumed, sounding ruder than she ever allowed herself normally to be.

"I'm a good listener, I'm told," the white-haired man promised.

"Thank you, but I don't want to talk about it," Julia scoffed, falling over onto her rear end, trying to dry her tears.

"Okay…I don't want to push you, but I'll be right over here if you change your mind," the man with the kind smile said as he began to move back toward a bench.

"Why? Why is all of this happening to me? I'm not a bad person," Julia muttered.

The man turned around as if a window had been opened. "I wish I could answer that for you. I don't know you well, but no one takes so much upon themselves that doesn't care. No one knows why things happen. We sometimes never find out the reason."

"Why not? Is this some evil plan God has to destroy me? Why, why would He do this to me? To my family?" Julia demanded.

The man hesitated for a moment, feeling the despair resonating from Julia, studying the moment and considering the words he would send forward. "I don't know. I wish I could answer that question, and I know it doesn't seem like it now, but there's always a plan. I say that from experience. Something I personally had to learn the hard way."

Julia looked at him with disgust. Almost as if he were the cause of her pain. "Yeah, well, I thought you'd say that. Let me guess. You're the chaplain here?"

"Yeah, afraid so. Guilty as charged," the chaplain in the plaid shirt admitted.

"Well, you have been absolutely no help. You can't even tell me why, huh," Julia said, putting her hands on her forehead and bringing her legs before her, searching for an answer in this small courtyard below the waving palm trees.

"I'm afraid not. I know you don't want to hear this, but He hasn't left you."

"Oh, no. Are you a parent, preacher?" Julia chastised.

The preacher bringing his compassionate eyes up to hers, answered, "Yes, I am."

"Then you know. You know what you would do for your child. Can't He take me instead?"

"No, I'm afraid not. And yes, I do have some experience with this. My son was taken five years ago, and not a day goes by that I don't ask that very question."

Julia hesitated, ashamed of what she had said. Knowing there was no way to take the words back, as they were now out in the open, drifting. She penalized herself for being so heartless. "Um…I'm…I'm so sorry. I didn't know."

"I know, child. How could you?"

"Then why? Why do you believe?"

"Because I don't know the whys. I don't know the reason, but I believe in the plan. Oh, I can't say I have stopped asking why, but I know one day I will know the answer," the preacher explained.

Julia, disgusted, threw her arms down to her side and looked off into the distance. "Yeah, well, I'm not sure I can wait that long."

"What's your child's name?"

"His name is Bobby."

"I'll pray for him."

"You do that, preacher, because I'm all prayed out."

The preacher touched Julia's shoulder and prayed a heartfelt prayer for her, "Lord, please bring Bobby back to his mother's arms, healthy, wise, and knowing he is loved by You. We believe in Your miracles, and one is needed for this family. In Your name, we pray. Amen."

Surprised by his kind gesture, Julia looked up at the stranger and said apologetically, "Thank you."

"You're welcome," the pastor said as he moved toward the glass door. "I'll be in the chapel until seven tonight if you need to talk. People tell me I have a good ear for listening."

"Thank you," Julia said, sniffling. "Thank you for listening to me."

"Hey, that's what I do," the pastor said with a wink as he reached for the door handle. The pastor then walked back into the hospital, leaving Julia sitting alone in the courtyard.

Julia stood up, walked over to the bench, and sat down. Feeling the sun lighting up the area around her, she shut her eyes and felt the warmth of the rays falling upon her face. There was a large man-made waterfall next to where she was sitting, and she sat and listened as the rushing water made its way over the large rocks, racing down toward the larger body of water that was surrounded by concrete.

The palm trees swayed in the cool breeze of the day, shuffling their branches in the wind. She looked up into the sky and shut her eyes tight as the musical whistles of the birds in the trees united in a beautiful chant of wind, water, and warmth. Each note distinct as it melted into her soul, allowing her to breathe deeply. Julia threw her head back—the way she did when she was a small child—and breathed in the red, white, and orange images that danced behind her closed eyelids as she sighed, absorbing the light of the day, and for one single moment, she was at peace.

After several deep breaths, Julia commanded her body to make its way back to her mother's room. When she reached her mother's floor, Julia caught sight of Lisa in the hallway.

"Lisa!" Julia shouted louder than she meant to as all the hospital staff turned around in response to the loud cry. Julia, forgetting where she was for a moment, moved swiftly toward her friend. Lisa had to literally catch Julia in her arms as they embraced in a long hug.

Julia pulled back, wiping tears from her eyes, "It's so good to see you."

"How you doin', my friend?"

"Not well. It's all, all of it; it's been so crazy," Julia said, whimpering, letting go, feeling safe to let Lisa see that side of her. The side she hid from everyone else.

"I saw your mom. She's not as talkative as she used to be."

"I know. We don't know what to do. She's given up. Oh, Lisa, I can't lose her and Bobby, too."

"Haven't heard from him, huh."

"Nope. I…I just don't know what to do. What could have possessed him to…to do this?"

Lisa stepped back, taking a look around the hallway as if debating on her next words.

"He's not your son anymore. You have lost him to something that controls him. Something, I'm sorry to say, that means more to him than you all do. I know. I grew up with an addicted father. There's nothing on God's green earth you can do until he decides he wants help."

"Oh, I know that. You think I don't know that. But he's my son, Lisa. I can't just sit around and let him fall deeper into this evil."

"Yes, you can," Lisa said, turning to look straight at her friend. "Julia, you have raised that boy the best you could. He's been hurt. I know. Scott leaving was a blow to all of you, but you made it out."

"I know, but…"

"But nothing. Bobby has just gotta make that choice too. And he will. I'm praying for all of you all. Especially for Carmen in there. She's something. It's their decision, Julia. Not yours."

"I know. My head tells me that, but my heart keeps saying to do something."

"I know. I know you do. We moms always want the best for our kids."

"Yeah, we do."

"Honey, there is nothing you can do for your mom or your son until they decide to start living again. You can try, but it may end up killing you too."

Julia looked up at her friend and took a deep breath. "I have to do something."

"Okay, then you pray. That's about all you can do. Listen, I have been there. You can wish until you turn blue, but that ain't going to change a single thing. You got to let them go, girl."

"That's easier said than done."

"I know. But, I, for one, don't want to lose my friend."

"Well, I don't want that either."

"Okay then," Lisa said, drying Julia's eyes with a tissue, "Hey, I've been meaning to tell you. I've seen that guy around. The one with the young girlfriend."

"You have? When?" Julia asked, bringing a tissue up to blow her nose.

"At work. He doesn't know I've seen him, but he comes around. I think he's looking for you."

"Really?"

"Yep. Boy, is he fine. If your mother wasn't in the hospital and your son a drug lord, I'd be going after him my own self."

And Julia laughed for the first time in a long time. "Oh, Lisa. I needed that. What the heck am I going to do?"

"You are going to keep going on; that's what you are going to do. I can't afford to go find any other best friends if you are sent to the looney bin," Lisa said, smiling and placing a hair behind Julia's ear. "Now, you can do this, Julia. I'm here if you need me. I'm always here. You understand."

"I do. Thanks, Lisa."

"You're welcome. Well, get on in there. Your daughter is there waiting on you. She was dropped off by that other guy you rejected. Why can't I get just one guy? Here you had two guys fighting over you, and I can't get one date. Now, how fair is that?" Lisa said, winking at Julia.

Julia just smiled.

"You call me if you need anything, hon. You hear? And give that good-looking guy, the one not dating your daughter, a call."

"I'll think about it," Julia said.

"Okay, then. I'm out of here. You call if you need anything." Lisa then walked down the hall flirting with one of the young male doctors, turning back to wink at Julia. And Julia just smiled.

Just then, Julia's cell phone went off, and she looked down, seeing that it was Scott.

"Julia, I think I have found him again, but I don't think he will come with me. Well, I was thinking…maybe if you come down here. I hate to ask you, with Carmen being in the hospital and all, but I don't know what else to do. I know he won't listen to me. He should be here any minute. He usually always arrives here around this time."

"Okay, where are you? I can leave now. Lauren's here. She can stay with Mom."

"I'm at the old Empire Theater. It's boarded up now, but there's a lot of drug traffic going on here. People are entering and leaving like it's a freakin' bus station or something."

"What day is it? What day is his court?" Julia said, brushing her hair out of her eyes, trying to think of how many days it had actually been.

"It's Thursday, Julia. He has to be there tomorrow morning."

"Okay. I'll be right there," Julia said as she hung up with Scott.

"I heard," Lauren said behind her. "Go, Mom. Get Bobby and bring him home. If I go, I might kill him, and that wouldn't be good for anybody."

"True. Okay, if you're sure you're good to stay here?"

"Yeah, I got Grandma. You go get my brother."

"Okay, sweetheart. I'll try my best. I better go. I'll call you later."

Julia then made her way out of the hospital. Her mind drifted as she looked around at the city that continued to live, even though she felt like everything around her was dying. Regardless of all the craziness happening around her, she had always loved living in San Diego. She loved everything about it. She loved the sandy beaches and the blue ocean as far as the eye could see. The beautiful sun that slowly set each day was something that, even as a child, she cherished.

The outdoors used to be her refuge. Her favorite place to write. She and Ritchie would go to the park or the beach and find a quiet spot. He would take a nap, and she would sit and write and observe the world until they were ready to go. As a writer, she found that it gave her inspiration. The sadness, the happiness, the anger, and the joy of it all were what she loved so much. Right now, that world seemed a million miles away. Back then, she felt as if she could've sat and watched this world forever.

Julia sat at the stoplight and wondered when was the last time she had sat on her beach. She couldn't even remember. Maybe Lisa was right. Julia's mind began to wander as she thought about the last time she had felt truly happy or even the last time she had laughed uncontrollably, and for some reason, at that moment, she thought about Andy.

Once Julia arrived, she parked across the street from the theater. The theater, which the city chose not to renovate, used to house magnificent plays and various performing troops from a bygone era. The outer exterior was still in very good condition, except for the random graffiti that was sprayed across some of the outer walls. The inside, Julia hadn't seen since she was a small child when her mother used to take her to the movies. At that time, the city had converted the facility into a movie theater.

There were magnificent high ceilings covered with vivid paintings and massive chandeliers that hung from golden arched coves. Gold, being the prominent color, was displayed on the handrails and accents along the walls and ceiling.

The theater used to have a deep red carpet that stretched everywhere, even walking into the individual theaters. Julia had always wished she had enough money to buy and restore the old facility. Right now, it is being used to house the homeless, drug users, prostitutes, and the mentally ill. Now, Julia thought, it was being used to house her son.

Scott pulled up beside Julia, startling her at first, her nerves already on edge. He quickly got out and came over to get in her vehicle.

"I've been watching the place for a day or so, and he has been here twice now, always at the same time of the day. I tried to speak to him both times, and he just blew me off. I can't get past the doormen standing right over there." Scott pointed to two large men standing outside the backdoor smoking what looked to be marijuana.

"Well, what do we do, go ring the bell? Is he in there now?" Julia said sarcastically.

"No, if I'm right, he should be showing up at any moment. He usually comes walking up the back with another man, and they both go in and come out a few minutes later. Where they go from there, I'm not sure."

"Okay, let's get closer," Julia said, removing the keys from the ignition.

"No, if he sees you, I think he might run. We'll have to take him by surprise."

"Well, can we stand behind the trees over there?" Julia asked, pointing to the trees along the alley.

Scott surveyed the alley and sighed. "Okay. That might work. Julia?"

"Yeah," Julia said, still trying to visualize how this would all play out.

"Thank you so much for coming. I know it was a lot with Carmen being in the hospital and all. You have to believe if I thought he would come with me, I would have done this on my own."

"No, I get it. He might come with me. Or I might drag him into the car, kicking and screaming," Julia said, becoming irritated with all that Bobby had put them through.

Scott, realizing that Julia had no idea of what Bobby may be capable of, tried to warn her, "Now, don't try anything crazy with him. He's not who you think he is anymore."

"He's my son, Scott. I can drag him or knock him in the head if I need to. I carried him for nine months, for Christ's sake. I think that gives me the right."

Scott hesitated, realizing that this was a losing battle with Julia. "Okay, but I just want to warn you…"

"I know…I know…I get it. I know that probably wouldn't be the wisest thing to do. But he's lucky that I don't have a baseball bat in the car right now."

"Huh…oh." Scott grinned. "Are you sure you are okay to do this?"

"Scott, I'm okay. Really. Don't you go worrying about me. I need you to concentrate on our son right now."

"I am. Why do you think I'm out here?" Scott replied.

They sat watching as people entered and exited the building. They were all being let in by the two men at the door. There didn't seem to be any police in the area, which was strange since this was a known drug facility. All of this certainly did not make Julia feel any better about her son being a part of this world. He was already in danger of doing real-time if he got caught dealing or using again.

If ever there was a time for a miracle, it was now. If ever there was a time Julia needed a helping hand, it was now. She sent up a silent SOS into the atmosphere and waited again for an answer. Her faith and her hope were running low, but her love was at two hundred and twenty-five percent because she would never, ever give up on her child. Not ever.

Julia sat there thinking that no one would be taking her son, not in her lifetime. Not if she had anything to do about it. And if so, it would be over her dead body.

CHAPTER NINETEEN

Julia and Scott's plan was to make their way to a trash dumpster next to some trees just off the alley. They both felt they could get there without being seen by the two men at the back door. This location would give them a better chance of reaching Bobby before he reached the rear entrance.

Scott led the way, grabbing Julia's hand and pulling her toward the alley as they moved forward. Julia—feeling that the hand-holding was unnecessary—continually shook her hand loose.

"I'm just trying to help you," he whispered.

"If you want to help me, just keep your eyes on those guys at the back door, so I can get close to Bobby. I can handle Bobby. I just can't keep my eyes on them."

"Alright, alright," Scott conceded.

"So, they just come up on foot?" Julia asked, surveying the alley.

"Yeah, they usually walk up right over there," Scott whispered, pointing to the north side of the lane. "They're not usually in the building very long."

The alley was right behind the theater. There was a loading dock on the south side where props used to be delivered. The dumpster was below the loading dock, a few feet away from the back door of the theater.

Julia and Scott kept their heads down and waited patiently, hoping not to be discovered before they could reach Bobby. Scott looked up over the dumpster and saw two men walking down the sidewalk, just across from the parking lot where they had parked their cars. One of them was Bobby. He didn't even notice his parent's cars as he walked by. He was too busy conversing with the man beside him. Scott noticed that they were both carrying backpacks this time.

He nudged Julia as she looked over and spotted Bobby. Without any notice, Julia moved out from behind the dumpster. She moved so quickly; Scott had to scramble to get up in order to follow behind her.

"Julia, wait," Scott whispered.

The two men at the door, who were dressed in black boots and camouflage pants, saw the couple come out from behind the dumpster, and the larger man, wearing a black bandana, jumped over the concrete wall and landed on the paved surface. He proceeded to make a bullseye right toward Julia and Scott.

The confrontation happened so fast that no one had time to think, as time was sent into fast-forward. Bobby looked over just in time to see what looked like his mother running up toward him. He grabbed at his backpack, making sure it was steady on his back. He thought about running but saw the larger security guard heading right for her. He reactively moved toward Julia, trying to head off the certain collision between her and the guard.

"Tony, I got this. I know these people," Bobby said, holding back the large man with one arm while grabbing Julia to hold her back with his other arm.

"No, you don't got this. You know the rules. No outsiders. And that includes these two tourists."

"I got this. I'm coming in. It's cool, man. They're nobodies."

His partner in crime, a brown-skinned young man wearing a black beret and displaying tattoos up and down his arms, rolled his eyes and pulled Bobby toward the theater by his T-shirt. "Come on, man. We don't have time for this."

Bobby held his ground, snatching his friend's arm from his T-shirt and then rotating his head back and forth from his parents to the guards, seemingly unsure of what to do.

The other security guard approached Scott and looked him up and down. He lunged toward Scott as if to try and scare him. Scott flinched but stood his ground as the large man smiled and headed back toward the doorway, "You got one minute to get them out of here, Bobby, or all hell is going to break loose."

"I told you, I got this, man," Bobby said.

The security guards then walked toward the back door, keeping their eyes on Julia and Scott.

"Bobby, we need you to come home. Your court date is tomorrow. You have to be there. What are you doing with these people?" Julia said, more terrified than she thought she would be from the run-in with Bobby's business associates.

"Mom, you have to get out of here. These guys don't play."

"I'm not leaving here without you," Julia said, shaking off Bobby's arm and looking back and forth between Bobby and the theater security.

"Mom, you can't help me. You can't save me. Please, you have to consider me no longer your son." And he turned toward Scott. "And I was never yours. Now, please, just go. Get her out of here. Why would you bring her here?"

"Don't tell me you are not my son. I carried you for nine months, and I'm not letting you go. You have to be in court tomorrow. Now you're coming with us," Julia said, grabbing Bobby's arm, accidentally knocking the backpack off his back. And before they knew what was happening, the security guards appeared to flash to their location.

"I told you to get the heck out of here, Mr. and Mrs. Smith!" the nameless security guard said, pulling out a handgun. He grabbed Scott by his neck, pointing the gun at his head. Now you can go walking, or we can carry you out of here. What will it be?"

Julia looked at Bobby as the world began to spin; everything went fast forward. "No, stop, please," Julia cried, turning toward Bobby. "Is this what it has come to?" Julia asked, just as Tony grabbed her arm and pushed her down onto the pavement.

Bobby grabbed Tony's arm, pulling it down, "Tony, I got this. They're not a threat. Just give me a second to deal with them."

Tony reacted to Bobby's words so quickly; Bobby didn't even have time to duck. Tony brought his arm back, hitting Bobby full-force in the nose, sending him backward about two feet, his nose now bleeding down his shirt.

Time started to spin as Bobby jumped back up and tried to move in between Scott and the other security guard.

Tony looked over at him. "You going with them?" Tony asked. "Because I can take the merchandise in, no skin off my back. I can take care of all three of you."

"No, man. They're leaving. Just don't touch them. They're leaving," Bobby cried out, trying to convince him while wiping the blood from his nose. "Get the heck outta here!" Bobby screamed at Julia.

The other guard threw Scott down to the ground, face first, right next to Julia. Scott's head made contact with the pavement first before his body rolled to a stop.

Julia looked up at Bobby while trying to help Scott sit up.

She couldn't believe what Bobby was allowing to happen to them. Her body felt so heavy she couldn't rise from the pavement. Still confused, Julia tried to form words, words that would reason with him.

"Okay, but I'll be back. I'll be back tomorrow and the next day and the next day after that, and they'll have to carry me out of here in a bag before I let you go," she cried.

"That can be arranged, Mrs. Smith!" Tony screamed out. "Bobby, get your sorry self over here?" Tony screamed out in a chilling tone.

"I'm coming, man. Chill," Bobby said, wiping his nose with his shirt. He moved toward the back door looking back every once in a while to make sure that his parents were leaving. Bobby then turned back around and mouthed the words, "Mom, you have to go."

Julia picked herself up.

Scott tried to lift himself off of the ground, struggling to stop his nose from bleeding.

"Grandma's in the hospital. She's had a stroke!" Julia screamed out.

"A stroke?" Bobby shouted back as he stopped walking, looking back toward them.

"I want Grandpa's ring back. I'll be back for it," Julia said, not sure why she had brought the ring up at that moment. Julia turned to help Scott up. "If you won't help yourself, I expect you to help Grandma. She's very sick. I want the ring by tomorrow. Do you understand me?"

Bobby's eyes narrowed. "Grandma?"

"Yes, you heard me. Grandma," Julia cried, trying to hold back tears.

"I'll try," was all Bobby said as he turned to head toward the back door of the theater, Tony pushing him from behind. Bobby turned back once before heading in.

Julia helped Scott over to their cars. Scott's lip was bleeding. His lower jaw was covered in blood, and his shirt was now stained around the collar. Julia helped him into his car and took some tissues out of her car, and placed one on his lip.

"I'm so sorry, Julia," Scott said.

"There was nothing more you could have done," Julia responded. "I think I have some band-aids in my glove compartment. Let me check."

"You are such a good mom," Scott said, with tears in his eyes. "I was so wrong."

"I know, Scott," Julia said, tears making their way over her cheeks as she tried to wipe them away. "But this is not about you, and it's not about me. It's about our son, and he needs us. So, don't fall apart on me. I need you on this one."

"I won't let you down. Do you think he will bring it?" Scott asked.

"The ring?"

"Yeah."

"I don't know," she said as she bandaged Scott's lip the best she could.

"We need to get out of here. Those guys may be back, and I don't want them near you," Scott said.

"Yeah, I guess," Julia answered, now looking around the car, wondering if the guards, or possibly Bobby, had followed them.

Scott could sense that she wanted to run back in there. He grabbed her hand as she was cleaning him up. "Julia, these people don't play around. Don't even think about it," he said.

Julia looked at him, feeling his concern for her safety, and for a moment, she remembered why, at one time in her life, she once loved him.

"I'm not. I just can't…"

"I know…. It'll have to be another day. We'll get him back," Scott said, grabbing her hand. And she let him. "We will. I promise."

CHAPTER TWENTY

"Did you see him?" Lauren asked as soon as Julia returned to the hospital.

Julia placed her things down and peered over at her daughter. "Yes, we did. It didn't go well," Julia said, rubbing her arm where she had hit the pavement.

"But tomorrow is his court date. Augh...maybe I should've gone," Lauren said, throwing her head back.

Julia looked at her with a face Lauren hadn't seen since she snuck out of their home to meet up with friends at a football game when she was supposed to be grounded. "I don't want you around him. You have to think about the baby."

"I'd be fine. Bobby's my brother. He wouldn't do anything to hurt us."

Julia looked at her as if she didn't know what to say and put her hand up to her mouth to try and stop the tears. "I'm not sure about that anymore," she sniffled. "I just don't want you around him. I'm going to bring him home. It'll take time. But as God is my witness, I will not let them have him."

Lauren came up to Julia and hugged her, and they stood for several minutes quietly crying and rocking each other, looking over at Carmen.

"I'm sorry. I've just been very emotional lately," Lauren whispered.

Julia smiled. "I so understand. I was the same way."

"I literally cry over everything. I'm going to drive Brad insane."

"Oh…I think he understands," Julia said, placing her keys in her purse.

"Maybe, if this were his baby," Lauren said unexpectedly. "I wish that were true. I'm not sure what he's going to do," she whispered. "I'm sorry. I didn't mean to bring that up. I know you have so much on your mind right now. I'm fine."

"Oh, sweetie, it'll all work out," Julia said, placing a loose strand of hair behind Lauren's ear.

"It's so unfair to him, Mom. I mean raising someone else's child," Lauren said softly so that her grandmother wouldn't awaken.

"Sweetheart, people do it all the time. They adopt children all the time that are not theirs."

"Yeah, but this is different. Brad would have to live with my mistake."

"What?"

"No, not the baby. I mean Jake."

"Sweetheart, Brad's an adult man. He knows what he's getting into."

"I know. It's just you were right about him. I'm just starting to care for him so much. It really scares me. I'm not sure I could handle losing this one."

"You won't. You won't," Julia said as if she were trying to convince herself. "It'll all be okay," she said while rocking Lauren in her arms like she did when Lauren was three-years-old. "It'll be okay. I promise you, one way or the other. We Melrose women are a tough bunch." She smiled.

Lauren smirked, letting out a giggle, wiping the tears from her eyes.

* * * *

Julia observed her mother waking up throughout the day but could still see that she had no inclination to live. Carmen lay in bed, rolling her head back and forth across her pillow as if she were trying to shake off the realities of this world. Then there were other times she would face the window, stretching her neck to hear the birds chirping outside, gazing at the clouds floating by.

Lauren brought Carmen's bird clock up to the hospital, hoping that the sounds of home would somehow spark some type of awakening in her grandmother. The clock would go off every hour on the hour, and Carmen would habitually turn her head towards the chirps and then as if on cue, stare back off into space as if she had given up all hope.

When the clock chirped, you could see in Carmen's eyes that she was thinking about her birds at home. Julia reinforced to her mother that she and Lauren were making sure that the birds got fed, but Carmen still refused to acknowledge her daughter. She acted as if Julia and Lauren weren't even in the room.

As the day went on, Julia insisted that Lauren return home to get some sleep, fearful that Lauren was doing too much. After she left, Julia walked around the room as the clock ticked away. She stared at her mother as if she were trying to get inside her head, determined to understand the reason for her defiance. She had just about enough of the people around her giving up. She wasn't about to lose her mother, too, not without a fight.

"Mom...Mom, I know you can hear me. The stroke did not affect your hearing," Julia blasted.

Carmen rolled her head away from her daughter.

"Okay, Mom. If you are going to give up, so am I. I'm just going to quit my job and lock myself in my room," Julia said, looking back at her mother for a response. "You don't think I haven't thought about that? Just checking out. Like you obviously have. Oh, and I'm going to marry the first guy I meet on the street who has no job and move him in with us too. How would you like that?" Julia said, and Carmen glanced her way, rolling her eyes. "Mom, I know that you're in there. They can't feed you with this tube forever. Well, they can, but it's awfully expensive, and the cost will make your hospital bill outrageous. What will you do then…huh?"

Julia looked for a response, but Carmen continued in her zombie-like state.

Julia plopped down on the vinyl chair and stared at her mother's motionless body. She brought her hands up, pushing her fingers through the loose strands of hair, turning to stare out the window, trying to figure out what her mother was looking at. Disgusted, she threw her hands down to the cushion, pushed herself off the chair, and headed closer to her mother's bed and the endless beeping of the machines that surrounded her.

Julia had made a video on her phone of her mother's birds. She placed her phone in front of her mother's face so that she could not avoid looking at it. Carmen automatically rolled her head away in the opposite direction. Julia moved the phone from side to side as her mother continued to avoid the screen.

"Do you hear them, Mom? They are saying that they miss you," Julia said. "And I'm getting really tired of feeding them. They bite the heck out of my hand," she complained. "In fact, I'm thinking I'm going to stop feeding them because they are such a nuisance. How do you like that? What are you going to do about it, Mom? Are you just going to lay there and let them die?" And still, Carmen did not respond. "Mom, answer me."

Frustrated with the continued silence, Julia lifted her hand up and threw her phone at the oversized recliner as the birds in the video continued to chirp. The phone bounced against the back of the cushion and landed just on the edge of the seat.

"Fine…fine, fine, fine!" Julia cried out. Upset, she grabbed her phone and fled from her mother's room, suddenly finding it hard to breathe. She ran past the nurse, who had gotten up to see what the shouting was about. Julia walked the unending maze that made up the different sections of the hospital. She struggled to walk straight as the relentless episodes of the day came back to her over and over again. Julia found herself having to grab at the wall as she walked, afraid that she might faint.

She made it to the community restroom down the hall and opened the door slamming it behind her. Her body collapsed as she melted down the tiled wall forming a pool of agony on the floor. Julia lay there sobbing quietly, trying not to make too much noise. She placed her hand over her mouth, holding back the scream that formed at the bottom of her throat.

After a few minutes, she forced herself to stand and stood looking at the image staring back at her in the mirror. She wiped the mascara from underneath her eyes and splashed some cold water on her face, pulling back the loose strands of hair from her eyes.

"What are you going to do?" she said to the image. "Just let everything fall apart?"

She took one more look at the beaten image staring back at her and brushed her hair back, straightening her shirt and brushing her hair down at the sides. "Well, you have certainly made a fine mess out of all of this," she stated to the image staring back at her. She took a deep breath and slowly opened the bathroom door, making her way out into the hallway.

Julia followed the geometrical shapes embedded in the blue carpet and made her way down the long and winding hallway, thinking she might possibly go to the cafeteria to get some coffee. She was halfway down the hall when her phone lit up. She looked down and discovered that it was Scott calling her. Sighing, she quickly answered her glowing phone.

"Julia?"

"Yeah," Julia said, exhausted.

"I wanted to let you know that I hired a lawyer to represent Bobby. Are you okay? I can barely hear you."

"I'm fine. What does that mean? I mean, what if he doesn't show up?" Julia asked, trying to clear her throat so that she could be heard more clearly.

"Well, I'm going to try and get him an extension if he doesn't show up. I was talking to the lawyer, and he said he might be able to get an extension if he claims Bobby has to be at the hospital due to Carmen having a stroke. The lawyer will paint a picture of your mom wanting Bobby right beside her. It may not work, but it could buy us some time to bring him to his senses if that's possible. It's worth a shot, don't you think?" Scott asked.

"Well, at this point, I guess we don't have any choice. But what if the judge doesn't approve the extension?" Julia asked.

"Well, then we're sunk," Scott said. "A warrant will be issued for his arrest, and he'll do real jail time. I mean…what else can we do?"

"I don't know. I just can't think about all of this right now, Scott. At this point, I'm not sure what the right thing to do is."

"Well…hey…I was just wondering…do you want me to bring you dinner or something? I mean, I can bring it for you and Lauren. I know you both are spending a lot of time at the hospital and have a lot on your plate right now. I just thought maybe I could help, somehow."

"No, but thank you, Scott. I'm just going to grab something at the cafeteria. It allows me to get away for a little while. Sometimes, I just need a break. Lauren went home anyway. I wanted her to rest."

"Well, do you want me to bring you something other than hospital food? I could go to that sandwich place you used to like," Scott asserted. Again, Julia could hear the apology in his voice, that tone that said, I'm so sorry for screwing up your life, and how can I make it better.

"No, I'm fine, Scott. But thank you. Just please worry about the lawyer. And thank you for that."

And Scott took every kind word from Julia as if it were a gift. A gift of hope that someday she might forgive him and let him back into her life. "Not a problem. I'll let you know what the lawyer says about our chances in the morning. I'll see you at the courthouse."

"Great. See you then."

Julia made her way to the cafeteria and sat against the windows, looking out onto the blue sky she loved so much. She saw people walking to and fro along the concrete path, set inside a garden that was designed as an escape for family members who needed time to think. Benches—that called out to the passersby—were strategically placed along the walkway. This tiny refuge was an oasis in the middle of their desert.

Julia thought about Bobby and his reaction when they showed up so unexpectedly in his new world. She could sense that the drugs hadn't completely taken him over. She felt the Bobby that she knew as her son was still in there somewhere, down deep inside. The one that cared about his family. At least he had tried to protect them, even if he didn't come home with them, Julia thought. She tried to see his reaction as positive. She tried to see it as a sign that he wasn't completely lost to them yet. At this point, Julia grabbed onto any speck of hope that she could, limited as it was, regarding Bobby's current situation.

Later that evening, Lauren returned to the hospital, against Julia's wishes. She came by herself and explained that Brad couldn't get away from the base. Lauren seemed to be in good spirits and demanded that Julia—who looked extremely exhausted—head home and get some sleep. Lauren said she would wait there with her grandmother until late in the evening and then head home herself.

Reluctantly, Julia agreed, starting to feel the ramifications of the last couple of days catching up with her. So much so that she was finding it hard to keep her eyes open.

When she arrived home, and after checking on Carmen's birds, Julia went to her closet and uncovered her secret box of notebooks. She looked over some of her past writings and cuddled up in bed, placing a notebook on her lap as she often did when the world around her somehow just didn't make sense.

She had been writing for several minutes when she suddenly looked up and stared at the drawer that held her past, maneuvering her eyes back and forth between the drawer and her notebook. Without warning, she lifted the notebook over her head and threw it across the room, straight toward the innocent dresser. The notebook crashed against the front of the dresser with its pages flaring and landed hard on the carpet.

Julia fumed. She had always turned to that harrowing picture, the past continually haunting her. It was time to let it go, she reasoned. She couldn't bring him back. She couldn't change the past. There was nothing left but to move forward. And maybe, just maybe, the picture was the source of her misery. The piece that kept her from being truly happy.

She got up and crept toward the drawer that entombed her past. She opened it and took out the folder, still wrapped in plastic. Ripping the outer plastic off, she stood looking at the folder that contained her beloved and slowly opened it, removing the picture of Ritchie that made her gasp every time she saw it. She held the picture in her hands as all the memories came flooding back at her. The two wonderful years she spent with him before he was stolen away from her. That smile. Those eyes that haunted her. She took the picture in her hand and was about to rip it down the center when something crashed against her bedroom window. The force was so loud Julia jumped, causing her to drop the picture. She watched as the picture floated slowly across the room, back and forth, until it landed right beside the window.

Astonished, Julia made her way toward the picture at the foot of the window. She picked it up, bringing it back to her chest, hugging it as tears ran their course, making their way down her already flushed cheeks.

She slowly opened the curtains to see a tree limb outside of her window, hitting the side of the house. Looking out into the distance, she thought she saw a glow that slowly dissipated, heading toward the sunset, and she thought of Ritchie again.

She fell to her knees next to the window and leaned against the wall, hugging the photo in her arms, bringing it close to her chest as she began to sob and scream out into the silence.

"I miss you so much. Why? Why did you have to leave me? I needed you. I still need you. I have made such a mess of my life. What happened? You left me here all alone. It wasn't supposed to be like this," she said, wiping the tears from her eyes.

After a few minutes, she got up and walked over to the dresser, picking up the black folder. She placed the photo back into the sleeve and closed it. She slowly dropped the folder back into the plastic bag and placed it carefully back into the drawer, covering it with her clothing.

Sobbing, Julia made her way back to her bed and tossed back the covers, climbing into bed fully clothed, weeping until she fell asleep.

As Julia slept, she entered that stage of sleep where images begin to appear, working their way into your unconscious. Circles and shapes encircled her subconscious, forming images from long ago.

She saw herself moving through a crowd of people while music played all around her. She had to walk toward the center of the floor to find some open space; the crowd was so thick. Suddenly, a light flashed above her head, and she threw her head back, looking up at the ball, flashing multicolored lights over the entire crowd as the music became louder and louder. The music was so loud that Julia had to cover her ears. She saw an image dressed in a white shirt and black pants heading toward her. He was carrying sunflowers, which were Julia's favorite. The vibrant yellow color glowed underneath the light, and then she saw that smile and immediately knew it was Ritchie.

He handed her the flowers and said, "I love us."

And Julia kept repeating, "I love us, too."

But something kept pulling Ritchie back. She grabbed at his hands, dropping the sunflowers, which appeared to float toward the floor, one by one, spreading out as if they were knee-deep in a meadow. Ritchie started to float backward, and the crowd around them began to gather, blocking them from reaching one another. Julia tried to push through them, but they wouldn't allow her to move an inch. She struggled to fight her way through the crowd, but the crowd just became thicker and thicker. And suddenly the music stopped. A silence followed as the crowd parted. Ritchie looked back at her as a door opened, and a bright light flashed into the room like a flashlight in the darkness of the night.

Julia screamed out, "Ritchie, wait for me. Where are you going? Hold on!"

Ritchie turned around once again. She saw that he had tears in his eyes.

Julia screamed out again, "Wait for me. What's wrong?"

Ritchie just smiled and pointed toward the dance floor.

Julia looked over at the dance floor, and there was another man there dancing with a red-headed woman. The man turned around and started to walk toward Julia, but she paid no attention to the stranger and turned back and looked toward Ritchie, who was grinning with tears running down his face. He then blew her a kiss and went through the door frame, the door slamming behind him.

Julia screamed out, "Wait, don't go! Don't you love me anymore?"

Julia then felt someone tapping her shoulder. She turned around and recognized the stranger's eyes. It was Andy. He was twenty-two years old again. He said, "I would like to dance with you."

Julia looked back toward the closed doors and started running toward them. She had to fight her way through the crowd but suddenly broke through, reaching the large black doors with four engraved squares lining either side of the door with protruding large gold doorknobs.

She began to bang on the doors with both of her fists, crying out to the silence. She screamed and screamed until she had no voice. Finally succumbing to exhaustion, she collapsed onto the floor, sitting in front of the doors as all eyes were turned toward her.

She watched as her audience slowly turned and walked away from her, one at a time, until there was only one man standing in the middle of the floor. It was Andy. He was older now. He stood there with his hand extended for her to join him.

Julia sat there on the floor whimpering as she reached out toward Andy, expecting him to join her, but his image slowly faded into the darkness. She then brought her hands back into her chest, clenching her fists, and the lights dimmed, and the only sound that could be heard was the sound of her tears as they made their way down her cheeks, splashing onto the black marble floor.

CHAPTER TWENTY-ONE

The sun rose on the next day, creeping into Julia's room. Her pillow was wet. Tears sat embedded in her eyes. The dream—if that's what it was—seemed so real. It was almost as if she could breathe in Ritchie's cologne. She remembered the soft touch of his hand over hers. She rose slowly, remembering details and moments, afraid of what the dream meant.

She showered and dressed, trying not to concentrate on last night's dream, knowing that it would slowly fade—as most dreams do—into the realities of the day. She had to focus. She had to check in on her mother and make it to the courthouse by mid-morning, so she would be there for Bobby's hearing.

And then there was the issue of the ring. She told Bobby that she would be back for it. She secretly hoped that he would bring her mother's ring to the courthouse, but if not, she had her mind set on somehow locating him to get the ring back.

Throughout the morning, she continually texted Bobby the time and place of his court proceedings, not sure if the texts were getting through to him or not.

As she was about to leave, she got a call from the hospital. Frantic, Julia juggled her phone as she heard an unfamiliar voice coming through the receiver.

"Hello, yes, this is Julia Melrose," she said.

"Hello, Mrs. Melrose; this is Kelly, your mother's nurse. The doctor has asked me to call you. We need you to come to the hospital as soon as you can, please. Your mother is refusing any medical treatment, and we need to know what you want us to do."

"I'll be right there," Julia said as she hung up with the nurse. She clutched her keys and sprinted to her car, jumping in and hitting the gas pedal, checking her phone from time to time to see if she had received a response from Bobby. When she arrived, she parked in the hospital's parking lot and had to push past several people in order to get to her mother's room. Just outside the hospital room, her mother's nurse stopped her before she could enter.

"I want to warn you that your mother's not acknowledging anyone. We've had to use restraints on her hands until the sedative kicks in. She keeps trying to remove her IV. I just wanted you to be prepared. She is not responding to anyone at the moment. Your daughter is also on her way. I called you both. So please, be gentle; she's not in a good place right now."

Julia, taken aback by the nurse's remark, reflected on her words. *Is she saying that I'm not being gentle?* Part of Julia did want to go in and give her mother a good swift kick in the rear end, but the other part of her just wanted to crawl in bed beside her and become as comatose as she was.

Thoughts made their way through Julia's mind as she entered her mother's room. *How dare she decide to leave the family of her own free will? How dare she not take them into consideration? What did she think she was doing?* Julia took a deep breath as she turned and nodded to the nurse, and slowly made her way into the hospital room.

The door inched open, squeaking so loud Julia thought surely her mother heard it. And there she was, lying there, stiff as could be. Her eyes were wide open, looking at her bird clock. Waiting for the seconds to signal the end of another hour. The end of another moment that she was stuck here in this bed, in this strange place, in this strange body.

Carmen's blank stare said it all. She was at the mercy of all who surrounded her. Deciding her future for her. And now her daughter was here, feeling robbed of her once-strong mother.

Julia watched as her mother slowly gave up. Choosing not to live. Julia thought that maybe if she were lying there, she would be making the same choice her mother was. After all, her mother had done her job and raised Julia and her sister. Maybe she would just have to accept her mother's decision not to live. She would have to accept that to her mother, her current way of life was no way of life at all.

Her mother's hands were restrained beside her as tears slowly made their way down her cheeks.

Julia came up beside her. She had no more words. Tears started to form, making their way down to meet her mother's tears as Julia gently took her mother's bound hand into hers. "I'm so sorry, Mom. Tell me. Tell me what you want me to do. I'm sorry I'm being selfish, but it's true. I don't want to lose you. Tell me. Please tell me what I can do."

Carmen's tears began to gush out as she stared out into the unknown without a word to her daughter and without hope for the future as the people around her were forced to let go. Carmen had already begun the process, and to speak to her daughter now would only be backtracking. She had made her decision, and they would all just have to live with it. They would all have to learn to live without her.

Julia sat rubbing her mother's hands and her hair, hoping, praying that Carmen would come to her senses and somehow want to live again. Julia found herself staring out the same window that her mother did. Maybe her mother was doing the most sensible thing. Maybe life just didn't want them anymore. She found herself sinking deeper into a pit of guilt and blame as she thought about her son out on the streets in search of a drug that he loved even more than he loved her. Her mother was lying there before her and had given up on life, unable to move the right side of her body, robbed of her speech, and looking at being cared for the rest of her life. Unable to do all the things she used to do.

Julia started to accept her fate and the fate of her mother because she knew...she knew that had it been her lying there, she would be doing the very same thing her mother was doing. She would be giving up.

When Lauren arrived, Julia was sitting in the vinyl chair, staring out the same window her mother always turned to. They both looked frozen in time, as if a cold chill had entered the room. As if death was whispering to both of them.

Lauren frantically spoke to her mother, reminding her of the hearing that was about to begin, "Mom, you need to be at the courthouse at eleven, right?"

Julia, realizing Lauren was in the room, turned toward her daughter, still in a daze. "Yes, that's what your father said."

"Well, you only have an hour to get there."

Julia did not respond.

"Mom, are you listening to me?" Lauren repeated, concerned for her mother's well-being.

"Yes, yes. I'm sorry. I just..."

"Mom, you have to be there in case he shows up. Do you want me to go?" Lauren offered.

Julia, finally hearing the urgency in her daughter's voice, came out of her fog. "No, I'm sorry, sweetie. I'm going. Ahhh...I'll text you once I get there and let you know how it turns out," Julia said, slamming the footrest of the vinyl recliner down and picking up her purse.

"Okay. Are you sure you want to go?"

"Yes, yes. If he does show up, I'll need to be there to help arrange things, and I don't want you to get all worked up."

"Okay, but you are scaring me a little right now. I'm not sure you should be driving," Lauren said.

Julia looked over at Lauren, then looked down at her daughter's pregnant little belly and said, "I'll be all right. I'm just not sure how this is going to turn out. I can't lose your brother too."

"I know, Mom, but I can't lose you," Lauren pleaded.

Julia was so dumbfounded by her daughter's statement that she shook her head as if forcing herself to concentrate on the world before her. Was she giving Lauren the impression that she didn't want to be around? Was her daughter thinking that she didn't want to be around for her? In all the craziness, Lauren had gotten misplaced once again. She was the strong one who always did the right thing. She was the one that Julia could usually depend on and the one that got pushed aside. "I'm so sorry for making you feel that way, sweetie. I'm not going anywhere."

"Well, that's good to know. For a minute there, I thought I had lost you too."

"No…no," Julia said as she tried to think of something redeeming in her life right now. Something that would give them both hope. And it came to her. "After all, I have a grandchild to spoil." And Julia smiled for the first time that day.

"Oh, oh…" Lauren said, reaching down toward her pooched belly.

"What? What is it?"

Lauren then grabbed her mother's hand and placed it on the center of her belly. "He's moving. See…" she said.

"Oh, my gosh. He is," Julia said, rubbing her daughter's pregnant belly. Realizing that the baby, who was at first thought of as a mistake, may now be the only thing keeping her family sane at the moment.

Julia left the hospital, trying to concentrate on what lay ahead of her. She remembered her mother's words the day she had to confront Bobby about his addiction, and she realized that she was doing the exact thing that her mother told her not to do. She was taking on all of their baggage, and now she was taking on her mother's baggage too. She couldn't control Bobby, Lauren, her mother, or even Andy. She could barely control her own life. And no matter how she tried to control the situation, ultimately, it was up to her family to decide their future.

If her mother wanted to end her life today, then that was her decision. There's no way Julia was able to control that. She would just have to accept her actions as a plan. A plan she didn't understand yet. But how to do that was the obvious question. If she was going to be able to stand up to all the craziness that was bombarding her, she would have to rely on a power greater than herself. She entered her vehicle and bowed her head over her steering wheel. She prayed for the first time in a long time for an outcome that seemed impossible to her at the moment. An outcome that would only come from letting go.

CHAPTER TWENTY-TWO

After Julia arrived, she maneuvered herself through the crowd of people at the courthouse. She found Scott waiting just outside the courtroom with the lawyer he had hired. The lawyer was younger than she expected but was dressed very professionally, wearing a blue suit and matching tie. Scott was also dressed in a dark suit. Julia had grabbed the first dress she could get off the hanger that morning, anything that she didn't have to iron. She adjusted her dress, fixing her hair as she walked up to the two men.

Scott noticed her right away as she entered the magnificent corridor. He seemed glad to see her. Probably because this meant he wouldn't have to handle all of this on his own. Julia saw him light up as soon as she was in view.

"Julia, Julia, over here," Scott announced to the corridor, motioning for her to come over and join them. As Julia came up to the two men, Scott grabbed her arm, bringing her close to him as he introduced her. Julia wondered if Scott had misled the attorney into thinking they were all still one big happy family.

"Ron, this is Julia Melrose," Scott said. "Bobby's mother."

Julia carried on the façade, thinking that this might somehow help Bobby. She shot out her hand to meet Ron's. "So glad to meet you, Ron. I hope you are going to be able to help us today."

"Nice to meet you, Julia. I'm going to give it my best. Any news from Bobby? Have either of you spotted him on the grounds?"

"Not yet," Julia and Scott said almost in unison.

Julia and Scott took a moment to scan their surroundings, hopeful that their prodigal son had made his way to the courthouse to hold himself accountable for his actions. Secretly, they also both hoped he would show up because it would also prove to the world and to themselves that they weren't these horrible parents who had led their son astray. It would prove that maybe they hadn't failed.

Julia looked around at the grey concrete walls accented with black cast iron lighting that looked to be remnants of the long-ago twenty's era. The ceiling was magnificent and stretched up for what seemed like miles. Chandeliers hung from spider-like indents that multiplied and covered the entire corridor. Large windows faced the busy street that awaited them, set in black metal frames.

The massive entry doors opened, welcoming the many people that awaited their fates. Scott and Julia looked around desperately for any sign of their son. They were met with face after face, but Bobby was nowhere to be found. They were surrounded by strangers, searching for someone—just as Julia and Scott were—hoping to find that individual that would answer their prayers.

One by one, the other parties around them found themselves relieved to be joined by the person that held their hope in their hands. At the last minute, the person they needed most arrived and joined them, and they entered the courtroom in confidence and solidarity.

Julia and Scott continued to scan the limited area as their attorney spoke with the court officer, trying to make small talk in order to hopefully buy them a little more time. Time that they so desperately needed. But the strangers just passed them by, and the lights turned dim as they checked the large clock on the wall that slowly made its way to their destiny. He had not come.

They had failed each other, and they had failed their son.

Their heads hung low as they dragged themselves toward their attorney, meeting his eyes as he glanced over at them. "Well, I guess it's plan B," the young attorney said. Scott looked over at Julia, wanting to comfort her but afraid to reach out. He grabbed her hand at one point, and she did not have the strength to take it back. She looked down at her hand, unable to feel his touch anymore.

They entered the back of the courtroom and sat halfway down. The judge came out of a room behind his bench. Their lawyer sat, sketching down his plan on a piece of scratch paper.

They sat and watched as the judge determined the fate of the others around them. He was a hard-nosed judge who demanded proof of every minute aspect of the case. Julia's hand began to shake as she witnessed the tears and heartbreak of those around her. Case after case was presented to the judge, and he would hear no excuses.

Their lawyer turned to them unhopeful of a positive outcome, and then their name was called. Julia thought she was going to pass out as Scott helped her to a stand, and they made their way to the front of the courtroom to face their executioner.

"Bobby Melrose," the clerk called out.

They all shook their heads yes.

"Which one of you is Bobby Melrose," the judge asked.

Their lawyer spoke up, having instructed them to let him do the talking.

"I am his attorney, Your Honor. I am asking for an extension of this case due to extenuating circumstances. You see, Bobby's grandmother had a stroke earlier this week and is in critical condition at St. Francis Medical Center. Bobby has been requested to stay with her due to her severe condition."

"Requested? Requested by whom," the judge roared out.

"His grandmother has requested that he not leave her side, Your Honor."

"What? Do you have a doctor's written statement of this so-called request? Some type of proof that he is needed there?"

"Ahhh, no, Your Honor, but I do have his mother and father here, and they will vouch for his whereabouts. The patient in the hospital is Mrs. Melrose's mother, Your Honor."

"Well, I'm very sorry to hear about your mother's recent stroke, Mrs. Melrose, but I'm not sure I can do much for you all without a written statement from your mother's doctor."

"I'm sorry, Your Honor." Julia suddenly felt herself blurting out at the obvious annoyance of their attorney. "I didn't know I was supposed to bring one."

"So, your son has no intention of showing up for his hearing?"

Scott then spoke up this time, "I'm Bobby's father, Your Honor, and no, he won't be here. His grandmother is not doing well, and the only thing that seems to give her any peace is her grandson, our son, Bobby."

"Well, this looks to be a first-time drug possession with intent to sell. This is serious. I'm not sure why you all would show up here without your son, but he is a big boy. He needs to take responsibility for his actions, and I'm sure I'm not telling you anything that you don't already know.

"Yes, sir," Scott said as he put his head down for a moment, sighing, and then looked back up toward the judge.

"Your honor, the stroke was unexpected. No one could have known…" the attorney said, trying to salvage the situation.

"I know this, counselor. I'm an educated man, after all. But the law is the law. He was summoned to be here, and he's not. I'm not sure why he sent you two or why your lawyer would not stress the magnitude of him physically being present with everything that he is being charged with. That I leave on your shoulders," the judge said, looking at their attorney. "I understand that there may be reasons that I don't understand, and I am truly sorry for your mother, Mrs. Melrose, but I can't extend the hearing. A warrant will be issued for your son's arrest, and if found, he will come before me again, and we will relook at the case. But you obviously knew this was his last chance to regain any type of credibility that he was indeed sorry for his serious hurtful actions against an unsuspecting community. My judgment stands. Bailiff?" the judge signaled for the bailiff to show the family out of the courtroom.

Just as the words left his lips, the back doors to the courtroom swung open, and a young man with disheveled hair, dressed in jeans and a sweatshirt, emerged from the opening.

"Wait!" the young man said, trying to lay his tousled hair down.

"Who is that? Bailiff, remove that man!" the judge screamed out.

"Wait!" Julia said, looking at the judge. "That's our son. That's Bobby."

"What?" the judge said, irritated, looking down at the three people before him and into Julia's heartbroken eyes. "Come forward, son," the judge shouted at the young man. But Bobby stood in place with a blank stare. "I said get down here, now!" the judge screamed out.

The forceful tone of the judge seemed to jerk Bobby into a steady path forward as he made his way through the swinging gate that separated the judge from the people in the courtroom. He walked up and stood beside Julia, still not able to look her in the eye.

"Well, so you made it," the judge said.

"Yes, sir. I apologize for being late."

"Yes, your mother and father were just telling me how sick your grandmother is. I'm so happy you were able to tear yourself away. This might have gone really south for you if you hadn't. I should throw the book at you for arriving late in my courtroom. The only reason I'm not is that I think your parents have been through quite enough because of you. Your grandmother being sick was probably the last straw. I would imagine that you have them hanging on by a very thin thread right now, young man. You have no idea what you have put them through. Most kids don't."

Bobby looked up at the judge, hearing every word, and said to him, "Yes, sir. You're correct. I have put my parents through so very much." He stopped and looked at both of them. "And I am so, so, very sorry."

Julia immediately began to tear up as the judge sat and watched them all as if he was trying to sense what kind of a family was standing before him.

"Well, I will choose to ignore your tardiness to my courtroom because I believe your parents have probably been through enough, and with your grandmother being in the hospital and all," the judge said and looked directly at Bobby. "I am sure your poor mother here has been through enough. My judgment is for you to enter rehabilitation. But I promise you," he said, and the judge shuffled some papers around. "If I see you in front of me again, and I will make sure that it is me that you come before, it will not go as easy for you. You will do time. Do I have your attention, Mr. Melrose?"

"Yes, sir. You do," Bobby said, standing at attention and looking directly back at him.

"Okay, good luck to you all. See the bailiff. Next case," the judge said as he pulled another file from his stack.

The group headed out a side door. Their attorney took the lead, moving them toward a hallway outside the courtroom where they would wait to get the judge's orders. The attorney left to talk to someone behind a sliding glass window.

"Well, glad you decided to make it," Scott said awkwardly.

Bobby took a deep breath, and his parents were able to get a good look at him for the first time in a long time. He was thin and pale as if he hadn't eaten in days. Their once tall and broad son looked as if he had shrunk and shriveled up into a person that they would not have recognized. The dark circles under his eyes cried out from the lack of sleep. He had dirt under his nails, and his hair was disheveled and sticking out in all directions.

"I'm so sorry for everything that I put you all through. I didn't come to terms with my addiction until I heard about Grandma."

"What do you mean?" Julia asked.

"Part of me wanted to take off and go to the hospital right away, and the other part told me that I would die if I didn't use again. Part of me said that the meth was all that I needed to live. And that's when I knew. I knew I was an addict. Oh, my gosh, how bad is she?" Bobby said, worried about someone else for the first time in a long time. "I didn't mean to take those things. I just had to have it. I still need it. I have to get help. Can you get me help?"

Julia took Bobby in her arms as tears began to roll down her cheeks. "We will. We will get you the help you need. All you needed to do was ask."

"I know. I'm so sorry. I didn't mean to hurt her."

"I know…," Julia said. "I know."

"I'm sorry I was late," Bobby apologized.

"No, it's fine. The important thing is you made it," Scott said.

"There was something I had to do before I got here. I wasn't sure if there would be time afterward." Bobby reached down and took a gold ring out of his pocket. "I had to get it back. I'm so, so sorry," Bobby said, hugging Julia.

Scott stood looking at the two of them. Not sure if he should join in. Not sure if Bobby would allow it. So, he just watched the two of them. Envious of the relationship that Julia had built with the children, but also so thankful for it.

The attorney returned to the group. "I have been instructed to admit him to the Westchester Rehabilitation Center. I'm sorry, but we have to go now," the attorney said.

"I can't," Bobby said.

"What?" Julia asked. "But you just said."

"I have to see Grandma. I have to tell her. I can't go until I do," Bobby insisted.

The attorney looked at all of them. "I have two hours to get him there. The hospital is on the way. Let's go."

The four of them hurried out of the large doors and down the grand steps of the courthouse. They made their way to the hospital, where Julia's mother lay unresponsive. They made their way with what little hope they had. The ring and Bobby. But would this be enough to restore Carmen's faith in a world she was trying so desperately to forget?

CHAPTER TWENTY-THREE

When they arrived at the hospital, Bobby wondered if he could truly face his grandmother again after all he had done. He listened as his mother retold the story of the past couple of days. The days when he was lost to them. He felt the weight of guilt slowly consuming him as Julia explained how his grandmother had given up on life. She explained how no one could seem to reach her. Not even Lauren. And as he heard those words, he knew. He knew he had been the one that started his grandmother's downward spiral. The drugs, the stealing, the constant lies to those who would have given him anything, and he looked away from the hospital, not sure he could go in.

"She's waiting for you," Julia muttered.

"But what will I say? How can I make this better?"

"You'll find the words. I have confidence in you," Julia said, brushing Bobby's unruly hair from his eyes.

"Okay, I know…I know this is something I have to do."

They made their way in through the automatic doors and headed up the escalator to an elevator that stopped on the fifth floor.

Lauren was sitting in the recliner studying when the group made their way into the hospital room.

Bobby glanced at Lauren, who sat up in her chair, surprised to see him as she whispered, "You're back?" She then waved her hand in front of her face as his stench followed him through the door. "What's that smell?" she said before she realized that the smell was originating from him.

Bobby gave her a slight nod and made his way over the gray tile while trying to adjust his sweatshirt as he smoothed back his hair before he faced the woman who had helped raise him. The woman who had raised his mother.

Carmen loved both Lauren and Bobby very much and always doted on them. She gave Bobby the hardest time due to his inability to grow up, but he always knew that she loved him. He knew she would have done anything for any one of them. And she had.

Bobby came up beside Carmen's bed as she gazed out the window of her room. She often dropped into a type of trance, watching the birds fly close to the building, sometimes landing on her windowsill, chirping as if the hours on the clock had somehow come alive. As if every bird condemned to the clock somehow grew wings and sailed out of the confines of this small room, away…far away from the room's sadness.

Bobby instantly sensed his grandmother's sorrow. Her disappointment. He immediately knew why she saw no point in going forward with a life where half of her body was no longer a part of her anymore and where her grandson chose a life of drugs over those that loved him.

He stood next to her bed and took her hand in his, squeezing it tight.

And for some reason, Carmen turned her head toward the image beside her as if she knew who would be standing there before she saw him.

"Hello, Grandma," he said, smiling. "Now, before you say anything, I want you to know that you are the reason I've come back. I heard your voice calling to me, even when I was doing all that stupid crap. I heard you. I heard you calling me home." Bobby then reached into his pocket and brought out the gold ring that was engraved on the inside and placed it in his grandmother's right hand, shutting her fingers tight around it. "I'm so sorry, Grandma. I'm so sorry that I hurt you. Please forgive me. If I could take it all back, I would. I wouldn't blame you for hating me…"

To everyone's amazement, Carmen opened her right hand, maneuvering her arm slowly so she could drop the ring onto the bed, and then she slowly lifted her hand up to Bobby's face and rubbed the side of it with the backside of her hand, dropping the stubborn hand to the bed as she mumbled, "Bbbb oy, do…do you…need…a…a ba…th."

The whole room let out a roar of laughter and tears as Bobby leaned over the railing taking his grandmother into his arms. "I know. I know I do, Grandma."

Carmen, making a face due to the smell, used her good hand to move Bobby away from her. "O…kay…o…kay," she said, and she picked up the ring with her good hand. "I…it's…a…b…about t…t…time," she stuttered.

And these were her first words. Somehow the laughter that filled this small hospital room floated out of the doorway and into the corridor, where the nurses and doctors heard it and were drawn into the room of the woman who had decided not to live. They all stood there looking in and wondering what had brought this room back to life.

Another face poked his head through the door, and Julia looked over at him. It was the pastor she had met in the courtyard. He smiled at her, and Julia returned the gesture with a slight grin. The pastor then pointed at her and winked, and slowly turned away, making his way down the long corridor.

Carmen looked around at all of them, annoyed that she could not get up, and announced to the room. "I…I'm hu…hun…gry."

"Oh, Mom!" Julia said, with tears in her eyes, walking to the other side of the bed, hugging her.

Carmen's nurse then moved closer into the room and stood next to Julia, giving her a one-armed hug. "We can start her on a liquid diet. I will get a hold of the doctor."

"Nooo…l…liq…qu…id," Carmen said, hitting the sheets of her bed, as the group started to roar with laughter.

Bobby then kissed his grandmother's hand and whispered in her ear. Carmen leaned forward to see a man in a suit standing behind him. "I've got to go for now, Grandma. I've got to go get myself better, but I'll be back. I promise."

Carmen looked at the man behind him, and she waved him off. She tried to speak but couldn't get the words quite out, "B…bbb."

"I'll be back before you know it," Bobby said. "And I expect you to be at home."

Carmen looked up at her grandson and mouthed, "D…on't m…m…ake me c…come…afer…y…you."

"I won't, Grandma. You just get better. And eat, eat," Bobby said as he took one more look at her and turned to exit the room.

Julia followed them out into the hallway. They could hear Carmen getting upset about having no food in front of her, which made Julia and the others smile.

The nurse walked up to Julia and said, "It should be right up. We are going to take it slow to see what her body will allow."

"Thank you so much," Julia said, still overwhelmed by everything that had just transpired.

"But it's a good sign that she wants to eat," the nurse said, smiling at the family and squeezing Julia's arm.

"Yes, yes, it is," Julia answered her, wiping away a tear that had made its way down her cheek.

Julia and Scott walked Bobby and their attorney down to the hospital entrance. As they walked, Julia reflected on all that had happened in such a short amount of time. It appeared to her that the winds had finally changed. It seemed that she had her family back. Saying goodbye to her son again was not going to be easy, but she knew that it was the only way to make sure that he got the help that he so desperately needed.

Scott stood looking at Bobby, not knowing what to say when Bobby spoke up.

"It'll be okay. I'm done with this crap. It won't be easy, but I refuse to let it control my life anymore. I've got to get help, though. Man, this crap, the drugs, still keep trying to draw me in. Every moment gets harder and harder. But I promise you, both of you," and he looked at his parents, "I won't let this crap take me down again."

At that moment, Julia noticed Bobby's hand starting to twitch, and he had sweat beading across his forehead. Bobby quickly used the bottom of his sleeve to wipe away the moisture. Bobby's head then started to jerk back and forth toward the door, almost as if he were contemplating whether or not he wanted to go through it.

Julia knew she had to let him go. Julia hugged Bobby and told him, "It'll be okay. We are so proud of you. We'll be waiting for you to come home."

Bobby pulled away from her. "Thanks, Mom." He tried to discreetly hold onto his rebellious arm, summoning it to lay still. "I love you."

"I love you too, sweetie."

Bobby then turned toward Scott, "I'm…I'm sorry, Dad. Thank you for not giving up on me."

Scott felt the tears start to roll down his cheeks. "And I'm sorry, son, for not being the father you needed me to be. I would have never given up on you. You're…you're my son, and you will always be."

The three of them embraced. Bobby looked up at them both and suddenly pulled away, leaving out the revolving door with his attorney as they made their way to the parking garage and eventually out of his parent's sight.

Scott and Julia stood watching them until they could no longer see the shadows dragging behind them.

At that moment, Scott turned to Julia and looked her in the eye, and said, "I'm so sorry for everything I've ever done to you. Can you please forgive me?"

Julia looked back toward Scott as if she suddenly recognized him again. In that rare moment, she saw the man she had known when she was young, the man who truly had once loved her, and she said, "I already have."

Scott took two steps toward her as Julia reactively stepped back.

"You've done such a great job with the kids. They are good kids. I just wanted you to know that," Scott said.

Julia smiled. "Thank you."

"And I know you'll never believe me, but…"

Julia then narrowed her eyebrows.

"I've never stopped loving you…"

CHAPTER TWENTY-FOUR

It would be two months before Julia's mother would return home. She was sent to the rehabilitation facility for intensive physical therapy. When the day came for her to leave, the staff was sorry to see her go. Carmen always seemed to have the whole facility rolling in laughter. She took on each new challenge with the determination of a woman half her age. She told every last one of the staff that she would be walking out of those hospital doors, so they didn't need to bother bringing up the wheelchair because she would have no use for it.

Her walking increased steadily, and before no time, she was eating on her own, but her speech was slow to return. Frustrated, the staff and residents would often see her hitting the arm of her wheelchair as she stumbled on words that she had said all of her life. Her right arm also fought her for control as she continually struggled to lift anything with it.

Carmen was eventually released as an outpatient. She said her goodbyes to the staff. There were lots of hugs and tears. Julia watched as her mother visited each room that day as the patients waved goodbye, and the staff rejoiced in her recovery.

During this time—with everything that was happening around her—Julia found little time to think about the dreams she had put on hold. Her hopes and dreams were again placed on a shelf—where she often kept them—as she put the needs of those she loved before herself.

Those dreams again sat there, waiting for her to pick them up again, knowing that she was slowly running out of time.

Julia was either at rehab, working at the department store, or checking in on Bobby's status. It had been nearly two months since she had seen her son. She was only able to speak with him over the phone once a week. She used any free time that she had to research how to help her son through his recovery once he was able to return home.

On one of their many calls, Bobby informed Julia that he had gotten through the detox stage and was hoping to be released as an outpatient soon. Julia thought he sounded more and more like his old self. Yet, she did not let her hopes get too high. As she researched more and more about this disease, she discovered that the chance of him relapsing was pretty high.

She met with Scott a couple of times for lunch to try and form a plan for Bobby once he returned home. They had never discussed the words Scott had spoken to her the day that Bobby entered treatment, and Julia had no need to bring it up. She secretly hoped that they could somehow remain friends after everything they had been through.

The rehabilitation center where Bobby was receiving treatment recommended that he start attending Narcotics Anonymous or NA meetings as soon as he was released. She and Scott had both kept in contact with his doctor in regard to what they would be looking at during his never-ending recovery. The doctor stressed, and so did Scott, that once an addict, always an addict. It never went away like the flu or pneumonia. It wasn't suddenly cured like cancer. Drug addiction was something always there in the shadows, calling out to him. It was going to be a lifelong fight, and the winners were the ones that realized the never-ending battle that they faced.

Whenever Julia was allowed a moment to herself, her mind tended to drift off to a comforting smile that she tried to keep hidden down deep, away from those who knew her. The smile was hidden so deep that even she resisted acknowledging her true feelings.

In the past, it had always been Ritchie's beautiful smile, but these days she couldn't shake the warm smile and touch that she had experienced with Andy. He had even made his way into her dreams most nights. Each dream more vivid than the one before. They were usually at the dance club. Forever young and full of life, Andy would come to her, his hand extended, always with the same statement, "I would like to dance with you."

Ritchie was always in the background, watching as if he were somehow protecting her. She would take Andy's hand, and then Ritchie would head toward one of the exits, turning to stop and smile at Julia before he went through the door. Julia was unsure what all this meant, but it had been weeks since she had visited the black folder hidden deep in her drawer.

Julia found herself stealing secret moments by locking herself in her bedroom. She would take out her laptop and begin pouncing on the keys, trying to keep up with all that was pouring out of her. All the tragic events around her became her stories. Lauren's pregnancy, Bobby's drug addiction, Brad's affection for Lauren, her mother's illness, and her unexpected fascination with Andy all came spilling out onto the page.

Several times a day, Julia found herself imagining what Andy was doing at that exact moment. She wondered if he ever thought about her at all. She often thought about what would have happened had she not chased him away. This new type of haunting was unfamiliar to her. This dream was all too real. This dream was one that she felt she could reach out and touch. One that she was afraid would bring her more devastation than the short time she had with Ritchie. After all, the past could no longer hurt her, but this reality was all too tangible. This reality could rupture her broken heart all over again, leaving her to bleed to death.

These days, work was a sanctuary for Julia. There, she didn't have to think about anything but what was right before her. Lisa was a godsent.

She was there for Julia on her good days as well as her bad. She had a way of making Julia forget about all of her troubles. Well, at least most of the time.

"So, how are things?" Lisa asked Julia daily the moment that she set eyes on her.

"They're good. Mom is home and doing fairly well. I leave her with her meals made, and she sits in front of the television and eats and eats. I don't know what is in the medicine that they prescribed for her, but she is eating like a horse. It's like she is playing catch up."

"Oh, my auntie did that. She had a stroke and was eating my cousin out of house and home. We didn't get it. And the woman never put on an ounce. Go figure," Lisa chuckled. "My cousin said it got so bad that her mother would end up ordering pizza before dinner and then would sit down for a full meal with them. What the heck was up with that?"

"Wow. My mom is probably headed in that direction, but I'm actually just glad to see her eating. So, I don't say a word."

"I get you, girl," Lisa chimed in as she laid her arms across the glass perfume case, leaning into the conversation. "As long as they are healthy and getting better, don't rock the boat. I'm praying for you all."

"Oh, thanks, Lisa."

"So, I've been meaning to ask you, did you ever get a hold of that good-looking guy you were kind of hot and heavy with before all this craziness happened? I haven't seen him around, and you haven't mentioned him lately."

At the mention of Andy, Julia began to sort through some of the perfume sets on the glass shelves, straightening the boxes as if she were trying to avoid the question. "Oh, I don't know. You know, he seemed perfect, but you never know. I told you that we knew each other when we were young, didn't I?"

"What? No, you didn't. Tell me more," Lisa exclaimed, shooting up to a stance and looking around to make sure there were no customers in her area and that Dan, her supervisor, was not anywhere to be found. "I got time."

"Well, you know I told you Ritchie and I would hang out at that dance club all the time."

"Yeah, yeah, you told me. Go on…"

"Well, turns out Andy was there."

"Where?" Lisa asked, her eyes widening.

"At the club. He had even asked me to dance."

"You're kidding me."

"No. I didn't remember him at first, but now, it's so weird."

"What…what's so weird?"

"I see him so vividly now in my dreams. It's like he's right there every time. He's there watching me dance with Ritchie, and it's like he doesn't give up."

"Oh, girl. That's a sign," Lisa gasped, folding her arms across her chest.

"What? A sign of what?"

"A sign that you better give him a call."

"I don't know. I mean, Bobby is supposed to be getting out soon. Lauren is not far off from having the baby. I'm goin' to be a grandma."

"A hot grandma."

Julia rolled her eyes at Lisa. "Oh, you. I just don't have time for anything…you know, like that."

Lisa walked forward, pointing at Julia like she was her third-grade school teacher. "Have time for what? For you? Let me tell you something, my friend. You may have it in your head that you somehow don't deserve this guy. That time has somehow left you behind. I believe you have nothing but time for this guy. We have one run-through, my dear. One chance at this thing we call life. You better take advantage of it. If you don't, give me his number. I'll be giving mister wonderful a call."

Just then, Dan, Lisa's supervisor, came around the corner as Lisa quickly grabbed the shirt she had laid on the counter and walked across the floor to hang it back on the rack as if she were headed there the whole time. Lisa then nonchalantly walked back toward her register, smiling and complimenting Dan the whole way.

Julia smiled, putting Lisa's words on rewind over and over again in her head. Maybe she should give Andy a call. If she just wasn't so dang embarrassed about their last conversation. She had pretty much told him never to contact her again, even after all that he had done for her. How could she face him again? Anyway, he had probably moved on to another young girl, someone half his age, who had no idea what the '80s looked like. The only thing his current girlfriend probably knew about the '80s was that she was born in that decade.

Julia made her way home that evening and went into the house, predicting that she would find her mother right where she had left her—in the recliner. Wondering if her mother had tried to do too much during the day was always one of Julia's fears.

Lauren and Brad had called Julia earlier and were on their way over to Julia's house. Brad had offered to attend Lamaze classes with Lauren. They were planning on stopping by Julia's house that evening to pick up a blanket that Lauren had left at the house to take with them to their second Lamaze class.

Julia was growing more and more fond of Brad and how deeply he appeared to care for Lauren. In spite of the awkward way that they had met, this unusual group all seemed to be forming this strange little family.

How could someone not love Lauren? Julia thought. She was this great ball of sunshine, so full of life. So ready to take on the world. Everything that Julia once was. Well, except for the whole single mother thing.

When Brad and Lauren arrived, Julia had just sat down to watch a television program with Carmen. She brought Carmen a warm cup of tea, and they were practicing Carmen's vocal exercises. Not that Carmen was a great patient. She often got weary of the exercises and would refuse to do them. Julia tried to be patient with her, but sometimes her mother took stubbornness to another level.

"Okay, Mom, say cheese for me. Ch…Ch…Cheese…"

"Nooo…"

"Mom, we are almost done. You have to do these vocal exercises if you want to improve your speech."

"I…I'm goo…d," Carmen responded.

"Oh, Mom, come on."

"I…al…ready…di…d"

"Oh really, when?"

"Whi…le," and she pointed to Julia, "you w…ork."

"All right. I don't have the strength to fight with you tonight."

Lauren and Brad arrived just in time to catch the last few minutes of Julia's debate with Carmen.

"Hi, Mom," Lauren said. She then turned her slightly expanding belly to greet her grandmother, who was sitting on the other recliner. "Grandma, how are you doing? Are you doing your exercises?"

"Ye…s…yes," Carmen said before Julia had time to answer.

Lauren then looked at Julia.

"Yeah, she said she practiced all day before I got here," Julia responded, too tired to argue anymore.

"Grandma?" Lauren said, looking directly at her.

"W…hat? I…I…did," Carmen added.

"Okay, well, I hope so," Lauren said sternly.

"Hello, Brad," Julia added, not wanting him to feel ignored. "Are you two off to the hospital?"

"Yeah, we figured we would get there early so that we could sit up front. Last time we got there right on time, and I got shoved into a corner," Brad advised.

"Yeah, poor Brad here was practically pinned against the wall, so we don't want to repeat that scenario," Lauren chuckled.

"Well, how are you feeling, sweetie?" Julia asked.

"You know, so far so good. My feet have been a little swollen, but nothing terrible. We found out the sex…" And Lauren looked at Brad. "I mean, I found out," Lauren restated as if she realized she was putting Brad in the equation with the baby.

Julia watched as Brad reactively took Lauren's hand and looked her straight in the eye. "No, we found out."

Lauren then turned toward Julia, who was trying not to show any emotion, fighting back tears as she watched Brad take Lauren's hand into his. Lauren and Julia gave each other a glance that only they two could share in the realization of what this meant to Lauren.

Lauren then beamed, "It's a boy!"

Julia jumped up from her recliner and leaped over to where Lauren and Brad were standing, taking Lauren into her arms. "Oh, I'm so happy for you." And she looked over at Brad and drew him into the group hug. "Happy for both of you."

"H…ot Dig…it..y," Carmen attempted to yell out as she slapped her leg. "A…l…little…b…boy!"

"That's right, Grandma," Lauren said.

"He…'ll be a han…ful." Carmen chuckled.

"Yep," Lauren said. "Somehow, I always knew it would be a boy."

For several minutes, the group talked about what lay ahead for Lauren and the delivery of Julia's grandson, and Lauren then excused herself for another bathroom trip.

"Sorry, got to go again."

"I get it," Julia said. "I was the same way with both you and your brother."

After Lauren left, Brad moved close to Julia and asked her a question she wasn't expecting. "So, what happened between you and Mr. Wonderful?"

"Who?" Julia asked, not realizing who he was talking about at first.

"I think his name was Andy."

"Oh, yeah, Andy."

"Yes, that's him. So, what happened?"

"I just didn't have time. You know, with Mom and Bobby and everything."

"Oh…I understand. So, what's stopping you now?" Brad grinned.

Julia was a little set back by Brad's comment as she stared back at him. "You know? I'm not sure."

"Well, think about it. You don't run into a man that looks at a woman the way he looked at you very often. Just sayin'. From a friend to a friend." Brad smiled.

Julia smiled at Brad. "I will. And, let me tell you, Lauren is so happy…"

Brad put up his hand before she had time to finish. "I feel truly blessed to be involved with your daughter. I know it's crazy. I know it's a little weird, but it's like, I don't know, like it was always meant to be. Like me meeting you that night was a means to an end. It's a little unnerving. My fear is she is going to get tired of me hanging around."

Julia said, "I don't see that happening."

"Hey, we can only take it day by day. But you, my friend, are letting go of something that might be really great. Now…what are you going to do about it?"

Julia grinned, not sure how to respond. "I'll give it some thought."

"You do that," Brad said, as Lauren came into the room unaware of what had been said, curiously looking at both of them.

"What?" Lauren asked.

"Nothing…nothing, dear," Brad said.

"Y…eah…what…talk…bout," Carmen said, feeling like she was being ignored.

"It was nothing, Mom," Julia said, turning to see her mother reaching for the remote control. "Well, you two better get going. I don't want Brad here stuck in a corner. He's way too large to be squeezing back there." Julia urged them along.

"Okay, Mom. Are you okay?" Lauren asked.

"I'm perfect, sweetie." And she winked at Brad. "Well, mostly."

"Okay, well, we have to go before we're late. I love you," Lauren said. "Bye, Grandma!"

"Bye...b...ye," Carmen stuttered.

Later that evening, while Julia was putting Carmen to bed, the voices of the day kept dancing around in her head, "Andy, Andy, Andy." But what everyone didn't understand was the toll Julia felt it would take on her to let herself fall for someone again. Or maybe she was just afraid of the possibilities. It's understandable. Ritchie, Scott, Andy... they all ended badly. Maybe love was just not in the cards for her. And what about all she had said to Andy the last time she saw him? She was horrible. Even after all he had done for her. How could she ever face him again? How could he ever forgive her?

One thing Julia was sure of was the realization that she wasn't going to let life just happen to her anymore. She had to take control. She had to choose her own destiny this time around. She came to the conclusion that she needed to find herself before she could ever think about letting someone get close to her again. Whether it be Andy or anyone else. Besides, she was running out of time to go after her dreams, and Julia knew better than most that time, after all, was obligated to no one.

CHAPTER TWENTY-FIVE

The day finally came. The day they at one time thought would never become a reality. Bobby walked out of the rehabilitation center tired but with a joyous smile on his face. He rubbed his unshaven face instinctively with his fingers every few minutes as if it were a nervous habit he had picked up. He instantly grabbed both of his parents and squeezed them with all his might, his breath traveling down between them. Bobby then quickly kissed Julia on the cheek and threw his head back, taking in a deep breath of air.

"Well, looks like this is it. I made it."

Scott and Julia looked at each other, not sure how to respond. Scott then said, "Yes, and we are so very proud of you."

Julia followed Scott's sentiment, "Yes, Bobby. We are very proud of you. But you know, you have a long road ahead of you."

"I know. I know, Mom," Bobby said, still scanning his surroundings. "And isn't it a beautiful day to get started? Shall we?" Bobby said, bowing and pointing toward their vehicle as all three of them slowly moved toward the car, arm in arm.

Scott had a job waiting for Bobby as soon as he was released. It was a job working in the warehouse of one of the larger furniture stores in town. Scott sold furniture items to the store for one of his clients and was good friends with the furniture store owner.

Bobby, who was a fast learner, and had a gift for gab, was soon a favorite with most of the staff.

Bobby appeared to have a new outlook on life. He was determined not to relive the decisions that started him on the downward spiral toward the world of drugs. As time went on, the nightmare was slowly fading from everyone's memory, and by all outward appearances, Bobby was developing a love for life again.

He was slowly starting to find himself once more.

"I'm moving out," Bobby said to Julia one Saturday morning while she was getting ready for work.

"Do you think that's wise? You have only been out a couple of weeks," she said, trying to find the right words to say to Bobby without revealing how terrified his last comments made her feel.

"I know, Mom. I know I've only been out of treatment a short time, but I'm attending daily NA meetings like my therapist recommended, and I think I'm going to be okay. No…let me put that another way. I've decided I'm going to beat this."

Julia looked at her son, who—for some reason—somehow seemed like less of a boy and more of a man.

"I can do this, Mom. I have to."

"I know you can. I've always known that, but it's just so soon."

"I need this. I need you to believe in me. I can do this on my own. I won't let you down again."

Julia then took his arm. "I'm your biggest fan. You know that. I just worry. Mothers worry," Julia said, turning to look Bobby in the eye. "Okay, so…then…where will you look for a place?"

"There are apartments near the furniture store that look promising. If I get one close enough to work, I could even walk. Who knows, I might even start jogging before work at the fitness center."

"Jogging? You?"

"Yep, jogging."

"That sounds wonderful," Julia said, trying to sound as if she expected him to have come so far, so soon, when in reality, she had her doubts.

"I can do this, Mom."

"I know, I know you can. It's just…"

"I know. I failed you all before, but I'll never let that happen again. Look…" Bobby said as he reached behind him and pulled out his wallet. He opened it and pulled out two pictures. "Lauren gave these to me."

Julia looked at her son with her eyes narrowed as she looked down at the pictures.

"It's for me to always remember."

"What do you mean?" Julia asked, staring down at the pictures in her hands, noticing that they were both pictures of Carmen.

"One is before I came back. See…" Bobby said, pointing at the picture in her right hand. "She had given up on life. I had taken that from her."

"No," Julia replied.

"Yes, I did, Mom. I can own up to it. But look at this one." And he pointed to the other picture. "This was when I came back. When I returned Grandpa's ring to her. Look…it is a completely different woman. I know that I also did this," Bobby explained.

"Yes, you did. These are good reminders."

"Exactly. I will never hurt you all again. It's a promise I made to myself."

As Bobby walked away, he placed the pictures back in his wallet, and Julia knew. She knew he was being truthful with her. She saw it in his eyes. He had lived through the darkness and had come out somewhat scathed but with possibly a new outlook on life. One he might not have had had he not lived through this ordeal. In a way, he had possibly grown up through this experience. He now knew what he wanted out of life. And what he didn't. At that moment, in a small way, Julia felt she somehow envied him.

After Bobby moved out and Carmen started to get around better, Julia found herself with time on her hands. She would walk past the remote control to the television and stop and stare at it. She would look up at the old bird clock that would begin to chime the hour and knew that her favorite television show, *One Moment in Time*, was about to begin. She would sometimes pick up the remote and play with the buttons, looking at the television screen, and then would toss the remote back into the empty recliner.

In the evening, she would head off to her room, where she would be found most days clicking away on the keys of her laptop. It had become a kind of spiritual journey with her most nights. The screen would light up, and she would sit there staring at the blank page for only a moment before the words would start to pour out, leaving her fingers struggling to keep up with all the stories that were flooding out of her. She would get so lost in the written word that Carmen would sometimes have to come and tell her it was time to eat.

One evening, Carmen stood at Julia's door shaking her head in disbelief, slowly trying to put together the words that fought against their release. "W…wha…t are y…ou do…ing in there?"

"Oh, Mom, sorry, I lost track of time," Julia would answer.

"Wh…at are y…ou do…ing on tha…t stu…pid th…ing?"

"I'm just jotting down some notes, you know, from the day. Recording stories before I forget them."

"W…rit…ing again?"

"Yeah, Mom, I'm writing again," Julia answered.

Carmen stood there in shock and smiled. "T…hat's good. A…bout t…time."

"I know, Mom. It is about time."

Later that night, Julia started surfing the internet and made her way back to the university website that she had visited what seemed like ages ago. She started searching through the screens and suddenly found herself on the admissions page again. After she stared at the page for about twenty minutes, skimming through all of the requirements, she brought up her application for admission and found that it had not expired.

She decided to begin again. The dream that she thought she had said goodbye to, oh, so many years ago, was still living deep inside of her, longing for its release, and this time Julia was not going to let anything or anyone get in her way.

Once her family and friends found out what she was doing, they encouraged her. The excitement she felt to be going back to school was overwhelming. It was like being reborn again, with all the uncertainties and limitations behind her.

The department store was willing to work around her school schedule, which enabled Julia to take classes that were offered during the day.

On her first day of school, she got up early and nervously packed her backpack. Random thoughts went through her head of the failure that could strike at any moment, but she pushed those aside, repeating a phrase that went through her head randomly whenever she had any doubts about what she was doing. The soft voice inside her head told her, *If not now, then when?* And the voice in her head would repeat this phrase over and over again until she didn't even notice she was doing it anymore.

It was fall. The landscape of the city campus was in full bloom and swaying in the breeze that swam in from the coast. Julia pulled into the university parking lot and watched as the young students swarmed the many sidewalks on their way to their futures. The mixture of concrete and landscape was natural to the university, which was located in the heart of San Diego. New modern architecture gave way to desert-like landscaping of native plants. This landscape fought for life against the desert conditions, which left emulating the natural ecosystem the only obvious choice.

Julia looked down at what she was wearing. She had worn her trendy black slacks and one of her favorite flowy white blouses so that she could head to work directly after class. It was one of her more casual outfits, which she hoped would allow her to blend in with the younger students.

She felt a newfound confidence bubbling up inside of her. A belief in herself. A knowing that she belonged here. That the limits had somehow been lifted. That these were indeed her people, the people searching for more. The people who were determined to see their dreams come true. And she was one of them and walked among them, once again.

She could hardly breathe with all the promise that her next few steps brought her. She held her breath as she opened her car door and took her first steps out into the sun of this new day.

She walked almost as if she were being lifted from the pavement, joyously aware of her surroundings. She placed her backpack on her back and gazed into that marvelous sun, closing her eyes for just a moment to feel the warmth and the light descend upon her face.

Afraid that she would be late, her feet picked up a quick rhythm as she struggled to breathe in and out with every new step. She finally made her way to the doors of Chamberlain Hall. This was where the English Department was located and where most of her classes would be held.

The magnificent gray stone glowed in the sunlight, and the sun's rays reflected off the glass of the large wood-framed doors. She passed through the doors, stepped onto the marble floor, and made her way to the stairs trying to keep pace with the young students around her.

Julia was so preoccupied with her surroundings that she didn't take notice of a large gentleman headed straight toward her. She was just about to ascend the staircase when she felt a hand grip her shoulder.

"Hey, don't I know you from somewhere?" the deep voice blurted out.

Julia looked up to see Brad standing over her, smiling.

Happy to see a familiar face, she stepped out of the flow of traffic, and they made their way over toward the wall where it was safe to stand without getting swarmed upon.

"I know. I'm finally here. Part of me feels so out of place."

"What? You will do great. Lauren told me you were starting today, but I didn't think I would run into you."

"So, are you on your way to class?" Julia asked, looking around at the others, hoping she didn't seem too much like a nervous mom.

"Yeah, I have algebra right now."

"Oh, thank goodness. I thought you were going to say poetry."

"Poetry? Is that what you are taking?"

Julia looked at him with her eyes narrowed. "And what's wrong with poetry," she asked.

"Nothing, nothing, just not my cup of tea."

"Well, I'm going to find out if it's mine."

"You'll do great," Brad affirmed.

"I hope so," Julia said, more aware of how out of place she was.

"You're going to knock 'em dead."

"Well, we'll see," Julia said nervously. "But, thanks."

As they waved goodbye, Julia climbed the stairs until she reached the third floor. She made her way down the large corridor as students revolved around her, bouncing into each other like a pinball machine as they made their way to their final destinations.

Julia stopped and looked up at the doorway, which read room 312.

When she entered the room, she was met by a distinguished-looking woman dressed in a soft peach blouse and white scarf who sat behind a large desk. Her hair was lifted behind her head in a twisted bun, and she wore glasses that sat on the edge of her nose. She had her chair turned sideways, facing the door so she could welcome everyone who entered the classroom.

The woman took notice of Julia and asked her if she was there for the beginning poetry class.

Julia responded with a resounding, "Yes, I am."

"Well, welcome, and take any seat."

Julia took one of the desks in the front row because she had read somewhere that the closer you sit to the front of the classroom, the higher your grade would be. It was supposedly a proven fact that the students who sat in the front of the classroom started with A's, the middle desks made B's, and so on and so on. So, she promised herself, no matter how hard it was, that she would sit in the front row in all of her classes.

She placed her backpack and purse on the floor and took a seat just left of the center aisle. Julia tried to slow her heart rate down by telling herself to breathe in and out but had limited success. Her heart continued to pound away, ticking in rhythm with the sound of the second hand, which continued to make its way around the white-faced clock that sat over the professor's desk. After the last student had made their way into the classroom, the professor walked over to the door and checked her watch, closing the door behind her.

The professor made her way to the front of the desk and lifted her hips, sitting on the surface of the desk with her feet dangling in front. "So, you all have an interest in poetry." The professor went on. "Well, let me tell you, I share your interest. I'm a poet myself. I have been since a very early age, even before I knew that it was poetry that I was writing," the professor enunciated, to a stream of giggles from the class.

The professor went on to define her past and her recent publications. She discussed the various kinds of poetry that they would be concentrating on that semester, and she left them with a writing assignment, which Julia immediately got started on before they were all dismissed.

Julia was also enrolled in fiction writing that semester. She found this class to be her favorite of the two. Her professor was a published author and would tell his students about all the difficulties they would face regarding their chosen career path, but he also applauded them for being brave enough to follow their dreams. He was a gentle man that took an interest in Julia's writing from the start. Being one of the more mature adults in the room, Julia came in with a whole different perspective of the world. One that the other students had no idea existed yet.

Throughout the semester, Julia found her stories being read as examples to her classmates. Being separated by decades, the young writers around her sometimes struggled to understand the stories of a life that they had not yet lived.

Julia's fiction writing professor encouraged her to join the local writer's group on campus. Julia reluctantly agreed, thinking that she would be the oldest person in the group but was pleasantly surprised to find that there were several others in the group that were her age or older. Several older graduates often returned to the group, looking for the same validity and feedback every writer in the group so desperately sought.

Day after day, throughout the semester, Julia made her way to school and to work. She found herself running to her next class with the excitement of a child on Christmas morning. Such promise, such hope lay behind those doors she entered every day. She valued her experienced professors and the authors they brought in to speak to them.

She found herself writing with every free moment. Nothing was off-limits when it came to her stories. Julia's life—like most people—had given her a multitude of joys and trials, and they all came exploding out of her whenever she sat behind the keys of her laptop.

Julia learned more than she had ever dreamed possible in those precious few months and was surprised to realize that her first semester was behind her and she had received an "A" in both of her courses. Her eyes had been opened, and Julia found herself in a pool of joy. The joy that had been hiding behind those fear-filled gates of her past.

But there were still moments when no one else was around. In the silence, she felt something tugging at her. She knew something was missing. Memories gripped her in the middle of the night. Longings that she had tried to push aside the day that Ritchie died somehow resurfaced. Those feelings that she pretended no longer existed returned to her like a lightning bolt to her heart. Somehow, living out her dream, she realized that she was still very much alone.

CHAPTER TWENTY-SIX

Fall faded into winter, and Julia was elated to have her first semester behind her. She looked forward to the spring semester and had already registered for her classes. Each course she was taking seemed so beautifully phrased: world literature, women's literature, advanced creative writing, astronomy. They all seemed to sing a sweet song to her soul. She felt she was floating, soaring into her destiny. Julia calculated that if she pushed herself and included summer classes, she would graduate in two years if they accepted all of her initial courses from community college.

These were her thoughts as she walked toward the parking lot after her last fall final for the year. She had just loaded her backpack into the backseat when her phone lit up. She looked down to see Brad's name flash across the screen.

"It's time!" he said, bursting with excitement.

"Time?" Julia answered. "Oh, it's time. The baby is coming?"

Brad laughed into the phone. "Yes, Grandma. It's time. Get up here."

Julia raced through the city streets as stoplights and stop signs blurred in her rearview mirror. She frantically called into work, stumbling through the words on why she wouldn't be coming in. When she reached the hospital, she hurried to the front doors asking where the maternity ward was.

A hospital volunteer pulled out a map and guided Julia toward her destination. Julia found it difficult to maneuver through the many winding hallways and tried to follow the overhead signs that the volunteer had pointed out. She made her way up the escalators taking the elevators located on the north side of the hospital. She rushed in, hitting the fourth-floor button, afraid that she might be too late. She finally made it to the maternity ward nurse's station and was directed to the waiting room, where she found Carmen, Bobby, and Scott waiting for her.

Bobby had stopped to pick up his grandmother. Julia was so grateful because, in all the excitement, she had forgotten to even call her mother. "So, any news?" Julia asked.

Bobby walked over to her, "No, not yet. Brad's with her. He's going to let us know as soon as he finds out anything."

Scott made his way over to Julia, smiling from ear to ear. "Hello, Grandma!" he said, giving Julia an uncomfortable hug.

"Hi, Scott, or Grandpa," Julia replied, as she returned the awkward embrace.

"I'm so happy for her. And this guy, Brad, he seems to be a good guy. I think he really cares for her," Scott said as if he were taking credit for all of Julia's brilliant undercover work.

"I know. I love him too," Julia said, debating on whether or not to tell Scott how Lauren and Brad met. How Brad had been attracted to her first. But she decided now might not be the best time.

"Well, I take it we have you to thank for them meeting."

"Well, it's a long story, Scott."

"Well, we'll just have to get together so you can fill me in some time."

"Yep," Julia said, peering around Scott, not really focusing on what he was saying as she slipped around him and headed toward Carmen, who was sitting on the sofa behind them. "Mom, so glad you made it. I'm sorry I didn't call you, but I just found out."

"Oh…it…was…f…fine. Bobby…pic…picked me up."

"Wow, you are talking really well today, Mom. I'm so glad," Julia said as a nurse made her way into the waiting room.

"It's taking a little longer than predicted," the nurse said. She then asked who Lauren's mother was.

"I'm her mother," Julia said as everyone in the waiting room turned their heads toward her.

"She would like to see you," the nurse answered, already starting to make her way toward the waiting room door.

"Why, is there something wrong?" Julia asked as she made her way behind the nurse.

"Well, the baby has turned; he is now a breech delivery," the nurse replied to Julia. "We will have to do a C-section, and Lauren wanted to see you before the surgery. It's a really very common procedure," the nurse assured Julia. "The doctor is prepping right now. So, if you will follow me."

Turning to look back at the others with a concerned look on her face, Julia followed close behind the nurse as her words resonated in the small confines of Julia's mind. C-section…breech…common delivery… as scenes of her daughter's child, her grandchild, being brought into the world after Lauren has been cut open flashed through her mind.

When she reached the hospital room door, she saw one of the nurses exiting the room in a panic and felt an uneasy feeling settle into the pit of her stomach. When she entered through the doors, she caught sight of Lauren's hand resting inside Brad's. Brad stood caressing Lauren's hair out of her face with his other hand.

"Did you hear?" Lauren asked.

"Yes, I heard. It's going to be fine, sweetie. They do C-sections all the time. I promise you it will all be okay. It's a very common procedure these days."

"I know. It's just…he's turned the wrong way."

"And that happens," Julia said, now aware that the doctor had come into the room. "You and the baby will be fine," Julia said these words so confidently she almost believed them herself.

"It's a sign, Mom. He isn't coming out the way he was supposed to. He just turned. Why does this stuff always happen to me?"

"Sweetie," Julia said, pulling Lauren's chin toward her. "Everything is going to be fine. I promise. You have to believe that."

Lauren looked at her mother and then back at Brad.

"It's true, honey. It's going to be fine. We are right here with you," Brad said, engulfing Lauren's hand in his.

Julia, realizing the doctor was ready, squeezed Lauren's hand and kissed her on the forehead. "He will be here in no time, and we all can't wait to meet him."

Lauren grinned at her mother as the words floated down toward her, soothing her frazzled nerves.

One of the nurses then came up to Julia. "I'm sorry, but only one person can be in the room. Will it be Dad or you?" the nurse asked.

Julia looked over at Lauren and Brad and, without even thinking about it, announced to the room, "It'll be Dad. I'll see you after, sweetie. I love you." She smiled at them both, slowly letting go of Lauren's hand.

Julia made her way out of the room and stopped right outside the door to say a little prayer, "Lord, please don't make a liar out of me. Please be with them through all of this." She then made her way back to the waiting room and sat down next to her mother, taking her mother's hand into hers.

Carmen looked over at her and said, "What…s…wr…ong?"

"Nothing, Mom. It's fine. They'll be fine."

The clock in the waiting room came to a complete stop as all Julia could think about was the panic in her daughter's eyes.

Bobby paced the floor in front of them, grabbing magazines, pretending that he was reading them. Scott sat in the chairs across from Julia and Carmen with the pretense of watching the television on the wall as he checked his watch every few seconds. Everyone was uncommonly quiet as the room seemed to stop breathing.

After what seemed like hours, the same nurse returned to the waiting room and announced to the family, "It's a boy. He's fine and healthy. You'll be able to see them in just a little while."

Julia closed her eyes and gave a silent "hallelujah" under her breath. "Thank you," she said, looking up toward the sky.

About thirty minutes later, Brad entered the waiting room, wearing green scrubs, and said it was okay to visit Lauren and the baby briefly before they moved Lauren. He then walked directly over to Julia and Carmen, "We named him Charles or Charlie. It's what we plan on calling him. It's my grandfather's name."

Julia stood and gave him a big hug, "I love that."

"Well, you all are welcome to come in for a minute. She's tired but excited to show Charlie off," Brad said to everyone.

They all moved toward the door and were shuffled into the large patient room for mothers and newborns.

Lauren looked tired but lit up as soon as she saw them enter the room. "Well, I've been stapled up. They gave me some pain medicine, so I am still kind of out of it. I may not be awake for long," she said.

Julia and Scott watched as their eldest child became a mother. They peeked into the rollable, metal baby bed that held the tiny human with blonde hair and gray eyes. Julia reached out toward Charlie's tiny fingers as they wrapped themselves around her finger, and she felt a surreal feeling of looking into the future. A future filled with soccer games, t-ball games, plays, and music recitals. She stared at her brave daughter and Brad as they comforted one another; their eyes glazed over from many happy tears.

After visiting for a short while, the group was led out into the hallway to give mom and baby some time to bond and feed. The doctor wanted to give Lauren time to recover from the surgery, so the nurse recommended that everyone leave and return in the morning.

As they all made their way out of the hospital, Bobby took off ahead of them, pushing Carmen in a wheelchair like she was a racecar driver at the Daytona 500. He took Julia's keys as he passed her so he could help load Carmen into Julia's car. Bobby, feeling elated from the birth of his nephew, tried to do an impromptu wheelie with his grandmother's wheelchair.

This action led to a slap on his arm from his grandmother, who hollered at him, "Let...m...me...down!"

Scott followed along, kind of straggling behind at first, stating that his car was parked in the same lot. He caught up with Julia just as Bobby raced by them, placing his grandmother in the lead and swiftly exiting through the hospital doors.

"Well, we did it, Julia."

Julia turned to look back at him, grinning. "Yes, we did. We are officially grandparents."

Scott then smiled and said, "Yes, we are officially old."

Julia smiled back at him. "Speak for yourself, Grandpa. I'm never going to get as old as you."

Scott stood for a moment, looking at her, "I bet you won't. Anyway, ummm...how would you like to grab some dinner?"

Julia lowered her eyebrows, thinking about what he had just said as if she hadn't heard him correctly. "You mean you and me?"

"Yeah, I mean you and me. How about it?"

"Sorry, Scott, but I have to get Mom home. She's really tuckered out, and I'm not sure where Bobby has taken her, so I better get out there."

"Oh, yeah, well, maybe another time."

"Yeah, I'm so tired. I bet Bobby might join you, though. You should ask him."

Scott stood there for a minute and then grabbed Julia's arm to stop her from exiting. "Julia?"

"Yeah," Julia felt herself saying reluctantly, as all she wanted was to get home and relax so she could get back to the hospital early in the morning.

"You know, if I could do it all over again…"

And Julia stopped at the door with her back to Scott. She felt him walking up behind her, and she turned slightly back toward him while reaching for the handle on the door, thinking she could probably make an escape before he said anything else to her.

"I should've never left. I know that now. It was the biggest mistake of my life. If I had to do it all over again, well, it would have been different. I just wanted you to know that," Scott said.

Julia turned around and, without thinking, said the first thing that came to her mind, "I know it was, Scott. I've always known that." And Julia walked out of the door, leaving Scott standing behind her, heading straight toward her car, and she didn't even look back once.

CHAPTER TWENTY-SEVEN

Charlie came home with Lauren, a bouncing, healthy baby boy. As the weeks passed, Julia thought it was strange, but she began to see resemblances between Charlie and Brad. It was more Charlie's mannerisms she acquainted with the resemblance. The squinting of his forehead or when Charlie lowered his eyebrows just reminded her of Brad.

Lauren was a fantastic mother. Shortly after Charlie's birth, she told Julia that she had decided to only take one online class that semester and finish up her degree over the summer and fall semester to possibly graduate that winter.

Julia was overjoyed to see her daughter finally happy. Brad was everything she could have asked for in a father. He was attentive, affectionate, and most of all, he loved Charlie.

He was always referring to Charlie as his little quarterback. Lauren was so, so in love. It showed in everything she did. Everything was for her new family. Julia could tell that Lauren wanted her relationship with Brad to be more. Julia just wasn't sure how Brad felt about his new instant family.

To her knowledge, Lauren and Brad had never discussed marriage, at least not seriously. I mean, she couldn't blame Brad; he walked into a situation that was probably the furthest thing from his mind. Being a father to someone else's child. She wondered what Brad's plans for her daughter and grandson were. She prayed a lot for Brad and Lauren. She wasn't sure that Lauren could survive a heartbreak like this one should he decide to walk away, so Julia stayed close, just in case. Just in case, she would have to pick up the pieces.

Julia returned to work and school and found it hard to find time to visit Charlie, let alone babysit. She loved being with Charlie, but it was just so exhausting with school and work. She found she had little time for anything else.

Yet, she couldn't seem to shake a feeling of overwhelming sadness that would creep up on her at different times of the day. Oh, she did an excellent job of hiding it from those around her. It was when she was alone that the shadow of loneliness crept up on her, like a thief in the night, wrapping its long arms around her, declaring that she had no one.

It was a kind of hollow feeling, like something was missing.

"I know what's wrong with you," Lisa said.

"Nothing is wrong with me," Julia responded while wiping down the glass counter just as Annie came around the corner on her way back from the restroom.

Annie, overhearing the two friend's discussion, interjected, "Something is wrong. You just don't seem to be yourself. I have felt it too."

"That's what I told her," Lisa agreed.

"Guys, I'm fine. I'm just tired. You know I'm working and going to school. And I'm a grandmother."

Suddenly, a gentleman in a suit with black hair that was slightly graying on the sides passed by them. Julia looked over at him with anticipation until the man turned around, and it wasn't who she thought it was.

Lisa looked at the man passing by and said, "Um…hum…I knew that was it."

Annie looked at Lisa, "What…what's it?"

"She's thinking about that guy."

"What guy?" Annie asked.

As Julia rolled her eyes.

"The one in line waiting to get into the '80s Explosion. The one with the young girlfriend. Boy, don't you keep up with any of this?" Lisa said, looking sternly at Annie.

"No, I never get in on any of the current gossip working back in jewelry," Annie grumbled.

Julia looked at both of them, walked over to a box of new perfume sets, and started to unload them into the cabinets, trying to seem uninterested in her friend's conversation. "That's not it. I'm happy. I have my job. I'm back in school, and I'm loving getting back into writing. My daughter is happy…well, she's happily seeing Brad for now, at least. I have a new grandbaby, and Bobby is doing well. Guys, I have everything I've ever wanted."

"But you don't have that guy. What's his name again?" Lisa asked.

Julia looked at her as if she was debating on whether to tell her his name or not.

"You might as well tell her, Julia; she won't leave you alone until you do," Annie said, raising her eyes over the rim of her glasses.

"His name is Andy, okay," Julia said while folding up the used cardboard boxes.

Lisa snapped her fingers as if having a sudden epiphany. "Yeah, Andy. That's him. Your blast from the past." Lisa chuckled.

"What do you mean blast from the past? She knew him before?" Annie asked, checking her watch.

"Yeah, get this. They knew each other way back. I mean, when this one was like nineteen or twenty. He used to try and get her to dance with him," Lisa said, nodding her head in affirmation.

"What? Oh my gosh, that's a sign," Annie exclaimed.

"That's just what I told her," Lisa said.

Julia rolled her eyes and walked back over toward her friends. "A sign of what? That you both are losing it? He's happy with his young teeny-bopper girlfriend. He hasn't even tried to contact me."

Lisa leaned into the counter, looking straight at Julia. "Well, didn't you kinda dump him?"

"Well, yeah," Julia said, stopping to consider all that had happened between them. "I guess you could say that."

"Well, what in the world would make you think he would try and contact you after you told him not to?" Lisa questioned, crossing her arms in front of her.

"I don't know. It doesn't matter anyway," Julia said, looking around at what else needed to be done. "It's over. I've got too much in my life as it is. Let's not confuse things."

"I bet that's not what Michelle would do?" Lisa said, sauntering by Julia while pursing her lips and raising one eyebrow.

"What, who's Michelle? Does she work here?" Annie said, confused.

"No…no! Michelle's her favorite character on that stupid soap opera she likes to watch all the time. What's it called? *Time for You to Get a Life* or something like that."

"No…it's called *A Moment in Time*," Julia said, irritated. "Besides, I don't even watch it anymore."

"Huh…well, it's about time. And it's about time you take charge of your life. I can tell you like this guy," Lisa said.

Julia's mind drifted off to the time when she saw Ritchie standing outside the department store hugging Andy. Andy glowing in a unified light like he was some type of an angel or something. And the time Andy took her to the drug park to help her find Bobby, safely getting her to leave as Bobby walked away. She dropped her head back disgustedly and then looked back toward her friends. "Ahhh…why are we talking about this? It's too late. I said too many hateful things. How could I ever face him again?"

Annie looked at her and walked over, and took her by her shoulders. "It's only too late when someone else has him. Until then, honey, it's up to you." She looked at Julia and then back at Lisa. "I have to get back, ladies. Julia…"

"Yeah…"

"I say go for it. But no one can do that but you, sweetie. I'll see you, girls, later. Let me know how this turns out, for goodness' sake. The jewelry department never has this kind of excitement."

"Bye, Annie," the two women said in unison.

"Why don't you give him a call?" Lisa asked, looking at her watch and checking her counter for customers that might be waiting.

"I…just can't. I wouldn't know what to say," Julia said, picking up a dust rag.

"Well, how about if you just kind of run into him? Would that work?" Lisa said, raising one eyebrow.

Julia stood for a moment, squinting her eyes as if she were in pain. "Ohhh…well…I guess so. But how would I do that?"

"Well, what does he do?" Lisa asked.

"He owns some fast-food restaurants."

Lisa stood and looked at Julia with her eyebrows gathering above her nose, dropping her jaw. "Say what?"

"Yeah, that's what he told me. And he used to play professional baseball with the Padres."

"So, you are telling me that you let a rich, former professional baseball player that has been crazy for you since you all were teenagers get away?"

"Yeah, pretty much. But…"

"But what? And this better be a very big what."

"He sees me as I was when we were young. I'm just not that girl anymore. I mean, look at me," Julia said, throwing her arms down toward her sides.

"What? Look at what? You almost hooked up with your daughter's boyfriend, who is mighty fine, if I do say so myself, and at least fifteen years younger than you. You look almost ten years younger than you are. If I was a guy, I would be dating you."

"What?"

"And Julia…"

"Yeah,"

"You're amazing, girl. When are you going to start seeing that? Everyone else around you can see it but you."

Julia looked back toward the counters, jugging a dusting rag in her hand, "Do you think he could still like me?"

Lisa took two steps toward her friend, "Girl, this guy is crazy about you. That's if he hasn't hooked up with some young thing trying to marry him for all of his millions."

Julia looked at her with a question mark across her face. "You think he has millions?"

"Probably not, but we can be hopeful, can't we?" Lisa said as she started to make her way back over to the women's department.

Julia smiled. "Yeah, I guess so."

"Well, leave it all up to me."

Julia anxiously twisted the dust rag in her hand. "Leave what up to you, Lisa?"

Lisa glanced around and saw Dan, her supervisor, heading over to her area. "Just leave it to me. It will all be okay," she said as she double-timed it back to her counter.

"Don't you do anything crazy," Julia begged.

"Who, me? Never…" Lisa said, smiling as she walked up to a customer, browsing through some clothing in her section, and offered to help her.

Julia stood shaking her head. "What's she getting me into now?" she mumbled.

Julia headed home after work, trying to process all that her friends had said. Was she lonely? She had thought about Andy quite a bit since starting back to school. She wondered what he would think of her choice to finish her education. She wondered if he would be happy for her. She often daydreamed that she would see him across the campus, standing there, as he does with his hand in his pockets, his jacket pulled up over his wrist, as he gave her that look. That look that said she had his full attention even though he was standing there listening to someone else.

"Wow," Julia said aloud. "I do miss him."

Julia arrived home and changed her clothes, climbing into bed with her laptop and backpack right beside her. She had a story due in her advanced fiction writing class and had decided to write about a family's experience with a drug-addicted son. There were many tears involved in writing this story, but Julia knew this was a story that had to be told.

She got caught up in her story and skipped dinner, choosing to snack on some veggies and a peanut butter and jelly sandwich so she could continue to write.

Carmen came in and said goodnight to her as she headed off to bed.

Julia's eyes grew heavy. She often took a break from writing by playing music on her computer. Feeling a little melancholy from the day, she looked up a song she had intentionally chosen not to listen to because of the memories that were associated with it. It was hers and Ritchie's song.

She slowly typed in the name of the song as the lyrics took her back to a place she often avoided. The past. The song was "Endless Love," sung by Diana Ross and Lionel Richie.

As she listened to it, she remembered that Ritchie had said that he liked the song because the guy singing it shared his name, but Julia knew better. Ritchie would sing it to her as they danced, and it seemed to always make its way onto the radio when they happened to be in the car, driving to the beach. She hadn't listened to it since the day that Ritchie died.

His mother unknowingly played the song at his funeral as a way of telling Ritchie that he was her endless love. His mother had no way of knowing that it was Julia and Ritchie's song also. When it was played, Julia broke down and had to be carried out of the room by several family members.

As the song played, tears rolled down her cheeks, and she found it hard to breathe as a cold breeze entered the room. Feeling tired, she turned off her computer and placed her head on her pillow, staring at the drawer that contained her past, her Ritchie. Her eyelids suddenly became very heavy, and she was forced to close her eyes, drifting off into a deep sleep.

"Babe!" Julia heard a voice calling to her. "Babe!" the voice said again.

Julia brought her head up from her pillow. Her backpack hit the floor, and she grabbed at the bed, frightened by the sound of the bag crashing onto the carpet. Her laptop sat next to her with a black screen. She opened her eyes long enough to notice that she had forgotten to turn off the lights. She made her way to the wall and hit the light switch, and the room went black, except for the thin stream of moonlight that made its way into her room. The moon was so bright it seemed to draw Julia over to her window. She stared out the window, mesmerized by the largest moon she had ever seen. The moon was so large it appeared as if she could reach out and grab hold of it. When she squinted, she could almost make out the surface features of the moon displayed in pale shades of peach and alabaster.

She closed her shades and made her way back to her bed, and got underneath the covers, resting her head on her pillow.

"Babe?" she heard again.

Julia's eyes flashed open, and she immediately sat up, grabbing at the mattress. She then noticed a small bright light in the corner of her room that seemed to be intensifying into a large oval glow with flares of light being released in all directions, like Fourth of July sparklers.

"It's me," the voice said.

Julia closed her eyes, putting her hands over her ears and holding them there tight. When she lifted them, he was standing there in his white suit and black satin shirt, smiling at her with all of those teeth.

"Is it really you?" she said.

He walked toward her with one hand in his pocket and the other hand stretched out as if inviting her to come closer.

She reached out toward the translucent hand and felt a tingle in her fingers as her hand passed through his. His smile suddenly drooped as he sat down on the bed next to her. His eyes flashed a serious tone as he said, "I want you to be happy."

"Then why did you leave me?" The words escaped before Julia had time to stop them. As if they had been there waiting for the twenty-five-odd years since he had vanished, for a time just like this.

"I didn't want to, babe. You have to believe me," he said, trying to rub her cheek as the translucent hand lit up her eyes. "You know, I never meant for you to die along with me."

Julia looked up at him and said, with tears in her eyes, "I know."

"He's a good man, Julia. Give him a chance."

"Who, who's a good man?"

"The guy at the club. He wanted to dance with you, but I would never let him. Now, he deserves you. Back then, not so much." Ritchie smiled.

And Julia smiled back at him, wiping a tear from her eyes. "I'll always love you. You know."

"And you will always be my endless love. I wanted you to know that."

"And you will always be mine," Julia whispered, a tear making its way down her cheek.

"Oh and…," Ritchie said as he tried to lift a piece of hair from her eyes, his glowing hand only managing to light the side of her face.

Julia gazed up at him, her eyes squinting from the bright light.

"Keep living, keep writing, babe…do it for me."

"I'll try," Julia said.

"No, live, my love. Promise me. I want that for you." And Ritchie smiled as his image slowly disappeared, his voice echoing through the room.

"I will try…"

CHAPTER TWENTY-EIGHT

Julia woke up to a tear-stained pillow. She looked around her room for remnants of Ritchie. A smell. A touch. A shadow. But the room felt as empty as she did. She sat up in her bed, snatching a tissue from the box on her nightstand. "Well, I think I'm going crazy," Julia said to her silent room as she blew her nose into the flailing tissue. Just as she said those words, the screen of her laptop automatically came alive, and the screen lit up and started playing their song, "Endless Love."

Julia looked around the room as if she had seen a ghost, slowly lowering the laptop lid and sending out a question into space, "Ritchie?"

Forcing herself to get out of bed, Julia headed for the shower. She was scheduled to work that day and contemplated calling in but decided work might keep her mind off of things she needed to forget. She turned the shower knob to hot and heard the roar of the water. It flooded out of the showerhead, hitting the tiled floor like heavy rain on asphalt as the steam started to rise. Julia stood in the flow of water, allowing the moisture to sink into her skin. She pulled back her hair from her face allowing the warm water to run over her forehead moving her face in and out of the flow as the water stung the closed lids of her eyes. She placed a hand on the wall, feeling the sleek, cool tile beneath her fingers. She breathed in heavily, trying to catch her breath as her chest felt weighted.

Angry, she hit the wall with her fist as tears formed once again. The tears blended into the rush of water as Julia wrapped herself in her arms, her back hitting the wall as her face fell forward. "Why?" Julia shouted into the unknown as the water seemed to wash away the night.

Once again, she faced another day. Another day without Ritchie. Another day she would spend alone. Was she really as dead as Ritchie stated? Had she given up on life? She leaned her body against the shower wall as she contemplated the words of a ghost, a lost love, the only man she thought she would ever love. Had she stopped trying? Is that why Ritchie had come back? Was she letting him down once more? And worse of all, was she letting herself down, forgetting that she once had a dream worth fighting for.

She began the route to work as she had every other day of her life. Almost on autopilot now, her mind took over, and every twist and turn of the road was unnoticed anymore by the occupant who had made this trip a thousand and one times before. She pulled into the parking lot, trying to dry her eyes. She had just exited her car when she ran into Lisa.

Julia dried her eyes, not wanting to discuss the night with anyone. Wanting it to fade from her thoughts so she could pretend that it never happened. As they made their way into the shiny glass doors of the department store, Julia's glazed eyes went unnoticed by Lisa, who was rambling on about her plan to locate Andy.

"I can't do it," Julia protested, trying not to burst into tears.

"What are you talking about? We haven't even tried yet. You haven't tried yet."

"I told you. I can't do this."

"I know it's not easy, girl. I know you are taking a chance, but I want this for you. Heck, I want it for me. We can't stop living. If we do, we die," Lisa preached.

Julia flashed back to the words Ritchie had said to her, "*I never meant for you to die along with me.*"

Julia discreetly wiped a tear from her eye. "Well, what's your plan?" she asked, sniffling and throwing her head back to prevent any more tears from making their way down her cheeks.

"Now you're talkin'. That's the girl that I love."

"It hasn't anything to do with you or me. I just made a promise to someone."

"Well, hallelujah to whoever that was, because girl, have I got a plan for you," Lisa said as they made their way into the store.

Julia placed her belongings behind the perfume counter and walked back out to where Lisa was standing.

"Are you okay?" Lisa asked, noticing her friend's grim expression.

"I just had a long night, that's all," Julia said.

"Okay, well, this will brighten your spirits. My plan is to meet up with him at a Padres game."

"How do you know he even goes to the games?" Julia asked.

Lisa stared at Julia, hanging her head to the side. "Girl, the man used to play for them; he is guaranteed to have season tickets. I would bet money on it. I just need to find out what box he's in."

Julia took a deep breath and sighed, "Okay, that doesn't sound too crazy. I like baseball. You like baseball. We could be there at the same time he is."

Lisa began to shake her head slowly in agreement with Julia, pointing back and forth between Julia and herself. "Yes, now you're reading me. Now, just to find out where his seats are. That's the hard part," Lisa said. "Don't you worry, though. I know people in low places. I got your back on this, girlfriend."

"Yeah, that kinda worries me but…go ahead."

"Now you're talkin'. Oh, and keep your schedule open this weekend," Lisa laughed, slapping her hands together.

Julia stood in front of Lisa, lowering her eyebrows. "That soon?"

"Yeah, that soon. Men like him don't stay single long, honey, and there are lots of money-grubbing, you know, women out there, so we have to move fast. Take my word on this."

"Okay...matchmaker." Julia laughed, her worries slowly melting into the hope of a promise of meeting Andy again. "Against my better judgment, I will leave it up to you. But please, let's try not to make fools of ourselves."

"That's just a part of love, Julia. You have to make a fool of yourself. Otherwise, what's the fun of being in love," Lisa said as she danced toward the women's department, placing her belongings behind the counter and giving Julia a thumbs up from behind the register.

"Oh, what have I got myself into," Julia whispered to herself.

Julia couldn't shake the feeling that Ritchie was somehow watching her. That it wasn't just an accident that had brought her and Andy back together again after all of these years. She felt an overwhelming affection for Andy. One that she hadn't felt since Ritchie. But could he ever forgive her? Forgive her for letting him go. That was the question weighing on her heart.

The weekend finally arrived, and Julia rolled up in front of Lisa's house on a sunny Saturday afternoon, unaware if Lisa was able to arrange for tickets near the so-called "Andy's Box" —as they were calling it—or not. Lisa came out of her home dressed head to toe in brown and gold Padres gear. She had the baseball cap, the T-shirt, the knee-high socks, and a large foam hand that she refused to take off.

"How are we supposed to be incognito with you dressed like that?" Julia asked.

"What? This is what everyone wears. Do you think it's too much?" Lisa asked, surprised by Julia's gaze.

"No, no. At least Andy will spot one of us. But I'm not sure it will be me." Julia laughed. Julia was wearing her jean shorts and Padres short sleeve jersey that Lauren had given her. She wore her white tennis shoes and pulled her hair up into a ponytail. "But at least I will be standing next to you when he sees you." Julia laughed.

Lisa opened the car door and hopped into the passenger seat. "Oh, whatever. I think I look cute."

"Well, that's one word for it." Julia giggled.

"Yeah, well, you can thank me later. I have it on good authority that these tickets are just to the right of the clubhouse where Andy and his group usually sit. Girl, you will definitely owe me for this one."

"His group? He has a group?"

Lisa looked over at Julia as they began to pull away from the curb. "Well, I'm just guessing on that. He has a whole box, so I would think he would be inviting others."

"Okay. I'm not sure about this. He's going to know."

Lisa looked over at Julia, rolling her eyes. "What did I tell you?"

"What?" Julia asked.

"The whole fool thing." Lisa laughed, pushing Julia's side as Julia struggled to maintain control of the car. "No, I'm just kidding with you. Hey, we are just a couple of Padres fans that happened to have lucked out with these seats. How in the world would we know where he was sitting?"

Julia sighed out loud and took a deep breath while maneuvering the car into heavy traffic. "Yeah, you're right. There's no way we would know that."

"Right. So, let's just get there. But don't you go forgetting your old friend here the next time Andy introduces you to one of those fine-looking baseball players on the team," Lisa said, pointing toward herself.

Julia looked over at Lisa with her eyes narrowed.

"Me, Julia. Don't forget me," Lisa said sarcastically.

"Oh, yeah, sorry. I'm new at this."

"It's okay. I'll get you through it. Now let's get there before the game is over, shall we?"

When they arrived, the parking lot was full. It seemed that everyone in San Diego had the same idea as the ladies struggled to find a parking spot. They ended up having to walk for almost ten minutes just to reach the stadium. Lisa pulled out her tickets and stopped and talked to one of the ticket agents, thanking her for the great tickets as Julia heard the national anthem begin to play.

Julia, feeling extremely nervous, had to make a stop in the lady's room to check her lipstick and straighten her baseball cap. "You can do this. Michelle would do this. You are an adult woman in college, and you can do this," she said to the image looking back at her in the mirror. At that moment, an elderly woman exiting one of the stalls glanced over at her. Julia smiled at the woman and turned to leave the restroom.

The two friends made it to the third level and moved toward their assigned seats right next to the glass box. Julia was so nervous she started to pace back and forth at the top of the stairs, unable to move down toward their seats. Lisa strolled down the concrete stairs to get a better look and tried to nonchalantly glance into the box to see if she could spot Andy.

She spotted him almost immediately. Andy then spontaneously turned toward Lisa as if he had recognized her. She had to quickly put her foam hand up to block her face so that he wouldn't see her. Andy glanced over at the foam hand but, not noticing anything out of the ordinary, looked away.

Lisa took this opportunity to race up the stairs and grab Julia, pulling her out from behind a tall steel rail. "Okay, he's in there. Are you ready?" Lisa asked as she started to pull Julia down the stairs.

Julia looked down at the field and then around at the millions of people in the stands. "I don't know. I can't seem to make myself move forward."

Lisa placed her hands on her hips with the large foam hand sticking out of her side. "Okay…are you ready now?"

Julia grabbed at her hat nervously and shook her hands down by her sides while pacing back and forth. "Lisa, just give me a second."

Lisa tapped her foot. "Okay…now can we go?"

Julia laughed nervously, still trying to hide behind the steel pole.

Lisa grabbed Julia's arm. "Listen to me. He has no idea we're here. We have no idea he's here. It's all very innocent. Now let's go."

Julia looked over at the box and began to move out from behind the pole. "Maybe it'll look better if we have food in our hands. You know, like we just came from the food counter and are here just to enjoy the game like everyone else."

Lisa looked at Julia throwing her shoulders and head back in disgust. "Do you know how much they charge for food here?"

Julia calmed Lisa down by announcing, "It's on me."

"Okay, why didn't you say that? Let's go."

After waiting in line for twenty minutes and getting a couple of hot dogs and drinks, Lisa and Julia made their way down the aisle, trying to seem as natural as possible so they didn't draw any attention to themselves.

Looking at the tickets, Julia noticed that the seats were only two seats away from the box window. "We can't sit there?"

"Why not?" Lisa argued, thinking about her cooling hot dog.

"He'll know."

"Know SMO...get me to my seat. Excuse me," Lisa announced to the people in front of her as she made her way to their assigned seats. A hesitant Julia followed close behind, trying to stay behind Lisa's big foam hand. "Okay, we're finally here," Lisa announced to the crowd.

"Sit down, Lisa," Julia said, embarrassed.

"That's what I'm trying to do," Lisa said as she struggled to sit down without dropping all the items in her hands. Lisa immediately started watching the game as they both unwrapped their hot dogs. Lisa bit into the bun and declared, "Boy, was I hungry."

"Do you see him?" Julia asked.

"Who?" Lisa replied as if she had already forgotten why they were there. "Oh, yeah, sorry." Lisa bent forward and looked into the box to find Andy standing right in front of the window, just two seats away from them. "Oh, yeah. He's there all right."

"What's he doing?" Julia asked.

"He's watching the game. What do you think he's doing?" Lisa answered. "Wait...oh, no, he didn't."

"What?" Julia blurted out, trying not to look over.

"There's a girl. A young girl taking his arm."

Julia slumped down in her seat and tried to look casually around Lisa so she could get a better look inside the glass box. Just as she looked behind Lisa, her eyes met Andy's. Andy, recognizing Julia, immediately smiled and waved, pointing right at Julia as the young, attractive woman beside him also looked around him to see who he was talking about. Andy then gave a thumbs up and headed toward the clubhouse door as Julia struggled to get up from her seat.

"Where are you going?" Lisa asked.

"I'm trying to get out of here before he gets here," Julia answered as she made her way to the center of the aisle—irritating the people beside them even more—only to look up to see Andy standing at the top of the stairs.

"Too late," he said after overhearing her comment. The young girl they saw in the booth was standing right beside him.

Julia looked up at Andy and smiled, "Andy, what are the odds? How are you?"

Andy grinned and walked down a few steps as Julia walked up the stairs to meet him. Julia noticed how Andy's teeth gleamed in the rays of the sun, his thick hair blowing in the breeze. He looked different in his casual clothing. He was wearing shorts and a Padres jersey similar to Julia's.

"I'm fine. Oh, sorry, let me introduce..."

"No, it's fine, no need to..." Julia said, trying to look away.

"Julia, this is my niece, Alex."

Julia looked up at Andy and could feel her face starting to turn red. The heat from her face ballooned as she tried to fan her complexion, hoping that this would somehow help, but it didn't. "Oh, your niece. So nice to meet you, Alex. I didn't know Andy had family in town."

The young girl, excited to meet a friend of her uncle's, reached out her hand, "Nice to meet you, Julia. No, I'm just visiting. Uncle Andy was nice enough to let me and my friends stay at his place for a few days before school starts up again. He's just the coolest."

Andy smiled and gave his niece a tight squeeze. "No, I love having the company," he said. He then noticed Julia's red face and thought it was from the heat of the day. "Hey, would you and your friend like to watch the game from the box?" Andy asked. "It's air-conditioned."

Lisa, hearing this, turned around and shouted over the crowd, "We would love to!"

Andy smiled and helped Julia carry her drink as she was juggling it in her arms. "I guess we will," Julia said, trying not to sound too anxious.

"Great," Andy said. "Let me help you, Julia."

The four of them made their way to the private box. After sitting down, Lisa and Andy's niece got into a conversation about the game, allowing Andy to sit with Julia in the corner.

"So, how have you been?" Andy inquired. "I've thought about you."

"You have?" Julia said, her heart beating so loudly, she was sure Andy could hear it from the close proximity he was sitting to her, his hairy, muscular arm grazing her arm.

"I have," Andy said, now ignoring the game and putting his full attention on Julia.

"Uhhh…, Bobby's well and he came home."

"Oh, I didn't know that. That's wonderful. I'm so happy for you."

"And mom's a lot better. She is still doing rehabilitation but is as feisty as ever," Julia said. "How about you?"

"Oh, I'm just working. It seems to keep me busy enough. I thought about calling you but wasn't sure if I should."

"I want to apologize for what I said to you at the hospital that day. How I treated you…"

Andy waved his hand in front of him as if trying to stop Julia from finishing. "No, you don't have to. I know you were under a lot of stress, and I was probably just adding to it."

"No…no, you weren't. I don't know why I said those things; I just didn't…well…I just wasn't in a good place at the time."

"And now?"

"Well, I'm also better. Much better. Oh, and I'm back in school."

Andy turned his body slightly toward Julia and said, "You are? That's wonderful. Good for you."

"I know. I truly love it. I'm writing now. Did I tell you that I write?"

"No, you didn't. I'd like to read some of your work sometime."

And Julia looked deeply into Andy's eyes as he seemed to look right through her. He looked as if he were staring into her soul. As if he knew what she was about to say before she said it. "It's all been this kind of a whirlwind. I never thought I would ever be able to return to school, but here I am."

"I'm so happy that you are doing something for you. So, are all the college guys hitting on you?" Andy joked.

"Well…one or two. No, I'm just kidding," Julia said, nudging Andy with her shoulder.

"Well, I would be if I were them," Andy said.

"I can't believe I said those things to you that day. I had no right," Julia said, turning her head away from Andy to avoid his eyes.

Andy reactively reached over and gently brought Julia's eyes back up to his. "It's okay, Julia. I forgave you the moment you said them."

Just as Andy finished his sentence, the door to the booth flew open, and in stepped a full-figured young woman. She was wearing sunglasses and had her naturally wavy, brunette hair tied up in a bushy ponytail. Her white canvas tennis shoes were exemplified by her amazing tan. The woman narrowed her eyebrows and ripped off her sunglasses, throwing her head back as her ponytail shook like a stallion's tail. "Andy, who is this?" the young woman asked in a Spanish accent, pointing her glasses toward Julia.

Andy turned around as if he were surprised to hear her voice behind him. "Zoey..." Andy stuttered. "I thought you weren't coming."

"Well...I left you a message that I would be able to make it. I didn't hear back from you, so I just decided to show up. Who is this?" Zoey said again, looking in Julia's direction as if she had never laid eyes on her before.

Andy looked over at Julia and then back at Zoey, seemingly forgetting Julia's name in the heat of the moment. "Ahhh..."

"It's Julia. My name is Julia," Julia said, shooting out of her seat like a rocket and stepping up onto the bar platform where the door was located. "Well, I think that is my cue to leave," Julia proclaimed, embarrassed that Andy couldn't even remember her name.

Andy grabbed at Julia's arm as Zoey sauntered over to Andy, rubbing up against him from the side, fumbling her fingers through his hair.

"Andy, my love, can you get me a drink," Zoey said, glaring at Julia. "I am completely parched after that long walk from my car."

Andy wiggled his way out of Zoey's grip as he tried to catch Julia, who was now darting toward the door.

Lisa, who turned just in time to see Julia leaving, hurriedly shuffled up the stairs, explaining to Andy's niece how she was going to have to leave with her friend. Julia being her ride and all.

"Wait for me," Lisa shouted behind Julia.

"Julia, wait. I didn't expect Zoey to show up," Andy whispered behind Julia's ear. "She invited herself when I ran into her last week. After all, I hadn't heard from you in months. Please, be reasonable."

Julia looked back at Zoey, who was sitting on the back of one of the club seats, throwing her long thick ponytail behind her. "No, I'm sorry. I don't blame you for anything, Andy. I shouldn't have come. It's my fault. This was a mistake. It was all a mistake. I have to go. I'm so sorry, Andy," Julia apologized.

"No, wait..." Andy said as Julia made her way in front of him, wiggling her arm out of his grip.

Lisa came up behind them, making her way around Andy. "Sorry, we have to go. It was nice to meet everyone. Maybe we can do this again sometime?" Lisa proclaimed before exiting right behind Julia.

"Julia..." Julia heard Andy say just as the door slammed behind her.

"Now what?" Lisa said.

"Nothing. It's over. I messed it up. That's all. Let's just get out of here."

"Whatever you say, but this is fixable, Julia. The man did not want you to leave. How was he to know we were going to show up today? Give him a break, Julia. Didn't you hear him?"

"Yes, I heard him. I just want to leave, okay? I've messed things up again. I must look like such a fool."

"Only if you want to. This can all be easily straightened out."

Julia turned toward Lisa with an irritated look on her face.

Lisa threw up her hands in front of her, "Okay...okay...we can go. But you're going to regret this. Take my word for it."

Julia took one long last look at the door of the clubhouse and started to walk toward the exit. She heard a whisper in the wind, something tugging at her, an inner voice telling her to turn around. But she ignored the voice. Humiliated, she kept on walking, the voice slowly becoming just a hum in her ear.

CHAPTER TWENTY-NINE

Julia slept for a mere hour that night. She tossed and turned, reliving what she had said to Andy at the baseball stadium that afternoon. She dissected the whole scene in her head over and over again, wondering what she should have done differently. In her heart, she knew she should never have walked out of that stadium box.

But there was also a part of her that wondered if Andy still had feelings for Zoey. After all, Zoey was there. She was young and energetic. Beautiful and exotic. What man in his right mind would turn down an opportunity like that?

For the first time since Ritchie had begun to appear to her, she wished his spirit would suddenly materialize so she could ask him what to do. She had so, so many questions. Ones she felt only he could answer.

Julia kept picturing the look on Andy's face as she flew by him. He looked as if he were losing his best friend. She remembered him grabbing onto her trying to prevent her from leaving as she once again dismissed him. She didn't even give him a chance to explain.

Julia's eyes met the first beams of light making their way through her blinds. It was the start of another day. She wondered if she should call Andy. Would he forgive her once again? Or would she be rejected because he had decided to return to Zoey? Could she take that chance?

Still, there was definitely some sort of connection between them. She could feel it. Or was it all just a figment of her imagination? She started to reach for her phone to check for messages when her phone began to vibrate. Julia's heart raced as she quickly looked down, thinking that it might be Andy. Her heart sank when she saw that it was Lauren calling. Julia glanced at the clock on her nightstand, which read eight in the morning, and knew whatever Lauren was calling about so early couldn't be good as she juggled the phone between her hands.

"Mom!"

"What?" Julia said, feeling the sense of urgency in her daughter's tone. "What is it? Is it Charlie?"

"Yes…no…it's Jake."

"Jake?" Julia said, almost forgetting who that was. "What? What about him?"

"He's back. He says he wants my car, the car we bought together, but then when I told him about Charlie, he decided he was going to try and get custody of him too."

"What? Did he know about Charlie before?"

"Well, no. I tried to get a hold of his mom, but she had changed her phone number. I didn't try after that. I was just kind of hoping he would go away, disappear, or something."

"Sweetie, you know that's not going to happen. So, he said he wants Charlie?"

"Yeah, what do I do?"

"Well, we'll have to get a lawyer. He's probably going to take us to court."

Lauren took a moment to let the words sink in. "Okay, Brad's here. He thinks this is just a ploy to get the car."

"All right. I'm coming over."

"Okay, Mom, and thank you," Lauren said, relieved that Julia was on her way.

Hanging up her phone. Julia's mind drifted to Jake and the fact that she had also utterly dismissed the fact that he was Charlie's father, hoping he would just somehow never return. That somehow Lauren and Brad would be able to move forward without the drama she knew Jake would bring should he find out about Charlie. Just as Julia's feet hit the floor, Carmen came to the door, having overheard parts of her daughter's conversation.

"What…What…hap…pened, now?" Carmen stuttered.

"It's Jake; he says he wants Charlie and the car. The car he and Lauren bought together."

"That…th…at…no…good. He…he…is no…good. I…will…take…care…of…him."

Julia smiled at her mother. "Thanks, Mom. But I'm not sure that would help. Or that we would get away with it. But a nice suggestion."

"It…c…cooould…work," Carmen said, now angry. "I…I know people."

Julia looked toward her mother with narrowed eyebrows as Carmen turned and walked away from her, heading toward the bathroom, mumbling something about a Frank and Bob that she would call.

As she dressed, Julia tried to remember the name of her divorce lawyer so she could give him a call. She was hoping she would never have to speak with him again, but here they were in another crisis. "What the heck?" Julia shouted out to the empty room.

After dressing, Julia headed to Lauren's apartment. When she walked in, she saw Lauren and Brad talking at the kitchen table. Charlie was being lulled to sleep in his swing.

"Did he just fall asleep?" Julia asked quietly.

"No, Mom. He's been asleep for a while. He should be up soon. He sure loves that swing you got him."

"Really? The swing was your favorite too."

"Well, we're not sure what Jake's going to do. He's on his way over here now to talk. We're hoping to settle this out of court."

"Well, I don't think that's going to happen, sweetie."

"Why?"

Julia put her purse down on the sofa and kneeled down to look at Charlie. "Because he has you right where he wants you. Do you think he even cares for Charlie?"

"He hasn't even spent any time with him. He walks in and tries to play with him but then hands him right back to me when Charlie starts crying," Lauren said, making her way to the kitchen table and plopping down on a chair.

"Has he asked to take Charlie with him?"

"No. Not yet. Besides, he doesn't have transportation or a car seat for his mom's car. And he says he wants my car because he said he paid for most of it! I don't know what to do," Lauren sighed.

"Well, how will you get Charlie around if you give him your car?"

"I don't know. Jake said he hadn't planned to stay around long because he wanted to get back to California for an acting gig, but now with Charlie here, he said he may have to stick around longer."

Brad got up and walked over toward the baby swing. He stared down at Charlie, watching the swing sway him to and fro, cradling the young infant. Charlie lay there, oblivious to the chaos that surrounded his future. Brad then spoke into the silence, "I seriously think he just wants the car. If we give it up, I think we may even get him to sign his rights away, but you all know him better than I do."

Julia peered over at Brad, who seemed so torn. He gazed down at Charlie as if he were his own flesh and blood. He loved this child with all of his heart. Julia could tell that Brad's heart was breaking just as much as Lauren's.

Lauren came up behind Brad, slowly caressing his back.

"Okay, let's all stay calm and hear what Jake has to say. After all, he is Charlie's legal father," Julia reminded them.

Lauren rolled her eyes at Julia and walked back toward the kitchen table, placing one hand on the table and the other on her head, rubbing her forehead, trying to stay calm.

Julia walked over to her. "It's true, sweetie. And maybe Brad is right. Maybe all he wants is the car. We'll have to wait and see. I still think getting a lawyer would be a smart thing to do."

Brad then turned around. "Yeah, babe. We're going to fight him on this. But if he pushes it, he has every right to see Charlie."

Lauren turned back around. "I know…I know he does. I'm not against that if he loves Charlie. But if he's doing this just to get back at me somehow, how can that be good for my son?"

The three of them stood there, knowing that Lauren was probably right but that their hands were tied. Julia watched as Brad slowly walked over to Lauren and tried to comfort her, taking her into his large arms as she disappeared into his chest. He rocked her as they began to sway in a kind of dance. This was the first time Julia realized how much Brad truly loved her daughter. This was the first time she felt an attachment between them. A bond that would lead them to face this life challenge together.

She glanced down at Charlie and prayed that this was not the first of many conflicts her little grandson would have to face. She didn't want this life for him. A father that would come in and out of his life as Charlie struggled to find out just where he fits in.

Suddenly, there was a rapping at the door as all heads turned toward the sound.

Lauren and Brad locked eyes. Brad threw his head back in disgust, looking at the ceiling. "I'll get it," Brad said, knowing it would be Jake.

After opening the door to mumbled hellos, the two men stood there staring at each other as Jake suddenly moved toward Charlie.

"How's my boy doing?" he said, grinning at Brad.

Lauren looked over at him. "He's fine, Jake. Like always."

"I know. I always knew you would be a good mother. I just wished you had told me about him sooner." Jake then looked over at Julia. "Hello, Julia."

"Jake," Julia said coldly.

"There was no way to get a hold of you, Jake. You didn't have a phone. Still don't," Lauren protested.

"I know. I plan to get one once I land a job in Los Angeles. Maybe Hollywood!" he said exuberantly. "That's why I need the car."

"It's the only vehicle I have, Jake. How am I supposed to get to school and work, let alone get Charlie to daycare?"

"I can watch him. You know, seeing that I don't have a car and all, I may have to stick around here longer. My mom would be glad to give me a hand."

These words left Julia, Brad, and Lauren standing silent, numb.

"Well, I can see the little tyke is tuckered out. I really just stopped by to see if you had made a decision on the car. But I can see you need a little more time to think about it. No hurry. I may just hang around the area now that I see Charlie may need me."

Lauren rolled her eyes. "You have never cared about anyone but yourself."

Jake looked over at her. "That's not fair. I didn't know about him."

"And now you do," Lauren said.

"Yes, now I do. I have to figure everything out. Not having a job does not help my situation. That's why I need the car," Jake said as if the only thing stopping him from being the hero his son deserved was his lack of transportation. Jake then hesitated as if waiting for the jury's decision. "Well, I'll let you all talk about it. I have no problem with waiting. I've waited this long. I'll check back with you all in a couple of days. Nice seeing you again, Julia."

Just as Jake was about to leave, Brad stepped forward. "Wait. We've discussed it. We'll sign over the car to you under one condition."

Lauren then moved toward Brad as he put his hand up in front of her, stopping her from reaching him.

"Well, that's great. What's your condition?"

"That you sign over all your rights to Charlie."

The room suddenly went silent, as if all the air had been sucked out; the last words lingering in the air. Everyone was holding their breath, especially Lauren and Julia, as all eyes were on Jake. Jake's eyes revolved around the room and then back toward Charlie. He seemed to be debating on his next move. It was as if a part of him wanted to stay and be a part of Charlie's life. Be the father that Charlie deserved. But the other part of him somehow knew that if he stayed he would only succeed in making things worse for Charlie.

And then there was the dilemma of his career. How could he become the actor he wanted to be if he had a child to take care of? And his eyes suddenly gleamed as if he had made a decision.

Jake glanced down toward Charlie and back toward the door. "I…I think that could be arranged," Jake said. "As long as I don't have to put up any cash for the lawyer. I would, but I'm getting an apartment and well…"

"You won't have to," Brad said, not skipping a beat. "We'll pay for everything."

Jake then immediately stuck his hand out toward Brad, "We have a deal. Besides I know he will be well taken care of. I know Lauren."

Brad then shook his hand reluctantly. "We can have the papers by the first of next week. Can you wait 'til then before you leave town?"

"I can do," Jake said. "I know you all will take good care of my son. And besides, I will be living so far away and it's just…"

"We totally understand," Lauren interjected.

Brad looked over at her, trying to hide his excitement. Both of them struggled to keep their feelings to themselves until Jake was gone.

"Well…," Jake said, "I'll see you all the first part of next week. Just let me know." He then glanced over at Charlie asleep in the swing. "Goodbye, little guy." He then walked out the door and out of his son's life letting the screen door slam behind him.

"Brad?" Lauren said with tears in her eyes.

"I just…I just couldn't let him take him. I don't trust him," Brad said.

Lauren turned toward Brad and he took her in his arms as they both looked over at the sleeping Charlie.

"Well...," Julia said, "I guess it's settled, Mom and Dad."

Brad relieved, smiled and looked toward Julia, "I guess it is. Oh, and Lauren," Brad said. "I'll get you another car, sweetie. I have some money saved up."

"No, you don't have to...," Lauren said. "I can try and save..."

Brad brought his hands up to her lips to stop her from continuing. "I know I don't, but I want to. Besides, how will we get Charlie around otherwise, huh?"

"I'll text you my lawyer's phone number as soon as I get home," Julia said as she turned toward the door. Just then, Charlie began to wake up. At that moment, Julia forgot she was leaving and dropped her purse on the couch, and went over to pick him up.

"What a big boy you are," Julia cooed over him as Brad and Lauren stood arm in arm and watched Charlie being loved on by his grandmother, who had forgotten that she was on her way out.

After playing with Charlie for about an hour, Julia said her goodbyes and headed out to her car. With all that had happened, she had all but forgotten about her run-in with Andy and Zoey. Coming out of the apartment door, she looked around at the noon-day sun and felt a warm breeze rush over her. She heard a whisper in the breeze and struggled to listen to what she thought was a voice calling out to her. In the whisper, she heard a phrase over and over again. The voice said, "He's here..."

"Who's here?" Julia found herself saying to the breeze.

And the wind picked up again. "He's here..."

Julia looked over toward the stairs and made her way down toward the parking lot and spotted a silver convertible parked at the bottom of the stairs. The glow from the sun was so bright Julia had to cover her eyes to see the gleaming vehicle below her. A man was sitting in the convertible and when he saw her coming down the stairs he removed his sunglasses and started to open his door. Julia's mouth dropped open. It was Andy.

Julia grabbed at her chest as she lost her breath the way that she did every time she was within a few feet of him. "Andy?" Julia questioned aloud. Julia grabbed onto the rail, afraid that her knees might give way. She was so shocked that she felt a little dizzy.

Andy stepped out of his convertible, hesitating for a moment, he finally made his way around the front of the car. He stood near the passenger side door as if waiting to see Julia's reaction to him being there.

"I had to see you," Andy shouted up the stairs.

Julia made her way slowly down the stairs, still not sure if it wasn't all just a dream. "But how did you know where I was?" she asked, suddenly realizing she hadn't told anyone where she was going.

"I stopped by your house. Your mother told me you were here. I just took a chance."

"Ohhh...," Julia said as her feet finally made it to solid ground.

"I just wanted to apologize for the other day. I didn't know Zoey was coming. I had run into her a couple of days before and told her about the game, and she sort of invited herself to join us. And at the time, I didn't think I would ever see you again."

"No, I'm the one who should apologize. You have every right to see whoever you want. After all, I am the one that broke up with you, remember?"

Andy smiled as he closed the gap between them. "Well, the specifics are a little fuzzy to me right now. I was just so happy to see you again."

Julia forgot to breathe as Andy moved within inches of her. She let out a sigh and looked around the apartment complex, unsure of what to say next as a wind came up behind her. The breeze was so strong Julia stumbled forward into Andy. He had to reach out and hold her up, afraid that she might fall into him.

"I'm sorry...," Julia said.

"It's okay. I got you," Andy said, as they were now so close Julia could smell the musky odor of his cologne.

"No, I mean for the other day and for what I said to you at the hospital. I'm truly sorry, Andy. Can we just start over? Is that possible?"

"I would like that," Andy agreed. "So, well, hello, my name is Andrew Harrington. I was wondering if you would like to have dinner with me tonight?"

As he spoke, his words got lost in translation as Julia stared at Andy's strong cheekbones and unshaven chin which left her in a sense of amnesia as she tried to remember what he had just asked her. Suddenly recalling his last words, she answered, "I would love to."

"Great," Andy said. "I can pick you up at six. Will that work?"

"Perfect," Julia said. "I have some homework I have to finish this afternoon, but it shouldn't take me long."

"Are you sure tonight will work? Because we could make it another night. I forgot you are a college girl now," Andy laughed. "It feels weird to say that I'm dating a college girl."

Julia giggled. "True, but somehow I bet you have said that phrase before." Julia winked at him.

"Well, I walked right into that one, didn't I?" Andy said, grinning. He then took Julia's hand into his, brought it up to his lips, and kissed the back of her hand ever so gently.

Julia became so frazzled at the feeling of his lips pressed against her skin that she felt weak in the knees. She tried to maintain her composure as Andy winked at her and made his way back around his convertible, seemingly excited about Julia's answer.

"I'll let you get to your homework," Andy shouted. "I'll see you tonight."

"Tonight..." Julia said in almost a whisper, waving her hand goodbye. She stood and watched as he sped out of the parking lot and down the palm tree-lined lane.

The breeze behind her suddenly subsided, and she lifted her face into the sun and spread her arms out like an eagle, screaming into the wind, "Yes! Thank You, Lord!"

CHAPTER THIRTY

When Julia arrived home, she was so elated by her rendezvous with Andy that she had a hard time concentrating on the short story that was due the next week. She sat down at her laptop and tried to focus but found it difficult and had to start over and over again because her mind kept drifting to Andy and what it would be like to spend time with him again. She felt goosebumps start to form on her arms every time she thought about him.

She was at the end of the story, the closing. The point when the reader is brought to the outcome. The time the writer allows them to see what was learned and what was lost. Julia was taken back to that time in her own life. A time when Andy was there for her. A time when she felt she could not go on alone. Her son lost.

As she wrote, tears ran their course, being wiped away by the hands of time. She dove deep into the heart of her characters, showing how just one act, one single act, affected so very many. The names and location were changed, but the emotions, the agony that the characters felt, were still so much a part of her. As she finished typing, she sat back and looked at the screen, exhausted and renewed.

It was the first draft, but she already knew that it would not change much. A comma here and there and some line editing, but all in all, she felt it was nearly perfect. The story was real, and it would connect with so many people who have experienced any type of life-altering struggle.

She saw her email light up just as she was about to abandon her laptop to get ready for her date with Andy. Julia noticed that the email was from her advanced fiction writing professor. He had sent her a link to a prestigious short story contest that he thought she might be interested in entering. He asked if she felt the story that she was currently working on was ready. Her professor had read the first part of the story and felt it had merit. His email explained that the contest deadline was two months away, which would give them time to review and edit the story. But in the end, he left the decision to enter the contest up to her.

The words on the screen became blurred to Julia as if someone had jumbled them up, making them unrecognizable. Julia reread her professor's email over and over again, trying to decipher his comments. He felt her story was good enough to enter this contest? He actually thought she had a chance of winning?

As she began to weigh the validity of her work and the true meaning it would express to others, the familiar voices in Julia's head began to rise. These voices she knew all too well. They were old friends.

These were the voices that continually called out to her and often told her that she needed to give up. The voices that said she was not good enough. These voices continually explained to her all the reasons why she shouldn't even try.

What if she didn't win?
What if they did all of this work for nothing, and the story was rejected?
What if people laughed at her?
Would she be labeled a fraud?

With all of these doubts stampeding their way into her thoughts, Julia emailed her professor back and told him she would review her story and let him know her decision. She then thanked him for notifying her of this opportunity.

Looking at the clock, Julia realized that she had only forty-five minutes to get ready for her date with Andy. Julia sat up in bed, staring at her closet, wondering what in the world she would wear. She felt as giddy as a teenage girl on prom night.

"What...are...you star...ing...at?" Carmen asked.

"Oh, nothing, Mom."

"Do...you...you want any...thing...to eat?"

"No. And, well...I have a date tonight," Julia said quickly, waiting on her mother's response.

"A...a...date? With...who?" Carmen asked, so intrigued she found herself inadvertently walking into her daughter's room.

"He's that guy that came by this morning."

"That...guy...tak...ing you...o...ut? I thought...he...trying to...to sell...in...surance...or something," Carmen sputtered.

"Thanks for that, Mom, but yes, he's taking me out. And why should that shock you?" Julia said as she walked into her closet.

Carmen opened her eyes wide. "He...he's sooo...ni...ce...to look at."

"Yeah, and guess what?" Julia said as she waited for her mother's response.

"What?" Carmen said, her eyes opening even wider.

Julia started to separate articles of clothing hanging in her closet, hearing the metal hangers scrape against the metal bar. "He's an ex-Padres baseball player, so you may have heard of him."

Everyone knew Carmen was a big Padres fan. She had been a fan of the team for as long as anyone could remember. At the mention of these words, Carmen's eyes lit up as her mind began to wander. "Whats...what...s...his...na...me?"

Julia smiled as she saw her mom's face glow with excitement. "Well, I mean, he doesn't play anymore, but, well, his name is Andrew Harrington, or Andy is what he likes to be called."

"How...the...eck...di...d...you...meet?" Carmen spitted out.

"Well, it's a long story, Mom. But actually, we met years ago. Before I was married."

"But...th...at...was...when..." And Carmen stopped, realizing that she had almost said his name, and she looked over at her daughter.

Somehow this information didn't seem to bother Julia anymore. "Yes, Mom. It was when I was with Ritchie. So, you see, Andy never really had a chance back then, but now he does. And well, I actually like him a lot. I think...I might be, well, I like him a lot."

"That...s...good...sweet...heart. Just...do...n't...scr...screw...it...up."

Julia frowned at her mother, but not even Carmen's words would deflate Julia's mood that day. The world was good, and it was going to stay that way.

As she continued to rummage through her closet, Julia pulled out her favorite navy-blue spring skirt, the one that fell just below her knees. She loved the way it bounced and swayed as she walked. She put on a freshly ironed, thin white blouse that buttoned up to her neck. She surrounded the sheer blouse with a cloth belt that was connected to the skirt, tying it around her waist.

She ran to the restroom and debated on blush and lipstick colors, choosing a more natural look. She began curling the ends of her hair and waited impatiently as she slowly moved around to each strand. Lastly, she sprayed on her most expensive perfume from the department store. She then stood back and looked at the image staring back at her. "Not bad if I say so myself."

Carmen was sitting in the living room watching television when Julia made her way into the room. Carmen's mouth dropped open as she watched her daughter drift into the room.

"Wow...," Carmen blurted out.

"You like it? Do you think it's too much?" Julia asked, turning to comb through her hair with her fingers as she looked into the entryway mirror.

"No...you...look b...beautiful."

"Oh, thank you, Mom. I hope Andy thinks so."

Carmen took out a notepad she had sitting next to her. She began to scan through some of the notes that she had scribbled down. "I…look…ed…im up. He…e…was quite…a base…ball…player."

"Well, you get to meet him in person in just a few minutes. He texted me that he is almost here."

"Oh…," Carmen said as her elated face was replaced with a look of disgust. "Oh…and…Scott…called when…y…ou…were…gone."

"He did? What did he want?"

"D…don't…know. He…want…ed…to…talk…talk to…you."

"Okay, well, I'll call him tomorrow. I bet it's about Bobby."

Suddenly there was a knock at the door. Carmen started to rise as Julia turned back toward her. "Don't be silly, Mom. I got it. You relax."

"O…kay," Carmen said, trying to sit up straight, ironing down her house dress and smoothing back the sides of her hair.

Julia opened the door and was immediately breathless as the image of Andy slowly formed through the light. He was leaning into the door frame with one hand extended over the top of the door. His jacket flapping in the wind. He turned slowly toward her as his gorgeous white teeth illuminated in the sun, and he said, "Hello, Julia."

Julia stood dumbfounded for a moment. After a few seconds, she suddenly realized that she hadn't answered him and quickly responded as if she had gotten lost in thought, "Well, hello you."

Andy then instinctively looked around Julia, sensing someone else was in the room, "Are you ready? Is your mother here?"

Julia, forcing herself to come back to reality, said, "So sorry, yes. I have a big fan of yours here, and she's dying to meet you."

Julia moved aside and let Andy move past her. He moved through the entryway, scanning the living area as if he were just as excited to meet an old fan. "Oh, really. Well, I always have time for those few fans who remember an old baseball player like me." Andy turned to the right and found himself in the living room. He immediately recognized Julia's mom as the woman he had spoken to earlier in the day.

Julia had never seen her mom so excited. Carmen couldn't seem to put two sentences together as she sat there stumbling over her tongue even more than she normally did after the stroke. "Hiii…I'mmm…Ju…lia's…"

And Andy marched right over to her, picking her up off the recliner, giving Carmen a big bear hug. "You must be Julia's beautiful mother. I believe I had the pleasure of meeting you this morning. I'm so glad to see you again."

"Th…anks," Carmen said, trying to sit back down, smoothing the back of her hair down in the process. "You…ou…played…for…for…the Padres?"

"Why, yes, I did. Julia must have told you. I didn't play all that long, but it was the time of my life."

Carmen smiled. "I…bet."

"Your lovely daughter here has finally agreed to go out with me. We knew each other way back. Back when she ruled the dance floor."

"Yes…yes…she…d…id." Carmen laughed nervously while straightening her dress and collar as if she had just met the president of the United States.

"Okay, Mom. We're going to get going. Do you need anything before I go?" Julia asked.

"No…no," Carmen responded. "G…go…go…have…a…good…time."

"Oh, we will," Andy said, taking Carmen's hand as she blushed. "It was so nice meeting you, Carmen. I hope to see you again."

"Oh…w…well…me…too," Carmen swooned, straightening out her house dress.

As the two exited the house, Andy immediately grabbed Julia's hand. "She's such a sweet lady."

"Oh, just wait until you know her better. That woman has a lot of spirit and can be really ornery."

"Oh, so that's where you get it." Andy winked at her.

Julia laughed. "Probably."

When they arrived at the restaurant, the sun was just starting to set behind the horizon. They stopped for a moment and watched from the sidewalk as the sun literally lowered itself into the ocean, moment by moment, inch by inch, in seconds, until all you could see was the remnants of the afterglow reaching out like spiked stars on the horizon as the purples met the yellows.

The couple sighed as they turned to one another and smiled. Andy reached down and took Julia's hand into his, sending small piercing tingles up Julia's arm as she looked down to see their hands formed into one.

The water gleamed like sheets of ice shimmering under the stars, foaming up near the shore. As they walked, they could feel the heat of the day cooling into the night.

"You look beautiful, by the way," Andy said, looking at her as if he was wondering if he should kiss her or not. Julia stood ready for the embrace as the moment was interrupted by another couple walking around them. Andy then looked down at his watch. "I guess we should probably go in."

"I guess so," Julia said as he led her onto the white wood porch that surrounded the restaurant, overlooking the coast.

Once inside, they were seated immediately by the maître d', who knew Andy by name.

"Good evening, Mr. Harrington."

"Good evening, Steven. How are you tonight?"

"Very well, very well. I have your table ready, overlooking the beach area." He looked over at Julia for a moment and smiled. "Please, be sure to walk out onto the deck and take in the sunset. It is remarkable."

When they arrived at the table, Andy walked over and pulled out Julia's chair as she sat down. They both stared out the window as the last remnants of the sun began to fade into the ocean.

"Would you like to go out?" Andy asked Julia.

"Could we? It's just such a beautiful evening."

"Sure, there's no hurry."

They both got up as a waiter headed their way but was stopped as Andy waved him off. The waiter lowered his head in recognition, turned, and headed back toward the bar.

Julia stepped out onto the deck, standing at the railing as the breeze from the ocean carried with it a hint of the sea. Julia, feeling chilled, rubbed both of her arms, trying to warm them as she looked out over the coast. Andy, noticing her attempt to warm her arms, walked up behind her and placed his arms over hers, trying to warm her. She took his hands in hers, laying them across her waist as they rocked back and forth, peering out toward the horizon, his head lowered and pressed to her side, rubbing his cheek against hers.

"Is there anything more beautiful than this view?" Julia smiled.

"Well, I can think of one view I like even more," Andy said, turning his head slightly to smile at her.

Julia smiled back.

The wind blew, lifting Julia's hair as Andy cuddled his cheek next to hers, standing directly behind her in a strong embrace that eliminated any space between them. Julia closed her eyes as they began to sway to the rhythm of the wind. Seagulls flew overhead. Andy stepped back for a moment to point toward them as Julia glanced up toward the dark shadows flying overhead, in and out of the breeze, floating down onto the shore.

Andy moved beside Julia, taking her hand in his. They watched as couples walked along the beach hand in hand. Andy then maneuvered his arm around Julia, pulling her into his side as they stared out over the ocean for what seemed like hours.

"Oh, how I have dreamt of this moment," Andy suddenly said.

"Dreamt of what moment?"

"Of you. Of us. Ever since the first time I saw you years ago. I still can't believe you are standing here right next to me."

"I never knew," Julia said.

"How could you? You had Ritchie at the time. I was just this weird guy who never had a chance."

Andy then turned to move a runaway strand of hair from Julia's eyes.

"I don't know what to say," Julia said.

"It all works out in the end, don't you think?" Andy asked.

Julia looked over at Andy wondering if he truly meant the words he was saying. At that moment, Andy leaned down slowly, narrowing the space between them. Just then, a waiter opened the door allowing another couple to come out onto the deck as Julia turned toward them, watching them walk by. They both then noticed the waiter looking out toward the deck, checking on them. They stared at one another as the moment seemed to have passed them by, leaving an awkward silence.

"Should we go in?" Julia suggested, seeing the candlelight from the tables peering through the glass that surrounded the restaurant.

"Only if you want to? Are you hungry?" Andy asked.

"Starving?"

"Well, then, let's go. I want to hear everything about what's been going on with you," Andy said while holding the door to the restaurant open for Julia.

"Well, there's lots to tell."

They made their way back into the restaurant. Andy pulled out Julia's chair and then sat down across from her. A lit candle flickered inside a small clear glass surrounded by multi-colored greenery. Soft music played in the background, and chandeliers sparkled overhead. The walls were lined with black and white pictures of Italy. Pictures of its history and culture were captured in these large snapshots. The images frozen in time for all eternity.

"So, what's new?"

"Well, my daughter had her baby, and it's a boy. His name is Charlie."

"Oh, love that name. And how are they doing?" Andy asked, taking a drink of his water.

"Really, well. And you remember Brad."

Andy choked a little on his water, bringing his napkin quickly up to his mouth. "Yes, I meant to ask you about that. Sorry, but maybe I have this wrong, but didn't he used to date you?"

Julia crossed her legs and grinned as if she were about to release world secrets, speaking so softly that Andy had to lean in to hear. "Well…it's kind of a long story, but in short, we never really had an official real date. He was interested, for whatever reason, but I knew he was way too young for me. Anyway…" Julia said, noticing Andy's eyes turn owl-like, "I also knew that he was this great guy. And he was looking for someone, and my daughter was looking for someone. And well, why not?"

"So, you set them up?" Andy said, leaning back in his chair.

"Well, kind of. Ahhh…pretty much, yes."

"So that day, the day at the roof theater, that was all a setup for your daughter?"

"Kind of," Julia smirked. "Ohhh, okay. Guilty as charged."

"You never fail to amaze me." Andy laughed out loud.

"Yes, I would have to say that was kind of strange, even for me. You'll get used to it," Julia laughed, flapping her hand forward in front of her face.

"Hey, I can't wait. So, they got together? But it hasn't been nine months yet if I am doing my math right."

Julia, now a little more embarrassed, was almost sorry she had brought it up. She was quickly learning how smart Andy was and how it didn't take him long to put two and two together. "Well, yes, you are correct. Charlie is not Brad's biological son," Julia said as quickly as she could.

"Oh, my," Andy said. "Now, I'm really impressed with Brad."

"Exactly, that was my thought. Anyway, I was the one that actually introduced them. I mean, Lauren is practically a clone of me, and Brad was attracted to me, so I figured, why not?"

"So, you introduced them, knowing that Lauren was pregnant by someone else?"

"Well, yes," Julia admitted, clenching her teeth, "guilty again."

Andy sat there grinning at her, shaking his head as if he had just discovered something else that he loved about her. "You must be some kind of mother."

"Well, a concerned mother, at least," Julia said as the waiter brought over a bottle of wine and filled their glasses.

"This is the bottle that you requested, Mr. Harrington. I will give you some time to look over the menu."

"Thank you, Henry," Andy said.

"So, you obviously come here a lot?" Julia said.

"Yes, I love the food. And I know what you are thinking, but you're wrong. I don't bring all my dates or women here. Most of the time, it's just me, or if my family is in town, I will drag them down here with me. I don't know. I just love this place. I will come to eat and walk on the beach. Read. It's kind of my oasis. Actually, I haven't brought many dates here at all."

"Really. Why not?"

"This place has always kind of been my getaway. I don't know. A place that was all mine. I just hadn't felt the need to share it. Until now."

"Well, that's a pretty good line, Mr. Harrington," Julia said while shuffling her menu between her hands.

Andy leaned in closer to her. "It's not a line. Not with you. I hope you can find it in your heart to believe me," he said. "I thought about bringing you here once."

Julia put the menu down and moved in closer to Andy. "Oh yeah. When?"

"Oh, about a thousand years ago. When I first met you. Way back when we were just kids."

"Really, you have been coming here for that long?" Julia said, sitting back up.

"I have. But you never gave me the time of day," Andy said, winking at her. "I meant to ask, and you don't have to tell me because I know it is none of my business, but whatever happened to the guy you were with back then?"

"Oh…you mean, Ritchie."

"Yes."

"He was killed in a car accident about two years after we met."

Andy's demeanor changed, and he sat back in his chair, not sure what to say next. "Oh…I…I didn't know. I'm so sorry." And then he said something not even Julia predicted. "I wish I could have been there for you."

Julia shifted in her seat and looked out over the restaurant, bringing her eyes eventually back to Andy, and she took a deep breath. "It was hard. I think he would have liked you, though."

Andy smiled at her and leaned against the table. "Oh…and how do you know that?"

"Let's just say I have my sources."

Just then, the waiter walked back up to the couple. "Have you decided?"

Andy smiled at Julia, and she nodded back at him. "I think we have," Andy said.

They ordered and drifted into a natural conversation. The two laughed throughout the meal like two old friends who hadn't seen each other in a very long time. They talked about the past and what they wanted for the future. Julia told him about how excited she was about her classes and how it has always been her dream to write stories, possibly even novels, and they found themselves telling each other things they hadn't felt the need to share with anyone before.

The conversation bloomed so naturally between them. It was as if they had known each other their entire lives. As if they had been waiting for this one moment in time. A time expected but unexpected all at once. As if this time were a predetermined destiny, one that most find never comes into existence.

"You should do it. You should submit your story," Andy encouraged Julia.

"You think so? But what if it is turned down? I don't know if I can take that kind of rejection. This story is so precious to me."

"But what if it's not, Julia? What if this is your time to do what you were always meant to do? You have to take that chance."

Julia dropped her napkin on her lap and brought her hands up to her chin, thinking about Andy's words. "I know part of me wants to, but then there's that part that says I'm just kidding myself. What makes me think I can write stories people want to read?"

Andy wiped his mouth with his napkin and leaned forward, laying his hand down on the table and taking Julia's hand into his. "Please don't take this the wrong way, but then why are you doing this, Julia?"

"What do you mean?" Julia said, somewhat bothered by the comment.

"I don't mean to be blunt, but really tell me."

"I do it so I can reach people. So I can help them with my stories. I do it because I love it."

Andy then hit the table with the palm of his hand, and Julia jumped a little, somewhat shocked by the gesture. "Well, then, I think you have your answer."

And Julia wrinkled her eyebrows, a little perturbed that Andy would be so blunt.

"Julia, if your stories aren't out there, then how will they help anyone?"

Julia sat there for a moment, unable to breathe, afraid that her heart might burst. This man, who made her tremble simply by his touch, had it all right. What was she doing this for if not to put the stories out there to be read by someone, anyone? And that's when the phrase came out from her lips as if it had been sitting there all this time, abandoned and forgotten, "If not now, then when?"

Andy looked over at her and said, "Exactly."

"You're right. I will enter the contest. Win or lose; I have to put myself out there. Otherwise, you're right; why am I doing any of this?"

Andy smiled at her and grabbed her hand, looking deeply into her eyes. "I believe in you."

"Thank you," she said, as she felt a blush coming on, and again could do nothing to stop it as she blossomed into a bright red complexion.

They finished up dinner with some ice cream and a stroll on the deck as dusk turned into night. Andy drove Julia home, understanding that she had school and work the next day. As they pulled up to Julia's house, Julia looked over at Andy, surprised that he had not tried to kiss her.

Andy looked at her taking her hand into his and leaned over the seat as their lips came close to meeting when he suddenly saw a shadow move behind Julia. He leaned his head around Julia to try and see who it was. "There's someone in your yard."

Julia twisted herself back around and strained to make out the shadow that was moving back and forth in front of her porch.

Andy reached for the door handle announcing to Julia, "Wait here."

Julia, puzzled as to what was happening, looked back toward the image, recognizing a familiar silhouette making its way into the light. "It looks like Scott. I wonder if something's happened."

"Scott? Your ex-husband, Scott?" Andy asked, with a jealous tone, letting go of the door handle.

"Yes," Julia said, irritated that Scott was there. "What's he doing here?"

"Do you need to go?" Andy said reluctantly.

"I suppose," Julia said. "I'm so sorry, Andy. I had a wonderful time."

"Do you need me to wait with you?"

"No…no. He's harmless. I guess I should find out what he wants."

"Well, for an ex, he sure seems to make his way back here a lot," Andy said in an irritated tone.

Julia, realizing that Andy sounded jealous, tried to calm any worries he might have. "You have nothing to worry about, Andy. It's nothing. I assure you."

"Well, can I call you tomorrow?"

"Yes. Please do." And Julia turned her head toward Scott and then back toward Andy. "I mean, I hope that you do."

"You can count on it," Andy said, trying to make the best of the situation.

Andy opened his door and walked around to open Julia's door as Scott stood looking at the two of them.

"I'll talk to you tomorrow," Andy said, lingering as if he wasn't sure what to do, but upon Julia grinning at him, reassuring him that everything was okay, he made his way back around to the driver's seat, got in, and pulled away.

Julia strolled toward Scott, who was pacing in the front yard as if he wasn't sure what to do.

"What's wrong?" Julia asked.

"I'm sorry. I didn't mean to interrupt your…your evening. I just need to talk to you. Can we talk?"

"Well, yes, come inside."

Scott followed Julia inside, neither one of them saying a word. She leaned down to turn on the lamp, sending out a small stream of light into the darkness. She turned around to find Scott standing right behind her.

"For goodness' sake, Scott," Julia announced in a whisper. "What is it?"

CHAPTER THIRTY-ONE

Scott stood uncharacteristically silent as Julia waited for some kind of explanation on why he had ruined what should have been one of the most memorable nights of her life. Not that this surprised Julia; he always somehow managed to get under her skin and spoil that moment that should have been a fond memory, stealing her joy once again.

Yet, Julia had to admit that Scott was also one of the most self-assured people she had ever known. She believed that this characteristic was what made him such an unusually gifted liar. Scott's charismatic charm was part of his appeal. Everyone was instantly fooled into believing his version of reality. True or not.

Maybe it was the fact that Scott somehow truly believed what he was saying; therefore, so did everyone else. Julia thought at that moment that his deception, this fantasy world, was probably how he got her to marry him. The lie that he would always love her unconditionally.

"I was looking at everything the kids are going through, and I can't help but feel I'm responsible. How did I make such a mess out of everything?" Scott said.

"Well, if you haven't looked lately, the kids are doing pretty well. I mean, Bobby has a job and has moved into his own place. He's gotten off to a good start, thanks to you. Lauren has Brad and now Charlie. I think the kids are doing okay, so you shouldn't worry about them. Is that what this is all about?" Julia asked.

"I've just been thinking about them...and, well, about us. I feel like they still need a father in their life."

"What do you mean, us? Why would you be concerned about us? And they have a father. You. What's going on here, Scott? I thought you were dying of something. Why would you just show up here? Did you not see that I was on a date?"

Scott looked at her as if her words cut him like a knife. "I know I probably don't have the right to ask, but I just wanted to know if there was any way this...you and me, could be salvaged. I wanted to see if we could possibly make this work and, well, maybe be a family again."

Julia felt numb. It was almost as if she had entered a tunnel, and Scott was standing on the other end shouting at her as she tried to figure out what in the world he was saying. "I'm sorry, but did you say what I thought you said? Do you mean after you went off and had your fun? You mean after I raised our children, you are asking me to take you back. Are you delusional?"

"Wait..." Scott said, holding up his hands in front of him. "Julia, hear me out. I made a mistake that cost me, well, us, everything."

"No, Scott. It didn't cost you everything. You had it made. All you had to worry about was Scott. I had to worry about the kids. You seemed to forget you had kids. And before that, you kinda forgot you had a wife right about the time you left me for Sky."

"You're right. I deserve that. It's just that I've changed. I could take good care of you. I see all that I gave up, and I'm so very sorry. You wouldn't have to work. I would take care of you, take care of everything. Let me try and be the husband that you deserved back then before I screwed everything up."

Julia walked over to Scott and looked him in the eye. "I never forgot we were a family. I never even forgot I was married; that was you. And for you to come here and ask me this. Do you know what I think it is? I think it's the fact that you can't stand to see me happy again. I don't want someone to take care of me, Scott. I can take care of myself. I think I have proven that. And now that I'm just starting to live again, how dare you try to take that away from me? I'm sorry, but I think you better leave."

Scott stood silent in the shadows, his body swaying, not sure whether to move forward or not.

Julia didn't say a word. She walked over to the front door and opened it. "You have a family, Scott. You have Lauren and Bobby; now, please stop worrying about me. Go be the father that they deserve. Oh, and if you didn't know it already, you're a grandfather. Charlie needs a great grandfather. Go and be that for him. They will always be your family. I'm sorry, but they're the ones you need to be concerned about, not me."

Scott walked toward the door and stopped when he reached Julia, "I'm sorry, Julia. You're right. I have no right to ask this of you. I guess I'm just finally realizing what I gave up."

After Scott walked out, Julia closed the door behind him, leaning her back against it as if the door would somehow tumble forward should she release it. She took a deep breath and felt a tear make its way down her cheek. She wiped it away and went to turn out the lamp as the room turned dark.

The next morning, Julia turned in her paper and spoke to her professor about submitting it to the contest. They agreed to meet once a week to review her story. Julia found herself at work later that day. She couldn't seem to concentrate, with all the promises that she felt her future held.

It was strange, but Julia could already envision her graduation day as if the day had already happened. The dream was so real; it felt as if she had already lived it a thousand times over. She pictured her mother and the kids in the stands cheering her on. Her professor shaking her hand as she crossed the stage and the look on her face as she accepted her degree. Yes, the dream was so real Julia could almost reach out and touch it.

She loved being a part of the university and thought she would possibly like to become an English professor someday. That way, she could constantly write and get paid to do it. Lisa stopped by Julia's department, as she usually did when they worked together, to get her daily dose of gossip regarding Julia and Andy's ongoing saga. Julia told Lisa about her little run-in with Scott after her date.

"He said what?" Lisa said. "Where is he? I want to give that no-good cheater a piece of my mind."

"No, it's fine. You would have been proud of me, though. I actually handled it."

"He has some nerve, coming around after all of these years. And yes, I am proud of you. About time." Lisa laughed.

"Thanks, Lisa."

"So, when's the date?"

"What date? What are you talking about?" Julia said, making her way around the counter.

"To your wedding, silly."

"Oh, Lisa, you watch way too many movies. We've only had one date, well, maybe two if you count the Chinese restaurant or the trip to the drug park, I guess."

"See, you two are already like an old married couple. Has he called you today?"

"Nope," Julia said as she heard her phone start to go off. She looked down at her phone and discovered it was Andy. "It's him," she said as if she were in high school and they were gossiping about her current boyfriend.

"Well, answer it. Hurry up so I can hear," Lisa insisted.

Julia hesitated, looking up at Lisa, holding her phone in her hand as it continued to ring.

"Okay, okay, I can take a hint. I'm going. I was going to help you out, but I see that you aren't interested, so I will be right over here working if you need me," Lisa said as she sauntered over to her department. "Some people are so ungrateful."

"Hello?" Julia said as she put some distance between her and her staff.

"Julia, how was school? Did you do your homework? I've been dying to say that to you all day." Andy laughed.

"I get a lot of that these days." Julia giggled.

"Hey, I know this is short notice, but I thought if you hadn't eaten, we could meet up after you get off work. Are you hungry?"

"You read my mind. I'm starving. Where do you want to meet? Oh, but, unfortunately, I can't stay out too long; I have another paper due tomorrow."

"Not a problem. How about Mexican? I know a great place close to La Jolla Beach. Do you want to check it out?"

"Yeah, I can meet you there. Just send me the address," Julia said as she noticed some of her staff looking her way.

"Will do. I won't keep you. I'll see you later."

Julia said her goodbyes and hung up her phone, looking around at the college girls who seemed to be standing around with nothing to do.

"Brooke?"

"Yeah," Brooke said as she stood checking her nails.

"Could you please get the new merchandise on the shelves? Have Taylor help you," Julia said.

Brooke immediately came around from behind the counter and strolled over toward the boxes, motioning for Taylor to come and assist her.

Julia, excited about her evening, waved toward Lisa, giving her a thumbs up.

Lisa responded by dancing next to her register.

Julia looked around her at the department store that had been a means to an end. It helped her survive when she most needed it. But it was far from her dream. She could almost taste what it would feel like to walk out those doors for the very last time, never to look back, running toward her future with no fear. Yes, this way of life had gotten her through, but she now realized she was not living the life she was meant to live. Julia had found her hope again, and she was determined never to let it die inside her ever again. Awakened, she was not walking toward her destiny; she was running.

CHAPTER THIRTY-TWO

Julia left work that day a little early just in case she had trouble finding the restaurant. She drove across town and headed up a long winding road that was lined with palm trees and goldeneye shrubs, which produced a bright yellow flower that is similar to the sunflower.

There was not a cloud in the sky. The road led to a hilltop overlooking the ocean. From a distance, Julia made out some type of red blots that lined the outside of a large white building at the top of the hill. As she got closer, she could see that the red blots were actually curved back chairs spaced about five feet away from each other. The chairs aligned the outside wall of the restaurant's large wrap-around porch.

Julia pulled up next to a sporty red convertible and noticed a man leaning against the driver-side door. The man had on a Padres baseball cap and thick black sunglasses, the kind you would see in a James Bond movie. She glanced over at him, and he smiled at her, accentuating his strong jaw and unshaven chin. Julia grinned at him, recognizing that beautiful smile.

"Wow, nice car," Julia said excitedly. She had secretly always wanted to own a convertible, and red was one of her favorite colors. "Exactly how many cars do you own?"

"A few. You want to go for a short ride before we eat?" Andy asked. "They said there was a one-hour wait, anyway."

"Sure," Julia said. She hopped out of her vehicle as Andy walked around his. Andy stopped just inches from her, signaling her to move before him as they made their way around the front of the convertible. Andy then bowed like a maître d' and opened the passenger side door for her.

"My lady," Andy announced.

Julia then noticed a large bouquet of pink-striped lilies surrounded by vibrant greenery sitting on the passenger seat. "Oh Andy, these are beautiful."

"They reminded me of you," Andy said.

"Well, thank you. They're beautiful." Julia picked up the bouquet and set them on the floor next to her.

Andy then skipped back around the front of the car, "So, shall we?" he asked.

"I'm ready if you are. Wait," Julia said, scavenging through her purse. She then took out a brown hair tie. "Let me get my hair pulled back before we take off."

Andy watched as Julia gathered her wavy brown hair into a ponytail. He flashed back to a night, long ago, when they were young, and Julia had come in with her hair all swooped up into a ponytail. Several loose ringlets fell around her face so naturally. He wanted so much to tell her how beautiful she looked that night, but Ritchie was always there, and they just seemed so in love. Andy figured at the time that it just wasn't in the cards for them.

He still couldn't believe that he was sitting right next to the girl he had fallen in love with all those years ago. He couldn't believe that fate had given him a second chance. He actually thought about Ritchie at that moment and thought how sad it was that he never got to see Julia become this beautiful woman.

"Are you ready?" Andy asked.

"I'm ready!" Julia found herself shouting.

Andy backed out and punched the gas pedal so hard that they both jerked back into their seats. Hearing the engine roar, they skidded out of the parking lot. It was strange, but at that moment, it was as if time went into reverse, and they were no longer these two people who had lived a life of disappointments, regrets, and celebrations. A time of lost loves, heartaches, and extraordinary moments. They were somehow taken back in time when they were both twenty-one again. There were no responsibilities, there were no histories, no deaths or bad luck, they were just young and alive, and no one could touch them.

Julia spontaneously flung her hands in the air and threw her head back, letting the sinking sun hit her face. Andy looked over at her, smiling, feeling his heart burst with excitement.

With the engine roaring, Andy drove up the highway heading toward La Jolla Beach. The sun was beginning to dissolve into the ocean as they both looked over toward the water, seeing the sun's reflection move over the surface of blue like a glistening sword. They headed up another hill and toward a beaming white cross that could be seen from miles away as they listened to the thunder of the engine, laughing at the recklessness of it all. The area was known as Mount Soledad Park.

"Oh, I love this park," Julia proclaimed.

"Let's stop. It has an unforgettable view."

"I'd love that," Julia said, giving Andy a reassuring smile.

"Oh, and if I hadn't told you. You look very beautiful tonight," Andy said, looking over toward Julia. "I can't believe that I'm here with you again."

"Why do you say that?"

"Well, I've wanted to tell you this for so long, but I was afraid you would disappear again. This will probably sound corny as all get out, but here it goes." And he hesitated, taking a deep breath as the wind rushed between them. "I've been drawn to you since the first time I saw you all those years ago. But it doesn't seem like that long ago because you are exactly as I remember you. Unfortunately, it was when you were

Ritchie's, and I'm sorry, I don't mean that in a bad way at all. I was just so jealous of him and how you looked at him because I wanted you to look at me that way too."

"It was so long ago. It feels almost as if it were a dream. One that I actually had tried so hard to forget. Until you," Julia said, looking over at Andy. "So, you felt drawn to me somehow?"

"Yes. Does that scare you?"

"Well, I'm not sure. I was with Ritchie at the time. I mean…I've sort of been his girl ever since. Even when I was married. Scott probably really never had a chance."

"And now?"

"I think I'm finding myself again. Slowly but surely," Julia responded.

"I'm so happy for you," Andy said, giving Julia a reassuring smile. "So, you never told me. What did Scott want the other night? Was it something urgent?" Andy asked, trying not to pry too much.

"I probably shouldn't tell you this, but he wanted to see if I would take him back. I'm sorry. I had no idea that was what he wanted to say to me. That came way out of left field, excuse the pun." Julia smiled. "I had no idea he still felt that way or ever felt that way."

"He still loves you. I can tell."

"No, you're wrong," Julia assured Andy. "I don't think he ever loved me. How could someone love another person and hurt them the way that he hurt me? I could never do that to someone I loved."

"No, I know you couldn't," Andy said, and he lifted Julia's hand to his lips, kissing her hand ever so softly, rubbing her hand against his unshaven chin.

Julia felt a tingle move down her arm as she tried not to blush.

"But, I think I know why he said it," Andy continued, shifting the convertible into low gear.

"You do?" Julia questioned.

Andy looked over at Julia with this look on his face as if he had known Julia and Scott all of their lives. As if he knew exactly what had gone on between them. *But how could he?* Julia thought to herself. She didn't even feel like she knew who she was with Scott during that time, oh, so, many years ago.

"He realized down deep inside that he gave up the best thing that ever happened to him. He gave you up."

Julia narrowed her eyebrows and smirked as if she didn't believe what she was hearing. She turned her head away and looked at the water and then turned back toward Andy.

Andy then continued, "And he can never change that. It was probably the biggest mistake of his life. I don't want it to be mine."

"What are you saying?"

Andy looked over at Julia and pulled the car into a nearby parking slot that looked over the coast, next to the ominous cross that sat above many brown stoned stairs.

The waves screamed out below, crashing violently against the shore as seagulls squawked overhead.

"I'm saying that I love you. I am sure of it. I fell in love with you a long time ago and have really never ever completely recovered. I am pretty sure I never will. And it's not that I remember you as you were, but more because I have seen what you have become. You are a mother, a student, and, yes, a grandmother, but you are so spectacular in everything that you do. You were then, and you are now. I'm sorry, I'm babbling."

Suddenly, without any warning, a rush of wind came up and blew Andy's baseball cap off of his head. "Oh my!" Andy said as his hat started to float through the air, heading across the parking lot. "I'll be right back," Andy declared as he quickly opened up his door, running after the renegade hat.

Julia suddenly gasped for air as she felt a burst of energy go through her body. She opened the car door, stepping out into the breeze, feeling something or someone drawing her out into the night.

Julia stood rubbing her arms, trying to warm herself in the breeze. She looked over at the massive cross, and it began to illuminate, setting off a glow across the sky. Julia narrowed her eyes, backing away from the car, as she turned toward the cross. She then saw a man walk out from behind the base. He was staring at Julia, his hair blowing in the wind as Julia held her breath.

"You know, I wasn't going to come," a voice rang out into the wind as he stepped out from the light. His skin glowed as he brushed back the side of his hair.

"You weren't?"

The image walked toward her, "He's good."

"Yes, he is," Julia said as she turned toward Andy, who was still in hot pursuit of his cap.

"He doesn't deserve you, though."

"No, but who does?" Julia smiled, shrugging her shoulders.

Ritchie laughed. "You could always make me laugh."

Julia put a strand of hair behind her ear. "This is goodbye, isn't it? Will I ever see you again?"

"You never know. I surprised you this time, didn't I?"

"Yes," she said, looking back at Andy.

"I didn't think it would be this hard to let you go," Ritchie said as he moved closer to Julia. "Go to him, babe. He's the one. The one who is finally worthy of you. Well, he's not me, but he's possibly the next best thing."

"Thank you," Julia said, turning her head toward him.

"For what?" He grinned.

"For loving me enough to come back. For letting me go. For helping me to let go."

They looked at each other for what seemed like hours, Julia studying every part of his face. She reached up to touch his cheek but found that her hand only passed through his translucent skin.

Ritchie leaned down and kissed her on the forehead, setting it aglow. He turned back toward the cross, slowly floating away. "Just remember who told you that they loved you first," Ritchie said, looking back once and winking at her, and then, he was gone.

Julia turned back to find Andy finally clasping onto his cap. She giggled as she watched him dust the cap off. She watched as he moved closer to her as she glared at the cross.

"What?" Andy asked as he turned to look at what she was staring at. "Yes, it is so beautiful, isn't it?

"Yes, it is," Julia said, tearing up. She looked up at him as her mind went blank. She couldn't breathe. Her eyes glazed over with tears.

Andy looked at Julia, pulling her face to his. "I'm so happy for me, for you. I don't need an I love you right now. I just need to know if your plans include me?"

Julia smiled, "Of course they do. I have it from a good source that you are the one. The one I've been waiting for. Are we crazy?"

"No, this is far from crazy. I found you again, and I'll never let you go. I plan to finish this dance with you, Julia Melrose. If you'll have me?"

"Of course I will. You're the one," Julia said as Andy pulled Julia into his arms, kissing her deeply, and the sun made its way down in the distance, slowly submerging into the sea, turning the sky a purple yellow. And Julia pulled back, looking deeply into Andy's eyes. "You're the one I've been waiting for. What took you so long?"

"I've always been right here. Right here, waiting for you." And he grabbed Julia and kissed her deeply as the cross lit up in a bright glow, like a firecracker in the night, and then suddenly diminished.

EPILOGUE

SIX MONTHS LATER

Julia came out of the church's backroom dressed in a mauve strapless gown with long white gloves that came halfway up her arms. Glistening windows were set on each side of the church's mahogany French doors. The light pierced through the glass and made its way over to Julia's eyes as she squinted to see the objects in front of her. She moved as if the church were on fire, holding a large bouquet of flowers in her hand as two tall men in dark suits made their way across the back foyer to where she was standing.

"What are you doing back here?" Julia said, scolding Brad.

"Lisa told me to come back here, something about you needing me," Brad apologized.

Lisa immediately looked at Brad as if he were insane and said, "Don't drag me into this. Julia, I thought you said you wanted them both."

"No, I meant for Andy to come back here, not Brad."

"Oh…my bad," Lisa said as she pulled Brad's arm leading him back into the sanctuary. "She's got those crazy eyes," Lisa whispered to Brad while turning him around and marching him back to the front of the church. "Better just do what she says."

"Mom!" she heard Lauren yelling from the back room.

"I'm coming…hold on. Everything's fine," Julia yelled back. She then turned toward Andy and whispered, "Honey, could you please go downstairs and tell the bridesmaids to get up here? None of them are answering their cell phones, and it's almost time to begin."

"They just don't want to be seen next to a beautiful woman like you." Andy smiled. "And can you blame them?"

"Oh…that's so sweet, honey, but I really need you to go get them, please."

"On my way, boss," Andy said with a salute.

"Oh, you," Julia said, pushing him on his way.

"Mom! What's going on? Where are they?"

Julia made her way back into the bride's dressing room, where Lauren was standing in a beautiful white ball gown. Her brown hair was curled into waves, pulled partially up, and tied on the top of her head with a cubic zirconia studded barrette that sparkled every time she turned her head.

"Wow, you look so beautiful, sweetie," Julia beamed.

Scott entered the room right behind Julia. "Oh my, aren't you a sight," Scott said as he moved closer to Lauren, attempting to place her in a massive bear hug.

"Dad! Please be careful. Sorry, my hair is hanging on by a thread here. I don't think she put enough hairspray on it."

"No, it looks beautiful, sweetie. You look beautiful," Scott said, trying to calm his daughter's frazzled nerves.

"Mom?" Lauren said, looking to Julia for confirmation.

"Your dad's right. You look stunning. It'll all be fine. I promise you."

At that moment, Andy made his way into the room, followed by five bridesmaids in navy blue tea-length dresses, each carrying a small bouquet. "I found them, dear!" Andy announced.

"Oh, thank you, honey. Okay, who has Charlie?" Julia asked.

Just then, Bobby came bouncing into the room, followed by a red-headed young woman dressed in a bright floral sundress and carrying a rambunctious Charlie. "Ashley has him, Mom. We're all good. Oh, and sis, you look decent," Bobby joked as Ashley pushed him with her free hand.

"Thanks, Bobby," Lauren said while laughing. "That's just what I needed to hear."

"What, babe? I was just kidding with her," Bobby said, apologizing as Ashley rolled her eyes, bringing Charlie closer to her.

"We'll have him in the front row, Lauren. Don't worry about a thing. I have his bottle all ready," Ashley assured her.

Lauren walked over to Ashley and hugged her and Charlie, "Thank you so much, Ashley. Especially for putting up with my brother."

"What?" Bobby laughed. "I never get any credit here." And he and Ashley exited the room with Charlie in tow.

Lauren took one last long look in the mirror. Julia walked up beside her, placing her head on Lauren's shoulder and hugging her from the back. "It's time, sweetie."

"Okay, we need to get to the front, honey," Andy advised, grabbing Julia's hand.

"Okay," Julia said, with tears in her eyes as she gave Lauren one long last hug before letting go.

"Well, I guess it's just you and me," Scott said as he watched Julia and Andy exit the room.

"Yep, Dad. You're finally rid of me."

"Oh, that'll never happen," Julia—looking back—heard Scott say just before she left the room. "You will always be my little girl."

"Oh, thanks, Dad. Okay. Let's do this thing so we can get this party started," Lauren announced while taking her dad's arm.

Julia and Andy walked in first, followed by Brad's parents. The bridesmaids walked down the aisle one by one. Julia looked back to see Lauren standing in the church's entryway with Scott. She flashed back to the tears they had shed when they learned about Charlie as she turned to look at the beautiful bouncing baby boy now resting in the arms of her son's girlfriend, who they all thought would never take him back. She watched the gentle way her son had his arm around Ashley as he played with his nephew with his other hand. The trauma from yesterday, all but forgotten.

Julia looked over at the handsome man standing next to her as Andy gently took her hand, asking her if she was okay as she whispered, "Yes, I'm with you."

Andy smiled, pulling her closer.

Julia's attention then turned toward Brad. She watched as his face lit up when he saw Lauren standing at the end of the aisle with her father. Lauren seemed as calm as a cucumber. She whispered to Scott and smiled as a song started to play overhead, and Julia heard the words start to drift across the sanctuary. The song was "Can't Help Falling in Love with You," but it was a version Lauren said was done by an artist named Haley Reinhart. The artist's soft wispy voice brought every heart in the room to an abrupt stop as everyone gasped at the vision of Lauren surrounded by the radiant light as she made her way down the aisle.

Julia felt tears making their way down her cheeks as she watched Lauren float by.

She watched as Brad took Lauren's hand from Scott's. Julia thought at that very moment that the world was now exactly as it should be. She looked over at Carmen shaking her head at her daughter, wondering what Julia was blubbering about. She turned to this man from her past who held her hand so naturally, as if somehow their hands blended into one, and Julia finally realized that she was completely, undeniably, happy.

After the wedding, the group made their way to the reception, which was being held in the heart of the downtown area. Julia had found a diamond in the rough. Surrounded by industrial business buildings, this unique venue captivated its attendees with a gold staircase and marble floors. A stage was set up for the wedding party that overlooked the dance floor. Windows made up the entire west wall with a lovely garden that set right outside the glass doors. Every guest gasped as they entered the two-story hall, which also had two balconies on either side of the large dining hall.

After dinner and when all the toasts were made, Julia watched as Lauren made her way up to the microphone to make some type of announcement, "Could I have everyone's attention, please? I have a special song that a gentleman has asked me to play for a very special lady, and if you don't mind, this couple will be the only two dancing on this one. Thank you."

Julia looked over at Lisa, who was sitting next to her, and asked, "What is Lauren doing?"

Lisa shrugged her shoulders and smiled. "I don't know, and just hold your horses," Lisa said with a wink. "I'm sure it will all make sense in a few minutes."

Julia, not sure what Lisa was talking about, turned to look for Andy. She narrowed her eyebrows as she heard a song from the past start to play. She recognized the song because it was quite popular when she was young. It was the love ballad "Right Here Waiting" by Richard Marx. She watched as a spotlight hit the middle of the dance floor, and she looked around again for Andy, and he was nowhere to be found, and all of a sudden, she saw him walking slowly out to the middle of the floor, followed by the spotlight. He was waving and motioning for her to join him.

At first, Julia shook her head no, and then she heard a voice beside her whisper, "Go ahead, babe. He's waiting."

Julia turned to see a dimming light in the corner of the room.

She stood up as Lisa pushed her forward, and she stumbled out onto the dance floor. Andy took her in his arms, and they swayed slowly as all the guests in the room seemed to disappear, and it was only she and Andy.

The words vibrated around the room as images of the past began to swirl around her, the ghosts of former dreams that haunted her every move since she lost Ritchie. Vivid images began to play in her mind of the dance club and Ritchie smiling on the beach. The car crash and the funeral that left her so broken. New images began to appear as she saw Andy so clearly at the dance club. The way he pursued her when she wouldn't give him the time of day. She remembered smiling at him once when he asked her to dance right in front of Ritchie. She remembered the way Ritchie smiled back at him and said, "Sorry, pal, this is my girl."

She remembered the devastating look on Andy's face as he walked away. She almost felt sorry for him at the time, but she didn't understand why.

As the song was coming to a close, she looked up at Andy, and he smiled at her and slowly dropped to one knee as the crowd took a deep breath. "Julia Melrose, I love you. I have waited a lifetime for you. Will you do me the honor of becoming my wife?"

The room started to spin as the crowd hummed, "Ahhhs" and "Ohhhs," and Julia looked for a face in the crowd, and in the back of the room, a light was blinking, and below the light, she saw him. Those teeth, that hair, that walk.

Time slowed as she released Andy's hand, making her way toward the light, almost floating, as she left the confines of the large room and saw him walking toward her in a cloud of smoke with that smile. The smile that would always melt her heart.

"I wondered if I would see you here," Julia said.

Ritchie smirked and smoothed back a piece of hair that was falling forward, looking around the room. "I always knew we would be here one day. I just didn't know it would be to give you away," he said, trying to pick up Julia's chin with a beam of light.

Julia sighed and looked back toward Andy, who was frozen in time. "He's a good man."

Ritchie looked over at him. "I know he is. He would have to be for my girl."

Julia's eyes filled with tears. "I will always love you, you know."

Ritchie looked away as if trying to hold back tears and then looked down at Julia, "Just remember who loved you first."

"How could I forget?" Julia answered.

"He's waiting, babe. It's time," Ritchie said as a beam of light formed behind him. "I will always be with you. Go, promise me you'll be happy."

"Will I ever see you again?" Julia asked, a tear making its way down her cheek.

"Sure. Sure, you will. I will be the handsome one in wings one day." Julia laughed.

"I have to go now. I know you are in good hands," Ritchie said as he slowly dropped the glistening light from Julia's hand and started to back up toward the bright light, never taking his eyes off of her.

"Thank you," Julia said as if it were an echo, and everything went black, and she found herself standing next to Andy once more as the song ended.

She looked down at Andy on one knee and then up toward the corner of the room where the light was diminishing. Andy took a deep breath as if he were no longer sure how she would answer. As if there was something stopping her.

"Yes!" Julia shouted.

And Andy took her into his arms and spun her in a circle until everyone became a blur, and the distant gleam dimmed and dissipated into the dark. Julia twirled around, seeing the world in images, and she knew she had finally entered the first moment of a wondrous, spectacular life. The life she had always dreamt about and had been waiting for her all of those years.

The life that she was always meant to live.

ABOUT THE AUTHOR

Stacy Thowe was born in Shawnee, Kansas. She graduated from Washburn University with a degree in English and Creative Writing. While raising a family, she began writing her first novel, *God Bless My Broken Road*. With God's intervention, she began writing a young adult fantasy series that she never had any intention of writing. *The Guardian Series* is a trilogy. She would say that all her writing is of God's hand.

www.ingramcontent.com/pod-product-compliance
Lightning Source LLC
LaVergne TN
LVHW090323051125
825063LV00042B/749